MIASM

MW01614328

By Lynn

Book 3: Hidden Agendas

Table of Contents

ISBN: 9781689988032

CHAPTER 1
MARION KAATON

At 07:00 on the first day Avery woke up to her little brown and white, floppy eared dog Dixie licking her face. Avery turned over and Dixie began to lick Ross' face. Today was a special day. It was Ross and Avery Lisano's first day working as private investigators, running The Van Wyck Detective Agency. Ross and Avery were more than detectives. They were a specially trained couple, a product of the high security CIA couples program.

Ross and Avery were members of Group Eleven, which was attached to the CIA Hackensack station, known to the public as the offices of The G.W. Scientific Research Company. The research was done in a highly secure location in Lodi, New Jersey.

Mr. Earl Sandman, a tall, stately African American man was their boss. He was never seen in anything but a suit and tie. He had been the head of the couples training program Ross and Avery attended when they first entered the CIA. He was adored by all who worked for him. Mr. Earl Sandman was the definitive father figure.

Both Mr. Sandman and Whitney Van Wyck thought working as private investigators was the perfect cover for Ross and Avery. As private investigators they could potentially venture where the CIA could not. Whitney Van Wyck, the owner of the agency and a long-time friend and asset to Mr. Sandman, was happy to have Ross and Avery running his operation. It was a win-win situation.

To save time, Ross and Avery jumped into the shower together. Lathering body wash on each other, they made love. Avery stood facing the tiled shower wall tightly holding the bar. She spread her legs, arching her back, as Ross wrapped his arms around her holding her breasts and entered her deeply from behind. They had just achieved their rhythm, when Avery's cell phone on the counter began bellowing out *The Hogan's Heroes* theme song. They were both almost there and ignored the intrusion. They exploded at the same time. The phone stopped but started again. Avery quickly wrapped a towel around herself to answer. It was Aunt Diana. "Hi, what's wrong?" Avery, spent and out of breath asked, "I hope it's nothing serious, dicey, or unpredictable." Avery put the phone on speaker so Ross could hear his aunt.

"No, there's no situation, nothing is wrong. Why are you so out of breath, Avery? Oh, never mind, I just wanted to inform you and Ross that I'll meet you at the agency this morning at 09:00 sharp to begin our first day."

"What do you mean *our* first day?" Avery was clearly dismayed. Ross began drying Avery off as she spoke to Diana.

"You and Ross need an office manager, and I'm it!" Diana stated emphatically. Ross was beginning to arouse Avery and she pushed him away.

"Does Mr. Sandman and Lester know about this? And, more importantly, does Whitney Van Wyck know about this?"

"Yes, Avery, of course they know, and quite frankly I'm surprised you didn't know," answered Diana, astonished that Avery was unaware of the setup. "Are you OK? You sound out of breath."

Looking at Ross she rolled her eyes. "Everything is fine. Ross and I are just rushing to get to the agency."

"I sincerely hope you and Ross were not planning on hiring a stranger for the position?" Ross was drying Avery's legs with a fluffy towel and began nuzzling her between her legs. As soon as Ross began using his tongue, Avery kicked him off, glaring at him.

Struggling to gain her equilibrium, she answered, "Honestly, the topic of hiring an office manager never entered our minds, but If we must have one, I'm glad it's you, Aunt Diana," Avery answered, defusing Diana's angst, but still glaring at Ross.

"Good! I'll see you two at the agency at 09:00. And Avery, I'll have a pot of coffee waiting for you." Diana ended the call smiling in anticipation of this new adventure.

Diana walked into the kitchen where her husband Lester was making coffee. "The kids are happy about our arrangement," Diana said smiling aware that she caught Ross and Avery in the middle of something sexual.

Lester smiled answering, "I knew they would be. It's better to keep it in the family. With you there they won't have to worry about their cover being blown." Lester pulled Diana into his arms. This was the first time in Diana's life she felt complete contentment.

Lester Ballantyne fell in love with Diana when they were both very young. By twenty, he had risen to Second Lieutenant in the army. He was deployed to an army recruiting center in Philadelphia. He had been there for only two weeks when she walked in. For Lester it was love at first sight. They became intimately involved resulting in Diana becoming pregnant. Lester begged her to marry him, but she refused, claiming it would be unfair. She did not love Lester the way he loved her. When their son Peter was born Diana gave him up to Madeline and Tom Lassiter, a couple who had one daughter, but could not have any more children. Madeline and Tom were very good to Diana over the years, keeping her up to date on Peter and sending her photographs. Diana shared everything about Peter with Lester.

She soon met James Kramer, a smooth talking, sophisticated, extremely good-looking CIA agent who recruited her from army counterintelligence into the CIA. Diana and James worked as partners, becoming a CIA operative couple and quickly married. They worked mainly in Russia and Eastern Europe. Lester never lost sight of Diana, always watching to protect her. He never trusted James. Eventually James' cover was blown. He was a double agent working for the Russians. By this time James and Diana had a son. James took their ten-year-old son Kevin into a car that he knew was wired to a bomb and killed them both. Diana was devastated but knew nothing about James and his treasonous activities. For years she believed that he and Kevin were murdered by a certain Russian agent, who Diana eventually killed.

Over time, Lester rose to the rank of general. Diana never officially left the army. Lester pulled her back into counterintelligence as a colonel. Now retired, both Lester and Diana remained with the CIA as overseers/handlers of the couples attached to Group Eleven.

Lester and Diana Ballantyne owned *The Double O Club* in Englewood, New Jersey. The "O" represented the words "only oldies." They served lunch and dinner with a full-service bar. Only music from past eras was played. In the two years it existed, the club had become extremely popular. On a Saturday night, one might wait two hours for a table. The club was Lester's dream, not Diana's. Now, working with Ross and Avery as part of their investigative team, Diana found her niche.

The comforting smell of freshly brewed coffee hit them before they opened the door. "Umm, my favorite smell," mused Avery as she and Ross stepped across the threshold into their new endeavor and cover. Diana and Lester greeted them with coffee and donuts. Whitney Van Wyck and his new wife Ernestine welcomed them with flowers and a fruit basket. Whitney and Ernestine Van Wyck were truly grateful to Ross and Avery for taking over the agency. It enabled them to fulfill their retirement dream of owning and operating a fifty-stall antique co-op on Route Seventeen in Paramus, NJ. All three couples were exactly where they wanted to be.

Whit explained the setup. The front room was the reception area where Diana would sit. There were two back rooms. One was an office for interviewing clients and working on cases. The other was used for storage and secure items and intel. There were no windows in that room as a precautionary feature. That room was always to be kept locked.

By early afternoon Ross, Avery and Diana were settled into their new surroundings. At exactly 13:00, the door opened. A well-dressed statuesque woman in her forties entered the office. Diana saw money as she quickly assessed the woman's expensively chic clothes, auburn shoulder length hair, and her downplayed jewelry, which, Diana knew was real.

From the moment Ms. Marion Kaaton entered the office, her expensive perfume drifted around her. Diana immediately recognized the fragrance. Dagmar, Diana's best friend, wore *Paris Noir*. There was no mistaking it.

Ms. Marion Kaaton was of Dutch origin. The Kaaton family came to New York in 1789 from Holland. Marion Kaaton was one of the wealthiest women in the United States. Her money was old money. From her family she inherited Kaaton Shipping Inc., which included a large import/export business and a fleet of ships. Marion's passions were Asian relics and her two teenage children, Roger and Denise Kaaton.

When there's a lot of money involved, it's sometimes difficult to know if you are truly loved by someone or you are deceitfully loved because that someone wants your money. Throughout her life, that was always Marion's dilemma. She wanted children but chose never to marry. Marion claimed she used a sperm bank to father her two children, both having the same father. Roger and Denise had been asking Marion to find their father. They convinced her that they had a right to know who he was. Marion said she tried to find him on her own but failed.

What brought Marion to seek professional help was an invaluable, irreplaceable Chinese statue. It was stolen from her home. "I want two things from you," she explained to Ross and Avery. "One, I want you to find my stolen statue, and two, I want you to find Kirby Lydell, my children's father."

"Are sperm banks allowed to give their clients the names of the sperm donors?" Avery queried.

Marion looked at Avery, surprised she would question that. "Well, whether they do, or they don't, I was able to get the name Kirby Lydell. I insisted on knowing the man who sired my children. My family is well known, and I am very rich. That may be why they willingly gave me what I wanted." coolly mused Marion as she looked around the office.

"Which sperm bank did you use, Ms. Kaaton?" Ross asked smiling politely at Marion.

Her answer surprised both Ross and Avery. "That is irrelevant. I gave you Kirby Lydell's name. There is no need to contact the sperm bank." Marion tried to hide her annoyance but failed.

Ross and Avery explained that her request involved two separate cases that needed to be dealt with individually. Marion look at them, smiled and said, "I have reason to believe there is a connection between Kirby Lydell and my stolen statue." Marion then admitted to having met Kirby Lydell in Atlantic City just before her statue was stolen. "It became crystal clear to me when I met Kirby Lydell in person that he was a very shady character." Ross and Avery said nothing but continued to listen. "Now, I want you to find him again. I know he is a professional gambler. He goes from casino to casino, from one gambling town to another. He's a high roller. When he's on a winning streak he lives high on the hog, but when he's losing he will do anything for money. Kirby Lydell sells his sperm and his blood whenever he needs money. He is a legitimate professional dealer but would rather gamble than deal."

"Does he know about his son and daughter?" Avery asked, suspicious of Marion's explanations.

"Yes, I told him about Roger and Denise, but he wants nothing to do with them."

"Does he have an alias, or more than one identity when he travels from one city to another?" Ross wondered.

Marion looked surprised answering, "I don't know. I never thought about that. Las Vegas would seem like the best place to begin looking for him, don't you think?" Marion asked sardonically, hoping they would take the bait and her case.

The entire Kirby Lydell story perplexed Avery. She was not buying it but decided to move on. "Let's talk about the missing statue," Avery suggested. Marion produced a photograph and handed it to Avery. The statue of a woman holding a small child was of Chinese origin, dating back at least five hundred years. It was made from black, green and red jade. Avery closely studied the photograph. She then asked, "Where did you find such a magnificent piece?"

"From the Smithers estate auction," answered Marion. "Clarence and Lillian Smithers were emissaries of the United States. In their travels all over the world, they acquired many beautiful relics and artifacts. They purchased that statue on one of their trips to Asia. Clarence and Lillian Smithers had one son, Clayton Emmet Smithers. He was living in London at the time of his fathers' death. He came home initially for the funeral but stayed on after his mother died suddenly. Clarence and Lillian died within four days of each other. That was so strange."

"Was there any sort of investigation into the causes of their deaths?" Avery asked, perplexed at the coincidental closeness of the demise of the elderly couple.

Marion thought for a moment. "No, I don't think so. I believe their deaths were deemed to be from natural causes. The Smithers were very good friends of my parents," Marion explained, sadly remembering. They sat in silence for a few moments. Marion continued. "It saddened me when I heard about the Smithers estate auction. Seeing so many pieces of furniture, paintings, relics and artifacts being auctioned off brought back so many memories of my youth when my parents and I would visit Clarence and Lillian."

"Who made the arrangements for the auction?" Ross inquired.

"I would assume it was Clarence and Lillian's attorney," Marion thoughtfully stated.

"Do you ever remember seeing their son Clayton when you and your parents visited Clarence and Lillian?" Ross asked as he leaned in closer to Marion.

"Yes, but I think I only saw him once or twice. I remember he was very stuck-up. He made it clear that he didn't want to be bothered with me. He attended some fancy boarding school because his parents were always travelling. My impression was that he was an angry unhappy child."

"Was he angry enough to murder his parents?" Avery asked directly, but with a hint of sarcasm.

Marion stared at Avery with a shocked look on her face. "I don't know," she answered, perplexed by the question.

"Tell us about the auction. Was Clayton Smithers there?" Ross asked.

"Yes, but I didn't speak to him and I don't think he saw me. If he did see me, he probably wouldn't have recognized me."

"But you can't be sure he didn't see or recognize you, right?" Marion didn't answer. "Go on about the auction and the statue," prodded Avery.

"I always loved the jade statue. I didn't care how much I had to bid to acquire it. A man kept bidding against me, but I was determined to win the bidding, which in the end, I did. What I didn't know at the time was that the man bidding against me was Kirby Lydell. I recognized him the moment I met him in Atlantic City, and I knew he recognized me. Neither of us acknowledged it." Again, the three sat in silence.

"Yes, I want to ask you about that," Ross said, paused, and then continued. "How did it happen that you met Kirby Lydell in Atlantic City, Ms. Kaaton?" Ross asked looking directly into Marion's eyes.

"It's very simple, really. I got his information from the sperm bank. I used a site on my computer which helps people find people. At that time, Kirby was living in Atlantic City. I called him, told him who I was, and he agreed to meet with me. It's as simple as that!" Marion exclaimed, as she sat back with a self-satisfied smile. Avery was beginning to get annoyed at Marion's sanctimonious attitude.

"You indicated that Kirby Lydell had a gambling addiction and he was always in debt. How could he possibly afford to bid on anything, much less a valuable statue?" Avery asked.

"He had to be working for someone who did not want to be seen at the auction. That's the only possibility I can think of," quickly answered Marion.

Avery continued her line of questioning. "Do you think the statue was stolen because it was valuable, or because something might have been hidden inside the statue, something of value, maybe something a foreign government would want?"

Marion's face turned ashen, "Do you mean that the statue could have been stolen by foreign spies who came into my home? Could Kirby Lydell be a foreign spy?" Neither Ross nor Avery answered, but just waited. Marion became unnerved asking, "Should I take this problem to the FBI or the CIA?"

Ross quickly answered, "No! Let us take care of the problem, for now. If we think the case should be handed over to the FBI or CIA, we'll take care of it." That was the right answer, the one Marion wanted to hear. Ross and Avery agreed to take both cases. Marion handed them eight thousand dollars as a down payment. The cost to Marion was dear, but she thought it was worth it. Both Ross and Avery agreed it would be best if Marion told Roger and Denise nothing. They were young teenagers and might become frightened. Marion agreed to honor their request.

"You asked if Kirby Lydell could be a foreign spy. Why would you connect him to spies? You really do suspect Kirby Lydell of stealing the statue don't you, Ms. Kaaton?" Avery asked.

"You make a good point, Avery," Ross said, looking at Marion.

Marion hesitated, then answered, "Well, he was there, at the auction, bidding against me for the statue. It just makes sense to me that he had to be working for someone unknown to us." Marion paused, and shrugged her shoulders, "I guess that's what you two need to find out," Marion smugly said off handedly, smiling as she got up to leave.

Ross and Avery did not know quite what to make of Marion Kaaton. They escorted her to the door, promising to be in touch. Once she left, they turned to Diana and asked her what she thought. The office had been wired so Diana could hear and see everything that occurred in the back office. "Yes, my darlings, I like it. I like it very much. There is something you should do immediately." Ross and Avery waited for Diana to continue. "You must find out which sperm bank Marion used and if Kirby Lydell actually did donate the sperm Marion claimed to have used. I can do that for you if you want," offered Diana.

"Yes, thank you Aunt Diana. I have the feeling what we have here is a complicated past history. Nothing felt exactly right to me," Avery admitted. Both Ross and Diana agreed. They all knew something was off. There were many pieces missing from Marion Kaaton's story.

They were sure the possibility was high that a foreign entity was involved in the theft of Marion Kaaton's statue. Diana decided to set up a meeting with Group Eleven that evening at the Hoboken safe house. She also asked Mr. Sandman to attend.

Included in Group Eleven were four couples with Diana and Lester Ballantyne at the helm as their advisors/handlers and Mr. Sandman as their boss. Ross and Avery, Albert and Sandra, Poppy and Lorelei, and Blake and Veronica made up the team. Each couple had their own special cover.

Ross and Avery were private investigators. Albert and Sandra owned a successful catering business in Hoboken known as *Albert's Garden Palace*. Poppy and Lorelei had a little boy still in diapers. Lorelei had become pregnant but suffered a miscarriage. They ran a cleaning service out of their house for private homes, stores, and office buildings. All four of their cleaners were CIA. Blake and Veronica maintained and were the key holders of the Hoboken safe house, while at the same time owning and operating a dry-cleaning business in Hoboken. Lester and Diana owned the very popular *Double 0 Club* in Englewood.

At 18:00 they were all seated in the living room of the Hoboken safe house eating cheese and crackers, drinking wine, and waiting for Mr. Sandman to arrive. He arrived with Esther Brouce, an attractive African American woman. Esther was Mr. Sandman's boss. She oversaw all stations in the north-east sector. They were happy to see Esther and welcomed her warmly. Earl Sandman and Esther Brouce had become very good friends. Their relationship was on the verge of becoming more.

After their meeting with Marion Kaaton, Ross did some digging regarding Kirby Lydell. Marion was right, he was a very shady character. Ross and Avery brought that information to the team meeting. Mr. Sandman knew the name Kirby Lydell. He was on the FBI radar, but not the CIA. Lydell had been involved in some unsavory activates working for the Mafia. His specialties were money laundering and petty theft. He was always in debt due to his gambling addiction. The Mafia owned him. Two questions swirled around Kirby Lydell: did he steal the jade statue? And if so, who was he working for?

Ross and Avery knew they had to find Kirby Lydell quickly. Once found, they needed to follow him closely to learn who he was entangled with. If it was a foreign entity the team would become involved. If it was domestic, Ross and Avery would take care of it themselves, asking Mr. Sandman's asset, Rocco DePalma, for assistance.

Clayton Smithers was the other question mark. Avery had the sense that all of these people, dead and alive, entwined around Marion Kaaton were connected. Avery was determined to unravel the knots.

Avery insisted that she and Ross immediately go pay Mr. Clayton Emmet Smithers a visit before he sold the estate and disappeared. Ross agreed.

They travelled to Hillshire in upper Westchester County. The Smithers estate was set back far from the road so it could not be seen. The mansion, sitting majestically atop a small hill, was a large red brick American colonial with black shudders. Ross pulled the car around the circular drive to the front door.

Stepping out of their car, they looked around and noticed two young Asian men pruning bushes and weeding a flower garden. The grounds were well kept which told Ross and Avery that money was not a problem. The butler answered the door. They showed him their credentials and asked to see Clayton Smithers. While they waited, they noticed the furnishings were sparse. Most everything had been auctioned off. The money from the auction went solely to Clayton.

Clayton Emmet Smithers greeted them from the top of the stairs. In his late forties, Clayton stood six feet tall with a well-toned, tanned body. His shortly cropped brown hair matched his brown eyes. A fleeting thought went through Avery's mind as he trotted down the long, wide staircase that he looked typically CIA. Clayton had a certain air about him that lead one to recognize he was well educated. His accent was almost British, but not quite. It annoyed him that Ross and Avery would question the cause of his parents' deaths, but he was willing to answer questions, thinking Ross and Avery were working for the Hillshire police.

Ross asked the first question. "Where do you live now and what do you do, Mr. Smithers?"

"I reside in London and I manage the London office of an import/export business."

Avery asked, "What's the name of the company you work for?"

Without thinking Clayton answered, "Kaaton Shipping, Inc."

Avery immediately jumped on it. "How well do you know Marion Kaaton?"

Clayton, without any hint of angst, answered, "I don't really know her at all. Her father hired me twenty years ago for his London operation." Avery was dubious of his answer. Both she and Ross were surprised that he didn't miss a beat when they revealed Marion Kaaton's name.

Avery jumped in again thwarting any question Ross wanted to ask. "Now, Marion runs the company. Surely you and Marion must have met for business purposes?"

Clayton's answer was simple, in fact too simple for Avery's liking. "She sends her New York people to London. She never comes herself." Clayton looked at Avery and then at Ross. After a moment he asked, "How do the two of you know Marion Kaaton?" Avery smiled, not answering his question. She was sure there was more to Clayton Emmet Smithers to be discovered. He seemed so CIA, but Avery was sure he wasn't. He lived in London. Maybe MI6, she thought.

There were no more questions forthcoming from either Ross or Avery as they stood up to leave. "Thank you for your time, Mr. Smithers. We'll be in touch," Ross stated flatly. Clayton bid them goodbye as he walked them out the door. He watched them drive away.

"What did you think, Ross?" Avery asked as they turned out of the estate onto the main road.

"Not much, Avery. I didn't believe a word he said," answered Ross with a disgusted look on his face.

"I want to contact Simon and Tessa in London. I have a strange feeling Clayton Smithers might be MI6," suggested Avery. Ross smiled and grunted, acknowledging Avery's suggestion.

When they got back to the agency, Diana had news. She had used her influence. So far in her investigation of the sperm banks in the tri-state area, Kirby Lydell was not registered, and neither was Marion Kaaton. Her quest was not complete, however. There were a few more sperm banks to check out. Diana was sure she would have the sperm bank investigation finished by the next morning.

Diana kept her word. The sperm bank investigation was completed, and nothing changed. Neither Kirby Lydell nor Marion Kaaton had ever been registered in any sperm bank. Diana called Marion Kaaton leaving her a message that Ross and Avery needed to see her immediately.

They didn't have to wait long. Marion Kaaton called The Van Wyck Detective Agency in a hysterical state. Roger and Denise Kaaton had been kidnapped and were being held by the Chinese. They wanted the jade statue in exchange for Marion's two children. Ross asked, "How did the captors relay that information to you?"

Between sobs Marion explained. "It was so strange. I was sitting on my terrace having my morning coffee when this drone swooped down and dropped the note right onto the table. It then immediately took off. While I was reading the ransom note the school called to verify that Roger and Denise were home sick. All I could do was scream and call you. Can you two please come over here, now?" Marion pleaded in a state of panic. Ross and Avery went into Manhattan to help Marion try to put the pieces together. It was now obvious that someone was watching Marion's every move.

With the kidnapping by the Chinese, the stakes were raised. Diana told Ross and Avery that it was time for the CIA to become involved. A meeting of the team was scheduled for that evening at the Hoboken safe house.

Marion owned a penthouse apartment in a luxury building on Park Avenue. Neither Ross nor Avery trusted Marion and the story she tried to sell them. It was time to confront her for the truth. They knew it was not secure to talk in Marion's apartment. Ross had done a quick check and was sure there had been bugs planted. They went to a nearby coffee shop. Marion became unnerved at the idea of someone watching and listening to her. She begged Ross and Avery to find the bugs and remove them from her apartment. Ross explained that if he did that it might mean a death sentence for her children. It would be telling the Chinese they were on to them. Ross strongly suggested they leave things as they were.

Avery was becoming quite agitated. She knew Marion was not telling them the whole truth or lying completely. She leaned forward, positioning herself as close to Marion from across the table as possible and whispered, "Do you realize what a dangerous position your children are in, if in fact they were actually kidnapped by the Chinese?" Marion stared at Avery not answering the question. Avery knew she had shaken Marion and continued. "In order to find your kids and return them to you safely you need to fess up and tell us the whole truth, Marion."

Avery's words stung. Tears began to run down Marion's face as she began to sob. "I don't think we should talk here, out in the open. Can we go to your office where it's secure?"

"Of course, we can," Ross quickly answered. They drove through the Lincoln Tunnel back to Hackensack. Diana was waiting for them. She knew what had occurred. "This is our office manager Diana. It's important she be a part of this," explained Ross, as he locked the door to the agency. They sat in Diana's area drinking tea. Diana insisted Marion eat a few cookies, explaining that the sugar would help her regain her equilibrium. Surprisingly, it worked. They did not push Marion but allowed her to tell everything at her own pace and in her own way. They knew Marion was extremely worried. She now understood the reality of what was at stake.

In her own time, Marion began to speak. "When I first came to you, I told you there were two issues I wanted dealt with. There are still two issues, but one of them has changed. I want you to find my children, but I still need you to retrieve the statue to save my children."

Avery jumped on the opportunity asking, "There is no record of either you or Kirby Lydell in any sperm bank in the tri-state area. Who is the real father of your children?"

Marion was startled, answering, "What do you mean? I told you, Kirby Lydell is their father."

Diana was itching to get involved but kept quiet. Avery became intense warning Marion that she needed to start telling the truth to save her children. "When you first came to us you said you were sure there was a connection between the theft of the statue and Kirby Lydell. Tell me about that connection. Did Kirby Lydell steal the statue? If he did, who was he working for? Who is the father of your son and daughter and how is he connected to all of this? These are the questions we need answered right now if you ever want to see your kids alive Ms. Kaaton. You came to us to solve your problems, but you lied. To what end, Ms. Kaaton, to what end?" By this time Avery was almost screaming at Marion. Diana put her hand on Avery's arm to pull her back. Avery began to calm down. But Marion Kaaton was clearly shaken, fulfilling Avery's objective.

Marion Kaaton was ready to reveal the truth. Ross, Avery and Diana sat waiting. Marion took a deep breath and began to explain. "The truth is that Clayton Emmet Smithers is the father of my children, but he doesn't know it." Ross, Avery and Diana stared at her blankly waiting for her explanation. "Clay and I were always attracted to each other. He was always trying to seduce me. When I finally decided I wanted children, I let him have his way with me until I became pregnant. I went back home to New York to have my baby. When Roger was a year old, I went back to London and picked up with Clay where we left off until I became pregnant with Denise. I went back to New York to have her, but I never returned to London. I always sent my New York people to deal with any business problems. Clay knows nothing of his two children, and that's the way I want it to stay," Marion strongly stated.

"Wasn't Clayton suspicious or at least surprised when you suddenly stopped seeing him?" Ross questioned.

"I think so because he called me a few times, but I was either too busy to take his calls or just ignored them," Marion coolly confessed.

Avery began to laugh at the absurdity of the situation. "That's horrible. How can you deny him of his son and daughter?" Avery asked, shaking her head.

"There is a valid reason," admitted Marion. "He has always and still is doing a terrific job running my London office. But I am sure he is involved in something else that is either dangerous or illegal. I do not want my kids involved with him in any way." It was then Avery was sure her suspicions about Clayton Smithers were right.

"It's too late for that kind of thinking, Ms. Kaaton. They are involved. You better tell us how everybody is connected. I think it's time we involve Clayton," stated Ross knowing he would be hearing from Simon and Tessa at any time with their answer. Ross was almost certain Clayton was MI6.

The three of them knew Marion Kaaton was hiding something important. Her children were being held to be exchanged for the missing jade statue, yet she was reluctant to reveal the missing piece of the story.

Diana knew she had to intervene. She took Marion's hands in hers, looked into Marion's eyes and calmly asked, "What's more important, the information you're keeping from us or Roger and Denise? If the intel you are keeping from us implicates you in any way, I ask you once again Marion, what is more important, you or your children?"

Marion looked up at Diana and began talking. "My company is losing money. Over the many years my family has been in business, my father and I, from time to time, for a price, have smuggled things into the country. Nothing illegal like drugs, but valuable relics and antiques. The Chinese knew we had done that for Clarence and Lillian. They approached me. They knew my company needed financing and offered me a legal offer. They would pay me a large sum of money to bid on the statue for them, acquiring it at any price, which I did. I was instructed to take it to their contact in Chinatown the next day. I would hand over the statue in exchange for the money they agreed to pay me. There was nothing illegal about my deal with the Chinese. That night the statue was stolen. The Chinese did not believe me when I explained what had happened. Kirby Lydell was bidding against me. I assumed he stole the statue, but why? He must be working for someone. That's all I do know, I swear it."

"Who contacted you when you failed to meet your contact with the statue?" Ross asked, beginning a line of questioning.

"I couldn't say. It was just a voice on the telephone."

"Were there any threats made involving you or your kids?"

"No, they said they would retrieve the statue another way. I did not feel threatened nor did I ever think for a minute that Roger and Denise were in any danger."

"Why did you make up all of that crap about Kirby Lydell? Why did you tell us he was the kids' father?" Avery asked.

"Just to hide the truth. He was the first person that came to mind," admitted Marion. Avery smiled, impressed at Marion's adeptness at lying.

Before Ross and Avery took Marion back to Manhattan, they instructed Diana to contact Clayton Smithers. She was to inform him that Ross and Avery would be back the next day because they believed his parents had both been murdered and they knew who killed them. Avery told Diana to then lock up the office and meet them in Hoboken. Ross was hoping to hear from Simon and Tessa before the team met but did not. Still, he and Avery believed Clayton was MI6.

By 18:00 Ross and Avery, Albert and Sandra, Poppy and Lorelei, Blake and Veronica, Lester and Diana, and Mr. Sandman were all seated in the living room of the Hoboken safe house. Ross began to explain the nature of the case. When the subject of Clayton Emmet Smithers came up, Avery took over. After she explained the circumstances she said, "And at first, I thought he was CIA, because he came across as *that* type, you know what I mean, right?"

"No, Avery, I don't know what you mean. What *do* you mean?" Lorelei smugly asked. Avery rolled her eyes, shrugged her shoulders, and looked the other way, ignoring Lorelei.

Albert leaned over to Sandra and whispered, "Here we go again!" Sandra looked at Albert, smiled and shook her head.

Diana was fuming. She had ordered Avery and Lorelei to work out their personal problems, never bringing them to work. "What we have here is a dangerous situation. Two young teens' lives are at stake. This situation is dicey and unpredictable, so please, try to focus," Diana stated, showing her anger.

Lorelei looked at Diana and whispered, "Sorry."

Ross continued to explain. "Tomorrow Avery and I are going back to Hillshire to talk to Clayton Smithers. I think he may have paid Kirby Lydell to steal the statue from Marion Kaaton. If he did, we need to find out why."

"The real question is why the Chinese are so anxious to get their hands on that statue that they would kidnap those two kids and threaten to kill them if Marion didn't produce the statue, which they believe she kept for herself? I am still not convinced that things are exactly as they seemed. Ross and I are anxious to question Mr. Clayton Emmet Smithers again," explained Avery, emphasizing his name, and avoiding eye contact with Lorelei.

Ross had left the room to answer his phone. When he came back, he announced, "My wife was right. Clayton Emmet Smithers is definitely MI6."

"I think the best thing for us to do is begin nosing around the Chinese communities to pick up any buzz about the two kids. Let's take the pictures Ross gave us and show them around," Poppy suggested.

"When showing the pictures to people, be very aware of how they react. Even a small thing like the raising of an eyebrow can tell you something," explained Lorelei.

"We need to find these two kids; however, I want you to stay put, Veronica. I just learned that Joey Jester and his gang are in the area and I do not want you taking any chances. You and Blake are off this one. Don't even go to the cleaners, Veronica, and that's an order. Blake can run the cleaners. You stay here, in the safe house," Mr. Sandman ordered. To the team, he seemed overly worried. Veronica picked up on that and promised to stay put. If she had to go out, she would use a good disguise.

The next day Diana opened the agency, Ross and Avery headed to Hillshire after giving their analyst Katrina a lead to work on. Albert and Sandra hit some of the Chinese communities in northern New Jersey. Poppy and Lorelei headed to Chinatown in Manhattan.

Ross called Marion on their way to Hillshire, telling her to remain in her apartment and not to allow anyone in. He was going to try to persuade Clayton to come back to Manhattan with them to talk with her. Ross told Marion it was extremely important to tell Clayton about his son and daughter. Clayton Emmet Smithers, Ross explained, may be the key to getting the kids back from the Chinese. Marion agreed.

When they arrived, Clayton was anxiously awaiting Ross and Avery. He ran out to meet them as they drove up. "Please tell me why you think my parents were murdered and who do you think murdered them?"

Ross got out of the car and immediately answered with, "First, we need to inform you that we know you are MI6. We are not with the Hillshire police. My wife and I are private investigators from the Van Wyck Detective Agency in Hackensack, New Jersey. We were hired by Marion Kaaton. A valuable Chinese Jade statue which she bought at your auction was stolen from her home. We think the Chinese may have sent someone here to see your parents. That person may have poisoned them making it appear like heart attacks, and then went in search of the statue," Ross explained.

"That all sounds absurd. I'm not sure what to address first," smugly answered Clayton. He then asked, "Why would the Chinese want to kill my parents? They were elderly and not able to defend themselves."

"I can't answer that right now, but we will find out who killed them, I promise," answered Ross.

"You said Marion Kaaton hired you?"

"Yes, and we need you to come back to Manhattan with us to meet with Marion. She needs to talk to you and tell you things," Ross said, peaking Clayton's interest.

"Does Marion really want to see me and what could she possibly have to say to me?" Clayton asked, almost to himself.

Avery walked up to Clayton and said, "You'd be surprised. She not only wants to see you, but she needs to see you."

Perplexed by the situation, Clayton answered, "OK, let's go see Marion Kaaton."

On their way to Manhattan Clayton asked, "What makes you two think I am MI6?"

Ross laughed and answered, "A little birdie told us."

Clayton smiled, sat back with his hands behind his head answering, "And I would bet that the two of you are CIA." Ross and Avery kept silent.

Avery couldn't resist the temptation. After a moment, she replied, "That's a compliment, thank you, Mr. Smithers"

"I'm right aren't I?" asked Clayton.

Avery quickly came back at him with, "Ask me no questions and I'll tell you no lies." Clayton laughed, knowing then who they really were.

As the three stood outside the door Clayton's stomach began to tighten. It was Marion, herself, who greeted them. For a short moment, before anyone spoke, Marion and Clayton stared hard at each other. "I was very sorry to hear about your parents. I have fond memories of visiting them as a child, with my parents," Marion stated somberly as she stood gazing at Clayton.

"Thanks, I appreciate that," he said, standing steadfast as he gazed back.

Ross and Avery gave each other a look. Ross immediately knew Avery was becoming uncomfortable. Her actions in such a situation could be unpredictable. Ross decided to move things along. "Why don't the four of us go inside and sit down. Marion, maybe you could ask your housekeeper to bring us some coffee," Ross suggested as he corralled them into the living room. Ross put his fingers to his lips indicating they stay silent. Ross quickly walked around temporarily disarming the listening devices he detected in the room.

"Of course," Marion answered as she walked into the kitchen to ask Yanyu to serve coffee and cake.

"You have two Asian gardeners I noticed working on the grounds. Who are they, Clayton?" Avery inquired.

"It's interesting you asked. Just before my father died, he told me that the gardening service he was using went out of business. The two men that are there now showed up before my father had a chance to hire someone else. My father assumed they were sent by the new service who was picking up the other's customers."

"What's the name of the new gardening service?" Avery asked.

Clayton thought for a moment. "I don't know. My father passed away just after they started." Again, he paused thoughtfully, sat down, and said, "My mother passed away shortly after that. Do think there's a connection between those two men and my parents' deaths?"

Avery answered. "There might be. I noticed that both men had the same tattoo, each on their lower right arm. I made a sketch. It looks like a sun, a circle with spokes. In the center is a red dragon. I gave the sketch to one of our best analysts. She came up with something very interesting. That tattoo represents a Chinese group known as the *Brotherhood of the Dragon's Revenge*. The group is dedicated to finding, recovering, and preserving all relics and antiques of Chinese origin representing the

Chinese culture and people, and punishing those who perpetrated any wrongdoing against the Chinese people or government."

"Then why didn't they just steal the jade statue. What's so special about it?" Marion began sobbing. "Why did they kidnap my children?" Clayton put his arm around Marion to comfort her and she leaned into him as she wept. Both Ross and Avery hoped the time had come for Marion to tell Clayton about his son and daughter. They waited, Marion composed herself, but said nothing.

Yanyu came into the living room wheeling a cart laden with coffee and a variety of pastries. Marion looked up and through her tears whimpered, "Thank you, Yanyu." The housekeeper turned to take her leave, hesitated, and began to leave the room.

"Yanyu, please come back," ordered Avery. The woman did as she was told. "You hesitated before you turned to leave. Please tell us what you know about the kidnapping."

Yanyu bent her head down, bowed to Marion and whispered, "I am truly sorry, Madame. My children are in grave danger and..."

Clayton stood up and stopped Yanyu from continuing by putting his arm around her. "That's fine, Yanyu, I'll explain the rest. I want you to hear this, also. Please, sit down," Clayton requested as he gently prodded her onto a chair. Clayton stood in front of them. "I am going to try to make a long story as short as possible. It's high time the story is told and put to rest. It is a story about revenge, unfair revenge. A very long time ago, during World War II, a Chinese man by the man of Woo Chen, was blackmailed by the Japanese to work for them as a spy. If he had refused, the Japanese would have murdered his entire family, including yours, Yanyu. Woo Chen did what he had to do save his family from certain death. Unfortunately, Woo Chen's capitulation meant the lives of hundreds, maybe even thousands of Chinese. Woo Chen was Yanyu's great uncle. Yanyu has two children a son, Bo Chen, and a daughter, Liling." At the sound of her children's names, Yanyu began to cry. "Please don't cry, Yanyu. Your children are quite safe and are in protective custody in London with MI6." Clayton sat down next to Marion and said, "Marion, the Chinese don't want your children..."

"Stop Clayton," interrupted Marion. "They are not just my children. Roger and Denise are *our* children. You are their father." Marion's unexpected revelation left Clayton speechless, but he began thinking, putting the pieces together.

"Why didn't you tell me? What kept you from telling me?" Clayton was feeling confusion, anger, and elation all at the same time. "I don't know what to say. I need time to process this."

"I'm so sorry, Clay, but I always suspected you were involved with something evil and very dangerous. I never imagined in my wildest dreams that you were MI6. I should have spoken with you years ago. Please forgive me. Please, save our children," begged Marion, as she wept.

Avery had become so emotionally involved in the scene between Marion and Clayton that she stood up and proclaimed, "I promise you Marion that Ross, Clayton, and I will do whatever it takes to save your children and to make sure that Yanyu and her children are reunited."

Clayton addressed Avery's proclamation. "Yes, Avery, but we must be very vigilant. The Chinese want revenge. In the statue the Japanese hid a list of all Woo Chen's descendances, including Yanyu. If the Chinese get the statue and retrieve that list, all of Woo Chen's relatives will be systematically murdered. In their mind that would be reparation for the deaths of so many. Killing all those people was also killing their families that would never exist. So, Woo Chen would never be allowed to have any family left alive as reparation for his treasonous acts."

"That's really tough stuff," stated Ross. He then looked at Avery and asserted, "Avery, it's time to quickly rally the troops." Avery silently agreed. Ross put a call in to Diana explaining what had occurred. Ross suggested Diana call Mr. Sandman for instructions. Ross agreed to stay at Marion's until he heard from Diana. Within ten minutes Diana called back. Mr. Sandman wanted to hold off until the statue was found. He suspected Clayton Smithers could accomplish that.

Clayton Smither's did accomplish that. He took out his phone and excused himself. Five minutes later he walked back into the living room smiling. "Kirby Lydell will be here in one hour with the jade statue," he announced.

Exactly one hour later, Kirby Lydell entered the living room, producing the statue. Clayton took the statue and carefully unscrewed the child's head where the list of names was hidden. It was empty. Kirby backed up towards the door. He put his hand into his pocket and produced the list. Everyone thought it was clever of him to have removed the list in case he was ambushed, and the statue was snatched from him. Kirby held the list up and announced, "Ladies and gentlemen, this list is for sale. I can sell it to you or the Chinese. Who wants to bid first?" Lydell asked smugly.

Avery became so enraged that without thinking she whipped out her gun and shot Kirby Lydell in the right shoulder and the left thigh, disabling him. It all happened so fast that all Kirby Lydell could ask was, "Hey, why the hell did you shoot me? I was only kidding!"

"Sure, you were, asshole," Avery answered sarcastically as she grabbed the list out of Lydell's hand and handed it to Clayton. Ross called an ambulance. The sirens could be heard coming closer. "The medics will be here soon, but you will be arrested," Avery explained. Ross then read Kirby Lydell his rights before he was formally arrested.

Kirby Lydell was treated and removed from Marion's apartment. Clayton stood holding the list of names. "I think we should burn this list and then return the statue to the Chinese. After all, it is rightfully theirs. I suggest we take it to the Chinese embassy and give it directly to the Chinese ambassador. I am confident if we do that, all will be resolved."

"What exactly does that mean?" Marion asked.

"It means we will get our children back and Yanyu will be reunited with her children. Believe me when I say that the Chinese do not want the blood of innocent American or British children on their hands." Marion threw her arms around Clayton and thanked him. Yanyu was sitting with her hands over her eyes. She looked up at Clayton and quietly thanked him.

Ross, Avery and Clayton went to the Chinese embassy. After explaining the situation, with the statue in hand, they were escorted into a waiting room and served tea. Within one hour, Clayton Emmet Smithers met his son Roger and his daughter Denise. Arrangements were made for Bo Chen and Liling to be reunited with their mother Yanyu.

At the same time, Albert and Sandra were sent to Hillshire to arrest the two gardeners for the murders of Clarence and Lillian Smithers.

The doorbell rang. Marion rushed, opened the door, and stood face to face with Roger, Denise, and their father. Ross and Avery stood behind them smiling. Clayton decided, with the approval of MI6 to send Yanyu's children to New York. Marion told Yanyu that they were all welcome to remain with her.

In the end, Clayton and Marion married. He resigned from MI6, moving back to New York to help Marion run Kaaton Shipping, Inc. They sold the apartment and moved to the estate in Hillshire, taking Yanyu and her children with them.

Diana was in the office when Ross and Avery arrived the next morning. "All's well that ends well," smugly said Ross.

Diana smiled answering, "That's what you think!"

CHAPTER 2
NIKA AND NATASHA

Ross and Avery walked into the Van Wyck Detective Agency to begin their day. Diana greeted them with a pot of freshly brewed coffee. After just having closed a difficult case the day before, they were hoping for a few days to rest and regroup. Ross threw up his arms and exclaimed, "All's well that ends well."

Diana smiled and said, "That's what you think!"

"What's that supposed to mean?" Avery asked just as Albert walked out of the bathroom.

Ross and Avery were both surprised to see Albert, but happy he took the time to visit their new workplace. "Where's Sandra?" Avery asked nonchalantly, as she poured herself a cup of coffee. "Who else wants coffee?" Avery asked, smiling at Albert. Seeing the look on his face, her smile disappeared. Albert explained that his visit was not a social call, but a call for assistance.

Ross walked over to Albert asking, "Where's Sandra? Does she know you're here?" Diana and Avery looked at one another, both concerned.

"No, Sandra does not know I'm here and for now I want it to stay that way," Albert said in a way that made it clear the situation was something Sandra knew nothing about. Neither Ross, Avery nor Diana spoke, but waited for Albert's explanation. He sat down, bent his head down and thought for a moment. When he looked up, Albert wore a cynical smile. He looked from Ross to Avery to Diana and said, "As Mr. Sandman would say, what I have here is a very sticky wicket."

Avery sat down and took a sip of coffee. "Sounds serious, what's up?"

Albert hesitated, but they patiently waited until he gathered his thoughts. "Twelve years ago, I met a beautiful young woman with whom I fell in love. Her name was… is Natasha." Albert stopped, anticipating a reaction to the woman's name. Diana took the bait.

"OK, I'll bite. Natasha is a Russian name. So, can we assume she was or is Russian?"

Albert looked at them and quietly announced, "Not *was* Russian, *is* Russian and she contacted me last night. I received a package in the mail containing a letter, and these," he explained handing an envelope to Ross. Ross looked at the contents of the envelope and handed it back to Albert.

Albert took the envelope back from Ross. He smiled and confessed, "I knew you, of all people Ross, would understand."

Avery and Diana looked at each other. "Would you mind sharing whatever this is with us," Diana insisted. Avery and Diana looked at the photographs, put them back into the envelope and handed it back to Albert without any comments. Not even Diana, who was never at a loss for words, knew what to say.

"Does she have a name?" Diana then managed to ask.

Albert gave her a crooked smile. "Yes, her name is Nika and she is ten years old."

Diana leaned forward towards Albert and said, "I have two questions. One, I assume Nika is your daughter and this is the first time you are learning about her? And two, is Natasha, who I assume is Nika's mother, a Russian operative?" Diana's eyes pierced Albert as she fleetingly thought, what is our group's obsession with the Russians?

Albert looked directly at Diana and shook his head yes. After a moment he said, "Nika is my daughter, but I'm not sure about Natasha. She was a Soviet operative when I was involved with her, but I don't know about now."

"Albert, just tell us how we can help you," Avery suggested.

"In her letter Natasha requested I meet her on the boardwalk in Coney Island by the old parachute jump. This could be a trap. If we could meet with Mr. Sandman, I would feel better. However, I do not want to drag Sandra into this until I'm sure it's safe," Albert explained.

"When is this reunion supposed to take place?" Diana asked, glancing at her calendar.

"Tomorrow at 13:00," Albert answered.

"OK, let me call Earl to see when he can meet with us," Diana said as she made the call. Ross and Avery pulled Albert into their back office.

"Albert, do you want Avery and me to go with you to meet Natasha to watch your back?" Ross ask as he put his hand on Albert's shoulder. Before Albert answered, Ross added, "Avery and I will go in disguise, just to be safe."

"Yes, please, and yes, you two going in disguise may be a good idea," Albert said, with a sense of relief. Diana poked her head in the door to inform them that Mr. Sandman was on his way.

While they waited Avery asked Diana, "What do you think about this Natasha?". Diana looked seriously at Avery and answered, "No Avery, I don't like; I don't like it at all." Avery stared at Diana, not knowing how to respond.

Mr. Earl Sandman walked into the agency with his usual sophisticated bearing. He got right to the point, asking Albert for the letter from Natasha. He studied the letter, seemingly reading it three or four times. Without speaking he put the letter back in its envelope. He began examining the photos of Nika. Sighing deeply, he handed the photos to Albert and asked, "Did you consider that she might be using Nika as bait?"

Before Albert had a chance to answer, Lester came bounding through the door holding a large bag of Diana's favorite smoked almonds from *The Nut Niche* in Hoboken. Seeing Mr. Sandman Lester exclaimed, "I'm sorry, am I interrupting a clandestine meeting?"

"No, not at all, in fact I'm glad you're here. I called a meeting for the team in Hoboken at 18:00. It's pizza night at the Hoboken safe house. The key holders are ordering in," Mr. Sandman said with a hint of levity.

Lester, on the other hand, became serious. He looked at Diana when he handed her the almonds, then looked at his colleagues and asked, "What's going on?" Without speaking, Albert handed Lester the letter and photos of Nika.

Albert watched Lester's face as he read the letter and scanned through the photos of the little girl. "It's quite a sticky wicket, isn't it Lester?" Albert asked.

"Don't worry, Albert. We'll all meet tonight." Lester put his arm around him assuringly. "We're a damn good team and we'll all be there to do whatever it is we need to do to help you."

"Thank you, all of you. Now the hard part. I need to go home and explain this to Sandra before our meeting."

Avery hugged Albert and said, "Don't worry, Sandra loves you very much. You two are a great team and have always come through for each other. She will come through for you now."

Albert hugged Avery back and thanked her for her support. "Well, my dear friends, wish me luck!" With those parting words Albert went home.

Albert's parents, Inger and Almund Goode greeted him as he walked in the door. They were playing with their grandson Albert Jr. who Albert and Sandra called Albee.

Looking around he asked, "Where's Sandra?" His mother Inger was so involved with the baby that she didn't hear him.

His father Almund laughed answering, "Your mother cannot get enough of that baby. Sandra is on her way home from some business regarding the catering hall. She should be home any minute."

"Thanks Pop," Albert said as he walked into the kitchen. Sandra walked in several minutes later. She picked Albee up, kissed him and handed him back to Inger.

Albert came out of the kitchen and took Sandra into his arms saying, "I am taking you out to lunch, if it's OK with my parents."

Before Sandra could answer, Inger and Almund readily agreed telling them to go out for some alone time. As Albert held Sandra in his arms, he whispered, "I need to talk to you. We need privacy." Sandra knew there was something odd happening. She acquiesced.

Ernst Culbert, the owner of the Hauf Brau Haus, greeted Albert and Sandra warmly. Albert asked for a private table. Ernst smiled obligingly and escorted them to a table in a back corner.

Sandra was certain Albert's objective was not to be alone for a romantic lunch, but something serious and possibly unpleasant. "Albert, I know something is happening and that you will tell me when you're ready. There is nothing you can't share with me. Remember when I shared my deepest secret with you and how loving and understanding you were? I love you Albert and there is nothing in this world that we can't work out together." He picked up Sandra's hands and kissed them, thinking how right Avery was.

Albert held Sandra's hands in his as he began his story. "Many years ago, long before I met you, or even Pat, for that matter, I met a young woman with whom I fell in love. Her name was Natasha. I was just becoming involved with the AFD in Munich. Natasha was a Russian agent attached to the Soviets. We had an affair for about six months before I was arrested by the CIA." Sandra did not comment but waited for Albert to continue, imagining the next part of his story would be difficult for him to explain. Albert took out the envelope containing the letter from Natasha and the photos of Nika. "What's in this envelope will explain the rest," he whispered, as he handed the envelope to her.

Sandra opened the envelope and read the letter Natasha had written. She took out the photos of Nika and began looking at them. Sandra smiled and said, "She's adorable, Albert. She has my color hair and eyes, but your face. What could be better?" Albert finally began to relax.

"Sandra, it all happened so long ago. I never knew Nika existed until now."

"That's right, Albert, it happened a long time ago, but now there's a little girl who's in trouble. She's your daughter, so we must help her," Sandra insisted. But on the inside, Sandra felt sad, like a failure because of her inability to give Albert a child of their own.

Albert picked up Sandra's hands again, kissed them and said, "Thank you my darling. I love you more than you could ever imagine."

"What's our next step?" Sandra asked forcing herself to smile to hide the sadness inside of her.

"The team is meeting tonight at 18:00." Albert laughed and said, "Blake and Veronica are serving us pizza. I want you to come with me to the meeting to know how this will all play out. Then, I want you to remove yourself from the situation. For your own protection, I never want Natasha or any of her people to ever see you. It's Mr. Sandman's orders!" Albert said to emphasize the point.

"Of course, I will go with you to the meeting, but I will not promise to not go with you to meet Natasha and Nika." Albert was not happy with that but decided to let Mr. Sandman handle Sandra.

At exactly 18:00, Ross and Avery, Albert and Sandra, Poppy and Lorelei, Lester and Diana, Mr. Sandman, and the two agents who had partnered with Veronica in the past, Barry and JB aka Johnny Boy, were all assembled at the safe house on Park Ave. in Hoboken.

Mr. Sandman was very clear on how this situation was going to be handled. His ideas were firm and they all knew it. Ross and Avery, and Poppy and Lorelei were to go in disguise, on foot with Albert to watch his back. All five would be wired. Mr. Sandman would be in a van with Barry and JB seeing and hearing it all play out. They were the extraction team.

The situation was extremely dicey and unpredictable because they did not know the opposing players. What made it worse was that it could all be a trap set by Russian adversaries. Based on this Mr. Sandman made his decision about Sandra. He refused to allow her to go, even in the van. Sandra was angry but realized it was for her own protection.

Mr. Sandman's next consideration was Nika. He had no choice but to let things play out, but he promised to do everything in his power to protect the little girl. "Nika is an innocent child either being used as bait to get to Albert, or an innocent victim caught up in espionage," he explained. This upset the entire team because their number one rule of law was never to use or involve any of their children in any way with their work.

The meeting between Albert and Natasha was set for the next day on the boardwalk in Coney Island near the old parachute jump. Everyone knew their function. Lester and Diana would be on monitors with Caeley and Katrina from the Hoboken house. They were their emergency backup. If things went sideways they would immediately send help.

By 18:45 every detail was set. Blake and Veronica came back with the pizzas, and dinner was served. Veronica ran upstairs to take off her short brown wig and the shoes that made her limp slightly. Joey Jester and his gang were back from Florida. Veronica had mistakenly fingered one of their men causing his death. They had wanted revenge, trying to kill Veronica. To protect her Mr. Sandman agreed to stage her death to take the heat completely off and close the case for Joey Jester. Even though this all occurred over one year ago, Veronica always had to be in disguise when she left the safe house.

Mr. Sandman ordered Blake and Veronica to remain in the safe house during the operation in case they needed to use the house to sequester Nika and Natasha.

At 13:00 the next day with everyone wired, the situation was under control. Ross and Avery and Poppy and Lorelei stood far enough away from Albert not to be noticed, but close enough to see him. Mr. Sandman, Barry and JB sat just off the boardwalk near the old parachute jump in a van with monitors enabling them to watch things unfold.

Albert paced back and forth, constantly scanning his surroundings looking for Natasha. Albert's heart was pounding as he remembered Natasha as she was the last time he saw her. She was so beautiful. He loved her even though she was a Russian operative. He knew she wanted intel about the AFD movement that had begun growing very large all over Germany, especially in Munich. Albert knew her motive was to develop their relationship to gather intel, but he didn't care. He fell in love with Natasha and always suspected she did not feel the same. Their relationship abruptly ended when Poppy arrested Albert. What Albert did not know was that Natasha was pregnant with his child.

Albert was lost in his memories when an elderly man approached him. The team saw what was happening and began to pay very close attention. "Where the hell is that woman Natasha?" Mr. Sandman said fearing it was a trap. They all listened intently to the old man as he approached Albert.

"Excuse me, Albert," the old man stated with a kind smile.

"Where is my contact?" Albert asked with authority.

The old man kept smiling. "She is fine. Please, come with me and you will be taken to her."

"Who are you and why should I trust you?" Albert demanded.

"You can trust me. She sent me. Please don't make a scene. Just come with me," the old man insisted. The old man began walking away and Albert did as he was told, he followed.

The team also followed. Ross, Avery, Poppy and Lorelei on foot. Mr. Sandman, Barry, and JB in the van. Lester, Diana, Caeley and Katrina watched and listened from the Hoboken house.

The old man led Albert to a building on Coney Island Ave. in Brighton Beach. Ross made sure to see which apartment they lead Albert into. He then went up on the roof of the building with binoculars and scoped the surrounding area for snipers or suspicious looking people. Avery cased the main entrance to the building while Poppy and Lorelei covered the basement exit and surroundings. The van was parked directly across the street from the building, enabling them to get out quickly if needed.

Neither Natasha nor Nika were in the apartment. An elderly woman was sitting at the kitchen table drinking tea when Albert and the old man arrived. Mr. Sandman's angst was growing. Poppy asked himself aloud, "What the hell is their game?"

"I don't know, but stay put," answered Mr. Sandman in such a way that both Barry and JB knew he was worried. "OK, folks, they're moving again, this time with an old woman. Keep on him and stay hidden," ordered Mr. Sandman as Barry started the engine, ready to move the van as soon as Albert and the old woman came out of the building. Mr. Sandman ordered Ross to stay on the roof until they were all at least one block away. Poppy and Lorelei were behind Albert and the old woman. Ross and Avery were one block behind them.

The old woman led Albert to a car. She opened the car door, Albert hesitated but got in. Ross, Avery, Poppy and Lorelei quickly jumped into the van. They followed the car to Sheepshead Bay, making their way to a narrow street with small bungalows. The old woman pulled the car onto a small driveway but did not turned off the engine. She turned to Albert and said, "There is a boat docked in the back of this bungalow. Get out of the car, walk through the bungalow to the back door. Go through that door and step up onto the deck of the boat. Wait there until someone comes to get you. Do you understand my instructions clearly, Albert?"

"Who are you people? And why am I being sent on a wild goose chase?" Albert's patience was running thin and his team knew it. Yet, Mr. Sandman ordered them all to stay put.

"Everything will become clear eventually. Please, just follow my instructions and all will be well," the old woman answered in a soft assuring voice. Albert knew he no choice but to follow through. He got out of the car and closed the car door. He looked around and saw the white van parked up the street. He felt more confident knowing the troops were right behind him.

Albert shut the car door expecting the old woman to go with him. Instead, she backed out of the driveway and drove off. He didn't move. He looked back at the white van but didn't make a move to go into the bungalow.

Watching Albert on the monitor Ross was becoming agitated. "What the hell is he waiting for. He's putting himself at risk standing out in the open like that." Ross was clearly upset.

"Take it easy, Ross, and that's an order," demanded Mr. Sandman. At that moment Albert began walking towards the van. "He's chickening out. You guys be ready to grab him and pull him in as soon as I give you the word," ordered Mr. Sandman.

Albert stopped midway between the bungalow and the white van. Suddenly, he turned and with purpose walked back to the bungalow and went inside. "I've never seen Albert hesitate like that before," Poppy said.

Lorelei answered her husband with, "Albert has never been in this kind of a position before." Avery was going to shoot a barb back at Lorelei but thought the better of it, keeping her mouth shut.

Albert stepped up onto the boat's deck and waited just as he was instructed. A younger woman came up on deck from below to meet Albert. "Come with me, please," instructed the woman. When he got below, Natasha was there to greet him. The woman excused herself and went back up on deck. Natasha and Albert embraced. She kissed him passionately and he responded. Albert pulled away. "Where is my daughter Nika?"

"All in good time, Albert. I am sorry about the wild goose chase, but Nika and I are both in grave danger. I can't take care of her properly anymore. You must take her. I have no family. You are her father and my only hope."

"Why are you and Nika in grave danger?" Albert asked bluntly.

"The Soviets are after me. I met this man, a Soviet, and I became involved with him. He turned out to be a traitor and they killed him. Because of my involvement with that man, they believe I am also a traitor. They want to kill me.

"Are you a traitor?" Albert whispered.

"No, I am a true Soviet!" exclaimed Natasha.

"In that case, I don't know how I can help you," Albert said looking away from Natasha.

"I am so afraid for Nika. Albert, I beg you, please take her. She is such a good girl and I am certain that you and Sandra will grow to love her."

Shocked, Albert asked, "How do you know my wife's name?"

Ignoring the question, Natasha explained, "Nika's full name is Nika Tatiana Goode. I have talked about you and showed her many photos of you. She will recognize you when she meets you, I promise."

"Are you sure of that, Natasha?" Albert whispered. He looked at Natasha and asked, "What if she misses you too much? What if she cries for you? How do we deal with that?"

"For her protection, for her safety, and for Nika to have a chance for a good life, I am willing to give up all rights to her. You and Sandra can adopt her legally. I love Nika so much that I would be willing to do that." Natasha was crying. Albert put his arms around Natasha to comfort her.

"Nika is my daughter, so yes Natasha, Sandra and I will take her and adopt her legally, if that's what you really want."

"Yes, Albert that is what I really want. Does Sandra know about me and Nika?"

"Yes, she knows about you and Nika." Albert hesitated smiled and added, "As a matter of fact, you and Sandra look a lot alike. When I first met Sandra, I couldn't believe how much she looked like you," Albert admitted. Natasha and Albert looked at each other. They inched closer and closer until they were in each other's arms kissing passionately. When they broke apart Albert said, "I was so in love with you Natasha that I couldn't see straight. What hurt was knowing that you didn't feel the same."

Natasha stroked Albert's cheek and said, "I wasn't allowed to feel anything for you or anyone else. But now I can tell you that I loved you deeply, Albert."

Inside the van, witnessing the scene between Albert and Natasha, Avery became anxious. "Holy mackerel, now what are we going to do? Listen to that crap and to make it even worse she looks just like…"

"Don't say it!" Ross yelled, cutting Avery off.

"Right now, we do nothing. What we are seeing is exactly why I didn't want Sandra here. We're going to wait and see how this plays out," calmly answered Mr. Sandman. Knowing how anxious Avery was becoming he added, "Don't worry Avery, I'll know when we need to grab him if it comes to that.

Before Albert had a chance to respond to Natasha's admission of her love for him, the woman came back escorting Nika down into the boat to meet her father. Looking at Nika for the first time Albert could not help but smile. Petite, with long sable hair and brown eyes, she looked like both Natasha and Sandra. Her face, Albert thought, was more his sister Ramona. His heart began to melt. He knelt in front of the little girl and said, "I am your Papa, Nika."

Nika looked at Albert exploring his face with her eyes. she then began touching his face. Nika took her time, touching all aspects of Albert's face as she did his pictures her entire life. The realization set in for Nika that this man was actually her father. Tears of joy flowed down her cheeks. Nika threw her arms around Albert declaring, "You really are my Papa. I love you." Albert held Nika tight. The connection was there. He knew without a shadow of a doubt that Nika was his daughter.

"I love you, too, Nika, my Nika, my beautiful daughter." Albert's emotions were running wild. A part of him wanted to run away from Nika and Natasha as fast as he could, putting them out of his mind, and the other part of him wanted to embrace Nika, saving her from harm and offering her a bright future. The latter seemed most probable. Albert knew in his heart that Sandra would grow to love Nika and accept her as her own child.

Mr. Sandman knew it was time for him to figure out the best resolution for the situation. He tuned into Albert's earpiece ordering him to bring both Nika and Natasha to the van. "Yes sir, thank you," Albert answered.

"I am hoping we can turn Natasha. We'll take her and Nika to a safe house for now," Mr. Sandman informed Albert. He then added, "We'll pull up in front of the bungalow. Come out as quickly as you can. I want to get the ball rolling."

"Yes, sir, will do," Albert answered. He turned to Natasha and said, "It's time for us to go. For now, I have arranged for you and Nika to be taken to a safe house. Once there, you will be able to make decisions rationally, not out of fear." Natasha smiled, silently agreeing. They walked out to the van with Nika between them, each holding one of Nika's hands.

Barry pulled the van up in front of the bungalow. While waiting, Mr. Sandman thought about asking Andrei to talk to Natasha to soften her up to be turned. On the other hand, he wasn't sure he was willing to put Andrei in that kind of danger. They were dealing with the same people who had kidnapped Caeley when she was eight months pregnant to use as a bargaining chip. So far, they have left Andrei alone, but he would weigh it out.

The safe house chosen was an apartment in Manhattan on East 24th Street and Third Ave. It was a small L-shaped studio with a galley kitchen and a small bathroom. It was mainly used to sequester one or two people for a short time. There were no holding cells or interrogation rooms. It was the perfect place for Natasha. It was decided that Nika would not stay with Natasha but would go immediately with Albert.

Albert and Natasha, together, explained to Nika why she needed to separate from her mother. Nika resisted going with Albert, but at ten years old and having lived in the shadows most of her life, Nika understood and acquiesced.

As they parted Nika clung to her mother crying. Natasha once again patiently explained that going with her father was the only way to keep her safe. To help Nika through the pain of separation, Natasha lied telling her the arrangement was temporary until the people who wanted to harm them were arrested. Albert was not happy about lying to Nika, but it was the only way to convince her to go. She took Albert's hand and left with him.

On the way back to Hoboken, both Avery and Lorelei tried their best to help Nika feel comfortable. Both women knew she was missing her mother, suffering from separation anxiety. Albert was hoping that Sandra would give Nika enough love and attention to fill the gap. He was happy his parents were still visiting. Perhaps Nika's newly found Oma and Opa would also help her to adjust.

When Albert and Sandra handed the Hoboken safe house over to Blake and Veronica, they bought a smaller brownstone on Garden Street near their catering hall, *Albert's Garden Palace*. The people who lived there before had converted the walk-in basement to a small apartment. They installed a new kitchen on the main level. Ramona rented the basement apartment from her brother and Sandra. This gave Ramona independence, yet preserving the feeling of security she still needed.

That evening during dinner, Albert and Sandra explained to Nika that they would have to enroll her in school. Sandra promised to take her shopping for school supplies and allow her to pick out pick out a few new outfits to wear. Nika seemed pleased but was not as enthusiastic as Albert had hoped. However, he knew she needed time.

Nika would have Ramona's old room. There was a ruffled bedspread on the bed and frilly curtains on the windows, all in soft pastel colors. Nika sat on the bed staring at nothing. Sandra sat down and put her arm around the little girl. She kissed her lovingly on the head and whispered, "I know this is hard for you, Nika."

Nika looked up at Sandra and said, "You look just like my Mama." Nika handed Sandra the photo of Natasha that she was holding. She smiled and examined the photo. Sandra had never seen Natasha. What she saw made her smile disappear and her heart pound. She knew Natasha had been Albert's first love. She knew it took Albert a long time to get over Natasha. She knew the reason Albert never married Pat was because he always hoped Natasha would come back to him. What Sandra just discovered was that she and Natasha looked like twins.

Instantly things changed for Sandra. She was numb and unsure of everything that was dear to her. It all seemed surreal. Serious questions arose for Sandra. Was Albert's love for her real or was he still in love with Natasha, the mother of his child that Sandra could not give him? When Albert made love to her, who was he with, her or Natasha?

Sandra needed to be alone. She needed time to think. She asked Inger if she would listen for Albee and care for him if he awoke. She locked herself in her bathroom and ran a hot bath. She sat soaking in a bubble bath for over an hour. Albert knocked on the door. It was locked. He was worried. Sandra never locked the door. She assured Albert she was fine, but she needed some alone time. She had taken the photo of Natasha with her. She kept looking at it, staring at it as if she expected Natasha to speak to her through the photo.

Albert had gone downstairs. Sandra felt she couldn't deal with the situation. She needed to get out, to get away from Albert. Getting out of the tub she dried herself off and threw on a sweat suit, socks, and sneakers. She quietly went downstairs and into the kitchen. Sandra grabbed the car keys and went down the back stairway to Ramona's apartment. She knew Ramona had classes and would not be there. She left through the basement door.

Once in her car she called Avery. "Avery, it's me. I need to see you and Ross. I'm on my way over."

"Of course, we're here. We'll be waiting," Avery answered. Ross walked into the kitchen. "That was Sandra and she was crying. She's on her way over now," Avery explained.

"Should I make a pot of coffee or take out the booze?" Ross asked with a straight face.

"What kind of question is that?" Avery asked, annoyed at what she thought was Ross' insensitivity to Sandra. "To me Ross, that question seemed insensitive. You were there. You saw how Natasha and Sandra look like twins. Sandra probably saw a picture of her and freaked out," Avery said, becoming a combination of anxious and angry.

"My point exactly, she might need a stiff drink?" Avery was dumbfounded. She looked at Ross, shook her head, and walked out of the kitchen.

Mindo was just coming down the stairs to collect George, Ross' father who was blind. George had been on a construction job in Syria. He was kidnapped by terrorists and blinded. He was rescued, but his eyesight could not be restored. Ross and Avery insisted he move in with them permanently.

"Mindo, Sandra is on her way over. Please take George into his room. Then go upstairs and make sure Ralf and Kimmy's bedroom doors are closed. I don't want them hearing anything upsetting," Avery whispered.

"What happened? Why is Sandra so upset?" Mindo asked, showing sincere concern.

"I'm not quite sure, but when I find out I'll let you know. After all, you are a part of our family and an integral part of Group Eleven," Avery said. Mindo was willing to help in any way possible.

Just as Mindo got George to his room, Avery saw the car's headlights pull into the driveway. She opened the front door only to meet a sobbing Sandra who shoved a photo into Avery's hand. "Look at that, Avery, he married me because I look like the love of his life who was able to give him a child without any problem at all."

Avery had never seen Sandra so out of control. All she could do was put her arm around Sandra and lead her into the kitchen. Ross had a pot of freshly brewed coffee ready and a bottle of whiskey out on the counter. As soon as they walked into the kitchen, Ross saw the condition Sandra was in. He asked, "Which would you prefer Sandra, Coffee or whiskey?"

"Whiskey, please Ross, and make it a double," Sandra managed to say through her tears.

"Sure thing," Ross responded as he gave Avery an 'I told you so' look as he poured Sandra a drink. She thanked Ross, sat down at the table, downed that drink, and announced, "I'll have another, thank you very much."

Avery walked over to Sandra, put her arm around her and said, "The only way you are getting another whisky is if you agree to stay the night in our guest room." Avery stood her ground and Sandra agreed.

Sandra began slightly slurring her words. "I would rather stay here, anyway. I don't want to even look at Albert right now. Let him worry about me. He probably won't care anyway now that he has her, the love of his life and the mother of this child. He just married me because I looked like his precious Natasha." At that point, Ross told Avery to handle Sandra herself.

Avery sat next to Sandra and gently said, "I know Albert really loves you and he married you for the wonderful woman you are *not* because you reminded him of someone else." Sandra was quite drunk.

"Oh, sure Avery, you would say that. Anyway, I'm too drunk to argue. All I want is for you to lead me to a bed, so I can sleep it off."

Avery put her arms around Sandra and helped her off the chair. "Come on let's go. I'll put you in the guest room, but you'll have to walk upstairs, with my help, of course."

As Avery helped Sandra up the stairs Sandra said, "Don't call Albert, let him wonder what happened to me. Let him worry, even though I know he won't because I know damn well that it's that damn Russian woman he really loves…."

"Sandra, stop talking, lie down and go to sleep," Avery insisted as she coaxed Sandra onto the bed. Sandra was asleep in five minutes. Avery covered her, shut out the light, and gently closed the door. Ross was waiting outside the door. Avery looked at him and said, "She was not ready to hear anything positive about Albert tonight."

Ross agreed and said, "I just got off the phone with Albert. He knows Sandra is here safe, drunk, and asleep."

Avery put her arms around Ross. "Let's call it a night. I'm exhausted." Ross agreed. They walked into their bedroom and quietly closed the door.

Very early the next morning Nika woke up and quietly crept out into the living room. She looked around surveilling the area. Seeing Inger's purse on a side table, she opened it, rummaged around, and took out twenty dollars. Nika put the purse back exactly as she found it and went back to her room.

Ramona was up and dressed. She had classes later that day and had homework to finish. She knew about Nika and was just getting ready to go up introduce herself when she saw the little girl sneaking out. Ramona threw on her jacket, grabbed her purse and began following Nika, but Nika caught on quickly. She looked backed at Ramona and began to run.

Ramona followed Nika onto a path train. Nika ran through the cars, but Ramona stayed a few paces behind her, keeping just far enough away to keep an eye on her. Once in Manhattan, Ramona ran fast, determined to catch up with Nika. Ramona knew Nika was headed to wherever

Natasha was. Nika tried to throw her off by running into alleys and through a park, where Ramona almost lost her. Ramona was furious and caught her by the arm when Nika dodged into a vacant lot with no way out. "I've got you, you little brat. Do you know who I am?" Ramona asked as she looked directly at Nika. Ramona saw herself in Nika's face and couldn't help but smile.

Nika relaxed and examined Ramona's face. "Are you Ramona?"

"Yes, I am your Auntie Ramona. Now will you please take me to your mother!" Ramona demanded.

Nika led Ramona by the hand straight to the safe house apartment where Natasha was hidden. As soon as Natasha heard Nika's cries, she opened the door. Ramona made her move, pushing her way into the apartment. Natasha instinctively knew who she was. "Ramona? You look just like Albert. And, he was right. Nika has your facial features."

"Right, and of course you're Natasha," Ramona answered.

Natasha smiled. "Thank you for following Nika to keep her safe."

"I didn't follow her to keep her safe, I followed her to see you." Ramona paused, looking Natasha up and down. "You do know, of course, that you look just like Albert's wife, Sandra?" Ramona asked with a hint of cynicism.

Natasha had a surprised look on her face. "No, I did not know that. I never saw a photo of Sandra." Natasha turned to Nika. "You disobeyed me. It could have been a bad person who followed you, not your Aunt Ramona. What you did, Nika could have cost us our lives." Natasha was clearly angry with Nika.

Nika was crying. I'm sorry, Mama, but I missed you so much. Sandra looks just like you, so it made it harder for me not to miss you. I just wanted to come home, Mama."

Natasha put her arms around her daughter, kissed her head, and said, "This is not our home, Nika."

Nika looked up at her mother, tears running down her face, and sobbed, "For me, home is wherever you are Mama. You are my home."

"Listen to me my darling daughter," Natasha said as she held Nika's face in her hands, "My life is not safe. I want you to be safe and have a chance for a good life. Your father and Sandra can give you that chance and I insist you take it." Natasha looked at Ramona, who was sitting at the table in the small dining area. "Ramona, please take Nika back to your brother and explain to him what happened here. Maybe you can help Nika adjust."

Ramona wiped the tears from her eyes. She stood up, walked over to Nika and put her arm around her. "I will do my best, Natasha, I promise," Ramona said as she pulled Nika close to her. "No more running away from me, Nika. Do you understand?"

"Yes, I promise, Auntie Ramona." There was something about the way Nika said that that made Ramona realize that Nika would be a challenge. Yet Ramona knew she and Nika would grow to love and respect one another. Ramona then decided that she would become Nika's teacher and protector.

"Go, Nika, go with your Aunt Ramona, you can trust her. I will see you again someday, Nika. I am your Mama and I will love you forever. Now go," prodded Natasha.

Natasha flung open the door ready to push Nika and Ramona out. Albert was standing outside the door with his fist in the air ready to knock. When he saw Nika he looked up, closed his eyes, and exclaimed "Thank God." He then realized Ramona was there. "What the hell are you doing here?" he asked Ramona.

"You're welcome, Albert," Ramona answered sarcastically.

Ramona smiled as they all went back into the apartment. She looked at Albert, raised her eyebrows and said, "Don't ask, it's a long story." Ramona then looked at Natasha. "I'm taking Nika back, now." She waited a beat or two expecting Albert to say he was going with them, but he didn't. Ramona took a deep breath and concluded with, "I'll see you back at home, Albert." Albert smiled and nodded affirmatively.

By spending a great deal of time with Veronica, Ramona began to develop a very suspicious nature. As they walked out of the building Ramona spotted a coffee shop directly across the street. "Come on, Nika, your Auntie Ramona is going to treat you to an ice cream sundae." Nika happily agreed. Ramona put her arm around Nika saying, "We'll sit and talk and talk while we eat our ice cream. We'll really get to know one another." Ramona's true motive was to see how long Albert would spend alone with Natasha.

When Ramona was a child, she remembered how in love Albert was with Natasha. She remembered sneaking into Albert's room when he was home for a visit. Ramona found photos of Natasha. She remembered how beautifully exotic looking Natasha was. Ramona was sure Albert loved Sandra deeply even though she and Natasha looked so much alike but wondered if Natasha could seduce her brother into bed. She was determined to time Albert, seeing how long he would stay with Natasha.

That led Ramona to start thinking about Arlo. She would have to find a way to rekindle their relationship. Ramona looked at her watch and realized she and Nika had been sitting there for close to two hours. Remembering their love affair, Ramona was sure Albert and Natasha were not just talking about old times.

They had not been talking about old times. After Ramona left with Nika, Albert and Natasha stood silently face to face. The moment Albert had dreamed of for years was now a reality. He moved towards Natasha and gently stroked her face with his fingers. Natasha responded by gently kissing Albert. Albert parted his lips and their tongues intermingled, dancing in each other's mouths. As they pushed together Natasha could feel his hardness pushing on her thigh. Natasha began to open his pants, groping for him. Albert threw Natasha onto the bed and began undressing her. She wanted him to touch her. She moved her hips and removed her panties pleading with Albert to touch her and bury his hardness inside her. Albert removed his pants. He kissed each of her thighs, slowly working his way up to her pleasure spot. Albert then eased himself inside of her as Natasha wrapped her legs tightly around him.

Albert and Natasha made passionate love. As they lay together, Natasha rested her head on Albert's chest. When two people who truly and deeply love each other make love, it doesn't matter how long it is before they come together again, it's always right. But for Albert something felt different, not right. Natasha sensed it. She began to kiss Albert's neck while she gently stroked him. He began to get aroused but stopped. Pushing Natasha's hand away, Albert got out of bed and began getting dressed. Natasha sat up and asked, "What's wrong? What are you doing?"

Albert looked into Natasha's sad eyes. "I'm sorry, Natasha, but I am completely committed to and deeply in love with Sandra."

Natasha was confused. "But Albert, I thought nothing changed. I was the love of your life. Don't you love me anymore?"

Albert chose his words carefully. "Yes, nothing had changed, but when I met Sandra, everything changed." Natasha's eyes welled up with tears. Albert went to Natasha, but she turned her back to him. Softly Albert whispered, "I'm sorry, Natasha," as he left, he closed the door behind him.

Albert walked out of the building feeling a sense of relief and guilt at the same time. He ran his hand through his hair and adjusted his belt. Now he was sure. There was no doubt in his mind. There was no doubt in Ramona's mind either.

Ramona took Nika back to Hoboken. She made Nika apologize to Oma Inger for stealing the twenty dollars out of her purse. Ramona replaced the money, telling Nika she would have to work off the twenty dollars by helping Ramona with her chores. She took Nika down to her apartment and made her wash her dishes and fold her laundry. Nika enjoyed being with her aunt so much that it did not feel like punishment. Nika asked Ramona if she could earn money by always helping her with her chores. Ramona happily agreed.

Sandra arrived home early from her night of heavy drinking at Ross and Avery's. Albert was not at home. She assumed he was at the catering hall. She took a shower, dressed, and went to meet him with the expectation of talking about their problems. Albert was not there. She waited for three hours and went back home fuming mad.

Ramona was helping Nika get ready for starting school the next day. Albee was napping. Inger and Almund were watching TV. Sandra was sitting in the kitchen drinking coffee. Albert walked into the kitchen. Sandra stood up and motioned for Albert to follow her up to their bedroom. She closed the door, faced Albert, and asked, "I waited for over three hours at the catering hall. Where were you?"

Albert quickly answered with, "I went to get Nika. Ramona saw her sneaking out of the house and thankfully followed her into Manhattan, back to her mother." Albert felt very guilty about sleeping with Natasha. He was not able to look at Sandra directly.

Sandra understood body language. She knew Albert was hiding something. Sandra stood up straight, looked directly at him, and asked, "Albert, did you sleep with Natasha?"

Albert hesitated, and not looking directly at Sandra stated, "No, I did not!" Sandra did not believe him.

"You're lying. I'm a trained CIA operative. Don't you think I know when someone is lying?" Without speaking to Albert, she walked into the bathroom, closing and locking the door.

Through the door Albert said, "I'm going to the catering hall, Sandra." When she was sure he was gone, Sandra called Avery.

"Hi, it's me. Listen, I need some space from Albert right now. Can I stay with you and Ross for a few days?"

"Yes, of course. But what happened? I assumed the two of you worked it out," Avery asked.

Angrily Sandra explained, "I'm sure he slept with that Russian woman that looks just like me. Nika ran back to her early this morning.

Apparently, Ramona saw Nika sneaking out of the house and followed her to the safe house. Albert showed up and told Ramona to bring Nika back to Hoboken. Albert stayed with the Russian. When he finally decided to come home, I confronted him asking if he slept with her, and he denied it. He lied. I did not believe a word he said. I can't be in the same house with him right now. So, can I please stay with you guys?"

"Sure Sandra. Ross and I will help you in any way we can. Go to my house now and I'll call Mindo and tell him to expect you. I'll see you later." Avery answered compassionately.

Relieved, Sandra answered, "Thanks, Avery. I'm on my way." Sandra left Albert a note on their bed explaining that she needed some space, away from him, to think. She told him she would be staying with Ross and Avery.

While driving to Tenafly from Hoboken, Sandra began to think about an old relationship she had before meeting Albert. She called her. "I'd like to speak to Congresswoman Weston. Just tell her it's Sandy."

A familiar voice evoked both fear and warmth into Sandra. "Sandy is it really you?"

"Yes, Pam, it's really me. I just wanted to tell you… I mean apologize about the way I acted when we meet unexpectedly two years ago. I'm sorry, I was awful."

"No, Sandy, you don't have to apologize. I understand why you left me."

"I'm glad you understand, Pam. You'll always hold a special place in my heart."

"You were the love of my life. Remember, Sandy, my door is always open to you. Is there any way we could perhaps meet for a cup of coffee and a raison bran muffin?"

"Yes, I would love to see you. I can't believe you remembered my favorite kind of muffin."

"Oh, my dearest, I remember everything about you. Lunch next Tuesday? I have a wonderful place in mind."

"Maybe, I'll look at my schedule and get back to you, OK?"

"OK, I can't wait to see you and catch up."

"I'll call you. Bye, for now, Pam."

"Yes, bye, just for now."

Ramona was upset with what she thought she discovered about her brother and Natasha. She went to talk to Veronica. Sharing a few secrets, the two had become very close. Ramona thought of Veronica as her big sister and confidante.

Veronica listened to the entire saga Ramona breathlessly spewed out. When she finished, Veronica took Ramona by the shoulders, looked at her sternly and stated authoritatively, "Ramona, if you know what's good for you, stay out of this."

Ramona sheepishly answered, "But I know Albert really loves Sandra."

Veronica sat Ramona down. "Listen to me, I know Albert loves Sandra, but they need to work this out themselves. You need to trust them, Ramona. If you inject yourself into their problem, you will not be helping. In fact, you might only make things worse."

"I know you're right, Veronica. But there must be something I can do to help them," Ramona said.

Veronica smiled. "In my opinion, there are two things you can do to help. Number one, stay out of Albert and Sandra's temporary problem. And number two, help Nika adjust to her new life. From what you told me she really took to you. Nika needs you Ramona. Be there for her in the same way I'm here for you."

Ramona hugged Veronica and said, "Thank you for putting things in perspective for me. I will be there for Nika the same way you are here for me."

Veronica hugged Ramona back stating, That's my girl!"

Albert's phone rang. It was Mr. Sandman. "Hello, Albert, it's done. It's all taken care of."

"Thank you so much. I really owe you one," Albert sighed.

"You owe me nothing, Albert. I was happy to help bring closure to this fiasco," Mr. Sandman said as he smiled broadly.

When Sandra arrived, Avery was waiting for her at the door. "I thought you would be with Ross at the agency, but I'm glad you're here."

"Diana was there and nothing of significance was happening. She and Ross both suggested I come home to give you some TLC."

Sandra pulled a large suitcase out of her car. "I packed for about a week, just in case. I hope you don't mind," Sandra asked, feeling a little embarrassed.

Avery picked up on that and took the huge suitcase away from Sandra. Carrying it into the house, Avery said, "Don't worry about a thing, Sandra. You can stay with us as long as you need to."

Following Avery into the kitchen, Sandra answered "Thank you, that makes me feel cared for."

Avery smiled and said, "I did something else that will make you feel cared for. I bought you your favorite muffins, raisin bran. Here, sit down at the table and we'll have coffee and muffins."

Sandra sat down at the table with Avery. "That's just what the doctor ordered," Sandra announced as she smiled thinking of Pamela Weston.

While pouring their coffee Avery asked, "Should I call Diana in on this? She's very good with this sort of thing. If it weren't for her, Ross and I would never have gotten married. Marco caused a lot of trouble between me and Ross and Diana straightened it all out."

"No, I just thought that maybe you and I could go together to see the Russian woman."

Avery smiled. "She does have a name, you know. It's Natasha."

"I know her name, but it makes me sick to say it," Sandra said with contempt. "Will you go with me, Avery?"

"Yes, of course I'll go with you. We might want to ask Lorelei to join us," Avery cynically suggested.

"No, I don't want to involve Lorelei. Just you and me. I want to see her in person and confront her about Albert. We promised to take care of her daughter. Now, I just want her to leave us alone."

Avery looked seriously at Sandra. "That's fine, but we better take weapons. She is an adversary. Natasha is a Soviet."

Sandra laughed, "Yeah, just promise me that you'll prevent me from killing her." They both laughed.

Avery and Sandra knocked on the apartment door repeatedly. Finally, they decided to pick the lock to break in. Natasha was not there, nor were any of her belongings. With weapons drawn, Avery and Sandra looked around carefully. They found the suicide note on the dining table. The note said:

> I realize that my life will end. Your people will jail me, or my people will kill me because they think I am a traitor. If I must die, I will die the way I choose to die.
>
> I love the ocean. I will walk out into the ocean at night on Brighton Beach and never come back. Please, Albert and Sandra, take good care of Nika and love her. Nika is a sweet, good child and now she is yours and yours alone. Raise her to be a good person.

Forever grateful,

Natasha

Avery and Sandra both read the note. Both shocked, Avery called Ross and Sandra called Albert. That evening they met with Mr. Sandman for closure. The case was closed.

On a cruise ship a woman stands looking out into the ocean. She opens her small case. She takes out an envelope and tosses it into the ocean. She takes out another envelope, smiles, puts it back and closes the case. She sits on a deck chair and takes two pictures out of her pocket. One she kisses, the other picture she glares at angrily. She puts both pictures back into her pocket. With a heavy heart full of vengeance, she takes a deep breath of the clean ocean air.

It was dusk. The boardwalk at Brighten Beach was deserted except for Ross and Avery, Poppy and Lorelei, and Blake and Veronica who stood guard. They watched while Albert and Sandra, with Nika carrying flowers, walked towards the ocean.

Albert, Sandra, and Nika stood at the ocean's edge on Brighton Beach. Nika threw flowers into the ocean, saying goodbye to her Mama. Albert and Sandra walked away from the ocean with Nika between them each holding one of Nika's hands.

CHAPTER 3
PAMELA WETSON

The Wisteria Café was a popular upscale restaurant in the Soho section of Manhattan. Sandra arrived ten minutes early. She went to the bar and ordered whiskey on the rocks. Sandra swirled the ice around in the glass. She began to feel vulnerable. Why did she call Pam? What was she doing here? No one knew where she was. "I'll have the same, whiskey on the rocks," a familiar voice seductively uttered over Sandra's shoulder, heightening Sandra's anxiety and insecurity. "Let's go to our table, shall we, Sandy," Pam suggested as she lightly touched Sandra's arm to lead her to the back of the café, through a door and out into an outdoor garden with trellises of different shades of purple wisteria abundantly hanging gloriously down.

Sandra stood in awe taking it all in. "Wisteria are my favorite flowers," she whispered.

Pam stood close to Sandra answering, "Yes, I know. That's why we're here. Every time I come here I think of you." As they were seated at their table Pam smiled asking, "It is beautiful, isn't it?"

"Yes, Pam, this garden is luminous. Thank you for suggesting we meet here," Sandra responded somewhat breathlessly. "Do you come here often?" Sandra asked realizing she was feeling a bit light-headed.

Pam sensed Sandra's mounting anxiety, choosing her words carefully. "This is a very popular place. My staff and I come here for lunch whenever I have business in Manhattan."

As they sat eating lunch Sandra was aware of three security agents placed strategically around to protect Pam, who was a New York Congresswoman. Sandra smiled thinking that Pam had no idea she was CIA.

"So, tell me Sandy, how is your catering business doing?" Pam nonchalantly asked, trying to keep the conversation light. That question revealed that Pam was keeping track of her. Sandra was not sure how she felt about that, but let it go. Sandra was also not sure if she should mention Albert but decided it would be the right thing to do.

"My husband Albert and I have done very well with our catering business. *Albert's Garden Palace* is a very popular venue for large events. I am quite proud of what we've achieved." With those words Sandra began missing Albert. She began to regret her impulsiveness in calling Pam because she was angry at Albert. She realized that she was, in a way, using Pam to get back at Albert for sleeping with Natasha. Sandra was now feeling confused and conflicted. She wanted to bolt but didn't.

"Tell me about your family, Sandy," Pam casually suggested, smiling, resting her chin on her clasped hands.

"Well, Albert and I have a daughter and a baby son. Albert's sister Ramona lives in our basement apartment, which is street level. We own a brownstone in Hoboken on Garden Street near the catering hall. Albert's parents are living with us temporarily until they return to Germany." Sandra did not elaborate.

"Are you happy?" Sandra knew Pam was sincere.

"Yes, I am very happy." Pam looked at her watch, but Sandra continued. "Pam seeing you like this…" Sandra hesitated, and Pam waited. "Makes me want to…" Pam took control of the situation.

Leaning forward, Pam held Sandra's hand in hers. "No, Sandy, as much as I may want to, we can't. You have a good husband, a family, and a great business. Don't fuck it up. We'll always hold a special place in each other's hearts." With those words Pam put a period at the end of that part of their relationship. Sandra was surprised. She felt relieved.

"My goodness, we've been talking so much that the time has flown by. I have a meeting uptown in an hour. Can we meet again like this sometime soon?" Pam inquired.

Sandra hesitated and answered, "Sure, why not. I'm glad we connected. I would like it very much if we could remain friends."

"I would like that very much, too," answered Pam, pleasantly surprised by Sandra's suggestion they see each other as friends. As they got up to leave Sandra paused and looked around at the wisteria garden. *The Wisteria Café's* garden, at that moment, became one of Sandra's favorite spots.

Sandra and Pam stepped out of the Wisteria Café onto the sidewalk. "Well Sandy, it's been so nice being with you."

"Yes, it has been nice. We'll do it again soon." Sandra noticed a red laser beam aiming down towards them from the roof of the building across the street from the Café. She pushed Pam down yelling, "Sniper get down." Gun shots rang out and people began screaming and running in all directions. Pam Weston's security guards were all wounded, two superficially and one critically. Sandra was laying on top of Pam to protect her. "Pam, I'm sorry I pushed you so hard. Are you hurt?" The police and FBI were now on the scene.

"How the hell did you know how to do that. How did you know there was a sniper?"

"Instinct, I guess," Sandra whispered.

"Bullshit but thank you for saving my life. And, no, I'm not hurt." The FBI whisked Pam away. Sandra stood and watched.

An FBI agent approached Sandra, "You'll have to come with me, Miss."

Her cell phone began to ring. She knew she had to answer but dreaded it.

"Hello Albert, don't worry I'm fine."

"Congratulations! You saved the Congresswoman's life. What the hell were you doing there with her, Sandra?"

"I'm not discussing any of this with you now. I'm being taken into custody by the FBI. Please, get Mr. Sandman and come get me."

"OK. I just want you to know that I love you."

"I love you, too Albert." Sandra ended the call. She told an FBI agent what happened and showed him her CIA ID. The FBI agent said he had to take her in. The FBI agent made it clear to Sandra that this was not a CIA matter and that she and the CIA should stay away from this case.

As soon as the attempted assassination of Pamela Weston occurred, Sandra knew who she would turn to. Her cell phone rang again. It was Avery Lisano, her teammate and best friend. "Hey, I'm fine. I was just about to call you. The FBI is taking me in for questioning. I just spoke to Albert. He's at the catering hall. He and Mr. S. are coming to collect me from the FBI. Then we'll come over to you."

"Yes, Sandra, please do. Ross and I will be waiting for you. Diana will be here filled with angst. By the way, what the *hell* were you doing with Pamela Weston?

"Yes, I want Diana there, too. Thanks, see you later." Sandra ignored Avery's question.

Albert was waiting anxiously for Mr. Sandman. He knew who Pamela Weston was and how she had fit into Sandra's life in the past. Sleeping with Natasha was impulsive, and he prayed his stupidity and lying about it to Sandra wasn't destroying his life with the woman he truly and deeply loved.

Mr. Sandman knew exactly where they were holding Sandra. He and Albert, with their CIA IDs had easy access to where Sandra was being held. Agent Henry Collins saw Albert and Mr. Sandman arrive. "Hello, Earl. Come on in, but just you."

Mr. Sandman saw Albert's anger rising. He put his hand on Albert's shoulder. "It's OK, son. We'll have Sandra out in a minute. You wait here and let me deal with Agent Collins."

"OK, you know I trust you completely. I'll wait here." Albert sat down, and Mr. Sandman went into Henry's office and closed the door.

"OK, Henry, I want my agent back. I don't play with yours and you don't play with mine. I want her back now."

"She needs to be questioned. She's a suspect. She was there!" Henry snarled.

"My agent is no more a suspect than your cat. For all you know, she could have been the target, not Pamela Weston. She saved the Congresswoman's life, for Christ's sake. I want her released into my custody now."

"I don't know that I can do that. How do you know I have a cat?" Henry smiled enjoying the momentary power he was enjoying.

Mr. Earl Sandman had enough. He whipped out his gun and pointed it at Henry. "You get my agent now or I'll find something to charge you with. And before you ask, yes, I am threatening you Agent Henry Collins" Mr. Earl Sandman and Agent Henry Collins stared each other down. Mr. Earl Sandman won.

"I'll go get her. Put that gun away," Henry said as he went to get Sandra. Sandra was brought out and ran to Albert.

Mr. Sandman looked at Agent Henry Collins and said, "You better find that sniper and solve this case or I will. You got that, Agent Collins?" He didn't wait for an answer. He walked over to Albert and Sandra. "Come on, let's get the hell out of here."

Mr. Sandman dropped Albert and Sandra off at their catering hall. They stood momentarily across from each other silently mapping out their apologies: Albert for sleeping with his former lover Natasha and mother of his daughter, Nika. Sandra for rekindling her relationship with her former lover Pamela Weston. Sandra had told Albert about Pam before they got married. Albert understood but never considered that Sandra would ever contact her again.

Sandra made the first move towards Albert. They were in each other's arms both apologizing at the same time. Albert stopped them. "Let me speak first. I love you, Sandra and have from the moment we met in

Nashville. You are nothing like Natasha. It's you who owns my heart, and only you."

"I was so confused, Albert. It was an impulsive move to call Pam. You own my heart, and always will. I love you, the life that we have built together, and I love our children, Albee and Nika. I hope I can be a good mom to Nika. She deserves that. I'm sorry I called Pam."

"You saved her life, Sandra. Maybe you were meant to be there."

"Maybe, but that doesn't matter anymore. We need to go see Ross and Avery at the agency." Sandra's cell phone rang. "Hi, yes Mr. Sandman, Albert and I are going over to the agency right now. Ross and Avery are expecting us. We'll connect with you later."

In the car on the way to the agency Sandra made a statement to Albert. "Under no circumstances do I want anyone to know the true nature of my relationship with Pam."

"I understand, Sandra. What will the story be?"

Sandra thought for a moment. "OK, this is it because it's true. I was a freshman at Vanderbilt and Pam was a senior. I pledged her sorority and she became my big sister. Pam graduated and went on to Law school. We remained good friends. Pam became a lawyer and I went on for my master's degree in criminology. Pam then turned to politics and ran for Congress. We kept in touch over the years on and off. Pam called me to meet for lunch because she had a meeting in Manhattan today."

"Is that really all true?"

"Yes, Albert, every bit of it is true. I'm just not telling about the other part. That's no one's business. I hate lying. It's better to tell the truth and omit a detail or two then to lie about everything."

"I hate lies too. I am so sorry I did what I did and lied to you about it.. I swear Sandra, I'll never do it again."

"I believe you and I forgive you. Now we need to put it behind us and help Nika adjust to her new life."

Albert looked at Sandra, smiled and asked, "You're the best. How did I get so lucky?"

Sandra smiled back at Albert answering, "You are a very good man, Albert, that's how."

Ross, Avery and Diana were anxiously awaiting their arrival. As soon as Albert and Sandra walked in Ross and Avery began bombarding Sandra with questions. Diana pulled herself together and yelled, "OK, shut up and sit down." They all obeyed instantly. Lester walked in as if on cue

48

with a box of pastries to go with the pot of coffee Diana had just made. "Oh, good Lester, I'm glad you're here, please stay." We have a situation on our hands."

"Yes, I know. I saw you on TV, Sandra. You saved that Congresswoman's life. I'm proud of you." Lester began passing the box of pastries around while Diana poured the coffee. Lester looked at Sandra quizzically. "What were you doing there, not that it's any of my business?"

"It's OK. Pamela Weston and I met in college. She was my sorority big sister. We've remained friends and kept in touch through the years. She had a meeting in Manhattan and asked me to lunch. It was a last-minute thing. That's really all there is to it."

"How long have you known the Congresswoman?" Avery questioned with a formal tone.

Sandra became defensive. "Don't you dare interrogate me, Avery."

"I'm not, Sandy."

"And don't you dare call me Sandy."

"I'm sorry, Sandra," Avery answered sarcastically. Diana watched the scene and decided she didn't like what she saw, at all. There was clearly more here, and Diana was determined to find out the whole truth.

Diana ventured to ask, "Does Pamela Weston know you're CIA?"

Sandra was stunned Diana would ask her that question. "Absolutely not. I feel like my best friends are all interrogating me, not helping me." Albert put his arm around Sandra to make her feel safe.

"Sandra has been through a lot today. Let's put things on the back burner until tomorrow," Albert insisted.

"Before you and Sandra leave, I'd like to make a suggestion," Diana stated.

Albert gave Diana a serious look. "What kind of suggestion?"

Diana looked at Sandra. "I feel very strongly that you and Albert should remove yourselves from this entire situation. For whatever reason, Sandra, I don't think you can handle it."

Sandra took a deep breath. "I'll sleep on it tonight."

Diana smiled, "No, Sandra, you are off it, at least for now. I care about you and I just don't think you can handle *this,* Sandra, whatever *this* is." Diana and Sandra locked eyes for a moment. Sandra turned and walked out of the Agency with Albert following close behind.

"What are we missing here?" Diana asked softly, almost to herself.

"I don't know, but we're definitely missing something, and I intend to find out what it is," Avery responded. Diana glanced at Avery sideways.

The next morning Diana and Avery ask Ross to stay at the agency while they attempted to go speak with Sandra. They decided not to call, but to just show up at Sandra's home. Sandra saw Avery and Diana approach her brownstone. "Oh shit, no!" Sandra bristled. Sandra opened the door before they reached the stoop. As Diana and Avery climbed the steps to the front door where Sandra was standing, Sandra apologized for walking out of the agency in a huff the day before.

Diana got straight to the point. "That's why we're here, Sandra. Can we come in?"

"Of course, please come in. I'll put up a pot of coffee. Albert's mother made her apple crumb cake. We'll have some. Believe me when I tell you it's the best."

Avery looked around and listened but saw no one and heard nothing. "Where is everyone?"

"Well, Albert is at the catering hall. Inger and Almund took Albee to the park, Nika is in school as is Ramona, who lives downstairs," Sandra answered with a touch of hostility Diana noticed.

Diana smiled, "That's good. We can talk freely. What can you tell us about Pamela Weston? Why would somebody want to kill her?

Sandra looked down, and then up, directly at Diana. "I don't know. Diana, you know I'm brave, but this scares the shit out of me."

Avery answered. "Yes, Sandra, you are brave. We've worked together for a long time now. We've been in many dicey, unpredictable and precarious situations. You've never been scared. So, what's scaring you, now?"

"Pam was my mentor and my friend. She helped me become the woman I am today. Avery, I feel I owe her. This is personal. Maybe that's the difference."

Diana cocked her head to the side thoughtfully. "Sandra, would you be willing to call Pamela Weston to ask her if she will allow you me and Avery to come see her?"

"Why? The FBI are working on the case. This is not a CIA matter," Sandra declared.

"You are absolutely right! But Avery and I work for a private detective agency. Neither the FBI nor the CIA have any authority over us. We are a private agency. Anyone can hire us to solve their case."

"Even Pam?" Sandra asked smiling as she got Diana's point.

Avery answered. "Yes Sandra, even Pam. She could hire us if she wanted to."

"I don't work for your agency, so I couldn't be involved with your investigation, Right?" Sandra queried.

Avery answered. "Technically, no you can't. But on the QT, well, who would know?" Sandra looked at Diana for her opinion.

"Avery is right. If Pam hires us she is hiring private detectives, and you as Pam's friend are a concerned bystander. You were there. You were a witness. As Pam's friend you could offer your help in a quiet sort of discreet way," Diana put forward seductively.

"Call Pam, Sandra. Tell her you would like to come to her home to see her with your two friends who happen to be private investigators. Tell Pam to tell her security people we are friends but instruct her not to mention that we are private investigators. The FBI doesn't like certain people treading on their turf," Avery asserted.

Sandra called Pamela Weston. She invited Sandra, Avery and Diana for lunch the next day. Now it was time to tell Mr. Sandman what was about to take place. Diana called him. They set up a dinner meeting at *Lester's Double O Club* for that evening in the secure private room. Albert and Sandra, Ross and Avery, Lester and Diana, Poppy and Lorelei, Blake and Veronica, plus Katrina and Caeley, their two best analysts would all attend the meeting to be briefed on the situation unfolding. Because Pamela Weston was a member of Congress the meeting was top secret.

Mr. Sandman stood up. "OK, everybody, listen up. This is very important. Technically, we're not allowed to work on this case. The FBI has this one. I've already had a run-in today with Agent Henry Collins when Albert and I went to collect Sandra.

Sandra said, "Yeah, he knew I was CIA. I showed him my ID and answered all his questions. I told him everything I knew at the crime scene. There was no reason for him to bring me in and put me in a cell at FBI headquarters. The guy is a real asshole." Addressing Mr. Sandman, Sandra asked, "By the way, how did you get me out of there so fast?"

Mr. Sandman laughed and answered, "Let's just say I worked my magic." Everyone laughed.

Jokingly and laughing Avery asked, "What did you do, pull a gun on him?" Mr. Sandman looked at Avery in awe, amazed that she guessed. But then again, that's what Avery would have done. Avery saw the look on Mr. Sandman's face and blurted out, "Oh my God, you pulled a gun on him."

"Yes, Avery, I did. He pissed me off. But, I got Sandra back, quickly. It's my word against his and it stays in this room. Now, let's get down to business. Katrina and Caeley, I want you two to dig up everything you can on Pamela Weston. Someone out there doesn't like her. See what you can find. Diana, why don't you take it now?"

Diana stood up and looked around the room at her colleagues. "We are in a unique position. Ross, Avery and I run a privately-owned detective agency. Anyone can hire us *privately* even if the FBI, CIA, or the police are working on their case. Sandra called Pamela and she invited Sandra, Avery and I to her home tomorrow for lunch, at which time we will ask her to hire us. If Pamela agrees, the Van Wyck Detective Agency will become your source for information. Sandra will work as your contact. Any information we obtain you will get through Sandra. It will be Ross, Avery, Lester, and myself working to get all information. None of you must contact the agency or us directly. Only go through Sandra. She will be getting all intel and evidence we collect and will give it to you secretly and discreetly. Are there any questions?"

"How do we go about contacting Sandra?" Lorelei asked.

"You don't. Sandra will contact you with anything we give her. We'll work all that out after Pamela agrees to hire us, as we assume, she will. Let's meet in Hoboken at the safe house tomorrow night," Diana answered.

"How about a lasagna dinner tomorrow night?" Veronica asked smiling.

Avery looked stunned. "Since when did you learn how to cook?"

"Diana gave me the recipe. I made it for Blake, and he loved it. Right, Blake?"

"I certainly did. My Veronica is turning out to be quite the cook," Blake answered proudly.

"So now I want to make it for all of you, OK?" Veronica asked looking around at her colleagues. They all agreed, and a dinner meeting was set for 18:00 the next night.

Avery, however, was feeling hurt that Diana would share their secret recipe with anyone else. Diana hadn't even given the recipe to Lorelei, who was her daughter-in-law. Avery began to wonder if Veronica was trying to get close to Diana for some reason. Avery became annoyed, thinking that Veronica had a mother and didn't need Diana in the same way she did. Avery's mother was never there for her. Diana had always been there for her through it all, as a mother would for a daughter. Diana had even told her so, saying those exact words to her, "Avery, you are the daughter I never had." For Sandra's sake Avery decided to tuck these feelings and concerns away until the Pamela Weston case was solved.

Pamela lived in a lovely home in Westchester county. As Diana pulled the car around the circular drive, Pamela opened the door and came out to greet them. Instinctively both Diana and Avery noticed Sandra and Pamela greet each other with a certain intensity. But under the circumstances that was to be expected.

Lunch was served on a brick patio overlooking the swimming pool which was designed to look like a natural pond. Pamela's maid served a lunch consisting of two platters, one of cold meats and the other a variety of cheeses. There were rolls, rye bread, plus a large tossed garden salad.

While lunching Diana asked Pamela a benevolent array of questions about her background and education. Before becoming a member of Congress, Pamela was an extremely successful attorney. She then became a county prosecutor, and then a judge. When Pamela ran for Congress, she skillfully won by exposing her opponent's dirty dealings with a certain foreign country. Her opponent was not arrested, but some of his people were. That last piece of information was enough for Diana to reveal the true nature of their visit. "Congresswoman Weston…"

"Oh, please, call me Pamela."

But Sandra took over, which Avery immediately thought strange. In situations like this both she and Sandra always acquiesced to Diana. "Pam, the real reason we're here today is this. Avery is my best friend. Diana, Avery and her husband Ross operate a private detective agency. Diana is Ross' aunt. It's a family-run business." Sandra was beginning to speak fast and breathlessly. Avery and Diana both picked up on Sandra's angst.

Diana tried to defuse Sandra's anxiety. "Yes, and because we are a private enterprise, we can explore in ways the police, FBI, or even the CIA can't. If you hire us I promise that we will find out who took that shot at you and who gave the order to do it."

"Please Pam, hire them," Sandra pleaded. There was a moment of unsettling quiet on the brick patio. Avery looked into Sandra's eyes and saw fear. Diana noticed Avery's questioning look. She looked at Sandra and saw the fear. Diana and Avery, at that moment, knew that there was, without doubt, something they were missing. What they didn't know was that Pamela also saw Sandra's fear. Pamela Weston signed the contract

Diana brought with her, hiring the *Van Wyck Detective Agency* to clandestinely solve her case. Diana excused herself. She left the patio to call Ross at the agency asking him to inform the team that Pamela hired them.

The lasagna dinner that night at the Hoboken safe house was on. When Diana came back to the table the maid was just serving coffee and dessert. Diana sat down and when the maid left she asked Pamela if she had any enemies. Pamela answered no, except for her opponent and his people who she exposed for their dealings with the Mafia and perhaps a foreign entity to collect dirt on Pam.

"Which foreign entity are we talking about, here?" Diana asked.

Pam hesitated to answer. "Maybe the Russians."

"Why would they go to the Russians?" Diana asked. To herself she asked quietly, "What' everyone's obsession with the Russians?"

"Inness Jones was trying to accuse me of selling the Russians certain intel that I was privy to," Pamela told Diana.

Diana was stunned. "What kind of proof did he have?"

Pamela looked at Diana, shook her head and answered, "None, it was lies, all lies. It came down to my word against theirs. The people made their choice at the polls. My opponent's approval ratings, even among his own party, plummeted. He blamed me. He even tried to sue me for deformation of character, but it never went anywhere."

"Would that be a reason for him to hire a hit man to kill you?" Avery inquired.

"I don't know. That would be a very drastic act." Pam replied.

"Inness Jones was your opponent, you said?" Diana asked.

"Yes, Inness Jones ran against me."

"Is there anyone else you can think of that would want to cause you harm?" Diana prodded.

Pamela hesitated, then said, "Only one other person. My step-brother, but I can't imagine he would want to hurt me in any way."

"I didn't know you had a step-brother, Pam," Sandra asserted.

"Yes, Holden Weston. My father remarried after my mother died when I was eight. Noreen came with a five-year-old son. Noreen's husband was in construction and fell off a building that was under construction when Holden was two. My father adopted Holden. He loved both of us. He always treated Holden like his own son, and Holden loved my father. In fact, Holden took over my father's firm after he died. My father left me this house and the bulk of his money. Holden got the business and all my father's stock holdings."

"What kind of business?" Avery asked

"Financial services," Pam answered.

"That sounds very fair to me," Sandra responded.

"My father left me ten million dollars plus this house. Holden was angry my father didn't leave him part of the ten million dollars. The company and all of my father's stocks probably add up to much more than that but are not as concrete as cold hard cash and a house." Pamela mused.

"Please give me Holden's address and phone number. I think we should speak to him," Diana pressed.

"Well, if you really think it's worth bothering Holden, then sure," Pamela ceded.

"Pam what's wrong with you? This is as serious as it gets. Someone tried to kill you," snapped Sandra, as she quickly stood up.

Pamela stood up and facing Sandra held up her hands in response to Sandra's concern. "OK, OK, I'll do anything you say. Sandy, please, I don't want you to worry like that." Sandra ran to Pamela and they embraced. Both Diana and Avery thought they saw, for a split second, what they were missing, but both pushed it aside. Avery, however, did not miss that Pam called Sandra Sandy.

Pamela and Sandra sat down, and Pamela began to explain. "The former Senator Kyle Ashley and I were friends in college. He was an honest politician but became money hungry. He got involved with the mob taking payoffs for favors. Many of these favors lead to illegal business dealings such as money laundering, protection, and drug dealing just to name a few. I testified against him which led to Kyle Ashley's arrest last month."

They sat in silence until Diana asked, "Is there any possibility that your brother Holden was involved with Kyle Ashley in any way without your knowledge?"

Pamela Weston was stunned. Diana was even more stunned by Pamela's answer, "I just don't know, but maybe."

Driving back from Westchester Diana called Ross and asked him to investigate the relationship, if any, between the former Senator Kyle Ashley and Holden Weston. Diana then asked Avery and Sandra if they picked up any feeling or sense about the brother Holden Weston. Avery and Sandra both agreed that he was worth looking into. They both felt something did not smell right. Sandra never knew about Holden, which was odd, Sandra thought to herself, considering the nature of her past relationship with Pamela.

The lasagna dinner was called for 18:00. Everyone arrived at once. The lasagna was exactly like Diana's. Everyone praised Veronica for her new-found cooking ability. Avery was the only one not smiling. She was incensed that Veronica wangled the recipe out of Diana in the first place. But to make matters worse, Avery never believed Veronica could actually make the lasagna, but Veronica proved Avery wrong.

On an intellectual level Avery recognized her feelings of jealousy, anger and insecurity were ridiculous, but on an emotional level Avery was jealous and angry, feeling that Veronica was infringing on her turf. There was a case to solve now, so Avery boxed up the negative, irrational feelings and tucked them away.

Mr. Sandman joined them in time for coffee and dessert. He fully approved of their plan. They began to discuss possible reasons someone might have for wanting to kill Congresswoman Pamela Weston. Ross did discover a relationship between the former Senator Ashley and Pam's brother Holden Weston, but no indication of any wrongdoing was found.

The questions now became who and why would someone want to kill Pamela Weston? Was it for revenge, money, exposing secrets, exposing illegal activities, or something unbeknownst to Pamela, herself? If it was the former Senator Kyle Ashley, he would have had to have given the order to kill Pamela from prison. Or, was it a mob hit without Kyle Ashley's knowledge? Inness Jones was now also a suspect. He lost the last election to Pamela. Or could it have been Holden Weston, Pamela's brother? It was then that Avery asked, "Are we one hundred percent certain it was Pamela who was the target and not Sandra?" Complete silenced enveloped the room.

After a few moments, Diana stood up answering, "Good question, Avery." Diana paused, looked at Sandra and said, "Avery made a good point. I think it best, Sandra, if you stay away from Pamela Weston and this case until we sort things out. Lester will become your contact. The club will be where you go to get your intel. Are there any questions?" There were none.

"Maybe you're right. Both Albert and I will stay away from this. Anyway, I have Nika to deal with. Ramona has been a tremendous help with Nika, but Nika is my daughter now."

The next morning when Ross and Avery arrived at the detective agency, Diana was just making the coffee. "I think you two should go to prison today," she said with a smile.

"Why, what did we do?" Ross joked, half believing, for a moment, that Diana was suggesting he and Avery be jailed. Both Diana and Avery laughed out loud, recognizing Ross' impulsiveness.

"Ross don't be ridiculous. Aunt Diana is suggesting we go speak to Kyle Ashley," Avery chided.

"May I also suggest, if there is time, you go see Holden Weston," Diana proposed. "But first go to Brooklyn to see Kyle Ashley. You never know, it might actually lead you to Rocco DePalma."

"If we do wind up having to use Rocco DePalma, Mr. Sandman should go with us. Rocco is his asset," Ross stated.

Diana jumped in with, "No, Ross, no. Mr. Sandman can never be connected to us in any way with this case. If necessary, I am sure Mr. Sandman will find some way to connect you to Rocco DePalma."

As Ross and Avery were about to leave the agency the phone rang. Diana answered it and held up her hand indicating for Ross and Avery to wait. They witnessed the color drain from Diana's face. Diana leaned on the desk and sat down. Ross and Avery rushed to Diana. She hung up the phone, looked at Ross and Avery and flatly stated, "Pamela Weston was murdered." Ross and Avery stood transfixed, staring at Diana with disbelief.

"How? What happened?" Avery managed to whisper.

"The housekeeper found her floating naked face down in the pool. The water in the pool was red from her blood. When the police arrived, the two security guards were both found murdered as well, hidden in the bushes. This changes our plans for today," Diana stated.

"This raises things to a whole different level. Now we are searching for a murderer," stated Ross.

Diana looked at Ross answering, "It sure does. I just decided that we need Mr. Sandman in on it now, but only clandestinely in the background for advice and guidance."

"I want to be the one to tell Sandra, if she hasn't seen it on TV already," Avery asserted. Without waiting for an answer, Avery went into the back office to call Sandra. Sandra did not hear about Pamela's death, but agreed to meet with Avery at her house. Ralf was in school, but Avery would make sure Ross kept Kimberly out of earshot.

Lester and Diana went to the murder scene at Pamela Weston's home. The area was swarming with police, but not one FBI agent was at the crime scene. Maria Sancho, Pamela's housekeeper, had worked for the family for many years. When Lester and Diana arrived, Maria Sancho was sitting on the couch in the living room crying and speaking to a police detective in Spanish.

Lester introduced himself and Diana as the private investigators Pamela Weston hired to find out who tried to kill her. Lester explained that he and Diana felt obligated to help the police since they were paid in advance. The police welcomed their help.

Maria Sancho spoke English and agreed to answer any questions Lester and Diana asked her. Diana, on a hunch, asked Maria if Pamela was alone the night she was murdered. Maria began to sob, explaining that Pamela's friend Claire was there, but disappeared sometime during that night. Maria knew that Claire was supposed to have slept over that night. Claire's suitcase and all her things were still in the house, but Claire was nowhere to be found. Maria cried saying Claire just vanished without a trace.

When Ross and Avery arrived Albert and Sandra were sitting in the kitchen with Mindo and George Lisano, Ross' father, who was blind. Immediately Avery announced, "Please everyone, I need to speak to Sandra alone." Without questioning, Ross plucked Kimmy up out of her highchair. They all left the kitchen. Avery got two glasses, put ice in them and took out the whiskey.

"What are we drinking to?" Sandra asked, cocking her head to the side, smiling.

"We're not drinking to anything. I'm just going say this. Pamela Weston was murdered sometime during the night or early this morning." Sandra stared blankly at Avery as if she didn't hear her.

"What did you say, Avery?"

"Sandra, I am your best friend. I know you heard me. Pamela Weston was found dead floating naked face down in her pool this morning. Now drink down that whiskey," Avery ordered. Sandra obeyed and in one gulp downed the whiskey. Avery drank hers and filled their glasses again. "Sandra please, talk to me about you and Pamela." Avery could see that Sandra was on the verge of tears. "Please Sandra, you must talk to me," Avery pleaded. "I can see you're in a lot of pain."

"I don't want to talk about it here. We have to go someplace more private." Sandra began sobbing uncontrollably.

"We'll go upstairs. Let me tell Ross that we require complete privacy, OK?" Avery gently asked Sandra as she stroked Sandra's hair. Sandra silently nodded. Avery opened the door and beckoned Ross to her. She explained the circumstances and asked Ross to keep everyone downstairs, especially Albert. Ross did not question Avery. He saw Sandra sobbing and the whiskey bottle on the table.

Avery and Sandra took their glasses and the whiskey bottle and made their way up to Avery's bedroom. They closed and locked the door. They sat in the two chairs by the window. Avery poured them each another glass of whiskey. "Avery, how was she killed?" Sandra asked staccato-like through her sobs.

"I am not sure, but I think she was shot and died instantly. I doubt she suffered," Avery assured the sobbing Sandra. Avery was not sure of anything but did not want Sandra focusing on how Pamela died or if there was any pain and suffering. What Avery needed from Sandra was information on the nature of Sandra's relationship with Pamela Weston.

Avery was beginning to suspect what had been between Sandra and the Congresswoman, but Sandra needed to tell Avery herself. "Now please, Sandra, tell me the nature of your relationship with Pamela Weston. I have to know the truth in order to start looking for her killer."

Sandra pulled a few more tissues out of the box, wiped her face and blew her nose. "Albert knows all about it. I told him before we got married. He didn't care. He said he loved me from the moment we met in Nashville."

"Yes, Ross and I noticed his affinity towards you immediately. Now tell me about you and Pamela," urged Avery.

"Albert is so wonderful, and I love him so much and the life we made together. But when Natasha and Nika came into the picture things changed. When I found out Albert lied to me, swearing he did not sleep with Natasha, and then finding out he had slept with Natasha, I was crushed. Even after Albert and I worked it all out after Natasha died, I still had anger buried deep inside me. She looked just like me, Avery. Nika kept staring at me. It was so freaky. Albert swears we were very different as people, but still, she looked just like me. Sometimes even now, I catch Nika staring at me. Anyway, I called Pam. I felt I needed to see her."

"Why didn't you call me? Why did you run to Pam?" Avery pushed. "Sandra, for God's sakes, tell me the truth about you and Pam. I don't want to speculate or guess. You need to tell me straight out." By this time Avery was almost yelling but pulled herself back.

"Damn you, Avery, OK, I'll tell you straight out. At one time, before Pam ran for congress, she and I lived together. We were lovers. OK? Are you satisfied now? You know my secret and it must stay a secret between us. Promise me that Avery, please?

"OK, I promise, but that's the big deal? Listen, I'll share something with you that even Ross doesn't know. I never had trouble attracting guys, but when I first started at West Point, the guys were always ragging on us woman. Well this one girl and I had an unusual attraction to one another. It quickly developed into sex. That lasted about four months until she was washed out of West Point. The whole army thing was not for her. That was the only time for me. But Sandra, I believe that people can have attractions for one another no matter what sex they are. So, you see, I get it. And now, we both have our soulmates, so who the hell cares?"

"Thank you for sharing that with me. I feel now that I can tell you anything. We're truly sisters," Sandra said with relief. Avery hugged Sandra.

"Yes, we are sisters and best friends. I feel I can be completely open with you, also. But now Sandra, we must find Pam's killer. That's our main goal and I'm going to need your help big time. I'll tell you what, let's sit down with Ross and Albert and we will both give full disclosure about having a close sexual relationship with another woman. I don't mind sharing that with Albert, and If I know Ross, it will probably turn him on." Sandra laughed at Avery's candor.

"What about Diana, Avery?" Sandra hesitantly asked.

"You know as well as I that Diana is very savvy. She hasn't said anything to me, but I'm sure she guessed the nature of your relationship with Pam. We need to sit down with her, too. She is an essential part of our team. We'll need her on this one."

"Avery, go get Albert and Ross. Let's get it over with right now," asserted Sandra. Avery smiled and went downstairs. She quickly came back with Albert and Ross, each carrying a glass. The four of them toasted their bond as best friends and team-mates. Sandra looked at Avery and said, "You do it. You explain it to them. You're better at that sort of thing than I am." Albert poured Ross and himself another whiskey. Without speaking, both men drank it down. All eyes were on Avery.

"I'm not going to make a big thing about this, I'm just going to say it because it might be relevant to the case. First, I must disclose that my first year at West Point I had a short sexual encounter with another woman. She washed out before the year was up. And second, Sandra had one with Pamela Weston before she went into politics. Ross and Albert stared blankly at Avery and Sandra. Finally, Albert smiled and addressed Avery. "I knew that about Sandra, but I did not know that about you."

Ross chimed in, "And I didn't know that about either of you. So, who gives a rat's ass?" Ross smiled seductively and confessed, "And besides, it kind of turns me on." Avery looked at Sandra and they both started laughing. "What's so funny?" Ross asked.

Sandra answered, "Nothing, except that Avery predicted that it would turn you on."

"Okay, now we need to get off this kick and get serious about finding Pamela Weston's killer," Avery ordered. All four agreed.

That night Diana and Lester invited Ross, Avery, Albert, Sandra, Poppy, Lorelei, Andrei and Caeley to meet at Diana and Lester's condo in Englewood. When everyone had arrived, Diana explained the plan. "We need to start exploring all avenues leading to Pamela Weston. Lester and I know that Pamela was not alone the night she was killed. We went to the murder scene to speak with Maria Sancho, Pamela's housekeeper. She revealed that a woman named Claire was with Pam the night she was murdered. It seems that this Claire vanished without a trace. Ross, Avery you two now need to go to Brooklyn to see Kyle Ashley. Ask him if he knew this Claire. Lester and I will go talk to Pam's brother Holden Weston to ask him about Pam's funeral arrangements. We'll all pay our respects. Poppy and Lorelei, wear disguises and meet us at the agency first thing tomorrow. We will take your pictures and present you two as detectives attached to our agency. I want you two to go pay Inness Jones a visit. He was her adversary when Pam ran for Congress. If all else fails, Lester and I will go see Rocco DePalma. Andrei, Caeley, you two rummage around the Russian community. Any names that come up, research them, Caeley. It's a long shot, but you never know."

"What does the Russian community have to do with Pamela Weston?" Caeley asked.

Sandra answered, "Albert and I just had a bout with Natasha and who knows how many others of them were involved. We have Nika now. Maybe they don't like that."

"That's ridiculous, Sandra," Albert spouted. "Nika is my daughter and now yours, too. That's the way Natasha wanted it."

Diana jumped on Albert's words with, "No, no Albert. You mustn't think like that. Anything is possible. They may, in some sick way, blame Sandra for Natasha's suicide."

"Oh my God, I never thought of that. I think we should put a guard on Nika just in case they try to take her away from us," Sandra espoused, breathlessly.

"OK, we'll do it now. I'll put JB and Barry on Nika. I don't want you to worry, Sandra. And guys. keep an opened mind." Lester added.

As Whitney Van Wyck opened the door to his Hackensack house where his detective agency was located, the comforting aroma of coffee brewing enveloped him. He knew Diana and Lester had arrived.

With steaming cups of coffee in hand, Diana explained the Pamela Weston case to Whit. What was unusual was that Pamela had given Diana a check for five thousand dollars as a down payment to solve her attempted assassination. Now, it was her murder they needed to solve. Whit agreed that because Pamela Weston paid them something in advance, it was now their obligation to solve the case.

Whitney Van Wyck had worked as an asset for Mr. Sandman for years before he had retired. He worked it out with Mr. Sandman that Ross, Avery and Diana would operate the agency, using it for cover as CIA agents. Whit was happy to have been able to reopen the Van Wyck Detective Agency again. Under the auspices of Ross, Avery and Diana the agency had become a thriving business.

A couple entered the agency as the three sat discussing the case. Diana jumped up saying, "Oh my God, you two look great!" Diana turned to Whit. "You remember my son Peter and his wife Lorelei."

Whit stood up, looked closely and said, "I would never have recognized either of you. Those are terrific disguises."

Poppy laughed explaining, "We had a little help from our friends, if you know what I mean."

Whit shook his head in amazement, answering, "Indeed I do!"

Lester led Poppy and Lorelei into the back room to take their pictures and give them their phony IDs. As they walked out of the back Lorelei asked, "Can you tell us about Inness Jones, the man Pamela Weston ran against for Congress?"

"I sure can," Diana answered and began to relay what Pamela Weston had told her, Avery and Sandra. "Inness Jones and his people paid a Russian agent big bucks to lie about Pamela Weston, accusing Pam of selling high level intel to the Russians. Through smart investigating Pamela Weston and her people proved it was all lies being spread to discredit her, so Inness Jones could win the race for Congress. It was Inness Jones who was discredited. His career in politics ended."

"So, you think Inness Jones had Pamela Weston murdered out of revenge for ruining his creditability and career?" Poppy asked.

"That's what you and Lorelei need to find out for us, son," Lester answered and continued with, "We'll all meet in the secure room at the club tonight at 19:00. I have to be at the club tonight because Arlo is taking Ramona into Manhattan for dinner and to see a show for her birthday."

"I'm glad Arlo and Ramona are together again. Arlo is in love with Ramona. He was so miserable when she was refusing to see him," Lorelei admitted as she and Poppy left to confront Inness Jones.

Lester called Ross and Avery to tell them to be at the club at 19:00 with the information they got from the former Senator Kyle Ashley. Lester reminded Avery to find out the connection between Kyle Ashley and Pamela's brother, Holden Weston. Also, to tell them anything he knew about Pam's friend Claire, if he admitted knowing her at all.

Ross and Avery arrived at the prison in Brooklyn where Kyle Ashley was being held. As they sat waiting for the guard to bring Kyle Ashley out to see them, Avery told Ross to let her do all the talking. Ross agreed. Avery had met Pam and he hadn't.

Kyle Ashley sat across from Ross and Avery. As soon as Avery mentioned Pamela Weston's name Kyle Ashley teared up. He swore to Ross and Avery that he valued and loved Pam as a friend. He knew she had no choice but to testify against him. Avery immediately knew that the former Senator had nothing to do with Pamela Weston's murder. Avery asked if Kyle knew that Pamela Weston was gay. He said he did. Avery asked him if he knew Pamela Weston's friend Claire. He said he did and described her as a good- looking woman with long dark hair, the same description as Maria Sancho gave Diana and Lester. He told Ross and Avery that Claire and Pamela had been lovers for about a year.

Avery then asked Kyle Ashley if he had any dealings with Holden Weston. He said he was acquainted with Holden and met a few people through Holden who contributed to his political campaign. Avery and Ross both concurred that Kyle Ashley had nothing to do with Pamela Weston's murder. But one thing was clear; Claire needed to be found.

Poppy pulled the car around the circular drive curving around the front of Inness Jones' home. Poppy and Lorelei, aka, Parker and Larina Lenox, rang the doorbell. A maid answered, and they showed their IDs to her asking to see Inness Jones. The maid, with an attitude, asked them what it was in reference to. Poppy smiled and told her it was none of her business. Both he and Lorelei stared her down. It was Lorelei's violet-blue eyes that got to her. She acquiesced and escorted them into a large living room to wait.

Within five minutes a large, rotund man, with thinning gray hair and black-rimmed glasses walked into the room. "I'm Inness Jones, and who might you be?"

Poppy spoke. "My name is Parker Lenox, and this is my wife Larina. We're private detectives who Pamela Weston hired to find out who tried to kill her. Now our job is to find out who did kill her."

Inness Jones looked strangely at them and blurted, "Well, hell, you don't think I killed her, do you?"

Lorelei instantly disliked Inness Jones and answered, "Did you kill her Mr. Jones?"

"I hear an accent. Where are you from?" Inness Jones smugly questioned Lorelei.

Poppy became annoyed. "That's none of your business. We are here to ask you questions, Mr. Jones. Now tell me about your relationship with Pamela Weston."

Inness Jones looked at Poppy and Lorelei with a smirk on his face. "You two are not the police, the FBI, or the CIA, so I am not obligated to answer any of your questions. Now, get the hell out of my house."

Lorelei stopped Poppy from leaving. "We know you bribed a Russian agent to accuse Pamela Weston of selling the Russians some sort of intel she had privy to. Isn't that correct, Mr. Jones?"

"I don't have to answer you," Inness Jones barked at Lorelei.

Her answer was, "You're right Mr. Jones, you don't have to answer us if you choose not to, but you will have to answer to the CIA Mr. Jones." Lorelei handed him a business card. Inness Jones read the card.

"The *Van Wyck Detective Agency*. Your name is not Van Wyck."

"If you change your mind you can reach us there. Good day, Mr. Jones," Lorelei said as she gently pulled Poppy out of the house.

When Poppy pulled the car onto the road, Lorelei said, "He is hiding something. I think we should suggest the CIA question him." Poppy agreed to bring it up at the meeting that night.

Lester and Diana sat in the garden of The Wisteria Café where Sandra and Pamela Weston had eaten lunch the day of the assassination attempt. They questioned as many of the workers as they could but got nothing new. Even so, Diana was amazed how such a beautiful garden could exist right in the middle of Manhattan. From the café, they headed to the Weston building to speak to Holden Weston, who was expecting them.

Holden Weston was waiting with his secretary when Lester and Diana arrived. He invited them into his office to a comfortable sitting area which was more conducive for an intimate conversation. "My sister Pam called me after you and your two colleagues left after lunching with her." Holden was addressing Diana. "Pam and I were close. She called me to tell me you would be interviewing me and apologized for pointing to me as a suspect."

"Are you a suspect, Mr. Holden?" Lester asked in a serious tone.

Tears welled up in Holden's eyes. "No, I loved my sister. Our father left Pam the house and ten million dollars, but what he left me is worth much, much more, not just monetarily, but he completely trusted me to take his place as CEO of Weston Financial Services. He built this business from nothing. It was his baby, and he handed it over to me. That meant the world to me. Pam never had any interest in our business and had no desire to learn about it. She loved the law and politics. Pam and I were never in competition with each other."

Diana leaned forward asking, "When is Pam's funeral, Holden?"

"The police are supposed to release her to the funeral home. They need about two days they told me. So, I guess between four and five days," Holden explained as he began chocking up. Holden put his hands over his eyes and began to cry. "I just can't believe my sister Pam is dead, I just can't believe it."

Diana moved over to the couch where Holden was sitting and put her arms around him. He leaned into Diana and wept. Diana rubbed Holden's back and told him to cry it out. "Thank you, I needed that. Since she died I haven't had the time to cry."

Diana handed Holden a business card. "If there is anything you need or want us to do to help you through this difficult time, just call me at the agency. Also, please let us know when the funeral is. What funeral home are you using?" Diana soothingly asked.

"Chadwick Funeral Home and Pam will be buried in Flower Hill Memorial Park. It's a beautiful cemetery near our family home. Both our mothers and our father are buried there as well." Holden handed Diana a business card from the Chadwick Funeral Home.

On their way back to New Jersey both Lester and Diana agreed that Holden Weston was no longer a suspect in the murder of Pamela Weston. They went back to the agency where Ross and Avery were waiting. Diana knew something was terribly wrong as soon as she saw the look on Avery's face. "Something is wrong what is it, what happened?" Diana asked, fearing the answer.

"We didn't want to tell you on the phone and knew you were with Holden Weston." Avery stared blankly at Diana.

"Well, spit it out, now!" Diana demanded.

"Claire Panetta, Pamela Weston's lover, was found dead in a dumpster in Brooklyn. She was shot first to kill her, and then her body was cut to pieces. But that's not the worse part," Avery said as she again stared blankly at Diana.

This time it was Lester who blew up. "Well what the hell was the worst part, Avery?"

"Claire Panetta resembled Sandra," Avery quietly announced.

"Oh my God, Sandra is the target. Call Albert immediately…" Ross cut Diana off.

Ross quickly explained, "It's all taken care of. Albert is with Sandra in their brownstone and we called JB and Barry to go to Nika's school to guard her when she comes out at three o'clock. And, Andrei and Caeley have been all over the Russian community and found nothing. Andrei said he is sure any orders to kill came directly from someone in Russia."

"But who does Sandra know in Russia? What's the connection?" Avery asked.

"That is what Andrei and Caeley cannot find out," Ross answered.

Lester asked, "What school does Nika go to in Hoboken? Diana and I will go get her and bring her home to Albert and Sandra. Nika knows us and trusts us."

Avery answered, "I'm sure it's school number nine on Willow." Lester and Diana ran out of the agency to get to Hoboken as fast as possible.

Barry and JB were standing across the street from school number nine when Diana and Lester arrived. Diana got out of the car, ready to grab Nika when she came out of school. The bell rang and within moments the street became crowded with parents waiting for their children. Diana tried to get as close to door as possible to grab Nika as soon as she spotted her.

The doors to the school opened and children began spilling out onto the street. Parents were yelling their kids' names. It was a swarm of people Diana had to push through when she spotted Nika, who had been told that Diana and Lester would be waiting for her.

Nika was just about to grab Diana's hand when someone behind Diana pushed her down onto the ground and grabbed Nika, throwing her into a car. Barry ran to Diana and JB got the plate number of the car. Someone near Diana helped her up, while Lester called the Hoboken police to block all roads out of Hoboken. Diana, Barry and JB jumped into Lester's car. Lester tried to keep up with the kidnappers.

Diana screamed, "Tell the cops not to shoot at that car because Nika is in there." The car with the kidnappers came to a screeching stop, spinning around at the roadblock. The man behind the wheel stayed in the car shooting at the police. The other man got out of the car with Nika, using her as a shield. Holding Nika, he inched towards the drivers' side towards the man behind the wheel. The police were told to hold their fire. In a flash, a gunshot was heard from somewhere behind the kidnapper's car. The man holding Nika was shot dead. Nika ran to Diana and the driver of the car surrendered. The driver of the car was taken into police custody. Lester went with the police to question the man. Diana drove Nika home with Barry and JB in the car with them for protection. Avery and Ross followed the police and Lester.

Nika ran to Albert and Sandra as soon as they entered the house. She was all excited about the adventure she just had. Diana explained what had occurred and was amazed that Nika was not scared to death. Diana said she needed to talk to Albert and Sandra privately. Almund and Inger took Nika into the kitchen for a snack. Albert explained to Diana that Nika was raised in an atmosphere of danger and had become very street smart.

Diana informed Sandra that they were positive that she was the target all along. It was difficult for Sandra to hear that, which made hearing about Claire Panetta even worse. But Sandra had Albert to bolster her. Now that Sandra knew she was the target, she knew she had to disguise herself whenever she left the house until the situation was resolved. Diana promised to have the people who were the disguise experts at the Hackensack station bring everything Sandra needed to the Hoboken safe house. From there it would be transferred to Sandra and Albert's home and none would be the wiser.

"What the hell are you two doing here?" Lester barked when Ross and Avery walked into the police station.

"Well that's gratitude for you," Avery barked back. "Who do you think killed that guy who was holding Nika?" Avery smugly questioned.

"That was you, Avery? Boy, you're a good shot," asserted Lester apologetically.

"That's what I do best," boasted Avery. Ross smiled proudly as he put his arm around his wife.

"I'm almost certain this guy is Russian and was ordered to take Nika away from Albert and Sandra for some reason. Can we get the cops to release him to us?" Ross asked Lester.

"I'm going to try. If I fail, I'll call Mr. Sandman to come down here and get him."

Avery stated, "This has now become a CIA matter. We should be the ones to interrogate him. By the way, Lester, where are Barry and JB?"

"They went with Diana to bring Nika home and then back to the safe house to prepare the basement for the Russian's interrogation," Lester answered.

The Chief of police came out of his office, inviting Lester, Ross and Avery in. "This is now a CIA matter and I would appreciate your cooperation by handing the Russian over to us," Lester suggested nicely, but with authority.

The Chief laughed saying, "It would be my pleasure. One less asshole for us to deal with. He's all yours. I'll have him brought up right now."

The Russian was sitting in a small room in the basement of the Hoboken safe house. He was seated at a table with both his hands and his feet bound, which was normal procedure for any prisoners. It was decided to have both Barry and JB interrogate him playing *good cop-bad cop*. They were the best. It was their specialty. The Russian scared quickly and divulged that the orders to kill Sandra did come directly from Russia. The sniper who murdered Pamela Weston and Claire Panetta was a woman named Anna Varvara. When Barry and JB pushed harder the Russian revealed that the man who gave the orders was a high-ranking Russian agent named Alexei Stamenov. He was in love with Natasha and blamed Albert for her suicide. Stamenov reasoned that by killing Sandra, Albert would suffer the way he is suffering. Barry and JB told the Russian that if anything happened to Albert or Sandra, they would kill Stamenov and his Russian assassin. They gave the Russian a computer and told him to communicate that to Alexei Stamenov. The situation was resolved for the time being.

CHAPTER 4
PRUDENCE KRULL

It was 09:00. Diana was preparing their first pot of coffee at the Van Wyck Detective Agency. Ross and Avery were in their back office settling in for the day. The phone rang. There was no number visible on the screen, which Diana thought strange, but she answered.

"Hello, Avery?" On the other end said a voice she could hardly hear.

"No, who's calling, please?" Diana asked

"I need Avery," the faint voice answered. Diana decided not to push it.

"Avery, someone is on the phone asking for you." Avery took the phone from Diana and in a cheery voice said "Hello".

"Help me, Avery, help me." The voice was very hard to hear yet, strangely familiar.

"Who is this? Who am I speaking to?"

"Help me please, Avery," the voice pleaded.

Avery was becoming a both upset and annoyed. "Who is this? Please tell me who I am speaking to."

Hardly audible, Avery heard, "Prudence, Prudence Krull." The phone went dead. The connection was lost.

Avery stood staring into the phone, confused. "Avery, are you OK? You look like you've just seen a ghost," Ross asked.

Avery looked seriously at Ross and uttered, "I didn't see a ghost, I just spoke to one, Prudence Krull, one of my childhood friends who died twenty years ago!" Avery walked over to Diana and asked, "Do you believe in ghosts?"

Diana saw by the look on Avery's face that her question was quite serious. "I don't know exactly how to answer that, Avery. I have had some things happen to me that were unexplainable, but ghosts, I don't know." Diana handed Ross a cup of coffee. She then turned to Avery and asked, "What just happen?"

Avery looked strangely at Diana. "That phone call was from Prudence Krull, a childhood friend of mine who's been dead for twenty years. Quite frankly, Aunt Diana, it's freaking me out!"

"I can understand that," Diana answered somewhat cynically. Diana then said, "Tell me about Prudence Krull and how she died."

"Her parents were Col. Arthur and Marjorie Krull. They lived on the base at Fort Benning, Georgia the same time we did," Avery explained. "Even though her father was strictly Army, he had a passion for sailing. He owned a large sailboat and went out sailing every chance he could."

"You know, now that I think about it, when we were all on the *Mystic Sun* sailing to Cuba to rescue those kidnapped girls, your father mentioned Col. Krull," Ross remembered.

Avery looked surprised. "Really? Although I shouldn't be surprised. Our families were very close friends. Being out on the ocean might have made my dad think of Col. Krull. My dad and I went sailing with Prudence and her dad a few times. Neither of our moms enjoyed it. I remember how much Mrs. Krull hated that sailboat."

"Yes, I do remember something about a family from Fort Benning perishing at sea in a boating accident," mused Diana, as she tried to remember the details.

"That's what was strange. I remember overhearing some of the adults talking at the Krull memorial service. Mrs. Krull hated sailing, yet she was with them when they died," Avery said. "The whole family wiped out. It was such a tragedy."

Ross took a large gulp of coffee and turned to Avery. "Maybe we should talk to your parents about the incident," Ross gently suggested.

Avery thought for a moment, answering, "We can call my dad, but my mom, I don't know. She's off in her own world, she always was. She probably blocked out all memories of living on army bases and the people she knew. She has a new life now with a new man. I'm sure she wants nothing to do with the past, including me," Avery said disparagingly.

"You don't know that, Avery. It wouldn't hurt to call her," Diana suggested.

"Aunt Diana is right. You should call your mother," agreed Ross. Avery tacitly agreed.

"There is one other person we should talk to." Turning to Diana Avery said, "As a matter of fact, Uncle Lester might know him. Gen. Irwin Ipswich. I'm sure he's retired now, but we should find him and question him about Col. Krull and his family. Gen. Ipswich was tight with my dad and Col. Krull."

"I'll get right on that. In the meantime, Avery, you and Ross contact you parents. Get as much information about the Krull family as they can remember," suggested Diana. "I'll call Uncle Lester at the club and get him into the mix," Diana said.

Lester remembered the Krull tragedy. He knew General Ipswich as an acquaintance. Diana asked him to get involved and he agreed to become part of the team. When asked about Gen. Ipswich, Lester remembered hearing that he had died suddenly of congestive heart failure. Lester checked, and he remembered correctly. Gen. Ipswich died suddenly twenty years ago.

Avery called her dad, Col. John Mueller, explaining the situation. He agreed to do whatever he could to help. He said, "I always liked Arthur Krull, but always sensed he was a bit off, as if pieces were missing. But, I never gave it a second thought. He was who he was. You know what I mean? I never thought much about it," he admitted.

Against her will, with Diana's prodding, Avery called her mother. Renee was very surprised to hear from her daughter. After explaining the situation, Renee told Avery that she was not interested in talking about her past life at Fort Benning.

Avery would not take no for an answer. She gently pushed her mother telling her how important anything she remembered might be. Renee reluctantly agreed.

There was one incident Renee thought of. She explained to Avery, "We lived two houses away from the Krull family. Marjorie Krull and I had become close friends. She always listened to me and was always very understanding. Her husband was in love with his sailboat and your father was in love with the United States Army," Renee sneered.

"Just tell me what happened, please," Avery asked, annoyed that her mother would say anything negative to her about her father.

Renee got the message and continued her story. "One afternoon, I saw Marjorie pulling into her driveway. I had just been to the market. At our last barbeque I had used a certain mixture of dry herbs in the potato salad. Marjorie loved it so much that I bought the mixture for her. I ran over to her garage when she pulled in to give her the herbs. I noticed what looked like dried blood on the floor of the garage. I told your father, but he told me I had to be wrong. He said many things could look like that," Renee remembered with a hint of contempt. Avery thanked her mother for her help.

Avery was intrigued by what her mother revealed. Col. John got back to Avery, taking a great interest in the phone call Avery received supposedly from Prudence Krull, a girl who had been dead for twenty years. Over the phone, he shared his impressions of Col. Arthur Krull with Avery. "Arthur Krull was, or at least appeared to be, an excellent leader and beyond reproach." Col. John did, though, side with Ross, feeling more intel was needed before they ran off to Georgia to examine a garage floor with luminol, a crystalline solid that detects traces of blood even if the blood is old and has been cleaned from the area.

Ross and Avery met with Diana, Lester, and Whit to decide how to move forward with this intriguing case. Whit agreed with Avery that if human blood was found on the garage floor, it might begin to lead them in the right direction.

"No bodies were ever found. There was no substantial proof that the Krull family really died," Diana suggested. She then asked, "If traces of blood were found, what did that actually mean? There are a lot of missing pieces to this puzzle," Diana stated.

Avery remembered that Prudence seemed socially challenged. It seemed to Avery that she was her only friend because their parents were friends. As far as Avery could remember Prudence had no other friends. She would come right home from school and stay in her house or go to play with Avery at her house. Avery frowned and said, "Prudence never invited me to play at her house. I was a child. I never thought anything of it. Now as an adult, I question that!" Avery strongly stated.

"What else stands out in your memories of Prudence and her family?" Whit asked.

Avery thought for a moment. "I don't remember them having any family. Prudence told me that both sets of grandparents were dead. Her mom and dad were both only children. She had no aunts, uncles, or cousins. Prudence, herself, was an only child. We always invited them for Thanksgiving and other holidays. I remember that every year between Christmas and New Years they went on vacation. Prudence told me they always took the sailboat and sailed down to the Caribbean every year." Avery stopped talking and began starring into space.

Giving her a few moments, Diana asked, "Avery, dear, what else do you remember?"

Avery began to think. "I don't know, it's all so hazy. Prudence told me about a family they stayed with on an island, but I can't remember which island."

"That's good, Avery. That's a good start," stated Lester.

Avery's mind kept jumping from Fort Benning to the Caribbean. "What is the connection between Fort Benning and the Caribbean?" Avery asked aloud.

Ross but his arm around his wife and asserted, "Don't you worry, Angel, if there is a connection we'll find it."

It was decided that it would be worth the trip to Fort Benning to begin the investigation into Prudence Krull. But first, Avery would speak to her parents again to gather any more intel that would help the investigation, beginning with her dad. Col. John had written down all his personal impressions and experiences regarding Col. Arthur Krull. He read them to Avery over the phone. "The main thing that stands out in my mind is that sometimes Arthur was very open and friendly. But at other times, he was inaccessible and aloof. It was as if he were two different people. I distinctly remember Arthur would never allow himself to have more than one drink on any occasion. It seemed to me that he always needed to remain in control. Some people are just control freaks."

"That's good. Is there anything else you remember?" Avery asked.

Col. John answered, "It was noted that there were more training accidents under his command than any other colonel in the Army. The Army chalked it up to coincidence."

Avery asked Col. John who else she and Ross should seek out regarding Col. Krull and his family. He suggested a Sgt. Leon Hester who was probably retired by now. He was Col. Krull's sergeant and aide.

It occurred to Avery that throughout her entire life it was always her father who came through for her. When Avery was arrested for shop lifting as a teenager, he came to bail her out and settle things with the judge. When she got pregnant at sixteen her mother declared that she couldn't deal with it. She turned her back on Avery. Her father came through making sure her abortion was safe.

Avery did not expect her mother to help any more than she had but was surprised when she did. What stood out most in Renee's mind was how much Marjorie Krull hated their sailboat. Renee explained, "I always wondered why Marjorie went out on the boat the day of the tragedy."

Avery asked her mother what her impression of Prudence was from an adult point of view.

Renee said, "I always felt sorry for Prudence because she looked so unhappy and lonely. I swear Avery, the only time I ever saw Prudence smile was when you and she were playing dress-up. I remember how Prudence always picked out the most colorful clothing."

That jarred Avery's memory. She remembered Prudence saying, "Someday I will be in a warm place and only wear tropical clothing." Avery remembered that Prudence tried to make everything into a sarong. Avery was beginning to think that a Caribbean Island was in the mix. That might be the key to finding Prudence.

In the meantime, Diana was trying to have the phone call from Prudence traced. She called Mr. Sandman, enlightened him on all the intel gathered, and asked if he thought the CIA should become part of the investigation.

His answer was simple, "Before I can determine that, Ross and Avery need to go to Fort Benning beginning the investigation there. They should go to the house the Krulls lived in and use luminol on the floor of the garage. If human blood is detected, collect a sample. Send it in and see if any matches are on file. They need to interview all personnel who knew the Krull family. Avery has good instincts. She usually knows when something is dicey, unpredictable, or false."

"I'll relay the message," Diana said, smiling. "Oh, Earl, I almost forgot. I've been trying to trace the phone number Prudence called from and was…"

Without letting Diana finish he answered, "No problem. I'll send over an expert as soon as possible."

"Thanks Earl, I knew I could count on you," Diana answered, relieved. Diana believed that was the key; finding out where Prudence called from.

Earl Sandman sat back in his chair at his desk, his hands clasped behind his head. What Avery's mother revealed intrigued him the most. He thought that Prudence's relationship to her parents was relevant. He sat wondering why Col. Krull, his wife and his daughter went out on their sailboat and never came back. As he sat thinking, Mr. Sandman began to believe that the possibility the Krull family was alive was real. It could have been an extraction by a foreign government, he thought. But by who and why?

Lester Ballantyne, being a retired general, knew many personnel at Fort Benning and other army bases around the country. Having been in counterintelligence, Lester had many contacts in the Army, as well as the other military branches. He was most interested in the Navy regarding this case. If the Krull family was alive, they had to have been picked up at sea and their sailboat destroyed to make it look like an accident. Lester, with an understanding of how extractions of this kind were conducted, suspected the Russian Soviets. But, to Lester, that seemed impossible. Arthur Krull was a high-ranking officer in the United States Army. He may have been kidnapped with his wife and daughter for intel or ransom, but no, not extracted. That seemed impossible to Lester. However, no ransom was ever requested, leaving doubt in Lester's mind. He contacted Earl Sandman. Group Eleven would be included in the mix, if necessary.

Ross and Avery headed to Fort Benning, Georgia. They would interview as many personnel as possible who knew the Krull family, keeping a list of any personnel involved with the Krull family. The intel would be sent to Caeley and Katrina at the Hackensack station to be analyzed and explored. Once all the intel was examined, they would see if the dots could be connected.

Lester would talk to all high-ranking officers in all branches of the military who had any connection to Col. Krull. To Col. John Mueller, this case was personal. He knew Arthur Krull not only as a fellow officer, but as a friend and neighbor. He had some vacation time available and took it. He was now fully in the mix. He flew up to New Jersey. Diana and Lester offered him their spare room. Ross and Avery had a full house.

Col. John would contact all personnel he knew at Fort Benning who had anything to do with Col. Krull. There were many personnel on the list. Some were still in the military, some were retired, and some dead. The causes of deaths and circumstances surrounding the deaths were scrutinized by Col. John. He had an odd feeling about two of the deaths in particular.

The first was the death of Keith Vance, an intelligence officer at Fort Benning. He and his son Colton reportedly died in a serious car accident. His wife Susan was not in the car.

The second was an army doctor, Captain Robert Oliver, who died in his sleep from an overdose of sleeping pills. The doctor's death was written up as suicide. When Col. John tried to find the doctor's wife Jane Oliver and daughter Gwen Oliver, he couldn't. They had simply disappeared. This revelation made all of Group Eleven stand up and take notice. It was revealed that Prudence used to play with Gwen Oliver.

Both Keith and Colton Vance and Robert Oliver died very soon before the Krull family's tragedy. The Army never connected any dots.

Ross rang the bell. They waited. Gina Comack, the wife of Maj. Lance Comack, answered the door. Gina, with her curly blond hair and green eyes warmly welcomed them. She expected them. Diana had called to explain the situation in a way that told her nothing. Gina Comack agreed to allow Ross and Avery to use luminol on the floor of her garage.

The result was positive. There were traces of blood found on the garage floor. Ross and Avery collected the samples and sent them off to be analyzed.

The results were stunning. It was human blood. Unexpectedly, there were two different types of blood found. Immediately Ross and Avery were able to find out what type of blood the doctor's wife and daughter had. It was a match, but with an added bonus. The doctor's blood type was A Positive, Jane's was B Negative, and their daughter Gwen's blood was O Negative. This was so rare that even though there was no DNA involved for identification, the rarity of the combination was a good indication that the blood they found was that of Jane and Gwen Oliver.

It was so bizarre and extreme to think that Col. Arthur Krull and his wife Marjorie would have murdered the doctor's wife and daughter. But, so far, that was where the evidence led. Now, Ross and Avery wondered if the doctor really committed suicide or died by having the pills forced down his throat, making it seem like suicide.

Ross and Avery looked into the death of Keith Vance and his son Colton. They died in their car when the brakes failed. It was dark, and they plowed into a large truck. Susan Vance was not in the car. Ross and Avery went to see her.

Susan Vance had never remarried and still lived near Fort Benning. Once blond, Susan's hair was gray. Her once sparkling hazel eyes were now dull and without expression. Twenty years had past since the car accident, but it still caused her pain.

Susan explained how shocked she was when the police found that the brakes in Keith's car were faulty and failed. Keith was fastidious about his car. She knew it had to be foul play, but the Police Dept. and the Army disagreed. It was written up as a tragic accident and the case was closed.

Avery gently asked Susan about her son Colton. It was very painful, but she was willing to answer any questions. Avery asked, "Was Colton friends with Prudence Krull?"

Susan was surprised by the question but answered honestly. "We were very friendly with the Krulls. In fact, our families were very close." Avery was shocked. Prudence never mentioned anyone else, ever.

Susan continued, "In fact the four of us, Keith, me, Arthur, and Marjorie used to tease Colton and Prudence saying that we were going to make an arranged marriage between the two of them." Susan began to cry. Through her tears she managed to say, "They are all dead except for me. I feel so guilty that I wasn't in the car with Keith and Colton." Avery put her arms around Susan to soothe her.

After they left Susan, making sure she was in a better frame of mind, Ross and Avery called Diana to report their findings. Diana clearly did not like it. "This is just the beginning, guys. You two need to follow this all the way to the end. Prudence somehow survived and is reaching out for help. You need to find her. The team and I will do everything we can to help behind the scenes. But Avery, it's you she needs to connect with in person. No matter where it takes you Avery, you and Ross must find Prudence." They knew Diana was right.

Lester had been digging deep, investigating Arthur and Marjorie Krull. Arthur and Marjorie were married in Seattle, WA and immediately moved east. Arthur had joined the Army. He was a model soldier and was recommended by many of his superiors for Officer Candidate School. He was always in the top five, rising to the rank of colonel.

According to past records, Lester found that both Arthur and Marjorie both lost their parents before Prudence was born. She was named after their mothers; Prudence Estelle. Both Arthur and Marjorie were only children. There was no family. That was literally a dead end.

Ross, Avery, and the rest of their team all agreed on one thing. The most important thing in Col. Arthur Krull's life was his sailboat. He went sailing every Saturday morning. Marjorie would never go with him, claiming to hate sailing. She would go, however, if Prudence spent the day with a friend.

Avery said, "I remember Prudence playing with me at my house. No matter how much fun we were having, she worried that something would happen to her parents at sea."

"I think it's high-time we find out more about that sailboat," stated Diana.

Ross and Avery went to the marina where Col. Krull kept his sailboat. They hoped someone would remember him. Someone did, an old salt of a man named Captain Hugo. He remembered that Col. Krull would take his boat out in any weather short of a hurricane. "Col. Krull claimed it cleared his head and renewed him," The Captain remembered.

Ross asked, "Can you tell us about the sailboat?"

"Sure can! That's one sailboat I'll never forget," said Captain Hugo. "She had a powerful motor on her and was quite sea-worthy, so I never thought much of it. What a tragedy that was, especially that they never recovered the bodies." Captain Hugo took off his cap and ran his hand through his hair shaking his head as he remembered.

Ross and Avery didn't know what to make of it. Avery asked, "What was his wife's attitude towards her husband's sailboat? Oh, and by the way, what did Col. Krull name his sailboat?"

Captain Hugo smiled. "She was called the *USS RUBY* and was painted bright red. His wife, well, she only went out with him sometimes."

Ross asked, "How long did Col. Krull usually stay out on the boat?"

Captain Hugo thought, and answered, "Most of the day almost every time he went out. If the weather turned nasty, he would come in." They thanked Captain Hugo. Leaving the marina Ross and Avery agreed they were lucky to have had the opportunity to speak to Captain Hugo.

Avery kept thinking about the name of the sailboat, *USS RUBY*. It was not unusual to give a boat a female name. She looked at Ross and asked, "Who the blazes is Ruby?"

"That, Angel, is the question we need to answer," stated Ross as he kissed Avery on the head.

Diana called to inform them that with Mr. Sandman's assistance, the CIA team was able to trace the phone call from Prudence. It came from St. Matthews, a very old Catholic Church in Castries, St. Lucia. Caeley and Katrina were able to scan the church and surrounding area, taking aerial photos. Across from the church was a park with a five-hundred-year old mimosa tree. That tree was a tourist attraction. Ross and Avery knew they had to go to St. Lucia.

On their flight Ross and Avery studied the aerial photos of St. Matthews Church and the surrounding area. There were beautiful gardens next to the church, but Avery was awed by the five-hundred-year-old mimosa tree in the park across from the church.

Avery read that St. Matthews was the largest Catholic Church in the Eastern Caribbean. "This church seems to also attract tourists who like the mimosa tree. That's good for us. It won't seem strange when we are seen poking around," whispered Avery.

"Just because Prudence called from that church, doesn't mean she's there," warned Ross.

"I know, but it is a place to start. We'll talk to the priest to see what he knows," answered Avery.

After landing in St. Lucia, they checked into a small hotel on a mountain overlooking the ocean. The view was breathtaking. Avery stood looking out across the ocean thinking how free she felt. At that moment Avery wished she could fly. Ross came up behind her, kissed her head, and told her their taxi had arrived.

Father Gabriel was standing outside waiting for them. A native St. Lucien, his skin was a soft brown and his smile was wide and welcoming. Avery immediately liked Father Gabriel and sensed he was someone they could trust. He led them around to the side of the church, through a door, into a hallway, and through another door into his office where he invited Ross and Avery to sit down.

"Thank you for agreeing to meet with us, Father Gabriel," Ross said.

"You're quite welcome and I won't beat around the bush," Father Gabriel said warmly as he leaned towards Ross and Avery, who did not respond but sat and waited. Father Gabriel continued, "Prudence has been coming to my church on and off for a long time. She is a very troubled young woman. She comes to me when things become too much for her and she needs to feel safe." Father Gabriel paused thinking Ross and Avery would respond, but they did not. The Priest continued, "She told me that you two are CIA and believed that if I allowed her to contact you, you would come to St. Lucia to save her. And, as God is my witness, here you are!" Father Gabriel declared, extending both of his arms towards Ross and Avery.

Ross and Avery were shocked that Prudence knew that about them as a couple, that they were CIA, and that they were working at the Van Wyck Detective Agency undercover as private detectives. "Father Gabriel, how does Prudence know all of this about us?" Avery asked, afraid of the answer.

Father Gabriel leaned towards Ross and Avery and stated, "I honestly don't know. I don't know much about Prudence, only what she tells me. I never ask her any questions." He paused and then inquired, "Is what Prudence told me true? Are you really CIA agents?"

They avoided the question, but instead Ross asked, "Can you please take us to Prudence, now?"

"Prudence is not here at the church. She left this morning and said she would be back by late afternoon," Father Gabriel answered. They thanked the priest and went back to their hotel.

The fact that Prudence knew what she knew unnerved them. They called Diana and Lester for their opinion and advice.

Diana and Lester were very clear, ordering them to leave St. Lucia immediately. They were sure there was a foreign government involved, leading Ross and Avery into a trap. They took the very next flight out back to Newark. Group Eleven was now definitely in the mix.

Group Eleven met at the Hoboken safe house. Lester announced a stunning revelation. "All personnel who were close to Col. Krull, his wife Marjorie and daughter Prudence died within a three-month period before Col. Krull left with his family on his sailboat, never to return. Avery and her family were the only ones close to the Krulls who were unharmed." No one spoke.

Diana continued, "It is clearly not safe for Avery, Ross, Col. John, or Renee to have any contact whatsoever with Prudence Krull until we understand the nature of the situation we're dealing with."

"Don't you think my mother is out of the loop? She's divorced from my father and is married to another man," Avery asked.

"Avery don't be so naïve. Your mother was a close friend to Marjorie Krull. She might still be a target," smugly asserted Lorelei. Diana looked towards Avery to see how she would respond to Lorelei's barb, but Avery did not respond. Diana smiled, proud of Avery for letting it go. She made a mental note to mention it to Avery later.

Ross and Avery were off the case. After much discussion it was decided that Poppy, Lorelei, Blake and Veronica would go to St. Lucia to extract Prudence. The four of them would go because they were not sure of the situation evolving in St. Lucia. If the Krulls were being held captive, it might take the four of them to extract the three Krulls successfully.

Ross asked Lester if he ever found Sgt. Leon Hester. Lester smirked, saying, "Yes, I did. I found him buried in the military cemetery behind Fort Benning. Apparently, he died of ptomaine poising. It seems odd, doesn't it?" Lester asked.

Avery, with a shocked look on her face excitedly asked, "Wait a minute, wait a minute. Are you suggesting that Col. Krull and his wife Marjorie murdered all of those people?"

Lester shook his head yes saying, "It is a possibility if they were foreign agents posing as US Army personnel."

"How could that ever happen?" Sandra asked.

"If they were implanted in the United States as a young married couple with all the appropriately falsified documentation, then it is possible," Lester answered, disgusted by the words he was speaking.

Diana saw where this was leading Lester. She stood up and adamantly stated, "Right now this is all conjecture. Even though it seems that all the evidence points in that direction, we should not jump to any conclusions. First things first. Let's extract Prudence from St. Lucia and bring her back here. Prudence is the key to all of this."

Mr. Sandman had been quiet up to this point. "Diana is exactly right." Pointing to Poppy, Lorelei, Blake and Veronica he ordered, "You four take our jet from Teterboro and fly down to St Lucia and extract Prudence Krull, and that's an order!" It was clear Mr. Sandman was upset.

"Yes, Sir. When do you want us to go?" Blake asked.

Mr. Sandman answered with, "Start packing. 06:30 the plane will be waiting for you to board." Mr. Sandman stood up, shook his head and to himself said, "Damn it," and walked out. The meeting was over.

Poppy, Lorelei, Blake and Veronica arrived in St. Lucia the next day. Mr. Sandman had arranged for them to be taken to a large house owned by his friend Bob, a retired CIA agent. The house was theirs for as long as they needed it. Their driver introduced himself as Tito, Mr. Sandman's cousin who instructed Tito to help them in any way he could. He handed Poppy a card with information on how to reach him. He drove them halfway up a mountain to a large house overlooking Castries and the port. There were two cruise ships docked in port. The view was awesome. Tito looked at the ships, smiled widely and pointing at the ships explained, "Yes, they are good for business. They will also help you four fit in as tourists." As he helped them in with their bags, Tito smiled widely again saying, "If you need me just call me."

They had given Tito copies of photos of Prudence at ten years old. That was all they had to go on. Tito said he would do some digging for them. He knew the people and he was one of them. He would prove to be an excellent asset.

The house was stocked with food, apparently ready for them. Mr. Sandman, anticipating the outcome, called Bob and made the arrangements for his people to use the house. They washed up, changed their clothes, made omelets, and called Tito. He drove them to St. Matthews Church.

Across the street from the church was the five-hundred-year-old mimosa tree which Avery had admired. Although the tree was a tourist attraction, what attracted people that day was a small combo standing next to the tree playing an interesting combination of Latin and Calypso music. They stood and listened for a while, enjoying the beat. There was a small pail next to the bongo player. Both Poppy and Blake put money in to thank them for their music. A large crowd began to form around the musicians. The four agents slithered out of the crowd, making their way across the street and into the church.

No one seemed to be around. Standing at the very back of the church scanning the area, they began searching, one couple on each side. Both couples were in awe of the magnificence of St. Matthews Church. It was large, more like a Cathedral. There was a long aisle down the middle with pews on each side. High archways framed the seating area. The walls and high domed ceiling were brightly painted depicting life on St. Lucia and the St. Lucian people within the boundaries of Catholicism. There were doors behind the high archways leading to unseen areas. They found nothing unusual in the sanctuary or on the altar.

Tito had been waiting outside. Veronica noticed him standing in the back. He caught her eye, motioning for them to come to him. He led them out of the church and into the car. As he started the up the engine he announced, "I have a lead for you. All three of them are here and have been for the last twenty years. I must also tell you that I am an investigator for the St. Lucia police."

"As Mr. Sandman's cousin, that doesn't surprise me. We're grateful we have your help," Blake said.

"So, Prudence and her parents, Arthur and Marjorie Krull have been living here on St Lucia for the last twenty years?" Lorelei questioned.

Tito quickly answered, "Yes, but you should pick up all three at once. If you pick up just the daughter, the parents will flee. Then, you will never get them." Instinctively, they all knew Tito was right.

Mr. Sandman agreed with Tito's assessment, ordering them to stand down momentarily. He thought they might be up against more than they could handle. He had to make a quick decision. He refused to allow The Krulls to escape. He called Group Eleven into his office for a quick meeting.

Col. John came along with Diana and Lester. He was raving mad. "I want to go down there and arrest that bastard and his wife personally. This is personal, Earl. Please, I need to go," Col. John pleaded.

Mr. Sandman shook his head no and answered, "No, John, I'm sorry, you are officially off the case. Besides you are much too emotionally involved." He smiled and said reassuringly, "Don't worry, we'll get them, John." Col. John knew Mr. Sandman was right. Agreeing silently, he sat down, taking a back seat.

Pacing back and forth, Mr. Sandman knew he had to make a quick decision. He stopped pacing, looked up and stated, "I'm the one going, and I'm going alone. Tito and I will find them. Poppy, Lorelei, Blake and Veronica will help extract them. The Krulls will be brought back and put on trial for murder and espionage." Before he left the room, Mr. Sandman smiled and said, "And, by the way, Tito is a detective and my cousin."

Arriving in St. Lucia early the next morning, Mr. Sandman ordered the pilot to be ready for a fast extraction on a moment's notice. Tito was there with outstretched arms, "Ah, it's been too long, Cousin Earl," Tito said as the two men embraced.

"I wish I was here for a social visit, but not this time. I need your help, Tito," admitted Mr. Sandman.

"Then you shall have it," Tito answered emphatically as they began the drive up the mountain to Bob's house. As they approached the house they saw smoke rising from the back yard. "It looks to me like they found the grill," Tito laughed.

"I sure hope so, I'm starving," Mr. Sandman answered.

After a hearty meal of steak, baked potatoes and a large fresh salad, they sat relaxed on the patio drinking coffee and eating rum cake. Mr. Sandman began to explain his plan of action. "The good news is, I don't think they know any of us, with the exception of me, possibly."

"Maybe you should go out in disguise," suggested Veronica.

"Yes, I intend to. My Cousin Tito and I have already discussed that. Show them, Tito," Mr. Sandman said with a big grin on his face. Tito walked into the house and came back with a large shopping bag. He pulled out a man's wig made up of dreadlocks, a pair of baggy shorts, and a brightly colored shirt. Mr. Sandman took the dreadlock wig and put it on. All six of them burst out laughing.

"That should definitely do the trick, Sir," Poppy exclaimed through his laughter.

"OK, now here's how it should work. Earl and I will go out on the street to try to locate Krull and his family." Looking at Blake and Veronica he said, "I think the two of you to go to the church to talk to Father Gabriel. He's a good man and you can trust him. He has helped us once or twice before, in the past. Make him understand that Prudence's life is in danger and that you need to get her away from her parents."

"Do as Tito says he knows this island and it's people better than any of us," Mr. Sandman instructed.

"Yes Sir," Blake and Veronica answered in unison.

Mr. Sandman looked at Poppy and Lorelei. "I want the two of you to stay here. Poppy, I want you to monitor me and Tito. Lorelei, you monitor Blake and Veronica. If things get very dicey, this is the number you will immediately call for help," he instructed as he handed them each a card.

"Yes Sir," Poppy and Lorelei answered in unison.

"Right now, I want the four of you to go throw all of you stuff back into your suitcases and put on travelling clothes. As soon as we find them, it will be a very quick extraction. We'll put your luggage, which I assume is not much, into Tito's car now. Sammy, Tito's colleague, will be here to wait with you. He'll drive you to the plane. Father Gabriel will drive Blake, Veronica and Prudence. Tito and I will take Arthur and Marjorie, or whatever the hell their real names are," Mr. Sandman venomously sneered through clenched teeth.

He went with Tito into marketplaces, restaurants, bars and other local hangouts showing old photos of Arthur, Marjorie and Prudence Krull hoping somebody would recognize them.

Blake and Veronica went to St. Matthews Church to see Father Gabriel. Mr. Sandman instructed them to make the situation clear to the Priest about Arthur and Marjorie Krull. They were to explain that Prudence's life was in danger and it was imperative they find her, bring her back to the United States and place her in a safe house.

Father Gabriel was enthralled in writing his Sunday sermon when Blake and Veronica found him sitting at his desk in his office. "Excuse us Father," Blake said as he and Veronica stepped into his office holding up their CIA IDs.

The Priest looked up. He smiled and then cocked his head to the side, looking confused when he saw they were CIA. He stood up and asked, "How can I help you?"

Blake and Veronica stepped closer to Father Gabriel's desk. Veronica explained, "We are here to talk about Prudence Krull."

"Please, sit down," invited the Priest. Blake and Veronica sat facing him. "Now, what is it you want to know about Prudence?" Father Gabriel asked.

"It's important you understand that Arthur and Marjorie Krull are wanted by the United States Government for murder and espionage," stated Blake.

Veronica continued, "We believe Prudence is in grave danger. She phoned one of our colleagues reaching out for help."

Father Gabriel shook his head and said, "Yes, Avery and her husband Ross. I have already met them."

"We need to find Prudence and protect her by bringing her back to the United States and placing her in a safe house to keep her from harm."

Father Gabriel stood up, walked around his desk, standing in front of Blake and Veronica. "I confess that Prudence has confided in me about her parents. The poor girl feels trapped by her circumstances."

"What are her exact circumstances, Father Gabriel?" Veronica asked.

"When Prudence was about twelve she found out that her parents were Russian spies and had been since they were implanted into the United States before she was born."

"Please, go on Father," insisted Blake.

"Prudence began coming to see me on a regular basis. She confided in me that many times she was afraid and felt unsafe and distressed. I gave her a safe space here in my church any time she needed it. She was constantly under guard. Prudence was free to go anywhere on the island of St. Lucia but was never allowed to leave the island. And this has been the way it's been for the last twenty years," concluded the Priest.

"If she has been kept isolated from the rest of the world, how did she know how to get in touch with Avery?" Veronica asked.

Father Gabriel sat back down behind his desk. He clasped his hands on the desk in front of him and continued the story. "Prudence could use the internet but only under the name of Nan Prince. She met many people, some with whom she became friendly. It was fine as long as she never revealed where she was or her real name. Finally, Prudence had had enough."

"I still don't understand how she was able to contact Avery?" Blake questioned.

Father Gabriel sighed and said, "Over the last twenty years the Krulls kept tabs on Avery and her family. As long as they believed they had died in a boating accident, the Krulls would leave them alone."

"No wonder they had to leave St Lucia so fast," Veronica said, almost to herself.

"That's how Prudence knew Avery was married, CIA, and worked at a detective agency, right?" Blake asked.

The Priest said, "Look, Prudence is an American citizen and now, as a grown adult, wants her life back. She wants to go back to the United States. That's why she reached out to your colleague. Prudence told me she was sure Avery would help her, and she was right, you are all here!"

"That's all very well and good, Father, but the bottom line is, where the hell is Prudence?" Blake was getting annoyed at the long drawn out story about Prudence. All Blake wanted was her location.

"The honest truth is that I don't know where Prudence lives," the Priest confessed.

Veronica was annoyed at Blake for showing his annoyance to Father Gabriel. "Thank you, Father Gabriel for breaking your rule of confidentiality and taking the time to explain things to us. It helps in our understanding of who Prudence is."

"Your welcome. I know what I did will only help Prudence in the end," Father Gabriel said as he walked Blake and Veronica out of the church.

By the time Blake and Veronica arrived back at the house they were surprised that Poppy and Lorelei had not heard from Mr. Sandman and Tito. But just as they began relaying their experience with Father Gabriel to Poppy and Lorelei, Mr. Sandman called to inform them that they had located the Krulls and ordered the four of them to stand down. They were to stay at the house until further notice. He commended Blake and Veronica for their interview with Father Gabriel.

The Krulls lived in a small fishing village. The people were very poor, and all lived in shanties that would be swept away with one good gust of wind. Most of the people went barefoot, they could not even afford a pair of shoes. A little way up the mountain stood a three-bedroom home that stuck out like a sore thumb. That was where Arthur, Marjorie, and Prudence Krull had lived for the last twenty years. They did what they could to help the poorest people in the village, but it was never enough. They themselves went without dinner a few nights a week so the poorest people could eat.

Arthur Krull still loved sailing. He forever longed for his sailboat the *USS RUBY*, but now owned a smaller, nondescript boat. He still sailed whenever he could. Arthur was older now and retired. He and his wife Marjorie had succeeded beyond their wildest dreams as Russian agents. Their reward was, at their own request, to spend the rest of their lives on the island of St. Lucia.

Twenty years prior, Prudence had discovered their radio, equipment and weapons in a hidden room in their basement. They then decided to be honest with Prudence revealing who they really were. They told Prudence their real names which were Boris and Tatiana.

Prudence refused to accept the truth reacting negatively and threatening to turn them in. They tied her up and locked her in her room until the next day. They sedated Prudence and the three of them took the *USS RUBY* out for the last time. A Russian trawler met them. They blew up Arthur's beloved boat making it appear that all three of them died. The Russian trawler took them to the island of St. Lucia where they lived peacefully for the last twenty years.

At almost thirty years old, Prudence had had enough. From the time she was eleven, tutors and private teachers had educated Prudence. She had always stayed to herself. She longed to be with people her own age.

She was born in the United States, that was her country, she was an American and would never consider herself anything else. Now, she was determined to go home.

Mr. Sandman and his cousin Tito drove slowly into the fishing village. They did not see much of anything going on. They spotted the Krulls house. There was a long, steep road leading up to the house. At the top, in front of the house was a circular drive. Tito pulled the car around, so it was facing towards the road to make a fast getaway if necessary.

They knocked on the door. Marjorie Krull answered the door. She stood staring at them, realizing she was looking into the face of a top CIA agent. Mr. Sandman knew she recognized him in some way, probably by a photo the Russians had of all known high-ranking CIA agents. Marjorie tried to turn and run, but Tito grabbed her by her arm and held her steadfast. Arthur saw what was happening. He bolted out the back door to an SUV parked facing forward on a different road. Mr. Sandman threw handcuffs at Tito, telling him to cuff her while he ran through the house and out the back door. He was too late. Arthur Krull had taken off. He quickly checked the house. Prudence was definitely not there.

Tito had already put Marjorie into the car. He tied her ankles together and put a gag around her mouth, so she couldn't talk. He was waiting for his cousin Earl, who jumped into the car saying, "Go fast, Tito. We still might be able to catch him." As they began driving down the steep road, they saw Arthur Krull's car parked at the dock the saw him untying his sailboat. By the time they got to the dock, Arthur had set sail, using the motor, taking himself, at full speed, out into the ocean. When he got far enough from the dock, Arthur blew himself and his boat up. Marjorie was screaming through her gag. Tito and Earl Sandman stood watching in horror as Arthur and his sailboat was swallowed up by the ocean. Prudence was nowhere to be found.

They began the drive back up into the mountains to bring Marjorie to Bob's house where Poppy and Lorelei waited for them. She would be brought back on the plane with them to Teterboro, but escorted directly to CIA headquarters in Langley, VA. Marjorie would be charged with murder and espionage.

When Blake and Veronica arrived at St. Matthews Church, the combo was next to the five-hundred-year old Mimosa tree playing the same combination of Calypso and Latin music. Inside the church, Blake and Veronica found Father Gabriel in his office. They told the Priest that Arthur Krull was dead, and Marjorie Krull was arrested. Blake explained that it was imperative they find Prudence, asking Father Gabriel to do everything in his power to help them find her. He knew her life was in danger, explaining, "There are other people who do not want Prudence to leave St. Lucia. She knows the entire Russian contingent. She knows them all and their families. Prudence has the ability to expose them all to the CIA if you find her and take her back to America." Blake and Veronica looked stunned.

"Do the Russians know we are here?" Veronica whispered to the Priest.

"I don't know, but if I had to guess, I would say no, they don't know you're on the island. Weren't the Krulls surprised when they were picked up?" Father Gabriel asked.

"Yes, but by now everyone must know that Arthur killed himself by blowing himself up in his boat," Blake suggested.

Father Gabriel looked out into the hallway. He closed his office door and said, "I think I know where Prudence may be hiding, but not the location. It's a cave she told me about. She found it a few years ago. The trouble is, I don't know the cave's location." The three of them sat in silence thinking.

Blake took out his phone and contacted Mr. Sandman. He relayed the intel Father Gabriel shared about the Russian contingent on the island now looking for Prudence. Mr. Sandman emphatically told Blake and Veronica to get to Prudence and take her straight to Bob's house where Poppy and Lorelei were waiting. Tito would have the house well protected by his people, all of whom were fully trustworthy. Mr. Sandman told Blake that they had Marjorie in custody and were on their way to Bob's house. As soon as Blake and Veronica picked up Prudence, they would all fly back, taking Prudence to the Hoboken safe house. Marjorie would immediately be shipped off to Langley.

Mr. Sandman knew that Prudence had probably been damaged by the life she was forced to live. What he felt she needed was to be with people who could give her a lot of love and understanding. The two people who could give her that were Katrina and Mother. They were told about Prudence and agreed to care for her, allowing her to live with them. Now it was just a matter of finding her.

Tito was driving, and Mr. Sandman was sitting in the back with Marjorie. They had to drive up and down steep mountain roads, some with very sharp turns. Coming around one of those turns there was a car sitting crossways, blocking the road. Two men got out holding semiautomatic weapons. They were Russians and they demanded that Tito and Earl Sandman surrender Marjorie to them. Tito and Mr. Sandman both had handguns. Tito was willing to rush them with the car, pushing their car off the mountain. Mr. Sandman thought it was too risky. They turned Marjorie over to the Russians.

Tito and Mr. Sandman chased the Russians up and down the winding, narrow mountain roads. They went faster and faster. Tito knew the roads and was used to racing up and down, taking the curves around the mountains. The Russians kept shooting at Tito and Mr. Sandman, but kept missing. Tito finally caught up with them and kept tapping their car. The Russians lost control. Their car skidded and rolled off the mountain and burst into flames killing Both the Russians and Marjorie.

Prudence was hiding in a small cave she had discovered ten years prior. She had never felt so alone and disparate as she was feeling now. She felt as if she was valuable prey and hunters were after her. Prudence had heard gunfire and an explosion. She didn't know what it meant or if it had anything to do with her family. Prudence was afraid to try to get to St. Matthews Church even though she knew she would be much better off there with Father Gabriel. If only Roxie would come, she thought.

Roxie, a twenty-year-old St. Lucian girl had also discovered the cave. One day they both went there at the same time. That's how they meet. Prudence had never shared any relevant personal information about her family. She knew better. Roxie and Prudence developed a warm relationship. They shared fantasies about their cave and the people who, long ago, may have discovered it. Who were those people? Where did they come from? Prudence was drifting off dreaming of tall ships with many sails blowing in the wind coming towards St. Lucia when she felt someone touch her shoulder. Prudence jumped, and her eyes flashed open. Roxie was bending over her smiling. "What were you dreaming of? It must have been something very nice. You were smiling and looked so serene I almost left you wrapped in your dream," Roxie told her.

Prudence was so glad to see her. She pulled Roxie down and whispered to her, "I need your help. My life depends on you doing something very important for me. Please, Roxie I need you to go get Father Gabriel and bring him here to escort me to St Matthews Church. There are bad people after me. Would you do that for me, Roxie, Please? Prudence begged.

Roxie hugged Prudence. "Why don't the two of us go to the church together, right now. We'll travel through the mountains until we get to Castries. No one will see us, I promise."

Prudence thought about it and said, "No Roxie, it's much too dangerous for you to be seen with me. I want you to go alone to Father Gabriel. Tell him my situation and he will know what to do."

"OK, I will go right now. Please stay here out of sight," Roxie said with a shaky voice. Prudence hugged her and promised not to move from the cave. Roxie did not take any shortcuts. She went directly to St. Matthews Church.

Blake, Veronica and Father Gabriel were looking at a map of St. Lucia when Roxie softly knocked on his office door. When Roxie opened the door and saw Blake and Veronica, her first instinct was to bolt. Father Gabriel sensed that, grabbed her arm gently, telling her to come in, that he was with friends. The Priest recognized Roxie having seen her with Prudence many times. As he escorted Roxie into his office he shut the door and said, "These are my friends, Blake and Veronica. Prudence is in big trouble. They are here to help me find Prudence. Please tell us if you know where she is."

Roxie was very forthcoming. "That is why I am here. Prudence sent me. She is hiding in a cave that she and I have been meeting in for years. She begged me to come here to bring you to her, Father Gabriel. She said that her life is in danger. Please come with me now," Roxie breathlessly requested. All three of them saw the panic on Roxie's face and the fear in her eyes.

Veronica looked at Roxie and explained, "If what you say is true, then right now Prudence is safe as long as she stays hidden in that cave."

Roxie's eyes opened wide. "Oh yes, she promised me she would. Prudence is very afraid. She won't leave the cave.

"Can you show us on the map where the cave is?" Blake asked Roxie.

Roxie looked at the large map of St. Lucia. "I'm good at reading maps. I think I can show you where the cave is." Roxie studied the map. Her finger going up and down the roads and mountains she knew well. Her finger stopped. "Here, this is where the cave is located," Roxie announced, looking at Father Gabriel.

Veronica looked at the Priest and asked, "You wouldn't, by any chance have any Nuns' Habits in the church, would you, Father?" Blake smiled knowing exactly what Veronica's plan was.

Father Gabriel also smiled answering, "As a matter of fact, we do. We have a convent called The Sisters of Mercy of St. Lucia. I know they will help us." Father Gabriel picked up the phone and made a call. He spoke in French. After he hung up he said, "The Mother Superior speaks French. Actually, she speaks five languages, but French is her native tongue. Sister Celeste will be here shortly with what we will need." Twenty minutes later Sister Celeste knocked. When Father Gabriel opened the door Blake and Veronica saw a nice-looking woman in her mid-thirties with short brown hair and sparkling blue eyes. She was wearing modern, but modest clothing. She introduced herself as she handed Father Gabriel a straw market basket and said, "We don't dress in these anymore, but we did save some of them. Some Sisters from other convents still use them. We have Sisters from all over the world come to visit. You can wear these habits without worrying. No one will think twice about it." There were three habits in the basket. Veronica and Roxie would each put one on and would bring the third to Prudence. It would be difficult trekking up the mountain to the cave in the habits, with their long skirts, but there was no choice. Disguise was the only way to help Prudence leave St. Lucia.

It was a long hard journey for Roxie and Veronica, but they eventually made it to the cave. Roxie went in ahead of Veronica. She called for Prudence to come out, telling her it was safe. Slowly, Prudence emerged from deep inside the cave where she had been waiting. Veronica was shocked when she first saw Prudence. Her dark blonde hair was dirty and disheveled, her clothes were practically rags, and she was filthy all over. Veronica's heart was breaking. It was very hard to believe that Prudence and Avery were the same age. Veronica spoke to Prudence in a soft soothing way so as not to frighten her. "Prudence, we will take good care of you, I promise." Veronica handed Roxie the basket and asked her to help Prudence put the habit on over her clothes. Prudence, as she put on the habit, asked about the explosion and the machine gun fire she heard. Veronica smiled, calmly telling Prudence not to worry about anything except getting out of St. Lucia safely. That answer seemed to satisfy Prudence.

Veronica then called Blake to say they were on their way down to the designated spot where he and Father Gabriel would pick up three Nuns. They went slowly, picking flowers, stopping to watch birds, stopping to pick wild berries and even wild mushrooms. They had to act as if they were exploring the mountain. It took a while, but the three Nuns made it down the mountain to the designated spot. They did not seem rushed. Father Gabriel got out and opened the back of his station wagon. Blake was sitting in the front dressed as a Priest. The three Nuns got in and they headed straight for the airport. Poppy, Lorelei, Mr. Sandman, and their luggage were on board waiting for them. Tito and his men were protecting the perimeter of the airport in order for them to take off safely. Father Gabriel drove directly up to the plane. Two Nuns and one Priest boarded safely. Father Gabriel would be sent a large donation to St. Matthews Church, along with a nice donation to Roxie and Tito.

On the trip home Prudence was told about her parents. Surprisingly, she took it well. Both of her parents were dead, but she showed no remorse, saying that they got what they deserved. Prudence began to relax and began to open up. She explained that for most of her life her parents kept her isolated, which concurred with Avery's recollections. Lorelei asked, "After all these years, why now? What made you hit the breaking point?" Prudence smiled slightly and took a deep breath. "I heard them discussing the possibility of the three of us going to Russia for good. That was it, I had had enough."

"How long ago was that?" Poppy asked.

"About six months ago. I thought it was just idle talk. But then the topic came up about three months later. That was when I decided I had better think about going home to America." Prudence looked so forlorn. Veronica couldn't wait to get her home and clean her up and get her a good haircut. She felt a strong urge she couldn't explain to take care of Prudence.

"But your parents wanted to go home to Russia, right?" Veronica asked.

"That's right." Prudence began to display anger towards her parents. "I was born in the USA. I grew up in the USA. I went to school in the USA, and I was an Army brat living on one army base after another. I am an American. America is my home, not Russia. I don't even speak one word of Russian. How dare they think for one minute that they could take me there without a fight." Prudence was yelling and very angry almost as if she were yelling at her parents. Mr. Sandman was happy. He now felt sure there was hope for Prudence.

"Everything will work out for you, Prudence, I just know it," Mr. Sandman said with optimism.

Prudence's anger turned to sadness. "Thank you, Mr. Sandman." Through her tears she smiled when she said his name. "I could use a good, peaceful sleep." Prudence said looking directly at him.

Mr. Sandman put his hand on her shoulder and said, "And you shall have it my dear, once we get back to the Hoboken safe house."

Her tears began flowing again. "I know my parents did evil things. It was not my fault. I had no idea who they were and what they were doing until I was eleven. I should have gone to Gen. Ipswich and reported them, you know, turn them in. But I was so scared, and they were my parents." Prudence began sobbing. Veronica put her arms around Prudence and told her to cry it out. That it was healthy to grieve for her parents.

Prudence kept chanting that none of this was her fault. Mr. Sandman had a hard time persuading Prudence that she should never blame herself for what her parents did. "Arthur and Marjorie were who they were. They did what they did back then because they were doing a job for their country. Back then, it was the KGB and The Soviet Union. You, Prudence, are who you are. You are an American and a very smart, good person. And finally, you are going home where you belong."

"I had to get out of St. Lucia before they dragged me off to Russia. They were leaving within a month. That's why I contacted Avery. I was desperate. I never dreamed she would even remember me, much less help me," Prudence confessed.

"Don't worry, Avery and her husband will be at the Hoboken safe house when we get there," promised Poppy. Prudence smiled at the thought of seeing Avery again after twenty years.

Mr. Sandman began to explain what would happen once they arrived at the Hoboken safe house. "The very first thing will be for you to be able to take a shower and change out of those rags. Then, If I know our Albert and Sandra, there will be a good meal waiting for you."

Veronica, in a sisterly way, offered to help Prudence with her personal hygiene, should she require help.

Mr. Sandman explained, "After a good shower, a change of clothes, and a good meal, I want to tell you how important it is for you to tell me the names of any known Russian agents on St. Lucia. You would be doing your country a great service." Prudence readily agreed. She said she would name names right now. Prudence outed about twenty Russian agents on the Island of St Lucia. He immediately sent the intel to his cousin Tito who was part of the St. Lucian police and military. He and his men would arrest them. The rest was up to the St. Lucien government.

Prudence looked worried and asked, "Once all this happens, what will happen to me. How will I take care of myself and where will I live?"

Veronica explained, "One of our agents, Katrina Duminski, is Russian but an American citizen. She and her mother, who we all call Mother, live in the area not far from the safe house. You will live with them for now. We are sure you will be well taken care of. One thing, though, Mother only speaks Russian, but wants to learn English. Maybe that would be something you could do for them. Teach Mother how to speak English. Maybe you could become her companion. Right now, it's very hard on Katrina. Mother refuses to leave the house without her. Katrina works every day. If you become Mother's companion and teach her English, Katrina would be very grateful. You will get room and board, TLC, and a small salary every week so you have some money. How does that sound to you?" Veronica asked.

"It sounds like heaven, almost too good to be true," Prudence answered. The wheels of the plane touched down in Teterboro Airport.

Agent Barry was waiting with an SUV. As soon as the plane landed, Barry drove up to the plane, enabling them to deplane and have immediate access into the vehicle, going directly to the Hoboken safe house.

Upon entering the Hoboken safe house, Prudence came face to face with Avery for the first time in twenty years. Veronica intervened. "Avery, I'm going to take Prudence upstairs to shower and put on clean clothes. Would you like to come up with us?"

Avery saw the answer in Prudence's eyes. "No, I'll wait down here with Ross and the others," Avery answered.

Veronica and Prudence came downstairs. Prudence was clean, wearing a dark gray sweat suit and sneakers. Her hair was washed and blown dry. Avery and Prudence became reacquainted. Avery promised she would check on her often. They both hoped for a new friendship.

Katrina and Mother had come when Avery and Prudence were talking. They walked over to Prudence and Katrina introduced herself and Mother, who spoke no English, only Russian. Diana, Lester, Albert and Lorelei all spoke Russian. Mother was very comfortable with them, but she wanted to learn English and become an American citizen.

The minute Prudence met Katrina and Mother, she liked them. Prudence knew she would feel safe with them. That was what Prudence needed the most, just to feel safe.

CHAPTER 5
VICTOR BEISSWANGER

At 04:00 Avery opened her eyes and sat up in bed. Ross was sleeping next to her snoring gently. She knew it was not Ross' snoring that woke her. Avery let herself wake up fully. There was something disturbing her. She realized it was the familiar feeling that someone was watching or following her. Avery got out of bed and walked over to the window. She saw a car pulling away from the curb directly across the street. She was stunned! She was right, someone was watching her, or Ross, or everyone living in her house. Or, was it just a coincidence and she was becoming paranoid?

There was no use trying to go back to sleep. Avery's mind was working overtime. She turned on her lamp and picked up the WWII spy thriller she was reading. Avery loved reading spy stories, especially WWII spy stories. Intrigued by that time-period, Avery's mind began to wander. There was such evil permeating the world in the 1930s and 1940s. In thinking about it, Avery concluded that there was just as much evil in the world today, the difference being technology. As technology changed, people changed. Avery loved history and comparing different eras in time. Her last thought was an age-old question. Why do human beings insist on killing each other?

The next thing Avery knew, Ross was shaking her to get up. She overslept. Ross went downstairs while Avery jumped in the shower. That same old familiar feeling still lingered with her. She didn't have time to ponder over it. Putting on clothes and getting to the detective agency on time was her main concern.

As Avery ran down the stairs she yelled the same thing she yelled every morning, "Where's my little man? Mommy needs her morning hug." Ralf came bounding out of the kitchen, running into Avery's arms.

Ralf was a miniature Ross. Sydney Brewer, Ralf's biological mother, abandoned him, leaving the scared little four-year-old boy on Ross and Avery's doorstep. He came with a small tote bag of old clothes and his birth certificate. That was two years ago. Ralf was now six, secure and happy. He adored Avery, Ross, Mindo, his grandpa George, and most of all, his two-year old sister Kimberly, who he called Kimmy.

Avery and Ralf walked into the kitchen where Ross was holding Kimmy as he gulped down a mug of coffee. Avery picked up their small brown and white dog Dixie to cuddle her. "Sorry I'm so late this morning, but I didn't sleep well last night," Avery explained as she put Dixie down, took Kimmy out of Ross' arms and kissed her.

"Mindo, please call Diana at the agency. Tell her Avery overslept, *again*. We'll get there as soon as we can," Ross politely requested. Avery was glaring at Ross for putting the blame on her for being late, even though it was true.

"Mindo, thank you so much. Because Ralf's school is closed today, I'll be home at lunchtime to take Kimmy off your hands, that is if nothing drastic happens this morning," Avery said smiling, as she handed Kimmy over to Mindo.

George Lisano, Ross' father, walked into the kitchen from the den that Ross and Avery had converted into a bedroom. George was on a contracting job building refugee camps in Syria. He was kidnapped by Isis but was rescued. He was permanently blinded by his captors. Ross and Avery insisted he move in with them permanently. Over time, George adjusted to his loss of sight. He and Mindo became good companions. Ralf loved his grandpa George. George was a good storyteller and Ralf an eager listener.

When Ross and Avery arrived at the Van Wyck Detective Agency Diana informed them that there was a bad situation brewing. Lester had called telling Diana to get over to *The Double O Club.* They locked up the agency and immediately left. In the car Diana explained that their entire group was to meet in the secure room at the club. Mr. Sandman was extremely shaken. Esther Brouce was on her way down from Connecticut.

While they waited for Esther Brouce to arrive, Ross, Poppy, and Albert scanned the room. To their dismay, they found a listening bug. Diana and Lester became angry saying that it would have been impossible for anyone to install a listening device without them knowing. Avery's eyes focused on Lorelei, but she made no accusations. Mr. Sandman searched again with Ross, to make sure there was nothing else.

Avery was concerned about Ralf and Kimmy. Diana assured her that Althea and Gabe were on their way to her house to care for them while Mindo attended the meeting. Mr. Sandman demanded the entire group attend.

When the entire group was finally assembled, Mr. Sandman took his usual stance, feet apart and hands behind his back. He was just about to speak as Esther Brouce, head of the entire northeast district and Mr. Sandman's boss, entered the secure room. She took a seat saying, "You go ahead. Earl, explain it to them."

There was worry in Mr. Earl Sandman's eyes and fear on his face, something they had never seen before. The tension in the room was high.

He looked at his group, his people, his family whom he loved and trusted with his life. He was about to inform them about the now present danger. "A CIA agent from another district contacted Esther to warn her that an agent somewhere in our district, is a traitor. But, it's even worse than that. The traitor obtained a flash drive containing the names and codes of all CIA agents in the northeast district. The traitor plans to sell it to the highest bidder. We must stop this treachery from happening. The flash drive has not been put out there yet, but it's just a matter of time. We must find this traitor, arrest him or her, and secure the flash drive."

Avery cynically asked, "How can you be so sure it isn't one of us? There very well may be a traitor among us," Avery said as she looked towards Lorelei.

Poppy lashed back with, "I do not want you or anyone else to make any more insinuations about Lorelei's loyalty to our family, our team, our group or the CIA. Is that clear?" Poppy demanded.

Avery smiled and answered, "We'll see."

Poppy answered with, "Lorelei and I both resent this. Lorelei is one of us, Avery, so get over it, I insist," snapped Poppy.

Before Avery had a chance to come back at Poppy, Ross stood up and sneered, "Don't you dare speak to my wife that way. She has right to her opinion and so do we all. And why can't Lorelei speak for herself? Why do you always have to be her spokesperson?"

Lorelei stood up and with tears in her eyes answered with, "I can speak for myself. I am not a traitor to my team, group, the CIA or my husband." No one spoke, it was true. There was a sliver of doubt in everyone's mind about Lorelei due to her not quite understandable relationship with Sergei Alexandrov, a high-ranking Russian agent. Lorelei had been spotted more than once walking in a park near the Russian embassy in Manhattan wheeling her son Peter in his stroller. Each time she was with Sergei Alexandrov, Peter's biological father.

Diana was annoyed. Lester put his hand on her arm signaling her not to get involved, but she did. Diana stood up and angrily said, "This is unacceptable behavior. I will not tolerate in-fighting among ourselves. You're all seasoned agents who, I am sure, understand what we're up against. Our lives are in jeopardy. We, as a group, must all be on the same page and in the right mindset. Now is the time to trust each other more than ever," Diana said looking directly at Avery. Avery knew she would have to speak to Diana privately. She did not trust Lorelei, and she never would.

Esther Brouce stood up and said, "I trusted Mr. Sandman when he told me that you folks, Group Eleven, are all one hundred percent beyond reproach. That's why we are meeting here instead of at the Hackensack station. I would hate to see any of you prove Mr. Earl Sandman to be a liar," Esther sternly stated as she glared at them. Esther put a period at the end of the Lorelei issue.

After a pause, Mr. Sandman stood up, took a deep breath, and took his usual stance, confirming the period at the end of the Lorelei's loyalty issue. "I want you all with Caeley and Katrina on this one. All personnel from every station in our district must be scrutinized. We will work from the top down. It would behoove us to clear as many station Chiefs as we can. We'll need the extra help. Once a station Chief is deemed clean, we'll hand his own station over to him or her. Any questions so far?" There were no questions. Mr. Sandman continued, "There are five stations in our district. I want all of you to investigate just the station Chiefs. We'll come together again here, tomorrow night to compare lists. If any name comes up twice or more, we'll dig deeper into that person. Are there any questions?"

Lester raised his hand and said, "Tomorrow meet here at 17:00, before the club gets busy and you will have burgers and fries on the house"

"There's nothing like greasy food to get one's juices flowing," Avery whispered to Ross.

Avery raised her hand and asked, "Will anyone have trouble with childcare tomorrow?" There was no problem everyone was set.

Mindo raised his hand and announced, "My parents, Althea and Gabe will be caring for Ralf and Kimmy. If any of you should run into a problem, just let me know. I'm sure my parents wouldn't mind taking on an extra child or two, or three". Everyone laughed and thanked Mindo.

Lorelei was very upset about the miasma of doubt Avery hung over her. She and Poppy decided to go for a drink. As she stirred her vodka gimlet, Lorelei looked up at Poppy, and with tears in her eyes said, "Avery is wrong!"

Poppy felt so sorry for Lorelei and so angry at Avery. "Avery needs to get her head screwed on straight."

Lorelei took a sip of her drink and said, "Avery never liked or trusted me from the time we met in Hoboken. Poppy, tell me, what have I ever done to Avery to make her feel that way?"

Poppy took Lorelei's hand in his answered, "Nothing at all. Avery is just a little crazy. She claims she senses things." They sat in silence for a while.

"I think she just picks on me because I'm German," Lorelei said, half smiling.

Poppy smiled answering, "No, I don't think that's it. Albert is German and Avery herself, is half German. No, it has nothing to do with that." Lorelei snuggled into Poppy.

"I don't get it. We've been on many successful assignments together without any problems. We work so well as a team. I Just don't understand Avery, at all," Lorelei admitted.

Poppy looked at Lorelei, took her hands in his and said, "I didn't tell you this because I didn't want you to be upset, but Sergei Alexandrov is on the loose again. Intel has him here in the New York area."

Lorelei leaned close into Poppy and begged, "Please, just keep him away from me. He'll try to contact me to see Peter." Poppy promised to do his best. Lorelei then suggested something that horrified Poppy. "Maybe we should just give him his son. That's what he wants."

"Why would you even consider such a thing? Peter Thomas Lassiter, Junior is my son. I am raising him. I am his father, not Sergei Alexandrov.

Lorelei stroked Poppy's cheek and kissed him gently on the lips. "I'm sorry, it was a stupid thing to say."

Lorelei offhandedly said, "Maybe we should try again for child of our own."

Poppy was stunned, asking, "Is that what you really want?" Lorelei just looked at Poppy and smiled a smile that was not convincing. It was that smile that made Poppy feel something he never felt before; unsure of Lorelei.

When they walked into their apartment, they expected to see Mrs. Grayson in her usual place on the couch watching TV and knitting. She was not there. The baby's room was empty. "Mrs. Grayson probably took Peter across the hall to her apartment. Let's go collect him," suggested Lorelei.

As they were about to leave, they thought they heard moaning coming from their bedroom. They rushed back to their bedroom and listened. It was coming from their closet. Poppy flung open the closet door and found Mrs. Grayson tied up and groggy.

Mrs. Grayson, sobbing uncontrollably, managed to confess that she never saw who hit her from behind. The next thing she remembered was waking up in the dark closet. She was sure Peter had been kidnapped. She explained that she was terrified because she was tied up in such a way that the more she struggled, the tighter the knots got. All she could do was wait until Poppy and Lorelei came home.

After soothing her, Poppy walked Mrs. Grayson across the hall to her apartment. He went in with her to assure her all was well. As he walked back into his apartment, to his amazement and dismay, he heard Lorelei speaking frantically in Russian.

Lorelei was very upset. He heard her say the name Sergei. Poppy couldn't believe his ears. Lorelei was talking to Sergei Alexandrov about the kidnapping. As he listened outside the bedroom door he heard Lorelei screaming at Sergei in Russian. She then began to cry. Poppy ran into the bedroom and grabbed the phone away from Lorelei. In an authoritative voice Poppy ordered, "Bring our son back, Sergei or when I find you, I swear, I will kill you to rid Lorelei of you for good!"

Lorelei was screaming, "No, no, you don't understand."

At the same time Sergei explained, "I don't have my son. It was not me I swear it. Listen to me Poppy. We must work together to find him. I will put feelers out there and so must you. This time, Poppy, we are on the same team." It was the tone in Sergei's voice that convinced Poppy that he might be telling the truth. He did not trust Sergei completely, and never would.

He looked at Lorelei seriously. He assumed she called Sergei when he took Mrs. Grayson back to her apartment. Poppy quietly asked, "Since when do you have Sergei Alexandrov's contact information? You obviously called him while I took Mrs. Grayson back to her apartment."

"I've had it since the last time I took Peter to that park for Sergei to see him, but it's not like that. Sergei is Peter's biological father. He wanted me to contact him for anything concerning Peter. I believed he kidnapped Peter. That's why I was screaming at him in Russian. He swore to me he didn't do it," Lorelei answered, sounding defeated as she sat down on the bed.

Poppy sat down next to her and took Lorelei in his arms. "I believe you, Lorelei." Poppy knew he was not telling the exact truth. Poppy began having small pangs of doubts and denial and that was not his style. They sat wrapped in each other's arms. Poppy whispered, "Don't worry, Peter is our baby. We'll find him. I'll call Mr. Sandman right now."

Poppy didn't have to call Mr. Sandman, he called Poppy, telling him that Ralf and Kimmy Lisano, Ross and Avery's son and daughter were also missing. Poppy told him that Peter was also kidnapped, but not by Sergei

Alexandrov. They agreed that the same people had probably taken all three children, but to what end?

They were vicious. Althea and Gabe Torres who were caring for Ralf and Kimmy, put up quite a fight, landing them both in the hospital with gunshot wounds. Althea's wound was superficial, but Gabe was fighting for his life on an operating table. George Lisano was found tied up and gagged in his closet. His hearing was excellent and from the sound of their voices, he was sure it was a man and a woman.

Poppy and Lorelei ran to the Hoboken safe house where the entire group was gathering. Mr. Sandman told Ross and Avery that Peter was also kidnapped, but not by Sergei Alexandrov. Poppy revealed that he spoke to Sergei and he was going to put feelers out and asked Poppy to do the same. Ross and Avery knew they would contact Andrei. If all else failed, Mr. Sandman knew he would need to contact Luka Ionovich.

Avery walked up to Lorelei and with tears in her eyes said, "God help us, Lorelei. Our children are being used for who knows what." Then, Avery hugged Lorelei and whispered, "If you had anything to do with this, so help me God, I will kill you!" That said, Avery walked to the other side of the room and sat down.

Diana had watched that scene between Avery and Lorelei. She walked over to Avery and sat down next to her. Diana whispered, "I know how hard this is on you, but please don't make things worse by taking it out on Lorelei. Remember, her child is missing, also." Diana was trying to remain strong by not crying, but her heart was breaking.

Avery turned to face Diana, looked directly at her and said, "Aunt Diana, I know she's Poppy's wife, but what do we really know about her? We've all been together from the beginning. She showed up in Hoboken claiming to have intel, which proved to be bogus. Next thing we know, Poppy announces that she is pregnant with his child and they are getting married. Her explanation was that she was a double agent working for us in Russia. Her proof, you know, the bra label, could have been taken from a real double agent."

"I hear you, Avery, and quite frankly, I don't disagree with you completely. But please, don't cause trouble within the group. Come to me first with anything regarding Lorelei. Please, promise me?" Diana asked.

Avery tried to smile. "You are my surrogate mother. I don't love or want my biological mother in my life. You're the one who's always been there for me. I love you, so I'll promise."

Diana smiled and said, "Thank you, Avery, and I love you just as much as if you were my own daughter." She patted Avery on the arm, got up and walked over to Lester.

Lester put his arm around Diana and said, "Well?"

Diana answered, "It's fine."

Lester answered, "Good, we don't need that now."

Without hesitation, Esther Brouce posted an urgent memo to each station in their district urging the misguided agent to come forward. Esther gave a number to call and promised there would be no repercussions. All would be forgiven if the agent contacted her within the next four hours. Three children of agents from the Hackensack station had been abducted. Esther was sure there was no connection between the stolen flash drive and the abducted children. She and Mr. Sandman concurred that the children were being held by an unknown entity. The person or persons were not part of the CIA." Mr. Sandman began calling each station Chief to assure that all personnel would read Esther's memo, and appeal to their perspective staff members to call Esther Brouce at her private number if anyone had any knowledge of any involved personnel.

Esther Brouce did not have to wait long. She received a call within two hours after the district-wide memo was issued. It was a man's voice. He was crying, saying he never imagined innocent children would be brought into the mix. The man would not reveal his name until he met face to face with Esther. She asked if Mr. Sandman could accompany her. The children of agents from his station were the ones abducted. The man did not object. They agreed to meet at the first rest stop going south from the northern end of the Garden State Parkway. Esther asked how she would know him. He thought for a moment and said he would be wearing a gray sweatshirt and a dark green baseball cap. The meeting was set.

Ross, Avery, Poppy and Lorelei insisted on going as back up, but Mr. Sandman forbid it. He would use Albert, Sandra, Blake, and Veronica for back up. Mr. Sandman ordered the rest of them to stay put in the Hoboken safe house. He felt it would not be wise for any of them to go home. They were dealing with an unknown entity who had already proven to be ruthless. Gabe Torres made it through surgery but was still listed as critical. Althea's arm would heal completely. Mrs. Grayson was traumatized and decided to move to Iowa to live with her daughter.

Victor Beisswanger was short in stature but in good physical shape. They saw him immediately. As Esther and Mr. Sandman approached, Victor stood up and handed Esther a brown envelope. His eyes began to tear as he said, "I am so very sorry, but I am a desperate man. May I please explain?"

"Yes, please do," answered Esther, motioning for Victor Beisswanger to sit down. Esther quickly looked inside the packet and recognized the flash drive. She felt the tension leave her body. She looked at Mr. Sandman, who got the message.

Victor Beisswanger wiped off his face and blew his nose into a paper napkin. "I lost my wife two years ago from a brain embolism. It was a terrible loss for me and our seventeen-year-old son Buddy. Since then Buddy is all I have left. Six months ago, he was diagnosed with cancer, leukemia, to be exact. He was doing well with the treatments until last week when they told me he needed a bone marrow transplant to survive. My insurance doesn't cover that. They denied him the treatment. I couldn't let Buddy die. I felt his life was worth more than mine." He stopped to wipe his eyes and blow his nose again. "I was truly stuck in a dilemma. I am not a traitor. I love our country, but I guess I love my son more. After I sold the flash drive and paid for Buddy's bone marrow transplant I was going to turn myself in. If Buddy died my life would be over anyway. So, there it is." Esther Brouce and Mr. Sandman were stunned. Victor continued, "I never imagined that other agents' children would become a part of my stupid scheme. I'm so sorry I've done this." Victor began sobbing again. "I just can't face losing Buddy, seeing his life snuffed out at such a young age. I'm beginning to question if God really exists."

Mr. Earl Sandman was beginning to ask the same question. He thought about the four million dollars sitting in the safe at the Hackensack station. It was money confiscated from a failed payoff that only he, Poppy and Richard Childs, his boss who was now dead, knew about. He took a deep breath and asked, "What hospital is Buddy in?"

Victor looked at Mr. Sandman questionably. "He's in Hackensack Hospital. They're the best for what Buddy has."

"I'll be right back" Mr. Sandman got up and left. He went out to their SUV. Blake rolled down the window when he saw him approaching without Esther. "Check Hackensack Hospital for a seventeen-year-old patient named Buddy Beisswanger who has leukemia. Walk in and stand at the door. Shake your head yes or no. I'll be watching for one of you." Mr. Sandman went back inside.

Five minutes later Blake came in. Mr. Sandman looked, and Blake shook his head yes. He turned to Victor and said, "Listen, even though you intended to betray us, no harm was done, and I understand your desperation. However, what you did was wrong. But, Buddy will have his bone marrow transplant. We'll pay for it. We will transfer you to our station in Hackensack and you will work for me. You will move to New Jersey to be near the hospital. You have to come with us now. You will stay at one of our safe houses."

Victor Beisswanger was sobbing. He took both of Mr. Sandman's hands in his, kissed his hands, and said, "My loyalty to you, Sir, is carved in stone. I swear I will never betray you or our country. I knew when I agreed to meet with you I wouldn't be going home, so I packed a suitcase."

Mr. Sandman put his arm around Victor Beisswanger, smiled and answered, "Good, because you, Agent Beisswanger, are going to help me catch some really bad people".

"I'll help you any way I can. What do you want me to do, Sir?" Victor sincerely asked.

Mr. Sandman looked directly at Victor and stated, "We are going to turn something unproductive into something good and extremely productive."

Albert and Blake checked Victor's car and suitcase. Albert drove while Blake sat in the back with Victor in handcuffs and ankle restraints. They would be removed at the Hoboken safe house. It was protocol. Mr. Sandman, Esther, Sandra and Veronica followed in the SUV. On the way back to Hoboken, Mr. Sandman explained his idea to Esther. She gave him the green light, agreeing that it might just work.

There were still no clues as to who kidnapped the children or where they were. Ross, Avery, Poppy, and Lorelei joined analysts Katrina and Caeley to search for any patterns or unusual discrepancies of all persons of interest, including Sergei Alexandrov and Sydney Brewer. They found nothing.

Ross and Avery had asked Andrei to help. Having left the spy business he lost all his status and clearance but promised to see what he could do. Andrei appealed to his old boss Mr. Ionovich. He came through for Andrei. What Mr. Ionovich told Andrei sent shockwaves through his entire body, like a bolt of lightning.

There was pounding on the safe house door. They all stopped and froze. Poppy, whispering, ordered, "Take out your weapons!" Ross and Avery positioned themselves on one side of the door, and Poppy and Lorelei were on the other side. Diana went with Katrina and Caeley down to the kitchen to get out if they had to. Lester answered the door with gun in hand.

"Who's there?" Lester asked.

"It's me, Andrei. Please let me in it is urgent." Caeley heard Andrei's tone of voice and immediately imagined that their daughter Riley had also been kidnapped. By the time Caeley ran up the stairs Andrei was in the house. "Caeley, Riley is fine, don't worry," were Andrei's first words to her.

Avery ran to Andrei and asked him what he found out. He saw the desperation on their faces. He decided to tell all of them, not just Ross and Avery. "You all better sit down. I went to Mr. Ionovich. We have a good relationship. I explained the situation. Sergei Alexandrov had no part in this. He, himself, called Mr. Ionovich to help find the children. I found out something that shocked me. There is a Russian spy, a Soviet, by the name of Alexei Stamenov."

"Yes, I know that name. I remember he tried to punish Albert by attempting to kill Sandra. He was in love with Natasha and blamed Albert and Sandra for her suicide," Avery remembered out loud. "What about him, Andrei?" Avery inquired.

"He was a double agent and gave up his alias years ago. His alias was James Kramer." The room was quiet.

Diana leaned against Lester and he against her. They were stunned and bewildered. Everyone was horrified at the thought of James Kramer being alive. "It can't be. He died in that car with Kevin. I know he did, I saw it with my own eyes." Diana felt weak. The room began spinning and she began to cry.

Lester held Diana tightly in his arms to make her feel safe. He pursed his lips in a moue of contempt and bellowed, "I'll find that bastard and strangle the shit out of him even if it takes me the rest of my life!"

"No, Lester, he is probably in Russia. Just leave him there, please." She turned to Andrei and asked, "He is in Russia, right?"

Andrei looked at Diana and said, "I will tell you what I know. His real name is Alexei Stamenov. He is involved with a woman named Anna Varvara." Andrei stopped. They all knew there was more but said nothing and waited for him to continue. "That woman Anna Varvara, that is the name she uses in Russia, Belarus, The Ukraine, and all of Eastern Europe. In Western Europe she is known as Beatrice Downing, and here she is Sydney Brewer."

"He's old enough to be her father, for God's sake," Diana blurted out.

"Yes, and they are here in this country. That was the last piece of intel I got on them," Andrei informed them.

It was at that moment that Mr. Sandman walked in with Victor Beisswanger, Esther Brouce and the rest of the team. They saw Andrei, looked around and knew something was going on or had gone sideways, but either way it couldn't be good. "This is Victor Beisswanger. He's going to help us get the kids back." Mr. Sandman introduced Victor on a positive note making their acceptance of him more palatable. He then asked, "What have you come up with so far?"

Andrei walked over to Mr. Sandman and extended his hand. Mr. Sandman shook Andrei's hand as he explained, "I was asked to help with this dire situation. I went to Luka Ionovich. He and I did some digging. An older agent named Alexei Stamenov, a treacherous Soviet, used an alias years ago. That alias was James Kramer." It took a few moments for Mr. Sandman to process the intel.

He looked at Andrei, then at Diana and Lester, then looking back at Andrei he asked with consternation, "Are you sure? James Kramer, Diana's first husband is *alive*?"

"Yes, I am sorry, but that is what I am telling you. He has hooked up with Anna Varvara, aka here as Sydney Brewer."

Avery became enraged, jumped up and said, "Sergei Alexandrov is a part of this treachery. He's a liar, those Soviets are all liars." Ross tried to stop her, but she pounced on him with, "No, Ross, you're not shutting me up this time." Ross backed down. He did not disagree with her. Ross let Avery loose. She looked directly at Lorelei. "Your ex-lover Sergei Alexandrov, the father of your son Peter, connected with Sydney Brewer, Ralf's biological mother who abandoned him, and Diana's first husband and misguidedly, the love of her life, I'm sorry Lester. The three of them stole our children, but to what end? We haven't heard from them. They must want something in exchange for our kids."

Lorelei vehemently defended Sergei Alexandrov. "I swear to you that Sergei is as upset as we are and is also searching for the kids. Sergei loves Peter, I know that. And I am also sure he would never harm Ralf or Kimmy." Lorelei's defense of Sergei Alexandrov and Poppy's silence made everyone sit up and take notice. It was at that moment that Poppy knew he had to do something he had been putting off.

"You are so fucking stupid, Lorelei," Avery spit at her. No one stopped Avery, not even Poppy. "James Kramer killed his own son without an ounce of remorse. I'm sorry Aunt Diana. Sydney Brewer would harm Ralf and Kimmy. She would do anything to hurt me in order to get Ross back."

"She never had me in the first place," Ross mumbled.

"Really, Ross? Don't give me that shit! You had a *child* with her, who I happen to love very much," Avery shrieked at him as tears streamed down her face. Ross knew not to answer. He shrunk deeper into his chair.

Mr. Sandman put a stop to Avery's tirade. "OK, Avery, you got it all off your chest now. It's time to get those kids back. I have a plan and Victor Beisswanger, here, is going to institute it for me." He paused waiting for someone to ask about the flash drive or who Victor Beisswanger was. He continued. "Victor will be joining our station. He is also a brilliant analyst. He gave us back the flash drive and offered to help end this crisis." Still no one spoke or asked any questions." Mr. Sandman was amazed but continued. "Victor is going to put it out there that the flash drive is for sale. Wouldn't Sergei Alexandrov, Sydney Brewer and James Kramer, or whoever the kidnappers are, love to own that flash drive?"

"In theory it's a great plan. We'll get many, many offers. How will we know who has our children?" Lorelei asked with tears running down her face.

"You see how fucking stupid you are Lorelei, that's the wrong question to ask. The right question is, if they don't know about the flash drive, which they don't, but have our kids, what is it they want in exchange for our kids? That's the right question to ask, Lorelei!" Avery was so worked up she was turning red.

Mr. Sandman smiled and put his arm around Avery. "I would bet my life that Avery is right. But I'm not sure about Sergei Alexandrov. Andrei could you please verify that information for us?"

"Yes, of course, I will try," answered Andrei.

"Now that there is a plan, Sandra and I will get some food for everybody. How about Pizza and Chinese just like in the old days?" Albert asked. Diana walked up to him and hugged him.

"That's great, thanks," Diana answered, giving Albert a not quite earnest smile.

Poppy walked up to his cousin Ross. "Can I speak to you privately?"

"If it's to complain about my wife, no." Ross answered without emotion.

"No, it's not. I need to check something, and I might need your help," Poppy explained.

Ross stood up. "OK, let's go down to the kitchen." Avery walked over to them. Ross knew how much Avery was hurting. He put his arms around her, kissed her forehead and said, "I need a few moments with my cousin. Ross gently cupped Avery's chin and pulled her face upward. I love you, Angel." Avery watched Ross and Poppy go down the stairs. She waited, and when she was sure she would be out of sight, Avery silently went to the bottom of the stairs to try to hear their conversation.

"OK, Poppy, what's up?" Ross asked.

"You know me, Ross. I have never allowed myself to go into denial about anything, and I am not going to start now."

"That's true, but what's your point?" Ross asked.

"As much as I hate to admit it, I am beginning to have that sliver of doubt everyone else has about Lorelei," Poppy admitted, as he looked down at the floor.

"OK, what do you want me to do?" Ross asked with consternation.

"I want you to check a number on Lorelei's phone; how many times she's called it and how many times it called her. Also, where the calls have come from. Will you do it, Ross? I just don't have the stomach to do it myself."

"No problem, just get me her phone."

"You'll have it by the end of the day," Poppy promised.

"It's Sergei Alexandrov, isn't it?" Ross asked. Poppy stared hard at Ross.

Without a sound, Avery ran back up the stairs. She heard the entire conversation, but decided to keep it to herself, at least for now.

Victor Beisswanger, in conjunction with Ross, Caeley and Katrina, put it out there loud and clear that the flash drive was for sale. There was a secure phone number for interested parties to call. The location of the caller was immediately pinpointed. Ross, Caeley, Katrina and Victor all had phones and computers linked to the given secure number as the calls came in. They were able to each answer a different caller at the same time.

The calls were rated in order of priority. Calls from Asia, Africa, Australia, New Zealand, or anywhere else in the Pacific west of Hawaii were rated as four, probably not being viable. Calls from Europe, including Russia were rated as three. Calls from Central and South America, Mexico, the Caribbean and Canada were rated as two. Calls from anywhere in the USA were rated as one, highest priority.

Andrei returned with two very important pieces of intel. Sydney Brewer and James Kramer were, as of an hour ago, placed in Los Angeles, and James Kramer was now using the alias Alex Stanton. Secondly, Sergei Alexandrov was in Moscow with his mother, who was suffering from bronchitis.

Avery argued that Sergei could still be in on the kidnapping in some way. Andrei assured her that they had Stefan and Liliya check it out. Sergei Alexandrov was definitely in Moscow caring for his sick mother.

Five minutes after Andrei revealed what he learned, Lorelei picked up her purse and went to the bathroom. Poppy led Andrei by the arm in the direction of the bathroom. Lorelei was talking in Russian to someone. Poppy motioned for Andrei to listen to Lorelei and tell him what she was saying.

Andrei began translating Lorelei's words. "She is asking Sergei about his mother. Lorelei is concerned about her health." Andrei stopped, listened and continued, "She is telling Sergei that we found the children and are going to rescue them." Again, he listened. "She told him no it's too risky. He wants her to do something or go somewhere." Andrei listened and said, "She is saying goodbye. We better hide." Andrei and Poppy slipped into an empty bedroom. They waited until they were sure it was safe. Poppy and Andrei went downstairs separately.

Poppy poured himself a cup of coffee and sat alone in the kitchen to try to sort things out. He tried to put things into perspective, but he couldn't. He needed to talk to his parents, Diana and Lester. He decided to wait until the children were back safely. Then, he would speak to his parents privately. He would then decide how to handle Lorelei. It was easy for Poppy to compartmentalize, but it was not easy for him to deal with the hurt he felt knowing Lorelei might be a fraud.

Veronica was on the phone with her best friend, Carole Cooper. She was connected with the Los Angeles station. Carole and her people would check out any leads regarding the whereabouts of Sydney Brewer and Alex Stanton, aka, James Kramer.

The point of the plan was to lure the kidnappers with the flash drive to find out what they really wanted, and their location. Carole Cooper and her team were ready to pounce.

They worked the four phones in six-hour shifts. The first day was a wash. But on the second day Mr. Sandman's lure worked. A man with a disguised voice called. He wanted to exchange the children for the flash drive and Albert. The call came from a private home in a residential section of Encino, CA. By the time Carole's team got to the house in Encino, the only thing they found were dirty diapers.

Lorelei sat quietly with her hands folded in her lap going deeper into herself. But Avery was becoming unhinged, pointing out that the longer it took the CIA to find the kids, the less likely they would find the kids alive, and hysterically asking, "And what the hell do they want with Albert?"

Avery began begging Mr. Sandman to bring the FBI into the mix. For Diana, that was the last straw.

Diana had to cajole Avery, who losing control and becoming hysterical, up to one of the bedrooms to lie down. Avery was distraught and emotionally drained, as they all were, but Avery was spiraling out of control. Diana convinced her to take one of her anxiety pills and go to sleep for a while. Diana stayed with Avery. Within twenty minutes, Avery was passed out. Diana covered her and went back downstairs.

Albert and Sandra were sitting with Lester and the rest of the team trying to figure out the connection between Albert, Sydney Brewer and Alex Stanton, aka James Kramer, aka Alexei Stamenov. Albert never met them and knew nothing about either of them, except what he learned from his teammates about his connection to Natasha. But that ended a long time ago.

Everyone was beginning to feel helpless. All they could do was to sit by the phones and wait. Ross was beginning to lose patience. Poppy sat next to Lorelei. He was eerily quiet. Diana sensed something was not right between Poppy and Lorelei but decided to stay out of it for now.

The call came in on Caeley's phone. Mr. Sandman immediately took it and put it on speaker. It was the same phone number, but not the same location. They were now in Glendale, CA. Their exact location was difficult to pinpoint because they were in a moving vehicle.

Both Diana and Ross were relieved that Avery was sleeping soundly with the help of one of Diana's anxiety pills. Ross went near the speaker and demanded, "Before we strike any deals with you, I want to speak to Ralf, Kimberly and Peter. I want to know they are safe."

"Hi, Daddy, it's me, Ralf."

"Ralf, you have to be strong. Are Peter and Kimmy there with you?"

"Yes, Daddy, Kimmy and Peter are fine, too. Please come get us because......"

Sydney Brewer got on the phone. "Hello, Ross, darling. If you want our son back along with the other two brats, I suggest you do exactly as you are told. Do you understand?" Ross felt the rage rising inside of him. "I want you Ross, the flash drive and Albert."

Poppy took over, fearing Ross would blow his top. "What do you want with Albert?"

There was silence. "Who am I speaking to now?" Sydney Brewer asked.

"I'm Peter's father. What do you want with Albert?"

"I don't care about Albert. It's my partner who has the beef with him."

Albert went over to the speaker. "OK, Stamenov, we've never met. What the hell do you want with me?"

The man's voice was clearly disguised. "It is because of you that I lost Natasha. She is missing. I know you fathered Nika, that wiseass kid of hers. You keep your brat Nika, but I want Natasha back," demanded Stamenov. For a fleeting moment Albert was proud of Nika. Obviously Nika got the best of Stamenov, at times.

Diana got up and walked over to the speaker. She knew, even with his voice disguised, it was James Kramer. Lester walked over and stood beside Diana with his arm around her. He whispered in her ear, "Do not let him get to you. Stay quiet. Do not let him know you're here." Diana turned into Lester and laid her head on his chest. Lester led Diana back to the couch.

Mr. Sandman whispered something in Albert's ear. Albert then answered, "OK, Stamenov, you win. Give the kids back and you can have me, the flash drive, and Ross. Where do we meet for the exchange?"

There was a moment of silence. Sydney Brewer answered. "Melrose Ave. at the Swing Diner, tomorrow at 16:00, exactly. We want Ross, Albert, with the whereabouts of Natasha, and the flash drive. That's the deal." The Phone went dead.

Mr. Sandman walked over to Diana and Lester. "We have pictures of Sydney Brewer. Believe it or not, we have no idea what James Kramer looks like. May we have a picture of him, please?"

Diana closed her eyes for a moment and said, "Well, unbelievably I don't have even one picture of James Kramer. All our wedding pictures disappeared shortly after our wedding. As a matter of fact, so did our photographer and his studio in a terrible fire. I have pictures of Kevin, and me with Kevin, but not one picture of Kevin with James. That was just another piece of my very complex denial."

"I'm sorry to hear that, Diana," Mr. Sandman said empathically.

While that was happening, Veronica was on the phone with Carole Cooper. Carole and her team devised a plan to get the kids back safely and capture Sydney Brewer and Alexei Stamenov.

Mr. Sandman ordered Ross, Poppy, Albert, Blake and Veronica to go out to CA on their private jet. They were to go immediately to the LA station to meet Carole Cooper and her team. The next day the plan to rescue the kids would be executed.

Avery was in a deep sleep but awoke to Ross rubbing her back. She turned to face him. Ross kissed Avery gently on the lips. He smiled saying, "I have good news. I spoke to Ralf. He, Kimmy and Peter are all fine. We know where they are and struck a deal to exchange the kids for Albert, the flash drive and me."

"What?" derided Avery.

Ross took Avery in his arms. Holding her close to him he whispered, "Don't worry, Angel. Mr. Sandman and Carole Cooper have a great plan in place. Poppy, Albert, Blake and Veronica will be going with me. I promise, we will bring our children back."

Avery smiled sweetly at Ross. "Please do!"

"You're very calm, Avery, and it's scaring the hell out of me. What's going on?" Ross gently asked.

"I was losing it when Aunt Diana brought me up here. She gave me an anxiety pill, and she was right. The pill knocked me on my ass. I desperately needed the sleep. Now that I am well rested, I am going to California with you."

"No, Avery. Mr. Sandman was very clear. Neither you nor Lorelei are permitted to go." Ross waited for Avery's rage, but was surprised by what he got.

She smiled at Ross and said, "He made the right call. The philosopher Kierkegaard once said, 'the most painful state of being is remembering the future,' or some thought like that. I trust you and our teammates to bring our children home safely." Ross had never seen Avery so calm in such a stressful situation, especially since it was hitting them so hard personally. In a way, it frightened him.

"I never knew you studied philosophy," Ross commented.

"You'd be surprised at the things I know, Ross. Ross grabbed Avery, pulling her towards him and kissed her deeply. She felt him getting hard and began to get aroused herself whispering, "I wish we could make love right now, but we can't." Avery pushed him away. "Now let's go downstairs," Avery said as she pulled a disappointed Ross off the bed.

Ross grabbed Avery by the shoulders and begged, "Please, Avery, I need you so bad right now. Feel how hard I am. Please Angel, a quickie like the ones we did in Germany?" Avery smiled and locked the bedroom door. Without speaking they quickly took off their clothes and got into bed.

Avery laid on top of Ross, his hardness on her stomach. With two fingers Ross got Avery ready. He rolled her over and with his knees spread her

112

legs, entering her easily. As they found their rhythm, Avery held Ross tightly and as they became one Avery whispered, "I love you so much, Ross.

"I love you so much Avery, Ross whispered right before they climaxed together. They kissed long and deep, savoring their moment of bliss. Ross pulled out of Avery and held her in his arms. "I'll bring them back safely, I promise," Ross assured her.

Avery smiled and stroked his cheek lovingly. "I know you will. I trust you, Ross." They got up, got dressed, kissed long and deep one last time, and went downstairs.

Ross pulled Poppy aside. "I'll have to check Lorelei's phone after we get back. There's no time now."

"Agreed, as soon as this whole thing is resolved," Poppy answered.

That night Ross, Albert, Poppy, Blake and Veronica flew to Los Angeles. When they landed, they went directly to the LA station to meet Carole Cooper.

The rescue on Melrose Ave. was a simple plan but would be an extravaganza. The plan was risky. They would get the kids back, which was their main goal, but there was a high risk of losing Sydney Brewer and Alexei Stamenov.

Carole Cooper explained she believed that sometimes through chaos comes success. She had a few friends in the movie industry. One of them was a director named Anton Ludnick, who was also one of Carole's most trusted friends and assets.

Anton Ludnick would arrive at 15:45 in front of the Swing Diner on Melrose Ave. with two busloads of people and a crew to shoot a generic street scene that could be used in almost any movie that needed a street scene. This kind of thing happened all the time in the Los Angeles area. The Swing Diner was a famous landmark on Melrose Ave. which made it even more plausible. A combination of CIA agents and FBI agents were intermingled with the actors.

Ross, Albert, Poppy, Blake and Veronica parked a delivery van in the back of the diner. Poppy stayed in the van behind the wheel. Blake and Veronica were dressed like the waiters in the diner but could not let the kids see them until the time was right.

Two actors playing customers would start a loud yelling match as a distraction. If needed, the actors would become physical for a bigger distraction. Blake and Veronica saw only Ralf. Four CIA agents were placed in the kitchen to help them out to the van in case of trouble.

At exactly 16:00 Ross and Albert entered the diner through the street crowd in the front. Ross spotted Ralf standing up in a booth looking around. He pointed him out to Albert. Neither Kimmy or Peter were visible. Ralf was alone. It appeared that somehow Sydney Brewer and James Kramer slipped away with the two toddlers and left Ralf alone.

Carefully Ross and Albert approached Ralf while Blake and Veronica scanned the rest of the diner. Ralf saw Ross and jumped into his arms crying. Ross held his son tightly and asked, "Where did they take Kimmy and Peter?"

Ralf was crying but managed to say, "To the bathrooms to change their diapers."

As Veronica and Blake approached, Ross yelled, "Diaper changes in bathrooms." They ran to the other side of the diner where the bathrooms were located. There was no sign of them. Every CIA agent checked every inch of the diner, but it was clear they had gotten away with Kimmy and Peter.

Ralf loved cars and amazingly, at six years old, knew every make and model. Ross and Ralf would often play name that car. Ross would point to a car and Ralf would name the make and model. He always got it right. Ross felt confident when he asked Ralf the kind of vehicle they were using. Ralf told Ross the make and model of the brown SUV they were driving. Ross called it in immediately.

An APB was put out. All airports, ports of entry, and both the southern border into Mexico and the northern border into Canada were covered by ground vehicles and helicopters.

Blake and Veronica were taken to a safe house with Ralf. Ross, Albert and Poppy insisted on working with Carole Cooper and her team to help find Kimmy and Peter.

Ross called Mr. Sandman to report the situation. He asked Mr. Sandman not to tell Avery and Lorelei that they only had Ralf and were still searching for the other two children. Mr. Sandman said he would not lie to Avery and Lorelei if they asked and wouldn't tell them he spoke to Ross unless they asked. He promised to call Ross back as soon as he heard from James Kramer and Sydney Brewer.

The call came. Mr. Sandman asked, "What happened? Why did you flee? Why didn't you take the deal?"

It was Kramer who answered. "We're not stupid, there was no deal. Your elaborate plan was ridiculous to even try. You get one more chance. If you want your two brats alive, you better follow our rules."

Mr. Sandman took a deep breath and said, "OK, spell it out. This time we'll comply. We'll come, hand over Ross, Albert and the flash drive. At the same time, you hand Kimberly and Peter over to us. The location of the exchange is your choice."

Brewer and Kramer then changed the deal. "We know damn well that you would never hand over that flash drive, and Ross and Albert aren't worth it. We want $2,000,000 in exchange for your two brats. We'll make the exchange at TBIT at LAX at exactly 17:00. One more thing, and this is a must. We will only make the exchange with Diana, no one else. Diana has to be the one. is that clear?" James Kramer demanded.

Mr. Sandman looked at Diana. She silently agreed to make the exchange. "OK, then, tomorrow TBIT at LAX at 17:00 sharp. Diana agrees to be there for the exchange," Mr. Sandman informed Kramer who answered, "That's good. I'm looking forward to seeing my old sex partner." Diana felt something stir inside of her but wasn't sure what it was. Lester also felt something, but he was sure of what he was feeling. He would have killed James Kramer right then if he had the chance.

Mr. Sandman called Ross. He ordered him and the rest of the team to stay with Ralf at the safe house. He was on his way to LA with Lester and Diana. He informed Ross that the deal changed for the better but would not divulge the plan. Avery begged Mr. Sandman to allow her to go. He denied her request.

What interested Avery was that Lorelei made no such request. She sat quietly, listened, and said nothing. It was then that Avery made the decision to watch Lorelei's every move without her knowing it.

Avery noticed Lorelei make a phone call. She watched Lorelei get herself together to go out. Sandra asked Lorelei where she was going. She told Sandra she was going back to her home to get things ready for Peter when Poppy brought him home. What Lorelei didn't know was that Avery tailed her.

Lorelei lied to Sandra. Avery followed her into Manhattan straight to the Russian Embassy. Avery thought Lorelei would go in, but she didn't. She waited by the gate until Sergei Alexandrov came out. Lorelei and Sergei hugged and went across the street to a coffee shop.

Avery waited in the shadows for Lorelei's next move. The couple left the coffee shop about an hour later, hugged, and parted. Avery followed Lorelei back to the Hoboken safe house and began keeping a log of Lorelei's movements.

Avery went down to the kitchen for a cup of coffee. JB and Barry were sitting at the table. JB and Barry looked at one another. JB asked, "Avery, were you ordered to tail Lorelei, also?"

Avery was taken aback by JB's question. "Why, were you?"

Barry answered, "Yes, as a matter of fact we were. Mr. Sandman gave us the order right before he left for LA."

Avery laughed, "So you were tailing Lorelei at the same time I was?"

"That's right," admitted Barry.

"Boy, you're good. I had no idea you two were there. Maybe the three of us could team up until Ross comes back with Ralf, Kimmy and Peter," suggested Avery.

"In what way, Avery?" JB asked.

"Look, I never trusted Lorelei from the moment I met her. I love Poppy and I don't want to see him hurt by a Russian agent who is pretending to love him. I want to find out the truth about her. Will you help me?" Avery asked.

"Do you really believe that Lorelei is actually a Russian Agent?" Barry questioned.

Avery thought about it. "I don't understand some of the things I've seen and learned about Lorelei. Poppy has an explanation for everything. Then, right before he and Ross left for LA, I overheard him ask Ross to check a certain number on Lorelei's phone. I'm sure it's Sergei Alexandrov's phone number, which tells me that now, even Poppy is doubting Lorelei's loyalty."

"How do you think we can help you?" JB asked.

Avery smiled. "Please, just tell me everything you find out about Lorelei. Today was the first and last time I can tail her. You two would be doing me a tremendous favor. I'll owe you, both of you. What do you say?" Barry and JB agreed.

While waiting at the safe house in LA, Poppy got a call. When the call ended he asked Ross if he could speak to him privately. They went into an empty room. Poppy smiled at Ross and whispered, "I finally got the word, Ross. Tim Van Wyck is one of ours. He is CIA working for the Russians as a double agent."

Ross patted Poppy on the shoulder. "Good job. Let's keep it just between the two of us."

"Absolutely," agreed Poppy. He then added, "It was actually through Tim that Liliya and Stefan were told to check the whereabouts of Sergei Alexandrov. It appears that Alexei Stamenov and Sergei Alexandrov are rivals on the same team, even though Alexei is old enough to be Sergei's father."

Ross smiled with satisfaction. "We may be able to use that intel to our advantage someday."

"Why not now?" Poppy asked. Ross smiled and waited for Poppy to continue. I'll ask Tim Van Wyck to inform Sergei Alexandrov that it was Alexei Stamenov who abducted his son. We already know that he and Sydney Brewer purchased airline tickets to London. That's a good way to start stirring the pot."

Ross laughed and said, "It sure is. I'm glad we're on the same side, cousin."

Poppy became very serious. "Ross, please do me one favor. When this mess is over, and we start investigating Lorelei, please keep Avery out of the mix."

"I'll do my best," Ross promised. They shook on it.

There was no way Lester would agree to let Diana go to LAX without him. Lester was armed and vowed to kill Stamenov if he posed even a hint of a threat to Diana or the children. Alexei Stamenov, aka, James Kramer, had caused his family enough heartache. It would cause Lester no remorse to take him out.

Mr. Sandman knew how volatile the situation could become. He allowed Lester to go only if he promised to stay out of sight. James Kramer and Lester Ballantyne were enemies in their younger days. Lester always felt that he and Diana could have had a life together if not for James Kramer. If Stamenov, aka, Kramer saw Lester it could cause a chain of events that could jeopardize the exchange and endanger Peter and Kimmy. Lester knew that and promised to stay out of sight.

Diana was riddled with anxiety by the thought of seeing her ex-husband and lover, whom she thought was dead. In her heart she knew that there had been something real between herself and James. He was a monster, faking his death and killing their ten-year old son. However, there was a very small part of her that longed for the days of heart-pounding dangerous missions and passionate lovemaking while facing death.

Diana was a seasoned CIA agent of more than forty years. She knew how to compartmentalize, concentrating on one thing at a time. She boxed up those other feelings and readied herself to face James Kramer for the exchange. Lester knew that about Diana and had total confidence in her. It was James Kramer he didn't trust.

Mr. Sandman decided that only Ross, Poppy and Lester would accompany him with Diana in the lead. It would appear she was alone. The four men would watch from a distance. Both Kimmy and Peter knew Diana and loved her. They would go to Diana readily.

The airport was extremely crowded at that time of day. Crowds supplied a measure of safety. Sydney Brewer and James Kramer would easily be able to slip into the crowd and disappear after the exchange. Mr. Sandman was aware of that but was willing to let them go in order to retrieve Kimmy and Peter safely.

Mr. Sandman alerted his CIA contact in London, as well as MI-6 Simon and Tessa, to be aware of their possible arrival. Sergei Alexandrov also knew Alexei Stamenov, aka, James Kramer and his cohort Beatrice Downing, aka, Sydney Brewer, aka, Anna Varvara would be arriving back on the continent. Now it was personal for Sergei. Stamenov had abducted and traumatized his son. He would make him pay.

TBIT, the international terminal at LAX was a plethora of rushing people. Diana's heart was pounding hard knowing she was minutes away from coming face to face with the man she had been blindly in love with, grew to detest, but at times lusted for. She stood in exactly the spot James Kramer designated.

Mr. Sandman placed himself, Ross, Poppy and Lester strategically around the area. Diana had on a wire. All of them could see and hear Diana easily, but she could not see them. But then, she saw him. Even though he aged he was still the sexiest man she had ever seen. He tried to play her, smiling that crooked smile she loved as he approached.

Diana's heart was pounding hard and her guts were churning, but on the outside, she stood steadfast like a stone statue. She refused to allow herself to smile back at this devil of a man. Diana pulled herself together searching for Kimmy and Peter. She did not see them or Sydney Brewer. Neither did Mr. Sandman, Ross, Poppy or Lester, who had his hand on his weapon.

As James Kramer sashayed towards her with his crooked smile, he said, "Well my dear, you're looking as delicious as ever."

What came out of Diana's mouth was even a shock for her. "Where are Kimmy and Peter? Did you kill them too like you killed our son Kevin?" His crooked smile faded. Hiding in the shadows, Mr. Sandman's heart fell into his stomach.

Mr. Sandman spoke into his watch to Ross, Poppy and Lester. "Shit, why did she have to say that? It might only antagonize him. Just be ready to grab the kids and run." All three agreed.

Diana then spotted Sydney Brewer walking towards them holding Kimmy in her arms and holding Peter's hand as she dragged him along. Both children were filthy. Diana wanted to grab them both and run but knew she would fail. She had to play it out the way they planned.

Sydney Brewer reached Diana and Kimmy cried, reaching out for Diana to take her. Peter strained and broke away, running behind Diana as she took Kimmy into her arms. Diana pushed the case of money towards James with her foot, but Sydney Brewer picked it up, turned and walked away.

Diana looked hard at James and then smiled. Without any emotion she stated, "We'll meet again, James. But next time, I'm going to kill you." Diana and James Kramer locked eyes for a moment before he and Sydney Brewer vanished into the crowd.

Diana took Kimmy and Peter and walked towards Lester. Ross and Poppy ran towards her to reunite with their children. Mr. Sandman was in a rush to get out. He explained that there were only piles of one-dollar bills adding up to about one thousand dollars in the case Diana gave them. "When they check the case, they will be raving mad and will probably come back at us. They will be arrested immediately," Mr. Sandman promised.

One week later, Avery and Ross hosted the monthly lasagna dinner. Everyone was talking, cracking jokes, and enjoying themselves. Ralf, Kimmy and Peter had been checked out by doctors and deemed unharmed physically. Diana, however, was worried about how their time in captivity would affect the three children over time. That was what troubled Diana the most. It was constantly nagging at her. It seemed impossible that the heartless monster who killed his own son to punish her did not do any psychological harm to Ralf, Kimmy and Peter, but especially Ralf, being the oldest and Sydney Brewer's biological son.

Lester sensed Diana's angst asking, "Are you all right, my darling?" He knew the answer. That morning he and Diana had a conversation about the children's mental health after such a traumatic experience. He told Diana they all needed to watch and be aware of any unusual changes of behavior, especially in Ralf. He assured Diana that it was not worth getting worked up over something that might not be an issue. Only time would tell.

"Only time would tell", were the words that haunted Diana. She was seething deep inside but could do nothing about it. She patted Lester's arm, looked up at him and smiled. "I'm fine, Lester, but I need to use the bathroom."

Diana stood looking at herself in the mirror. That was when her decision became unchangeable. She thought about Kevin, how sweet and innocent he was. Tears that had been pent up for over twenty years came streaming down her face and she allowed their release. This time Diana did not take an anxiety pill. She needed to feel her pain.

Opening her purse, she began rummaging through the contents until she found a soft leather pouch with a zipper. She unzipped the pouch and gently pulled the lining away from one side on the inside of the pouch. She extracted a small photo she had trimmed to fit into the lining. It was a photo of James Diana had taken many years ago when she and James were vacationing on the Black Sea.

Diana stood perfectly still staring at the photo of the young James with his crooked smile. Her mind wandered back to that vacation. She allowed herself to go deep into her memory bank, thinking of the hotel where they stayed. She thought of how alive she felt, how happy she was. She went deeper and deeper into her memory vault. She began thinking about his body, how he felt to her touch. Diana's eyes were closed thinking about how it felt when he was on top of her, starting slow and then… Someone was pounding on the bathroom door. It was Lester. She was quickly thrusted upward, out of her memory bank. "Diana, are you OK in there?"

At first it was hard for her to speak. "Yes, dear, I'm fine. I'll be right out." She stood for another moment looking at herself in the mirror. She picked up the photo of James, looked at it and began to put it back into the lining of the leather case, but stopped. Instead, she held up the photo of James with his crooked smile. Diana looked straight at James and stated unemotionally, "I promise, I *am* going to kill you!"

CHAPTER 6
MOTHER RUSSIA

Diana walked down the stairs to join the others. James *is* alive! She was resolved and at peace with the decision to kill James Kramer for killing their ten-year old son Kevin. The kidnapping of Ralf, Kimmy and Peter by James Kramer and Sydney Brewer gave Diana the push she needed. James deserved to die. Diana vowed never to allow any of their team's children to go through such an ordeal ever again. She walked over to Lester. He poured her another glass of wine. Holding up her glass Diana toasted, "To our family, especially the children."

As they clanked glasses Lester answered, "Amen!" It was 19:00 and Avery, Sandra, and Albert were putting out dessert. The smell of coffee permeated the air and Diana smiled, a smile of contentment and commitment to the promise she made to herself.

Sydney Brewer and James Kramer managed to evade capture in London. They disappeared either into Western Europe, Eastern Europe, or Russia. The CIA, MI6 and INTERPOL all had their eyes and ears open, but never caught a hint as to their whereabouts.

In Moscow it was 03:00. Yana Alexandrov was pacing the floor. Sergei promised he would be coming home. Her biggest hope was that it would be with her grandson. It was a complicated situation. Yana knew in her heart that there was no realistic solution. Yet, she strongly felt that because Peter was Sergei's biological son and her biological grandson, they had every right to have him in their lives. Sergei was her only child. Sergei and Peter were all she had left.

Yana's husband, Sergei's father, once held a top job in the Soviet government. The Alexandrov family had been a top-tier family from the beginning of the formation of the Soviet Union. With the collapse of the Soviet Union and the untimely death of her husband, all of Yana's friends had either left the country or died.

Yana was lost in her thoughts. The loud ring of the phone startled her. She jumped, but quickly answered. Before she had time to speak Yana heard, "Hello, is that you Mother?"

Yana heart lightened. "Yes, it's me."

"Don't be alarmed. I am sorry to call at such a late hour, but this will be the only chance I get. I have something to complete and then, I promise, you will see me walk through the door."

"Thank you for calling, Sergei. You know how I worry about you. Just be safe and come home soon. I will have all your favorites waiting on the kitchen table for you to gobble up."

"Thank you, Mother, I look forward to it," Sergei answered as he ended the call. He looked out of his hotel window and saw the Eiffel Tower in the distance.

Anna Varvara, aka, Sydney Brewer and Alexei Stamenov, aka, James Kramer parted in London. Sergei didn't care about Anna Varvara, but he followed Alexei Stamenov to Paris, where he saw him connect with two Romanian thugs. He wondered if they worked for Toma Bratu, an important and influential Romanian mobster.

The days were getting shorter and the nights were getting colder. It was the beginning of November and they began discussing Thanksgiving. Lester suggested the secure room at the club, but Diana, as well as Avery protested. Avery gave the order. "We are all going to be together right here in my house. But everyone has to bring a traditional Thanksgiving dish. Ross and I will supply a big turkey and a ham for those who don't like turkey."

Diana immediately volunteered. "Lester and I will bring my sausage stuffing and a few bottles of apple cider."

Then Avery added, "Everyone from Group Eleven is invited with their spouses, partners and families." They were all talking at once in the glow of a warm fire about what foods to bring, recipes, and desserts. Lorelei felt her phone vibrate. She excused herself and went upstairs to the bathroom.

Poppy motioned for Albert, who spoke Russian, to follow him. As Poppy walked up the stairs with Albert following, he caught a glimpse of the bathroom door closing. He turned and silently motioned towards Albert to listen through the bathroom door to hear if Lorelei was speaking Russian and if so, to translate.

Monday morning Poppy went to the Hackensack station as usual, but Lorelei complained of a sore throat. She called Peter's daycare facility explaining she would be home from work and did not need to bring him in. Lorelei walked into the kitchen, opened the refrigerator and took out the milk, thought for a moment and smiled. She called Poppy asking him to pick milk up on his way home. She then casually asked him, "Is Mr. Sandman in yet?"

Poppy was taken off guard. "Yes, he's in his office with someone. Why do you ask?"

"Oh, I was just curious to know what dish he was bringing on Thanksgiving, that's all. I forgot to ask him the other night." Lorelei felt the silent trepidation on the other end of the phone.

Poppy finally answered, "I'll ask him when I see him, Lorelei. I'll bring home milk. Feel better. I have to go to a meeting. Bye, sweetheart." Poppy hung up and immediately called Albert.

"Good, he *is* at the station!" Lorelei took the milk and walked over to the sink to pour half of it down the drain but stopped. It went against her grain to waste food. She poured half in a thermos bottle and took it with her when she and Peter left the house.

Poppy knocked on Mr. Sandman's office door. It opened quickly. "Poppy, I want you to meet an old friend of mine, Asa Page. Asa, this is Peter Lassiter, but around here we call him Poppy, and before you even ask, I'll tell you I don't know why we call him Poppy we just do!"

Asa Page stood up and extended his large weathered hand. "I'm happy to make your acquaintance, son. I know your mother, Diana, and heard a lot about you over the years."

Confused, Poppy responded, "It's nice to meet you, Sir. Everyone knows my mother." Poppy looked thoughtfully at Asa asking, "You're not *the* Asa Page, the legend? We all thought you were probably a myth, but here you are."

Mr. Sandman put his arm around Poppy. "That's right! He's real and temporarily out of retirement because he's going to help us. The thing is, this job, for us, is personal. To cover our tracks, Asa is going to hire the Van Wyck Detective Agency to track down Alexei Stamenov, aka, James Kramer. I've had just about enough of him. For your mother's peace of mind and safety and to ease your father's angst, I want him either arrested or taken out. Frankly, I prefer the latter."

Poppy looked hard at Asa Page. "What's in it for you, Mr. Page?"

Asa sat down. The friendly demeanor left his tanned wrinkled face. Poppy saw a sparkle in Asa's eyes. "Money, son, and the thrill of the hunt, plus the fact that I know the elusive Alexei Stamenov. I've tangled with him in the past and once even had a drink with him." Poppy's head was full of questions. The answers would come eventually, but not here and not now. Poppy instinctively knew that.

"Yes, Sir," was Poppy's response.

Lorelei wheeled Peter into Wood Park, easily finding the old stone structure that housed the public restrooms. She looked around but didn't see anyone. Lorelei did not know who her contact was. It was just a voice on the phone telling her where to go, when to be there and to bring her son Peter. She loved Poppy and hated deceiving him, but knew she had no choice. It was difficult, very difficult.

Lorelei felt a hand on her shoulder and spun around to face a pleasant looking older woman. The woman spoke softly in Russian. "He will meet you and the boy here one week from today, same time." The woman looked down at Peter, smiled, looked up at Lorelei and walked away. Lorelei stood in a trance watching the woman disappear as she turned a corner leaving the park. Peter began complaining, trying to climb out of his stroller. Lorelei took him out and they walked over to the children's play area.

Albert and Sandra were waiting for Poppy in his office. As Poppy walked in, he asked, "So, was I right, or not?"

Albert took a deep breath. "Yes, unfortunately you were right."

"How should we handle this, or do you want to handle it yourself?" Sandra asked, not making direct eye contact with Poppy.

Poppy knew Albert and Sandra were hurting for him. He also knew he could depend on them to do whatever he needed done. "I don't know what to do. I'm too close to the situation that I think is unfolding."

"Maybe you should sit down with Mr. Sandman and tell him what you think the situation *is* that's unfolding. He can then officially assign Sandra and me to the situation and you can bow out, which probably you should do," suggested Albert.

"I agree with Albert. At this point Mr. Sandman needs to know and you shouldn't be on this one. Anyway, who knows, it could all be for naught," Sandra added, trying not to sound grim.

"Why wait? Let's talk to him now," Poppy picked up the phone on his desk and punched in Mr. Sandman's extension. On the phone Poppy explained the situation he saw unfolding. He was still with Asa, but Mr. Sandman told them to come to his office. Asa was leaving when they got there. Poppy smiled, extended his hand and said, "It was a pleasure t meet you, Mr. Page. I hope we'll meet again in the near future."

Asa shook Poppy's hand. "I'm sure we will. Stay safe." Then, Asa made brief eye contact with Albert and Sandra. He quickly walked down the hall and got into the elevator before Poppy had a chance to introduce him. "Who was that interesting looking character?" Albert asked, his eyes transfixed on the elevator door.

"That was the legendary Asa Page," Poppy answered.

"Wow! I've heard stories but thought they were just that, stories," Sandra mused.

"What's he doing here? Was this just a social call or is he coming out of retirement to help with an assignment?" Albert asked.

"It's not for me to say, but we've got bigger fish to fry right now," Poppy answered as he opened the door to Mr. Sandman's office.

Asa Page stood in front of the Van Wyck Detective Agency. He went to open the door, but Diana beat him to it and opened her arms. "Asa, it's really you. When Earl called me, I couldn't believe it." Diana and Asa hugged tightly. "I 'll make a fresh pot of coffee, or would you prefer something stronger?"

Diana led Asa inside and sat him down on the couch. "Coffee would be great, with one or maybe two of those great-looking donuts over there," Asa answered as he eyed the box of freshly baked donuts.

Lester walked in just as Asa was biting into a donut. Diana jumped up to greet Lester and introduced him to Asa. She was surprised to learn that Asa and Lester had met a few times in the past. The two men shook hands. Lester poured himself a cup of coffee and asked, "OK, what or who is the situation? What are we doing, Asa?"

With another bite of donut filling his mouth and licking the sugar off of his fingers, he answered. "Earl wants me to hire your agency to find Alexei Stamenov. He says he's sick of his shit and wants us to take him out." Diana stared blankly at Asa Page, not quite believing what she was hearing.

Poppy, Albert and Sandra sat across the desk from Mr. Sandman, who had a slight inkling as to what this meeting was about. He listened to Poppy explain how he and Albert followed Lorelei to the bathroom at Ross and Avery's house as she answered a phone call from Sergei Alexandrov. Albert could hear enough to know that she was receiving some sort of instructions. Poppy then explained about Lorelei's excuse to stay home with Peter. Albert and Sandra took over describing what occurred at Wood Park. Sandra described Lorelei's contact. Albert explained that the woman instructed Lorelei, in Russian, to be at the same place in Wood Park in one week's time.

Poppy, Albert and Sandra silently waited for Mr. Sandman to respond. After a moment or two he stated, "This is all very interesting, but until something happens, there's nothing we can do." All three understood. "Keep me abreast of the situation. If we need to get involved, I promise, Poppy, we will," Mr. Sandman said assuringly.

"Thank you, Sir. We will keep on top of this and will keep you up to date," Poppy responded, trying to smile, but he was hurting inside. Poppy, Albert and Sandra stood up to leave. Mr. Sandman stood up, walked around his desk to Poppy putting his arm around him in a comforting way.

"Don't' worry, son. This situation will get resolved one way or another. I know how much this hurts you, but we must find out the truth, not just for your sake personally, but for the team's sake." Poppy shook is head in agreement, knowing Mr. Sandman was right.

Diana got up, walked over to her desk, opened the bottom draw and pulled out a bottle of expensive whiskey. "I keep this in there for an occasion exactly like this. I will help you find that bastard and do anything you need me to do to rid the world of that scumbag," Diana vehemently stated.

Lester turned to Diana and ordered, "You will not be a part of this in any way, and that's an order. Do you understand me?"

"I have to be the one to take him out," loudly stated Diana. "Lester, you are not going to order me around when it comes to James." Diana was having a difficult time staying in control. "James purposely killed our son Kevin and now, for Kevin, I must be the one to kill James. It can't be any other way." Diana held back her tears. "It can't go down any other way. I have to be the one. *Me* Lester. *I* have to be the one."

The door suddenly flew open. Mr. Sandman barged through. "Actually, Diana, neither you nor Lester are intended for this one. Ross, Avery, Barry and JB will work with Asa. They are my choices. My decision is final, is that clear?"

Diana remained staid. Seeing Mr. Sandman, she pushed Lester away and declared, "You had Asa wired so you could hear this conversation, Earl!"

"Yes, Diana, I did because I had to know exactly where you stand. You said something extremely incendiary to James Kramer at the airport in LA that could have compromised the safety of the kids. You're much too emotionally involved. I don't want you anywhere near this one, do I make myself clear?" It was hard for Mr. Sandman to say that to Diana. He knew she was in pain, how much she needed to feel vindicated, and mostly, how much she needed closure.

Looking down at the floor, Diana answered. "Yes, Sir." Diana knew she was not going to follow orders. Lester knew it, in fact he was sure of it.

Ross, Avery, Barry and JB walked through the door and stopped short when they saw the scene in progress. "Should we leave?" Ross asked as his eyes focused on Asa Page.

Mr. Sandman stepped up to Ross and put one arm around him and the other around Avery. "Asa Page meet four of my finest, Ross and Avery and those two characters are Barry and JB. They will be going with you to Paris."

"We're going to Paris? What's the situation? And who are you, Mr. Page?" Avery directly asked.

Mr. Sandman went on to explain who Asa Page was. Barry, JB, Ross and Avery all admitted they had always thought Asa Page was a fictional character. Avery laughed, admitting that she always thought the name Asa Page sounded like something out of a spy thriller. They were amazed he was a real.

Mr. Sandman explained that Asa would be hiring the agency to hunt down the psychopath who killed his own son Kevin. Asa is being hired to execute James Kramer for the murder of Kevin Kramer. Anger was rising in Diana's chest. "*I* am Kevin's mother therefore *I* should be the one to execute that bastard. It should be me, only me," Diana softly exclaimed through clenched teeth. Both Ross and Avery went to her to console her.

Asa pulled Mr. Sandman aside. "Earl, that woman needs closure, and for Diana the only way she'll get it is to kill Kramer herself. Come on, Earl, you know I'm right."

"I don't know, Asa. She said something that could have turned a safe exchange of the kids into an unnecessary tragedy. I just don't know if she can handle it."

Asa Page stepped closer to Mr. Sandman and whispered, "This is an entirely different situation and besides, Lester, Barry, JB and I will all be there. Please, Earl, I'm begging you, allow me to take Lester and Diana. You owe it to her." Asa whispered as he placed his hand on Mr. Sandman's shoulder.

Mr. Sandman closed his eyes in thought for a moment. "Against my better judgement, and with your solemn promise to keep things under control, I will relinquish Diana and Lester to you for this operation. But Asa, if I smell even the faintest scent of dissonance, the five of you will immediately be extracted even if the operation has not been completed. Do I make myself clear?" The two men's' eyes locked in mutual understanding and agreement. Mr. Sandman then whispered, "Just find that asshole and take him out. I want him dead!"

Asa Page and Mr. Sandman turned to face Barry, JB, Lester, Diana, Ross and Avery. Mr. Sandman smiled and said, "My dear old trusted friend here, Asa, has persuaded me, against my better judgement, that Lester and Diana should join him with Barry and JB in Paris instead of Ross and Avery." Diana was about to speak, but Mr. Sandman put his hand up and said, "Let me finish. If I have even the slightest inkling that things could go sideways, I will extract the five of you faster than you can blink. Get the message?"

Diana walked over to Mr. Sandman, looked into his eyes and whispered, "God bless you, Earl and thank you," Diana leaned up and kissed him on the cheek.

At dusk, Sergei Alexandrov walked out of his hotel into a misty rain falling on Paris. He had gotten a lead from an old friend as to the whereabouts of Alexei Stamenov, aka, James Kramer. Sergei was headed to Le Café Moreau where he was to meet his friend. His plan was to find Alexei Stamenov the next day, kill him and take an early morning flight directly from Paris to Newark International Airport before Stamenov's body was discovered, if it ever was discovered. But that was not to be. The intel Sergei's friend had gotten was false, in fact, purposely misleading. Alexei Stamenov, aka, James Kramer, had disappeared. Sergei went back to his hotel and changed his flight from Newark to Moscow. He would fly to Newark next week in time for his meeting in Wood Park.

The wonderful smell of freshly baked bread hit him the moment he opened the door. "Hello, Mother, I'm home as promised," Sergei shouted as he hung up his coat. Yana ran out of the kitchen and embraced her son.

"I am so glad you're finally here. I was so worried about you Sergei, more than usual this time." Yana led her son into the kitchen. Sergei was hungry so he dove into all his favorite foods his mother promised would be waiting for him. With satisfaction, Yana watched as her son eat heartily. She then asked, "Tell me honestly, Sergei, were you in danger in Paris?"

Sergei stopped chewing and looked up at Yana, surprised that she would entertain such an idea, but moreover, astounded that she knew he had called her from Paris. He swallowed his food and confronted Yana. "First of all, Mother, what makes you think I was in any danger? But more importantly, Mother, how the hell did you know I was calling you from Paris?"

"I have friends in high places," Yana coyly answered her son. But Yana knew that answer would not be enough for Sergei.

"Mother, what I do and where I go is never to be spoken about. Who is this friend who keeps you informed?" Sergei asked indignantly.

"It's your Uncle Eadric. Sergei, you must understand, I cannot live in constant fear of losing you like I lost your father. Please don't be angry with Uncle Eadric. He never gives me any details. He just assures me you are safe wherever you are in the world." Yana began to cry. "I sit here alone day after day. All of my friends have either left the country or have died. I miss your father terribly and you even more. The worst part is that I know I have a grandson I have never seen and it's killing me." Yana dramatically threw herself into her son's arms and sobbed, "Will I ever get to meet my grandson Peter before I die, Sergei?" As he held his mother close and comforted her, Sergei thought about how close Peter had come to losing his life when Alexei Stamenov and Anna Varvara held Peter and the two other children in captivity.

Sergei held Yana by her shoulders, looked directly into her eyes and strongly stated, "Yes Mother, you will meet your grandson Peter and his mother Lorelei next week, I promise." Sergei led Yana into the parlor, sat her on the couch and sat down next to her. He pulled a wad of cash out of his pocket and handed it to Yana. "Take this money and follow my instructions. You will have me, my son Peter and his mother Lorelei here next week. Then you will have a full house and will never be alone again." Sergei gave his mother the information she needed to prepare for Peter and Lorelei's arrival.

Lester, Diana, Barry, JB and Asa Page were meeting at the detective agency to discuss the upcoming operation. Mr. Sandman was not physically present but was wirelessly connected to them. He had been informed that their latest intel on the whereabouts of James Kramer was Paris, but that was unconfirmed. Agents in Europe were checking it out. James was now thought to be somewhere in the mountains in the south of Spain. Mr. Sandman wanted them to fly to Malaga, Spain that night from Teterboro on their unmarked private jet. The name Universal Tours would be painted onto the plane. It would appear that Asa Page was a tour guide taking four people on a private tour of Spain. Whit Van Wyck would sit in at the agency for Diana and Arlo would run the club for Lester while they were away. Their jet took off from Teterboro at 21:00 that night.

Sergei received intel the next morning that the CIA flew five agents, including the infamous Asa Page, to Malaga, Spain to capture or take down Alexei Stamenov. Even though Sergei knew he had to meet Lorelei in six days, he was instinctively pulled in the direction of Spain. He would let the Americans lead him to Alexei Stamenov. If the timing was right, he could still meet Lorelei on time. If it took too long to find Stamenov, he would back away from the chase to keep his date with Lorelei and his son Peter. If Diana Kramer-Ballantyne was part of the CIA team, Sergei knew James Kramer, aka, Alexei Stamenov did not have a chance in hell to survive after what he did to her by murdering their young son. This time, ironically, he and the Americans had the same goal, to eliminate James Kramer, aka, Alexei Stamenov.

Poppy walked into the house with a gallon of milk and vanilla ice cream, Peter's favorite. He opened the refrigerator and saw the old gallon of milk was over half empty. He poured all of it into a glass thinking that he had had a bowl of cereal that morning and could have sworn the gallon jug was almost full. Lorelei did not usually drink milk and Peter could not have consumed that much in a few hours. Poppy shook off his suspicion when Peter came running in to greet him with a big smile and hug. Lorelei was right behind Peter with her smile and hug. Poppy hugged Lorelei back but there was no smile.

The plane touched down in the early morning at the Costa Del Sol airport in Malaga, Spain. Their SUV was waiting for them. As Asa drove, taking the MA20 towards Torremolinos, it started to rain. The drive would have taken twenty minutes, but it began raining heavily. Asa, at times had to inch along because the windshield wipers almost made it worse. It took close to an hour to arrive at the Hotel Del Sol. They checked in, went to their rooms, changed into dry clothes, went back down and met in the restaurant. It was morning and the waiter brought them coffee, bread and cheese. Asa's contact was to meet him in the bar that afternoon at 12:00.

Albert, Sandra, Ross and Avery took turns keeping track of Lorelei. Avery never trusted Lorelei from the moment they met in Hoboken. While it was true that Lorelei was a trusted team member and had always come through on work assignments, Avery always suspected something was off with Lorelei personally. When Poppy was forced to reveal that Peter was Sergei Alexandrov's biological son that cemented Avery's mistrust and suspicious negativity towards Lorelei.

Lorelei was followed every moment of every day. At the end of each day the two couples met with Poppy to report Lorelei's activities. The worse part for Poppy was going home each night pretending everything was normal when, in fact, he knew when and where in Wood Park Lorelei and Peter were to meet Sergei Alexandrov. Despite it all, Poppy and Lorelei truly and completely loved each other. The more unspoken tension each felt, the more passionately they made love. In the moment, that was real for both of them.

Even though his instincts were to follow the CIA team to Spain, Sergei knew he had no choice but to fly back to New York. Sergei was now aware the CIA was watching Lorelei and Peter around the clock. He had to come up with a change of plans, throwing them far off the mark in order to easily collect Lorelei and Peter to transport them to his private plane in Long Island. All Sergei focused on was getting Lorelei and Peter safely back to Yana in Moscow.

The rain had stopped and by noon the sun was drying up the land. Asa Page sat in the bar of the Hotel Del Sol alone waiting for his contact. He spotted her immediately and rose to greet her with a warm smile. She returned his smile as she walked into his out welcoming arms. He hugged her tightly asking, "How are you Glenda? It's been a long time." He released her and they sat down. Asa ordered two Bloody Mary's.

Glenda stopped Asa before he continued speaking. "Don't worry, Sergei Alexandrov went back to Moscow to see his mother. He will not interfere with your operation."

"Thank you for that. The last thing we need is his interference. This time, Glenda, that bastard will be taken out by a very determined assassin with a justifiable beef. Do you know where Alexei Stamenov is?"

Glenda sat back, and with an air of superiority stated, "Actually, I do."

Sergei Alexandrov boarded his plane in Moscow with one purpose in mind. Having sent Glenda to Spain, he needed to figure out how to distract whoever was keeping watch over Lorelei and Peter. He could then bring them to the private airport in Long Island where his plane would be waiting, ready to fly them to Moscow.

He realized it would have to be a clandestine operation executed when Lorelei and Peter were alone. The planned meeting in Wood Park Glenda had set up was no longer an option. Also, he would need help, someone to distract the eyes that were on Lorelei and Peter. Sergei began to think of who he trusted enough to commandeer for the job. He closed his eyes, but who he saw, who he thought of was Lorelei.

Sergei allowed himself to drift back to the days when he and Lorelei were together. He loved her and the way he felt making love to her. He loved the very essence of her. They had been happy. Suddenly, she disappeared. The plane hit an air pocket and rose and fell with a jerk, snapping Sergei out of his memories of Lorelei. He called the flight attendant to bring him a double vodka.

Glenda left the bar walking swiftly out of the hotel. Lester and Diana were getting out of the elevator when Diana spotted her. "Lester, I'm sure I know that woman. She must have been Asa's contact." Diana saw Asa coming out of the bar and rushed over to him. "So, did she know where James is?" Asa knew Diana well enough to know that she was a straight shooter and expected the same from her colleagues. He told her the truth. "Yes, Diana, she knows where James is."

Diana's smile was his thank you. "Was that Glenda, by any chance?"

"Yes, it was. I'm surprised you remembered her after all this time."

"Tell me Asa, as a Russian agent what is *her* function? How is *she* connected to our operation?"

Asa looked at Diana and Lester, who was listening, and suggested they go into the restaurant for lunch. Barry and JB followed close behind. Diana pointed to a round table in a far corner of the room, asking if they might be seated there. The Saludador obliged and seated them. Diana wasted no time. "OK, Asa, now answer my question. Why is Glenda here? What is her function?"

Asa leaned forward and quietly explained. "Glenda actually works for Sergei Alexandrov. Up to two days ago, she was Sergei's eyes on Lorelei and Peter. Now, her eyes are on Alexei Stamenov. Peter is Sergei's son, as you all know. And, as you all also know, Alexei Stamenov, aka, James Kramer and Sydney Brewer kidnapped Peter along with two other children. Sergei wants James Kramer dead as much as you do, Diana"

"Oh, I doubt that very much. Besides, those are our children you're talking about." Diana snidely retorted.

"Yes Diana, I know and I'm very sorry the children were subjected to those two psychopaths."

"Are you saying that Sergei Alexandrov sent Glenda to help us find James?"

Asa snickered, "Amazingly yes, but with one caveat; Sergei knows you are first in line, but Diana, if you don't kill him, Glenda will."

"Not to worry, Asa. Point me in the right direction and *I* will kill him!" No one spoke, not even Lester.

Sergei Alexandrov stepped off the plane, got into the limo which was waiting for him and was taken directly to the Russian embassy in Manhattan. From the limo he called Anton Kristinoff who, many times in the past, assisted Sergei on his missions. He knew he could trust Anton as he had always been helpful and trustworthy in the past.

Anton Kristinoff was waiting. He greeted Sergei with a smile, a bottle of vodka and two glasses. The two men sat close together on a small couch that was tucked away in an alcove on the first floor of the Russian Embassy. Both Serge and Anton knew of two listening devices planted in that alcove. Sergei removed the one underneath the coffee table and

Anton removed the other in the lamp next to the couch. They looked at each other and quietly laughed, shaking their heads at the stupidity of it all.

Anton became serious and asked, "OK, Sergei, what kind of mischief do you have in mind for me?"

"I need a distraction, some sort of disturbance. Lorelei and my son are being watched around the clock. My goal is to extract Lorelei and Peter out of here and back to Moscow on my plane, which is waiting in Long Island and ready to go as soon as I give the word. I can't do this alone, Anton."

After a moment's thought, Anton asked, "What do you suggest?"

"Find out whose eyes are watching Lorelei and my son. Once you know that, you will be able to come up with an appropriate plan."

"Agreed, I'll get right on it. But Sergei, will you do something for me in return?"

"Of course, Anton, if I can. What do you want?"

Anton smiled slightly and sighed deeply. "I want to go home, back to Russia. I miss my family very much. Can you please do that for me Sergei?"

"Of course, Anton. Yes, I will arrange it. You will fly back to Moscow on my plane with me, Lorelei and my son."

Anton was so happy he almost cried. "Thank you, Sergei, thank you so much." Sergei poured each of them another glass of vodka and they drank to a successful operation. They replaced the listening devices before leaving the alcove.

It was 14:00 and they were on their way to Mijas Pueblo, a picturesque village of sun-drenched white houses on the side of a mountain. There, Glenda claimed, Alexei Stamenov, aka, James Kramer would be found posing as a local owner of a souvenir shop in the Constitution Square. James was half Spanish. His mother grew up in Malaga. She moved to Moscow when she married his father right after the WWII. She remained in Moscow until her death. Alexei brought her back to Malaga to be buried in her family's plot. Alexei came back to Malaga at least once every year to visit her grave.

As a young boy, his parents would bring Alexei for extended visits to his grandparents in Malaga. The small, ancient mountain village of Mijas Pueblo became his favorite spot on earth. He knew many of the locals and developed deep friendships with a few. Here, among narrow cobblestone streets, white houses with colorful flowers brimming over clay window boxes beneath wrought iron grates and second floor balconies, Alexei felt safe.

This intel did not surprise Diana. James always had a special affinity for Spain, but she never knew James was half Spanish. She never knew any of this. He lied to her about his parents, claiming they both perished in Europe as spies for the British at the hands of the Nazis during the war. James explained he was raised by his grandparents and when they died was passed from one aunt and uncle to the next until he was eighteen. He then joined the army. It was there, he told Diana, he was recruited into the CIA. Alexei Stamenov, aka, James Kramer was actually a double agent working for the Soviet Union. He used Diana as they worked together to gain access into the most secure places the CIA had in Russia and Belarus, all of which was the Soviet Union at that time.

Diana was determined that by days end James Kramer, the murderer of their son, would be slain. Asa, Diana and Lester all knew what James looked like, Barry and JB did not. Diana had no choice but to reveal her secret. Sitting in the back of the SUV with Barry and JB, Diana opened her small change purse and pulled the lining back, lifting out an old photo of her and James. "Here, you two, take a good look. He still looks pretty much the same, just older." Diana handed Barry the photo. He and JB studied it closely. Lester realized Diana actually had a picture of James after telling Group Eleven that no pictures of James existed.

"Give it here, let me see that," insisted Lester. Diana knew Lester was annoyed but did not realize he was also feeling betrayed. She had his picture stashed away all this time lying, telling everyone that no photos of James existed when in fact she had one securely hidden away. That was the first time he ever experienced Diana lying. Lester began to ask himself what else Diana might have lied about? He handed Diana back the photo without saying one word.

Asa felt the tension between Lester and Diana and knew he needed to defuse it. "OK, here's how we are going to play this out," Asa stated with authority. Instead of defusing the tension, he redirected it.

"Who made you the leader of the pack, Asa?" sneered Lester.

Asa knew Lester knew the answer, but answered him assuredly in a calming manner, "Earl Sandman made me your guide. But I am open to suggestions after you hear me out."

Lester backed down. "Sorry Asa, I'm just a little on edge."

"Don't think twice about it, Lester," Asa answered with a broad smile. He went on to explain his plan. "Since James knows Diana, Lester and me, it would behoove us to sit hidden away in some café. It would be best for Barry and BJ to find out which souvenir shop James owns."

Lester turned around to face Diana. "Why don't you give Barry and JB the photo of James you've secretly been carrying around with you, Diana?" Lester snidely suggested. Diana felt ashamed and looked the other way. She could not face Lester to answer his question. She silently extracted the photo from the lining of her change purse and handed it to Barry, who was sitting next to her. They rode in silence until arriving in Mijas Pueblo.

As they got out of the vehicle Diana grabbed Lester by the arm and held him back. Asa, Barry and JB gave them privacy to work out this unexpected issue between them. They turned to face each other. Diana looked Lester in the eyes and said, "I'm sorry I lied about not having a photo of James. I can't explain why I did it, but I am sorry. Can you please forgive me Lester?"

Lester took Diana in his arms. "Of course, I forgive you, but just tell me, how often do you look at that psychopath's face with that stupid crooked smile?"

"Never, Lester, never…well…only once. It was on a train late at night. I was with Ross, Avery, and Professor Paul Richards. We were travelling from Berlin to St. Petersburg. I couldn't sleep. I had never been in Russia without James, so naturally I began thinking of those days. So, I took out the photo and looked at James. You weren't there, technically speaking, remember?" Diana and Lester looked at each other and laughed.

"Did you really not know I was tailing you the entire time on that operation to extract Andrei?"

"A part of me thought it might be you, but I never believed you'd leave the club. So, no, I actually thought it was nuts for me to think it would be you."

Lester laughed, put his arm around Diana and led her away saying, "Come on my darling. *You* have to kill a madman!" With that said, Diana felt as if she was going to throw up.

Anton Kristinoff, loyal to his comrade Sergei Alexandrov, within hours, found the eyes on Lorelei and Peter. One couple, Ross and Avery Lisano, ran the Van Wyck detective Agency. The second couple, Albert and Sandra Goode owned and operated Albert's Garden Palace, a catering hall in Hoboken. Both couples were CIA, which would make creating a distraction or disturbance more difficult. Anton weighed it all out and came up with a plan he thought suitable. Lorelei did not know Anton, which Anton considered a plus. He would use that to his advantage.

Satisfied, he arranged to meet Sergei again in the alcove on the first floor of the Russian embassy in Manhattan.

On the table in front of them was a bottle of vodka, already half emptied and two glasses. Anton had removed the two listening devices before Sergei had arrived, enabling them to talk freely. Sergei listened to Anton's plan carefully, amazed at the simplicity of it and was satisfied. They drank to Mother Russia.

Lorelei had not been informed that Sergei was not going to meet her in Wood Park. She and Peter would go to the park as planned. Poppy would not be a problem. He would be at his job at the G.W. Government Scientific Research Company in Hackensack, trusting that his four comrades would be watching Lorelei and Peter. From that point Anton's plan would be executed, hopefully, with ease. Sergei approved and was eager to move forward, but knew patience and exactitude were his friends.

Asa went ahead to pick a suitable cafe for Diana, Lester and himself to sit and wait for Barry and JB to find James Kramer. He chose a café that was set up on a terrace overlooking the Constitution Square. From that vantage point they could see Barry and JB clearly.

There were many souvenir shops in and around the Constitution Square. Unless they were lucky it would take time for Barry and JB to find James Kramer. Asa, Diana and Lester settled down in the cafe with coffee and a platter of small sweet pastries.

Diana always complained that everyone ate much too much sugar, yet Lester noticed she was eating her fourth pastry and positioning herself to go for another. Lester touched her arm whispering, "Whoa, my darling. Aren't you overdoing the sweets?"

Diana sighed deeply. "No Lester, I need the immediate energy rush the sugar will give me to do the deed."

Lester smiled and patted Diana's hand. "OK, you know best. Just remember, Asa and I will be right there with you."

Asa agreed adding, "All you have to do is aim and pull the trigger. It'll be a fast, definite kill." The moment Asa said those words, Diana knew she couldn't do it. It shocked her, but she knew she couldn't do it. To make matters worse, she couldn't tell Lester or Asa. Diana sat silently struggling with her feelings.

The time came. Barry and JB found him. Asa paid the waiter and led Lester and Diana down the terraced steps into the square. Diana's guts were churning. She began to sweat, then shake. She grabbed Lester's arm, pulling him through throngs of people into a doorway. Lester shouted over the din of the crowd for Asa to stop. Lester looked at Diana and saw a part of Diana he had never seen before, the frightened child. Asa ran to them asking, "What's the matter with you two? We have to get to it!" Diana was shaking and couldn't speak.

Lester turned Diana towards him holding her by the shoulders. "Please, be honest with me. Tell me exactly what is happening. Where is your head at right now?"

"What the hell is going on here?" Asa growled, as swarms of people bumped into him from every direction, forcing Asa into the doorway with Lester and Diana.

Diana looked up at Lester and meekly stated, "Forgive me, Lester, but I just can't do it. Asa moved in closer towards Diana.

Leaning into her, Asa whispered, "If you don't do this you will regret it for the rest of your life, sweetheart." Asa couldn't hide his annoyance at Diana's sudden change of heart.

Lester agreed. "Asa is right. You said it yourself. You are Kevin's mother. It is your right to take James out. Why this lack of courage now?" Lester slightly raised his voice, asking, "What happened to that audacious woman who insisted she do the deed to avenge her murdered son?" Lester tone began to add anger to Diana's angst.

In a fit of rage Diana pushed Lester away and screamed, "Don't you dare talk to me about my murdered son. You were the one who planted the bomb!" Diana turned and ran up the steps back to the café.

Asa looked at Lester in disbelief exclaiming, "You planted the bomb?"

"It's not the way it sounds. I never dreamed in a million years that Kevin would ever be in that car. James murdered Kevin, not me and Diana knows that and forgave me a long time ago. I'll go to Diana; you go kill James. And Asa, make damn sure he's dead!" Lester turned and ran up the steps after Diana. He grabbed her arm and they sat down at the nearest table.

Diana's feelings were all jumbled up. She looked at Lester and curtly stated, "I am not apologizing to you!"

Lester took Diana's hands in his. "I'm not asking for an apology, nor do I need one. I understand and it's OK. Asa will do the deed."

"I'm so glad you understand because I don't," Diana stated sarcastically, pausing and then added, "I feel ashamed and disappointed in myself for caving in to…I don't know what. You say you understand, then tell me Lester, what the fuck happened to me? I'll never trust myself again."

Lester picked up Diana's hands, kissed them and said, "That feeling will pass. You are one of the most capable agents I've ever known. This one was different from all the rest. Give yourself a break. He was your husband; you loved him, and you have memories. Now remember this, James was ordered to kill you, but he couldn't kill you any more than you could kill him today. There's your proof that a part of him truly did love you Diana, just as a part of you truly loved him."

Diana was beginning to calm down. She smiled and leaned towards Lester. She stroked his cheek as she said, "Thank you, my love. You always know the right thing to say to me." Just as Lester was about to respond he saw Barry and JB running. He pulled Diana up as he stood up.

"Lester, Diana, get to the SUV quickly. We have to get out of here," Barry directed as he and JB ran towards the parking lot. Lester grabbed Diana and together they ran out of the café and down the terraced steps.

"Barry, where's Asa?" Lester asked as he and Diana ran towards the parking lot.

"He'll meet us, hurry up," Barry answered.

Diana breathlessly yelled, "Did he do the deed?"

"We think so," JB answered as the four converged in the parking lot near their SUV.

Lester was looking all around asking, "Where the hell is Asa?" As they were getting into the SUV Lester spotted Asa on the other side of the parking lot. Lester jumped into the driver's seat saying, "We'll pick him up over there. Is he being chased? I can't tell." Lester quickly drove to Asa who jumped into the back with Barry and JB. "Well, did you do the deed?" Lester asked as he drove out of the parking lot and onto the mountain road.

Asa began to explain. "James recognized me and headed towards the back door. I followed and was able to grab him from behind. I stuck a knife into him and threw his limp body into the dumpster behind his shop."

"But was he dead, Asa, did you check, was he dead?" Diana frantically asked.

"I stabbed him deep and hard. His body went limp. Who the hell had time to think? If you had done the deed it would have been an easy and definite kill. I didn't have time to shoot, I had to stab him. I had no choice. You did not come through, Mrs. Ballantyne!" Asa sneered.

"Lester raised his voice. "Leave her alone Asa. There's a lot here you don't know and can't possibly understand," Lester demanded.

Diana begged Lester to turn the car around to go back to find out if James was actually dead. She asked Barry and JB to go to the dumpster to check his body, if in fact James was still in the dumpster. Lester agreed when a booming voice sounded in each of their ears. "You will not go back. Enough is enough. I should have pulled you all out the moment Diana changed her mind, but I didn't. Now I am ordering you to go back to the hotel, pack up, check out and get back on our plane in Malaga tonight. That is a direct order. Do I make myself clear?" Mr. Sandman was clearly angry, but at himself for not trusting his own instincts to not send Diana. It went sideways as he feared it might and was not a definite kill. They were not sure James Kramer, aka, Alexei Stamenov was actually dead.

Ross and Avery and Albert and Sandra were in two separate vehicles following Lorelei but did not know her destination was Wood Park. Lorelei was going for her scheduled meeting with Sergei Alexandrov. Lorelei did not know that the plans had changed. Serge would never arrive.

Ross received a call from the Hackensack Police telling him that there was an occurrence at the Van Wyck Detective Agency and he and Avery were to go there immediately. Before Ross could ask any questions, the call ended. He called Albert to tell him there was an unknown situation at the agency. Albert told Ross he would keep him informed of their location at all times.

Just as Albert was ending his call with Ross, the Hoboken Police called Sandra to let her know that there was a break-in and a violent occurrence at their catering hall. Albert called Blake to keep his eyes on Lorelei while Veronica followed her. He explained there was a dire emergency at the catering hall and he and Sandra had to get there immediately. Albert called Ross thinking it was suspicious. Ross agreed, but said they had to check it out.

Blake told Veronica, while she was driving to Wood Park, that he just saw a man fold Peter's stroller and put it into the trunk of a limo. Lorelei got into the limo and it looked as if the man was putting Peter into a car seat. The man got into the limo and drove out of Wood Park. Veronica never made it there in time. The limo was equipped with a device to keep it off any radar. Lorelei and Peter were now off the CIA radar.

There was no occurrence at the Van Wyck Detective Agency, nor was there a violent robbery at the catering hall. They all converged with Mr. Sandman at the Hoboken safe house now realizing they were easily duped. Poppy was nervously pacing back and forth asking over and over how this could have happened? Everyone was waiting for Avery to snidely say I told you so.

Mr. Sandman put the order out to all operatives to check every airport in the metropolitan area for all private planes heading for anywhere in Russia or Eastern Europe. He posted agents at all three major airports with descriptions and photos of Lorelei and Peter, as well as Sergei Alexandrov.

Avery whispered to Ross, "Ask Blake if Lorelei appeared willing to go or forced to go?" Ross smiled, completely understanding why Avery asked him to do the inquiring.

"I have a question, Blake. As you watched Lorelei on the monitor, did she look like she went willingly, or was she forced to go?"

Blake was retrieving the video. "Here it is. Come see for yourself. It's hard to tell because we can't make out what the man is saying to her."

Avery blurted out, "Ross, we know who that is. That's Anton Kristinoff, Sergei Alexandrov's right hand man and best friend, isn't it, Ross?"

Ross leaned in looking closely at the screen. "Yes Avery, you're right, it's Anton Kristinoff."

"I would bet any amount of money that they are heading for Moscow. I believe that's where Sergei's mother lives. He and Lorelei are taking Peter there to see her."

Poppy exploded. "Oh, you would just love that Avery, to prove that Lorelei is an enemy agent who has used me to infiltrate our group." Poppy's scream was so piercing that Ross thought he might strike Avery. Ross and Albert each took Poppy by an arm and took him down to the kitchen.

To take the focus off of herself, Avery asked, "How did the Spain operation go, Mr. Sandman?" By the look on his face Avery knew.

"I ordered the five of them home. They are airborne now and will arrive in about two hours."

Sandra walked over to Mr. Sandman and asked, "She did do it, didn't she? That bastard is dead, isn't he?"

Facing the two women he confessed, "No, Diana couldn't kill him, but Asa stabbed him and threw his body into a dumpster. But damn it, Asa didn't check to see if he was dead or not. I should never have allowed Diana to go. This is my fault. Every instinct in my body was screaming no and I gave in, wanting to do the right thing. It was completely the wrong thing." Avery and Sandra did not answer. They each kissed him on his cheek and walked away.

Sergei Alexandrov and Anton Kristinoff arrived in Moscow with Lorelei and Peter the next morning. A car was waiting and took them directly to

Yana's apartment. Anton would stay until the next day when he would travel home to his family in Odessa.

Sergei presented Lorelei to his mother as the mother of her grandson Peter. Yana slowly approached Lorelei and hugged her. Lorelei hugged her back. Yana looked at Sergei, and then at Peter and said, "He looks just like you when you were a little boy." Yana picked Peter up and said, "I am your babushka and I loved you before I ever met you." Tears rolled down Lorelei's face.

Sergei answered his phone and walked into another room. He came back to Lorelei and said, "I'm sorry, something has happened that I must attend to immediately. I will be back in no more than two or three days." He kissed Lorelei on the forehead and began walking away. Lorelei grabbed Sergei's arm asking him where he was going. He answered with one word as he walked out the door, "Spain."

Avery was right. It was verified by a private airport in Long Island. Lorelei and Peter were kidnapped and taken to Moscow. Mr. Sandman called Mr. Luka Ionovich, who, while Russian, was not a Soviet. He wanted Russia and the Russian people to prosper through democracy and free enterprise. Over the course of time Earl Sandman and Luka Ionovich slowly became assets, and on some occasions, allies. This was one of those times. He promised Mr. Sandman to have Lilya and Stefan, a trusted couple who had worked with Ross and Avery, to do some reconnaissance work regarding Lorelei and Peter.

Mr. Sandman called Ross and Avery and Blake and Veronica into his office. Their assignment was clear. They were to fly to Moscow and bring Lorelei and Peter home no matter how they had to do it. Lilya and Stefan would meet them when they arrived by commercial jet in Moscow as the Carter family.

The flight was long and uneventful. Lilya and Stefan were genuinely happy to see Ross and Avery again, and were pleased to meet Blake and Veronica. On the way to the hotel, Lilya confirmed that Lorelei and Peter were staying with Yana Alexandrov at her luxury apartment. Sergei, however, left Russia. With a little digging Stefan found out that Sergei flew to Spain. Ross and Avery immediately made the connection and informed Mr. Sandman of this new and interesting development. Mr. Sandman thanked them but told them to focus on bringing Lorelei and Peter home.

The six of them sat outside of Yana Alexandrov's building in what looked like a delivery van. Yana and Lorelei came out of the building. Lorelei was wheeling Peter in his stroller. She and Yana were talking and smiling. Lilya and Stefan followed them. Ross, Avery, Blake and Veronica stayed in the van watching them on monitors. Lorelei appeared to be happy and at ease. Avery's blood was boiling, but Veronica suspected Lorelei might be putting on an act.

Yana and Lorelei came back with some groceries and went back up to the apartment. Avery, Veronica and Lilya went up to the apartment to get Lorelei and Peter, Ross, Blake and Stefan stayed in the van to monitor the operation as it unfolded.

Yana answered the door and Veronica immediately stuck her with her ring, rendering Yana unconscious. Lorelei acted happy, thanking them for rescuing her and Peter. Avery instructed Veronica and Lilya to hold Lorelei still. Avery slapped Lorelei hard across the face saying, "You, Lorelei, are nothing but a lying bitch traitor and I will attest to that at your trial." Avery then stuck her hand down into Lorelei's bra and pulled out the thin wire she kept there. Avery looked at her companions and sneered, "Lorelei keeps this for strangulation purposes, but I'll feel a lot better if I keep it in my bra." Lorelei yelled at Avery for treating her unfairly, insisting that Avery was wrong. Avery told Veronica to shut Lorelei up. Veronica stuck her with her ring and Lorelei collapsed onto the floor. Lilya picked up Peter and Avery and Veronica carried Lorelei out. Ross and Blake helped get them into the van. Stefan drove to the airport where they would take a flight to Berlin. Everyone had passports including Lorelei and Peter.

Lorelei woke up and Avery threatened to kill her if she opened her mouth. Lorelei believed Avery would do it. To assure Lorelei's silence, Veronica stuck her again with her ring. Lorelei was placed in a wheelchair. They had false papers for Lorelei stating that she was very ill and was being taken to Germany by her family for treatment. Mr. Sandman arranged for them to be picked up at the airport in Berlin by the US military and flown home in a military transport plane.

Mr. Sandman and Poppy were waiting for them when they arrived from Berlin. Lorelei ran into Poppy's arms. Avery carried three-year old Peter off the plane and handed him to Poppy. He looked into Avery's eyes and quietly said, "Thank you." Everyone was exhausted from the ordeal. Mr. Sandman ordered all of Group Eleven to meet the next evening for dinner in the secure room at Lester's club.

The entire team confronted Lorelei. Lorelei swore she behaved appropriately to keep herself and Peter safe. Lorelei said that she believed with all her heart that they would rescue her. The only one who believed her totally was Poppy. Everyone else had doubts, some more than others. Nothing could be proven.

Mr. Sandman received the call he was waiting for. There was no speaking, no movement until Mr. Sandman announced, "James Kramer, aka, Alexei Stamenov is officially dead. He was murdered in his hospital bed in Malaga, Spain by an unknown killer. Lorelei and Diana locked eyes.

CHAPTER 7
DR. MEYER HEMSLEY

Ross and Avery arrived at the Van Wyck Detective Agency at 09:00. Ross was just about to say his usual "All's well that ends well," when Diana Ballantyne, Ross' aunt and office manager put up her hand and stated, "Don't say it!"

Avery queried, "Why not, what's going on?" Before Diana had a chance to answer, Whitney Van Wyck, the owner of the detective agency, walked in with his wife Ernestine. They both greeted Ross and Avery with big smiles and a hug and a kiss for each.

While Ernestine poured coffee for everyone and plated up donuts, Whit explained, "I have a job for the two of you. Actually, it's a personal favor."

Looking at the plate of donuts Avery laughed and said, "It looks to me like Ross and I are being bribed. Those are our favorite donuts." She glanced over at Diana.

"Whit called me and asked me what your favorites donuts were, so I told him. Is that a crime?"

Ross answered with, "That depends on the reason we are being bribed!" Before Diana, Whit or Ernestine had a chance to respond, the door to the agency was flung open. As if going into hiding, stepped a short, round man in his mid-fifties, with thinning brown hair and wire-rimmed glasses. He was clinging to his briefcase, holding it against his broad chest as if it was about to be ripped away from him.

"Oh, Whitney, thank God I am in the right place," he gasped as he slumped against the closed door. He spoke with an accent that sounded like a mixture of different languages. Diana guessed it right. The man was Israeli, but originally from Romania. He noticed the donuts and snatched one without asking.

Whit walked over to him, put his arm around him and said, "I'd like you all to meet my cousin, Dr. Meyer Hemsley, a world-renowned genealogist."

Under his breath Ross mumbled to Avery, "I knew he had to be some kind of nerd."

Under her breath Avery responded, "That's the pot calling the kettle black!"

While everyone else was talking, Avery turned to face Ross answering, "You shouldn't talk. You're a computer nerd." Ross smiled, and Avery kissed him on the cheek as she went for a donut.

"Helping Meyer is the personal favor I need from you two, hence your favorite donuts," Whit explained, pointing to the plate of donuts that were nearly gone, thanks to Meyer.

"Whitney, please explain it to them. I need to rest. They're after me. It hasn't stopped since I landed from Tel Aviv," Meyer Hemsley complained as he lowered his short, round body onto the couch. His face was red, and beads of sweat were forming on his brow.

Diana stood up and questioned, "Who are the "they" that are after you? And, more importantly, why are they after you?"

He flailed his arms saying, "Whitney, again I ask you, please explain it to them."

"OK, Meyer, relax, I'll explain it," agreed Whit.

But Meyer continued. "You see, I could always count on Whitney to come through for me. Even when we were children. We came to visit, I was a fat boy with a strange accent, and I got bullied. But my cousin Whitney always stuck up for me. Why one time, he even got the shit beat out of him to protect me and I remember another time…"

"Enough Meyer," Whit chided as he took center stage.

Meyer laughed, "OK enough, I'll be quiet." Meyer promised, putting his finger over his lips.

Whit began to explain. "My cousin, as you all now know, lives in Tel Aviv. He put together a conference of genealogists from all over the world to hear his theory of how genealogy can bring about world peace. The conference will be held the day after tomorrow at the Madison Arms Hotel in Manhattan and will run for three days. Meyer needs protection from religious fanatics who are threatening to kill him."

Ross and Avery were beginning to wonder what kind of a crazy mix they were getting thrown into. Avery asked, "What, Dr. Hemsley, is your theory on achieving world peace that would anger religious fanatics?"

Whit began to speak, but Meyer Hemsley stopped him. "I will take over now. This is mine and I will explain it." All eyes were focused on Dr. Hemsley. He stood up and began to lecture, as if they were transported to a lecture hall. Pacing back and forth he explained, "I firmly believe that peace in the Middle East can be achieved through genealogy, or the understanding of genealogical backgrounds. Once the Jews, Christians and Muslims understand their true ancestry and origins, then, and only then, will peace be possible." Dr. Hemsley stopped pacing back and forth for a moment to gather his thoughts. "When everyone understands that all men originated from the same gene pool my theory will become clear and evolve into the truth." Again, he began to pace back and forth, stopped, and continued. "It was religion that caused the terrible rift between people. Once people can look at their origins in a rational way, without religion getting involved to skew the view, people will come to realize all of us carry common genealogical components that tie us together as human beings, making us akin to each other."

"In other words, we are all brothers and sisters," softly said Avery.

Meyer Hemsley sat back down, smiled at Avery, and answered, "Yes, my dear, now you've got the basics of it!"

Diana stood up again, walked over to Meyer Hemsley and sat down next to him. "Dr. Hemsley, you still have not answered my original question. Who are the "they" you think are after you?"

"Ah, but I cannot answer that question because I really do not know who they are."

Diana was becoming frustrated. "You must have some sense of who they are, Dr. Hemsley. At least throw us an educated guess," suggested Diana.

He looked at Diana and frowned. "Well, an educated guess? My disregard and contempt for religion has angered many religious fanatics."

Avery asked, "I can understand that, Dr. Hemsley. But, what makes you think they're after you?"

Meyer Hemsley was quick to answer. "I have received threats that if I allow the conference to take place, they will kill me."

Diana answered with, "Until we know who the "they" are, we have little means of protecting you."

Whit was beginning to get angry at his cousin Meyer. He Stood up and begged Meyer to cancel the conference if he truly thought his life was in danger.

Meyer flatly refused to cancel the conference declaring that he would not be put off by a few crazy religious fanatics.

Ernestine had not expressed her views until now, asking, "Meyer, are there any other groups, aside from religious fanatics, that would find your theory distasteful, or even abhorrent?"

"Let me answer that." All eyes turned to Ross. "I'd say the AFD or the White Supremist movement might be good suspects. Believe me, Avery and I have had a couple of run-ins with them." Ross turned to Avery, "And Avery, you know who could help us if that turns out to be the case?"

Avery smiled, emphatically stating, "I do, indeed." Diana smiled knowingly. It was Albert and Sandra that Ross was going to call. Both Avery and Diana deemed it to be the right move.

Ross and Avery explained that they would do what they could, but the CIA could not get involved with a private conference. Ross said they could alert the NYC Police and even the FBI, but until someone broke the law, neither could get involved.

"From where I'm sitting, I can see only one option, a private security agency," advocated Ross.

Avery added, "Yes, we will hire a private security agency to protect Dr. Hemsley, and at the same time we will investigate where the death threats are coming from."

"This is good. It sounds like we have a viable plan of action being hatched," Whit said with satisfaction.

"May I suggest, Ross, that we ask our teammates to join us for lunch?" Avery asked thoughtfully.

"Yes, Avery, I'll make the call," Ross responded as he walked into the back office. He called Albert asking if he and Sandra would meet him and Avery for lunch at *The Double O Club* that afternoon. Ross said he would then explain why they needed their help.

Once Whit and Ernestine took Meyer Hemsley back to his hotel, and Avery and Ross left to meet Albert and Sandra, Diana called her husband Lester. "Hi, honey, is the club busy?"

"Not particularly, why?" Lester questioned.

"I don't want to talk over the phone. Could you possibly come over to the agency? It's really important, Lester," Diana explained.

"How about I bring lunch?" Lester suggested.

"That would be wonderful. For me a large salad with grilled chicken would do the trick."

"You got it, my darling. I'll be there in half an hour."

"See you then, honey, and thanks," Diana said as she smiled thinking about how lucky she was to be married to such a great guy.

Albert and Sandra were sitting at a back table in a corner of *The Double O Club*. Ross and Avery arrived and were greeted by Arlo Gunther. A light bulb went on in Avery's head, but her idea was unconventional and would have to be discussed and carefully considered by the team.

Arlo was Lorelei's brother. Ross, Avery, Poppy, and Lorelei had witnessed Arlo fall into a deep hole. They were sure he had died. Arlo had not died but lost his memory. He was living as a homeless person. Avery spotted him while on an assignment in Carlstadt, NJ. Poppy and Lorelei rescued Arlo and gave him a second chance.

Before his accident, Arlo had been involved with the AFD. Lester hired him to work in the club, giving him a chance to turn his life around. As Diana had pointed out, it was a good way to keep an eye on him. Arlo proved to be a trustworthy, hard-working employee. He grew to love Diana and Lester and with their encouragement went back to school to work towards a degree in business.

Albert stood up when he saw Ross and Avery approaching. "Hey, guys, do we have a situation?"

As they sat down Ross said, "Yes, and I think you may be able to help us."

"What's it all about?" Sandra inquired.

Avery began to explain. "It's something our agency would handle, but it very well could become a CIA matter."

"Sounds intriguing," replied Sandra.

Ross and Avery explained about Dr. Meyer Hemsley, his theories, and about the conference to be held in Manhattan in two days. "The first part of the plan," Ross continued to explain, "is being taken care of by Whitney Van Wyck. He has a friend he has known for years who owns a security agency. Whit spoke to him. Ten of his friend's most trusted employees, in conjunction with the hotel security, are going to be at the conference to keep Dr. Hemsley safe. Diana is doing background checks on the five hotel security personnel as we speak."

Albert smiled, asking, "So what's the second part of the plan? I assume it will include me and Sandra?"

Ross smiled back, answering, "Avery and I need you and Sandra to help us discover who it is that keeps threatening to kill Dr. Hemsley."

"Dr. Hemsley's genealogical theory, I would imagine, would enrage any fanatical religious zealot, would it not?" Sandra asked.

"Yes, it would," agreed Avery. "But we would first like to rule out the White Supremists and the AFD. You might know how to go about that, Albert," Avery added.

Albert thought for a moment. "I've been away from them for a long time, but I could try."

"I had an idea. Let me run it by the three of you," suggested Avery.

"Sure, what is it?" Ross asked.

"Arlo Gunther, Lorelei's brother, used to be very involved with the AFD in Germany. He did, however, have contacts and knows people here. You could ask him to help you, Albert." Avery waited while Albert formulated his answer.

Albert looked over at Arlo who was working behind the bar serving customers. "I don't think so, Avery."

"Why not?" Avery asked, perplexed by Albert's answer.

"Because Poppy and Lorelei, with Diana and Lester's help gave Arlo a second chance, and he took it and is doing very well. I wouldn't want to bring him back into that element again. Let's leave Arlo alone. And besides, my sister Ramona is in love with him. That might go someplace. Let's just let Arlo live his life in peace."

"Amen", said Sandra.

"I agree. It would not be a good idea to involve Arlo in this, especially if it turns out that they are the people who are threatening Dr. Hemsley," Ross stated.

"OK, then, we'll leave Arlo alone. By the way, I didn't know Ramona was in love with Arlo," Avery derided. Avery's remark was ignored.

"Let's begin gathering intel immediately," Ross suggested.

Avery was not giving up on Arlo. "But wait a minute. We wouldn't ask Arlo to actually do anything, except to give us some names. We could call him over here right now just for names. He wouldn't have to be involved in any other part of the situation. In fact, we won't even tell him what the situation is about. All we would ask for are the names of a few preliminary contacts."

"Avery does make a good point. I don't know anyone here. All my contacts were in Germany. That was a very long time ago," Albert pointed out.

"Before we involve Arlo in any way, we might want to ask Poppy and Lorelei their opinion," suggested Sandra.

"No! This is not CIA business, at least not yet. We can't include anyone else from our group. Mr. Sandman will have our heads, or at least mine. I'm treading on thin ice with him most of the time as it is," complained Avery. They all laughed.

"Oh, come on, Avery, Mr. Sandman loves you," Ross said as he put his arm around his wife and kissed her on the head.

"He may love me, but his patience runs very thin with me at times," Avery confessed.

"That's because at times you've disobeyed orders," chided Ross.

"I disobeyed orders only once and there were dire consequences. You and I both paid dearly for that Ross," Avery reminded him.

"Oh, God, let's not go down that road, please," declared Sandra.

"Sandra is right. Let's just stay on track," insisted Albert.

"OK, then what about Arlo?" Avery asked, not giving up.

"If we asked him to name names, he's going to want to know what he's getting involved with. What do we tell him?" Albert asked.

"We don't have to tell him anything. Look, Arlo knows that Ross and I run a detective agency."

"How will you explain my involvement?" Albert questioned.

"You are making this too complex, Albert. You're German. Ross and I are simply asking you to supply us with a few contacts in the German community. We'll be asking Arlo to do the same, that's all," Avery explained.

"Avery is right. If Arlo gives us even one name, that could help tremendously with our intel gathering," Ross admitted.

"That's right, Albert. Arlo knows you're German. He'll automatically assume we're asking you for names too. It's very logical. Just play along with us," Avery urged.

"Sandra, what do you think?" Albert asked his wife.

"Now that I've heard Avery's argument, I think she may be right. Let's call Arlo over," Sandra suggested.

Ross stood up. "I'll go get him, but, no offense ladies, go take a walk. I think Arlo would be easier to work with if it is just me and Albert," Ross insisted.

"You're ridiculous, but probably right. Let's go Sandra." Avery and Sandra got up and left the club.

Ross walked over to Arlo who was wiping down the bar.

"Hey, Arlo, can I speak to you for a moment?" Ross requested. Arlo dried his hands and walked over to Ross.

"Sure, what can I get you?" Arlo asked.

"Names," Ross answered. Arlo looked at Ross perplexingly.

"What do you mean names?" Arlo queried.

"Would you join Albert and me over there?" Ross requested as he gestured towards their table.

"I'm working right now," Arlo explained.

"It's important, Arlo. I need you and Albert to help on a case I'm working on," Ross urged. Without saying another word Arlo followed Ross across the club, over to their table and sat down with Albert.

Albert had never seen Arlo up close long enough to study his face. It was remarkable how much of Albee he saw in Arlo, especially his violet-blue eyes. Inger Goode, Albert's mother told Albert, Sandra and Ramona that her grandfather had the same color eyes.

It was a big secret. Ramona spent one afternoon with Arlo engaging in wild, passionate sex. When she discovered she was pregnant, it was the perfect solution to Albert and Sandra's problem of not being able to conceive. During one of the group's monthly lasagna dinners, Albert and Sandra announced that Sandra's egg and Albert's sperm were combined and implanted into Ramona's womb. Ramona would carry Albert and Sandra's baby. As soon as Albee was born, Ramona handed him over to Albert and Sandra. The only thing Ramona was left with was tremendous guilt over denying Arlo his son. Ramona and Arlo were Albee's biological parents. Albee inherited Arlo's unusual violet blue eyes. It was a relief for Ramona to find out that her great grandfather also had those unusual violet blue eyes.

"Albert, I'm talking to you, what world are you living in?" Ross said nudging Albert.

"Oh. sorry, Ross, my mind was elsewhere," explained Albert.

"Apparently," laughed Ross. "What I need from the two of you are names, that's it."

"Names, whose names?" Arlo questioned.

"Look, it's no secret that at one time you were involved with the AFD both in Germany and here. I have a client whose life is being threatened we think, by them," Ross explained.

"I haven't been involved with them for a very long time. I can try to get some names for you if that would help," offered Arlo.

Ross thought for a moment. "No, Arlo, I do not, under any circumstances, want you out on the street trying to contact them again. It's too dangerous. I just thought if you knew anyone off the top of your head, you could give me the name."

"Maybe, I did hear about someone named Sabastian Meitzner. He was becoming and important figure, rising up in their organization a few years ago. In fact, I just saw a news special about Catalan, Spain. There is a movement there by some Catalonians for Catalan independence. Benet Horta, the man who is the head of that movement is living in exile in Switzerland. His cousin is Sabastian Meitzner. I don't know any more than that. I never actually met the man, but heard stories about him, about how part of his family was Catalonian from Spain. I hope I helped," Arlo said as he smiled and began to walk back to the bar but turned to face Albert. "By the way, Albert, how is your baby son Albee?"

Albert was taken completely off guard by Arlo's query. "He's fine. Thank you for asking"

Arlo smiled and answered, "I'm glad he's doing well. I'm in love with your sister Ramona, Albert, but I'm sure you know that."

"No, actually I didn't know that." By the way he answered, Arlo knew Albert was telling the truth.

"She and I are dating again. I 'm happy about that. Maybe you and Ross could put in a good word for me?" Arlo suggested.

Ross was becoming agitated and intervened. "I'm happy for you Arlo."

Albert, knowing the truth about Albee, felt sorry for Arlo. "I never interfere in my sister's life. I'm sorry."

"Thanks anyway." Arlo turned and walked back to the bar.

"Well Ross, what do you think?" Albert asked after Arlo was out of ear shot.

Ross looked at Albert. "Albert we're best friends and we've been through a hell of a lot together. Albee is your son, you and Sandra. Let's just put a period at the end of that right here and now."

"Thanks, Ross, OK," Albert answered.

"Now, about what Arlo gave us, it's a needle in a haystack, but it's worth looking into," Ross suggested.

"I agree," Albert concurred.

152

Lester walked into the agency just as Diana was hanging up the phone. "Well, all hotel security personnel are vetted and secured," Diana announced.

"I'm glad to hear it, but what are you talking about?" Lester asked. Diana began to laugh realizing that Lester knew nothing about the new situation.

"Let me explain our new situation. It's not a CIA problem, but the potential is there for it to become one."

"Um, that was a perfect lure, Diana, sounds very intriguing," Lester responded as he popped a piece of chicken into his mouth. "By the way, just before I left the club Ross, Avery, Albert and Sandra came in. Are they commandeering Albert and Sandra for this one?"

"I am certain they are. Here is the situation." Diana explained their entire encounter with Dr. Meyer Hemsley that morning. Lester sat back in his chair absorbing Diana's story.

"I don't know whether to laugh or take this situation seriously," Lester quietly responded.

"We need to take him seriously. He's been getting death threats since he landed here from Tel Aviv. I'm not so worried about the conference itself. Whit's friend owns a private security company. They will be there plus the five security agents from the Madison Arms Hotel."

"Sound pretty heavy duty, so what's the problem?" Lester asked.

"The problem is Meyer's down time. Granted, he's staying with Whit and Ernestine, but they can't be with him every second," Diana asserted. The door opened. Ross and Avery walked in.

"Uncle Lester, hi," Ross greeted him.

"We noticed you leaving with food and figured you would be here," admitted Avery.

"Are you in the mix now?" Ross asked, smiling cynically.

"I was lured very skillfully into the mix," Lester confessed.

"Thank you for the compliment, honey," teased Diana.

"You're welcome, my darling," Lester answering looking lovingly at Diana.

"Well, we obtained some very interesting facts from, of all people, Arlo Gunther," Avery informed them. She went on to explain the connection between AFD member Sabastian Meitzner and exiled Catalonian Benet Horta.

"Are you suggesting that something big might be brewing in Europe between these two cousins?" Lester asked.

"Yes, we think it might very well be the case," agreed Ross.

"So, if that is the case, who, specifically would you guess are the "they" that are threatening Meyer Hemsley?" Diana posed.

"The AFD, if I had to guess. The Catalonians have an air of superiority surrounding them. That's why they want to secede from Spain. Benet Horta is their leader even though he is living in Switzerland. Sabastian Meitzner, his cousin, might be fueling that fire. Meyer Hemsley's theory goes against their idea that one group of people are superior to the rest of humanity," Avery explained.

Lester was becoming very concerned. "I'm beginning to feel that this is much bigger than Dr. Meyer Hemsley. This all has a familiar ring to it. This kind of thinking could spread like wildfire throughout Europe. Remember, both Germany and Spain were Fascist countries. The seeds are there. They just have to be cultivated," Lester sadly suggested. There was no response to Lester's theory because they all believed he was right.

Ross asked, "You don't think it could be the Muslims, do you"?

"No, Ross, I don't. If it were the Muslims, they would have acted by now to stop the conference. No, it's not the Muslims," Lester firmly asserted. Lester continued. "I've been watching this situation in Spain with one eye. Now that you tell me about this Sabastian Meitzner, it feels right to me. We also need to check out the relationship between The Commander of the AFD, Berta Gruber, Sabastian Meitzner and Benet Horta." They all agreed.

Arlo was behind the bar at *The Double O Club.* A man came in and sat at the bar. Arlo felt his eyes and glanced over at him. He knew the man only because he attended a rally years ago and heard him speak. Arlo felt as if the man recognized him. He would deny it, of course, if asked. Arlo walked over to the man to serve him. The man looked at Arlo, smiled and said, "A dirty martini, please."

Arlo smiled, relieved, answering, Yes, Sir, coming right up."

The man sat smiling. Arlo could feel his eyes piercing the back of his neck as he prepared the martini. As Arlo walked towards the man with the martini the man said, "Have we met before?" Arlo began to feel nauseated but hid it well.

"No, Sir, I don't remember ever meeting you. Have you been in the club before?"

"No, this is my first time. It's your eyes, the color, very unusual. I have seen you, before," remarked the man.

"I am sorry, Sir, I don't recall ever meeting you. Many people have these color eyes. Elizabeth Taylor, the actor, for example, had these color eyes," Arlo said offhandedly. Arlo was smooth. He learned from Lester and Diana. Arlo had watched them deal with shady characters who occasionally came into the club.

"Sorry, my mistake," the man answered unconvincingly. Arlo asked the man if he wanted another martini. The man said no, got up and walked out of the club.

Arlo took out his phone and called Ross. Ross told Arlo he was with Avery, Diana and Lester at the detective agency. Ross put his phone on speaker, so they could all hear. "I have another name for you. Pablo Calla. He was just here at the club. Pablo Calla is Benet Horta's right-hand man, his second in command. He recognized me, but I denied ever meeting him. I met him about five or six years ago at an AFD rally. I can't believe he remembered me. It was my eyes he claimed to remember. I fluffed it off saying it had to be someone else who had the same eye color as me. He said he was mistaken, but I know he recognized me."

Lester took Ross' phone and took it off speaker. "Arlo, did Buster come in yet? Good. Tell him to take over the bar. You take the van and get over here right now. I don't like this. Leave the club immediately." Lester ended the call and handed Ross his phone back. "I don't like how this is stacking up," Lester said.

"No, I don't like it; I don't like it at all," Diana confessed. "This feels much bigger than just having to protect an old genealogist and his theories," concluded Diana. They were quiet, all drifting into their own thoughts.

Lester broke the silence. "Arlo is smart. He learns fast and applies what he learns well."

"What are you driving at, Lester?" Diana asked. Ross answered Diana's question by suggesting that they try Arlo out by including him on their investigating team.

"Wait a minute. I thought we, meaning you, me Albert and Sandra all decided not to involve Arlo in any way. Our goal was to just get names from him. Why are you changing the rules suddenly, Ross?" Avery asked, dismayed.

"Things have changed now. Arlo was recognized by someone dangerous. I'll call Albert. He and Sandra may want to come over now that Arlo is included," Ross explained.

"Really, Ross? That may be a reason for them not to want to come over," Avery jeered back.

"Don't start, Avery!" Ross ordered.

"What the hell is going on here? I want to know right now!" Diana demanded. There was no time for an answer. Arlo walked into the agency. The discussion was over. Diana decided she would speak to Avery privately.

Lester stood up, walked over to Arlo, and put his arm around him. "I'm glad you're here, son. Sit down." Arlo greeted Diana, Ross and Avery before sitting down. Lester continued. "We want you on our team for this case. Pablo Calla recognized you. You're a smart boy, Arlo and very resourceful. Ross can find out where Pablo Calla can be found. Would you be willing to cozy up to him, get on his good side to bring us information?"

Arlo seemed intrigued asking, "What kind of information?"

Lester smiled. "First and foremost, why is he in New York and/or New Jersey?

Arlo cocked his head to the side, smiled smugly and asked, "Are you asking me to become a spy, like the CIA?" It was the way Arlo asked that made Diana begin to believe that Arlo may suspect who they really were. Diana decided to squelch any conclusions Arlo may have come to.

Diana smiled sweetly at Arlo and said, "No my dear boy. Lester and I were in Army Counterintelligence and Ross and Avery are detectives, but spies, no, we know nothing about that. Our client is a genealogist who will be holding a conference at the Madison Arms Hotel in a few days. Some of his theories are controversial. He's been receiving death threats. We want to know if the AFD, Benet Horta and/or Pablo Calla are responsible for these death threats, that's all. It's really very cut and dry."

Avery smiled. "Don't believe her, Arlo. It's never cut and dry, but it is pretty straight forward."

Lester looked at Arlo and asked, "What do you say, son? We'll get you in, and we will make sure to get you out. Well, how about it?"

Arlo smiled smugly again, answering, "OK, count me in!"

Albert and Sandra walked into the agency just as they were all patting Arlo on the back.

Avery hugged both Albert and Sandra. "It turns out we don't need your help after all. Arlo was recognized when Pablo Calla, Benet Horta's second in command came into the club. Arlo agreed to infiltrate their organization to obtain certain information. We don't need you on the case."

Sandra hugged Avery, thanking her. Conversely, Albert was fuming mad. He did not like being tossed aside by the likes of Arlo Gunther. Albert looked at Ross and asked, "What the hell is going on here, best friend?"

Ross held Albert by the shoulders. "You are my best friend, and always will be. This was not my decision."

Sandra took over. "Please Albert, we have so much on our plate right now. Your parents are still here, we have Albee, and Nika needs a lot of attention, not to mention our catering business. Please Albert?"

Albert calmed down. "OK Sandra, you convinced me." They walked out of the agency. Diana knew something was afoot and was determined to find out what it was as quickly as possible.

Ross found out that Pablo Calla was staying at the Madison Arms Hotel. Ross came out of his back room and said, as he walked towards Arlo, "Pablo Calla is staying at the same hotel the conference will be held at in two days. We have to give you an excuse to go to the hotel right now to see him, but it has to look like a chance meeting."

Diana stood up. "Pablo Calla does not know me and has never seen me. I will go to the hotel and sit in the lobby. I will call now and reserve a room for Diana Nakos, my maiden name. I am your Aunt Diana and you came to pay me a visit. I am from Philadelphia and in New York to visit friends. I'll get this all set up." Diana walked into the back room where Ross had been.

"Wow, she knows what she's doing," Arlo exclaimed.

"Everything Diana told you is true. Her maiden name is Nakos, she is from Philadelphia, originally and she will probably have her best friend meet her at the hotel while you are with her. Just follow her lead and you'll be fine," Lester informed Arlo.

"Ross, should we wire him?" Before Ross had a chance to answer Diana came out of the backroom.

"Absolutely not! No wires. God forbid they find wires on Arlo." Diana was adamant. "Lester you are driving me, Arlo, and Dagmar into the city now. I can always count on Dagmar to play. She loves this stuff," Diana said laughing. She looked at Ross and Avery and said, "I'll be in touch."

Lester dropped Diana and Arlo at the Madison Arms Hotel at 16:30 and parked the car in a garage. Lester and Dagmar went to the bar in the Madison Arms Hotel.

Diana walked up to the desk to check in and get her room card. She smiled at the man and said, "You have a man registered in the hotel named Pablo Calla, do you not?" Diana held up her CIA ID card.

The man's smile faded. "How can I help you?"

"Call Mr. Calla. Tell him there is a message for him at the desk. You must insist he comes to pick it up himself. When he comes, apologize. Tell him you made a mistake. The message was for someone else." The man had such fear on his face that Diana felt sorry for him. "Don't worry, there'll be no trouble, I promise. It's not that kind of a thing. We just need to get him down here. Now, make the call." Diana watched and listened as the man called Pablo Calla down to the lobby. She then went and sat down. Arlo joined her, Dagmar left the hotel, and Lester remained in the bar to watch.

"There he is stepping out of the elevator," Arlo said.

"Arlo, you look like you're having fun," Diana stated.

"Actually, I am having fun," Arlo answered.

"You're not scared, are you?" Diana asked.

"Not at all." Arlo answered

"I'm so glad," Diana concluded.

Arlo felt a hand on his shoulder. "Well, what a coincidence, Arlo. We meet again."

Arlo stood up and extended his hand. "Pablo, what are you doing here?"

"I'm staying here. What are you doing here?" Pablo asked with a hint of suspicion.

"Oh. I'm sorry, this is my Aunt Diana. Aunt Diana, Mr. Pablo Calla".

"Nice to meet you Mr. Calla."

"Oh, please, call me Pablo."

Just as Diana was about to respond, Dagmar came bursting into the hotel lobby. With outstretched arms she yelled, "Diana, darling, it's been so long. How are you?"

"Dagmar, it's so good to see you," Diana exclaimed as she rushed into Dagmar's outstretched arms. Arlo could not believe the act they were putting on. Lester sat in the hotel bar laughing as he watched Pablo Calla take it all in.

Dagmar looked at Arlo and said, "No, this can't be little Arlo. My, you've grown up into such a handsome young man."

Arlo smiled, enjoying the performance. "This is My Aunt Diana's friend Dagmar. Dagmar, my friend Pablo Calla."

"Nice to meet you," Dagmar said as she shook his hand.

"The pleasure is all mine," Pablo responded.

Diana looked at her watch. She then hugged Arlo, saying, "Thank you for coming, darling. I'll see you tomorrow before I go home. Goodbye, Mr. Calla."

"Goodbye," Dagmar said as Diana whisked her away, out of the hotel. Lester stayed in the bar to watch Arlo and Pablo Calla.

"Pablo, I want and need to apologize to you for pretending not to know you at the club." Arlo was playing a part and it thrilled him like nothing he had ever done before.

"Why did you do that?" Pablo asked.

"Because of my boss. He is always chastising me for being too friendly with the customers. He says listening to their sob stories slows down business. Oh, he's a tough one, my boss. I always feel like I'm on the verge of being fired." Arlo was playing his part well, and he knew it.

"Why don't you look for a new job?" Pablo suggested.

"It's not so easy. I can't look while I'm working, and I must work to earn money. So, there you go! You wouldn't, by any chance, need any help with whatever it is you do?" Arlo was trying to come across as the perfect patsy. He was succeeding.

"Maybe," mused Pablo, who, unknowingly just opened the door for Arlo.

"What kind of business are you in?" Arlo inquired. "Whatever it is I could really use the extra money."

"I'm here on a security job for my boss. Maybe I could use your help. I'll let you know tomorrow, kid."

"I need to know now, Pablo, because I have to work out my schedule. I really need to keep my job at the club." Arlo almost begged. He knew instinctively how far to go.

"OK, Arlo, it's a one-shot-deal. I will need you to deliver something to this hotel the day after tomorrow. Once it's delivered, I will pay you five hundred dollars. How does that sound?"

Arlo wanted to try something but was not sure it would work. "Listen Pablo, I'm so broke. Sure, I'll deliver whatever it is you want delivered, but could I have two fifty now and two fifty after delivery?"

Pablo smiled and said, "I like you, Arlo, you got guts." He put his hand into his pocket and pulled out a wad of bills. "Here's three hundred. After delivery you'll get another three hundred because I like you, Arlo. Be back here tomorrow night at 9pm sharp."

"Thank you so much. By the way, what is it I am delivering?" Arlo did not expect an answer.

"That, my friend, is none of your concern. Just be right here tomorrow night at 9pm, is that clear?"

"Yes, don't worry. I promise I won't let you down," Arlo said, pleased with the way things turned out. Lester stayed to see if Pablo would follow Arlo. He didn't. Pablo went back up to his room.

Lester drove Dagmar home. He, Diana and Arlo went to the detective agency. Ross and Avery met them there. Diana and Lester congratulated Arlo for the wonderful job he did. It was decided that Lester, Ross and Avery would go back to the hotel with Arlo the next night. Lester would sit in the bar and Ross and Avery in the Lobby. Before they all parted, Diana asked Avery to have lunch with her the next day.

Diana told Avery to meet her at Mr. Chang's Chinese Restaurant. When Avery arrived, Diana was sitting at the usual private table in the back. Avery bent down and kissed Diana. Diana smiled and said, "I feel like boneless spareribs and steamed dumplings. How about you?"

"Sure, that sounds great. I know there is something on your mind. What is it?"

"You tell me, Avery. What were all those shenanigans between you and Ross about Arlo, concerning Albert and Sandra?"

"Ross forbids me to talk about it."

Diana laughed. "You see, for me that's a great opening. Since when could Ross forbid you to do anything?"

Avery sighed, "You got me there."

"Look, we're alone, just tell me. You know I would never betray your confidence."

"Oh my God, I know that Aunt Diana. It's about Albee."

"Albert and Sandra's little boy? What about him."

"Did you really buy that story they told us about Ramona's pregnancy?"

Diana threw her head back and closed her eyes. "No, Avery, I did not. But I swore to myself that I would respect their version of the truth as I respect them. You should do the same, especially since Albert and Sandra are your best friends."

"I did. It was all fine until I got a really good look at Arlo. It blows my mind how much the baby looks like him. What if Arlo notices that and demands a DNA test and he does turn out to be the father? He could take Albee away from Albert and Sandra." That would devastate them. It would ruin their lives, Albert's parents, Ramona's life…"

"Avery stop this right now. You are getting worked up over nothing. Now listen to me. Sometimes you say things to people out of a deep sense of loyalty, love and caring. But the way you say it does not reflect your true feelings. To someone who doesn't really understand you, you come across as a bitch, but you're not a bitch. In fact, you are one of the kindest most caring people I know. You have no idea how many times I've defended you because your words did not match your true feelings."

"I never realized that."

"Avery, I couldn't love you any more even if you were my own daughter. That's why I can talk to you this way. I will always tell you the truth."

Avery smiled and said, "I am so lucky to have you, Aunt Diana."

"Then will you do me one big favor? Try to get along with Lorelei."

"I am trying, but I'll try harder. She's a very hard person to get to know. She's so closed-up. It just feels like she has so many secrets hidden inside her that it's impossible to see the real Lorelei."

"I agree! But no matter who she is, Avery, Lorelei is still Peter's wife."

They arrived at the Madison Arms Hotel one half hour before Arlo's meeting. They went into the bar. Arlo ordered a drink and took it into the lobby. Lester, Ross and Avery sat at a table in the bar where they could see Arlo. Ten minutes before Arlo's appointed meeting with Pablo Calla, Ross and Avery meandered into the lobby and finally sat on a loveseat together sipping their drinks. They had a clear view of Arlo, as did Lester from the bar. At 9pm sharp, Arlo felt a hand on his shoulder. He looked up expecting to see Pablo Calla, but saw Sabastian Meitzner smiling down at him

This time, Lester had insisted Arlo wear a listening watch so at least he could be heard. Ross had printed out pictures of Pablo Calla, Sabastian Meitzner, Benet Horta and a few other of their colleagues. They knew who Arlo was dealing with but didn't know if Arlo realized it was Meitzner he was with. Arlo did know and played it very smooth. Arlo smiled asking, "Yes, can I help you?"

Meitzner sat down opposite Arlo. He looked hard at Arlo, studying his face. "My friend Pablo was right. You have very unusual eyes."

"Where is Pablo? I was supposed to meet him here at 9pm sharp," Arlo inquire without any emotion.

"Pablo is in his room. We will go up together to see him," Meitzner informed Arlo.

"What is your name, Sir? You seem familiar to me, but I don't know your name," Arlo asked. He knew it was Meitzner but loved playing the role he was playing. Arlo impressed Lester by how smooth he was.

"Shall we go? I will tell you my name upstairs," Meitzner responded. Arlo and Meitzner made their way to the elevator, along with Lester, Ross and Avery. Meitzner pushed the tenth-floor button. Ross pushed eleven. Lester got off on ten with Arlo and Meitzner.

Ross and Avery got off on eleven and ran down one flight to ten. Lester was waiting for them near the elevator. "They're in room 1012," Lester whispered. They positioned themselves near room 1012, but out of sight. They could hear every word said by everyone. So far, Lester was very pleased. He was certain it was Sabastian Meitzner and Pablo Calla who were planning something evil to happen during the conference. Lester, Ross and Avery all knew that they had to let it play out for as long as possible in order to discover their plot. Arlo was the perfect intermediary towards that end.

Sabastian Meitzner and Pablo Calla were stroking Arlo telling him they all knew about his history with the AFD. They said they thought he had been a good soldier and welcomed him back into the fold. Arlo played the game well but realized how lucky he was to have Poppy, Lorelei, Diana and Lester. They rescued him and gave him a chance to make a good life. He would do this for Diana and Lester and was determined not to let them down.

Pablo Calla handed Arlo another three hundred dollars, telling Arlo that he was to come back to the hotel the next day at noon. Arlo was told that he was to meet a man named Harry. He would be wearing jeans and a green shirt. Harry would hand Arlo another three hundred dollars and give him the message to be delivered along with the delivery instructions.

Arlo knew he was playing a dangerous game, but now it was different. He was on the right team. He felt a sense of comradery knowing Lester, Ross, and Avery were near by listening to everything being said.

Lester, Ross and Avery watched Arlo leave Pablo's room. He was not followed. Arlo got onto the elevator alone. Lester waited to see if anyone would follow Arlo. Ross and Avery ran down to the eighth floor to take the elevator to the lobby. Lester waited ten minutes. No one left Pablo's room. Lester walked up one flight and took the elevator from the eleventh floor. They all left the hotel separately.

Lester got his car out of the garage. He picked Ross and Avery up at the Port Authority bus terminal from which Arlo took the bus back to Englewood, NJ.

Arlo went back to his apartment. He was happy to be home. So far, he made some nice money. Arlo felt exhilarated knowing he got away with his charade a second time. Arlo's exhilaration was short lived. He saw the shadow of a man sitting in his living room before he even turned the light on. Then he saw the man. Arlo immediately recognized Benet Horta from the many pictures he had seen of him.

Arlo smiled, smoothly saying, "Mr. Horta, welcome to my humble home. What can I do for you?"

"I want to congratulate you. You have done very well so far." Benet Horta took out a wad of bills and offered Arlo another three hundred dollars. "This is to keep you happy, please take it. There will be five hundred dollars tomorrow when the message is sent." Arlo took the money but said nothing. He played the waiting game and won. Benet Horta kept talking. "The plan has changed slightly." Benet Horta stood up to face Arlo. "Harry can't make it tomorrow." Again, Arlo waited. "I am giving you your instructions now. There is a key to a locker in this envelope. The locker is in the men's' locker room next to the indoor pool at the Madison Arms Hotel. The package will be given to you by a woman who you will meet in the same spot in the lobby where you met Pablo and Sabastian. She will tell you her name is Marisol. Accept the package, take it to the locker room and open the locker. There will be five hundred dollars waiting for you. Take the money, place the package in the locker, lock the locker and leave the hotel. You job will be completed."

"That sounds easy enough. What happens next? Arlo asked.

Benet Horta smiled and said, "Don't worry Arlo, we will be in touch. You will be a useful addition to our organization. However, I warn you, if you screw us, you're a dead man." Benet Horta opened the door and left.

Lester, Ross and Avery sat in Lester's car near Arlo's apartment. As soon as Lester heard the plot, he contacted Mr. Sandman. Lester explained what had taken place so far. Mr. Sandman agreed that now it was time for the CIA to get involved. Benet Horta, Pablo Calla, Sabastian Meitzner, and the woman named Marisol were all foreign entities with questionable intents. Mr. Sandman also made it clear that until a crime was committed, no one could be arrested. He ordered Lester to collect Arlo and meet him at the detective agency. Lester then called Diana to meet them there.

Ross contacted Arlo. "Arlo, they may be watching your apartment. We need to get you out right now without being seen. Take your laundry basket and go to the laundry room. Lester will pull the car right up to the door. As soon you see Lester's car, hop in the back with Avery."

"OK, Ross. I'll see you in a bit." Arlo took his laundry basket and walked to the laundry room. Lester Pulled the car around the building to the laundry room. Arlo never showed up.

Arlo was sitting in the back of a car between Pablo Calla and Sabastian Meitzner. Two AFD thugs were in the front. "Where were you going, Arlo?" Meitzner asked.

"I was going to the laundry room to do my laundry." Arlo calmly answered, even though his blood was beginning to boil. "I'm not rich. I can't buy clothes the way rich guys can." His voice stayed and even.

"OK, Arlo, you'll stay the night with us. We'll put you in new clothes tomorrow," Calla said.

"And then you will deliver the message the way you were instructed. Take the five hundred that will be waiting for you and buy new clothes," Meitzner stated quietly as if talking to a child. "But for tonight, you will stay with us at the hotel."

Lester, Ross and Avery heard the entire conversation. Mr. Sandman and Diana were waiting for them noticing immediately that Arlo was missing. "What happened, where is he?" Mr. Sandman growled furiously.

"I'm sorry, but they managed to get him," Lester confessed sheepishly.

"Why in hell would you put an inexperienced kid into a situation like that? Whose idea was it to use him?" All eyes focused onto Avery. The silence became too much for Avery to tolerate.

Avery stood up. "Permission to speak freely Sir."

"Yes, Avery, speak freely," Mr. Sandman answered somewhat cynically.

"When I first suggested using Arlo, I never meant to put him out in the field. I only suggested asking him for names, so we had a way to start collecting intel. It was never my intent to use him as an asset on the street." Avery was angrily glaring at Ross.

Ross spoke up in defense of his wife. "Avery is right. She was not in favor of using Arlo as an asset in the field."

Diana was becoming upset. She had grown very fond of Arlo and was feeling the same kind of guilt she felt a few years ago when she sent Ross and Avery out to unknowingly to be used as bait. "Why don't we just put together an extraction team, go into the hotel and get him?

Diana's question surprised Mr. Sandman. "Let me spell this out for of you. We must assume the worst, that the message or package that Arlo is to put into the locker is a dirty bomb. At this point we cannot put in an extraction team. We need the military to send in an ordinance and demolition team to deal with whatever kind of bomb that package contains. The extraction team will be myself, Lester, JB and Barry. The rest of you are off it now, is that clear?" They all understood.

Two men and two women, in their bathing suits, coverups and flip-flops, each carrying a large brightly colored bag, made their way down to the Madison Arms Hotel pool for a swim. The two couples were laughing, talking and generally enjoying their vacation in The Big Apple. Mr. Sandman and Lester sat having coffee in the lobby of the Madison Arms Hotel. JB and Barry were each sitting outside in taxi cabs with their off-duty signs on.

Earlier that morning Lester and Mr. Sandman had spoken to the hotel manager. They showed him their CIA IDs and the manager agreed to comply with anything they needed. They now knew that Pablo Calla was still in room 1012. Sabastian Meitzner was in room 1014 and Benet and Marisol Horta were in room 1016.

Mr. Sandman had asked Blake and Veronica to sit in the lobby as back-up, if needed. They now needed Veronica. The hotel manager gave her a maid's uniform and a cart of towels and bathroom accessories. She was to change the towels in all three rooms to see where Arlo was being held.

When Veronica entered Pablo Calla's room she saw Arlo. He recognized her, did not show it, but was relieved that the troops had landed. Veronica reported that Arlo was in room 1012. She and Blake went back to Hoboken.

At twelve noon the conference started with a luncheon. Dr. Meyer Hemsley was there under heavy guard. He was not their only target. The entire populous of the conference was their target, regardless of who else was in harm's way.

Placed in the Lobby was a CIA collection team of eight men and women, posing as four couples. As planned, Arlo received the package from Marisol Horta. The CIA agents knew that Calla, Meitzner and the Hortas would check out by 11:00. The hotel manager was aware that the collection team would nab their catch as quickly and quietly as possible to avoid alarming hotel guests. Arlo would be unaware of the arrests and would continue with the plot.

Arlo made his way down to the pool locker room with the package and envelope containing the locker key. Lester and Mr. Sandman waited in a storage closet near the pool that Arlo had to pass on his way. As he passed, Lester pulled Arlo in and closed the door. Arlo faced Lester, sighed, and smiled. "Boy, am I glad to see you!" Arlo turned towards Mr. Sandman asking, "Who are you?"

Lester answered. "This is Mr. Sandman. He is CIA, Arlo. You have done very, very well.

"As we speak, Pablo Calla, Sabastian Meitzner and Benet and Marisol Horta are being arrested. The conference will go ahead as planned. However, the bad news is that what we think you have there is a dirty bomb that will probably be exploding soon," Mr. Sandman explained. Arlo's face turned ashen.

"There is a team of four military demolition experts waiting for you in the locker room. Give them the package and come back here to us," Lester instructed.

"There is five hundred dollars waiting for me in that locker. Do I have permission to retrieve it?" Arlo asked.

"Yes, but one of the team members should open the locker, just in case," answered Mr. Sandman.

"OK, Arlo, go! Come directly back to us, hopefully with the five hundred dollars," Lester gently ordered.

Arlo smiled and went to continue his mission. Without speaking or hesitation the team took the package away from Arlo. The four were clad in protective suits. "There is five hundred dollars waiting for me in this locker. Will one of you please get it for me?" Arlo asked handing them the key.

One of the women answered, "We will get it and give it to Gen. Ballantyne. You need to leave now. You are not in protective clothing, now leave!" Without questioning, Arlo left and went directly back to the storeroom.

Lester and Mr. Sandman grabbed Arlo and whisked him out a service entrance. Both Barry and JB were waiting. A shot rang out and Arlo slumped over. "JB and I will get him to the hospital, Earl. Go with Barry and explain things to Diana," Lester requested.

"OK, and keep in touch," Mr. Sandman demanded.

166

Veronica and Blake were picking Diana up to bring her to the hospital to wait with Lester. When Diana entered the car she saw Ramona was with them. "Ramona why are you here?" Diana questioned, showing annoyance.

"I'm here because I love Arlo. If he is going to die, he has to die knowing that I do love him." Ramona was sobbing. Diana put her arms around her to soothe her.

"I'm sorry honey, I didn't realize. As soon as they tell you he's out of surgery, you can tell him you love him." That brought a smile to Ramona's face and relief to Veronica. They rushed into the hospital to meet Lester and JB.

A doctor wearing surgical attire came to them. "He made it through surgery. It's touch and go, but he's young, healthy and strong. He should make it"

Ramona walked up to the doctor. With tears running down her face she asked, "Please, I must see him. I need to tell him that I love him. He doesn't know it, but he needs to know it, especially if there's a chance he could die." Veronica approached them telling the doctor she would accompany Ramona.

The doctor smiled. "As soon as he wakes up, I'll send for you." He turned and walked away.

By this time Ross, Avery, Poppy and Lorelei came running into the family waiting room. Diana stood up to defuse what she sensed would be a confrontation. "He's out of surgery and he's going to be fine," Diana calmly explained.

Lorelei was spitting mad. "What kind of a crazy scheme did you get him involved with that he got shot? Whose idea was it"? They all knew that initially it was Avery's idea, but said nothing.

Lester answered Lorelei. "He volunteered. He did us a great service. Your brother Arlo is a remarkable young man."

Lorelei was fuming. "He could die, and for what? Because one of you was stupid enough to put him out there?"

In a very calm, quiet manner Avery answered, "It was never my intention for him to go out into the field. The only thing I suggested was that we ask Arlo for names, so we could begin collecting intel."

"Oh, I should have known it would be you, Avery," Lorelei spit back at Avery.

Ross jumped in, "Now hold on, Lorelei. This was not Avery's fault. I was the one who allowed him out there, not Avery. So, if you have a beef, Lorelei, It's with me, not my wife."

Poppy put his arm around Lorelei. "Let's all calm down. I have two questions, however. One, was the outcome totally in our favor. Two, did they catch the person who shot Arlo?"

While Poppy was asking his two questions, Mr. Sandman walked into the room and answered Poppy. "The answer to your first question is yes due to Arlo's amazing competence. The answer to your second question is yes, they caught the shooter."

Poppy smiled and said, you see Lorelei, all is well. If he did so well, perhaps we should recruit him. He could go into training, come back a trained operative and join our group. What do you say to that, Lorelei?"

"Well, if that's the case, it's totally up to Arlo," Lorelei answered with a hint of cynicism, which Avery picked up on.

A nurse arrived to bring Ramona to Arlo. Lorelei started to go but Veronica held her back. "Let Ramona be the first person he sees. They really do love each other." Lorelei acquiesced, and Veronica walked Ramona to Arlo's room, but waited outside.

Ramona stood by the door for a moment looking at Arlo. She felt a tremendous mixture of love and guilt. She walked over to the bed. Ramona bent down and kissed Arlo gently on the lips. He opened his eyes, saw Ramona, and whispered, "I love you Ramona."

Ramona gently picked up Arlo's hand and held it against her cheek. "I love you, Arlo Gunther."

Arlo whispered, "Will you marry me? It will give me something to live for." Smiling, through tears, Ramona uttered yes.

It took Arlo about three weeks to recover enough to go back to work. He went back part-time until he regained all his strength. He bought Ramona a ring. They were officially engaged.

After about a month, when Arlo was almost fully healed, Lorelei and Poppy invited him out, but alone, not with Ramona. They brought him to the club. They walked directly into the secure room. All of Group Eleven was there to welcome him into the fold. Mr. Sandman walked up to them. He put his arm around Arlo. "This is CIA Group Eleven. We're kind of a special unit. Poppy is the head of this group. I am the Hackensack station chief. We think you would be a real asset to our group. Diana and Lester are the group's advisors." Arlo was speechless.

"All this time I was surrounded by CIA agents, including my sister, my brother-in-law, and my surrogate parents Diana and Lester, whom I love." Everyone began to laugh, including Arlo.

Lester put his arm around Arlo, "Well, what do you say son, do you want to join our group? You will have to go away for training. But when you return it will be as a trained CIA operative. Well, is it a yes or a no?"

Arlo looked around the room. He knew and loved most of these people. There was only one answer, and it was simply, "Hell, Yes!"

CHAPTER 8
HOPE, FAITH, GRACE, CHARITY

"Barnaby, hurry up, you're taking too long. We'll get caught!"

"Relax old boy, I'm trying to assess the best stuff to take."

"Find a bag or something and take it all, then let's get the hell out of here."

"OK, I got it all. Here I come. See, I told you mate, it was easy, let's go." The two men stole their way in the darkness, down the long winding staircase, exited out a back window, disappearing into the moonless night.

Grace Locklear, a charismatic, young woman, opened the door to her apartment. She crossed the threshold closed the door, and leaned against it, relieved to begin the end of her day. Grace threw her keys on a table near the door and walked into her bedroom. She took off her clothes and changed into sweats and slippers. Walking into the kitchen, she popped a frozen dinner into the microwave as she glanced at her mail she had thrown onto the counter.

Grace froze staring at the postcard. It was from Asheville, North Carolina, but that was not possible. He didn't live there, he never lived there, he never would have survived, but it was his handwriting. Why a postcard through the mail? Why not a phone call, an e-mail, or a text? Something was terribly wrong.

She had to handle this carefully. Grace sent her three teammates Hope, Faith and Charity a text message. They agreed to meet her at The Four-Square Diner in thirty minutes. Grace put on her sneakers and left her apartment, her dinner remaining in the microwave oven.

As the elevator door opened Grace's brother Joe came bounding out, almost knocking her down. They stood staring at one another for a brief moment. "Joe, what the hell are you doing here? And how the hell did you get passed my doorman?" Grace demanded to know. Before her brother had a chance to answer, Grace was pulling Joe into her apartment. "Well, what are you doing here?" Grace again demanded.

"I had to come in person. Something bad is happening at home, on the reservation. Our parents sent me to get you. All I know it that the trouble involves Tommy." Grace handed Joe the postcard she had just received.

"Tommy is at the University of Bucharest in Romania, Isn't he?" Grace responded, questioning Joe.

"Yes, Grace, as far as we know Tommy is in Romania. But we haven't heard from him in almost a month."

Looking at her watch, Grace said, "Listen Joe, I have to go out. It's important. Stay here, don't leave. I'll be back in about an hour." Grace remembered her frozen dinner. She took it out of the microwave oven and set it on the table. "Here Joe, eat this, it ain't bad." With that said, Grace ran out to meet her teammates.

Hope, Faith and Charity had been waiting ten minutes before Grace arrived. She spoke immediately and quickly. "This is personal, ladies. I need your help. My family is in some sort of trouble and I think it's serious. Will you help me?" Grace pleaded.

Hope leaned across the table, her thick auburn hair falling over her piercing green eyes. "Of course, we'll help you, Grace."

"What do you need? What's the situation?" Faith, a young attractive African American woman asked.

"We all stick together Gracie, no matter what. You know that. Now, just tell us the situation," Charity, a beautifully exotic-looking, young Asian woman said as she placed her hand on top of Grace's hand.

"OK, here it is. My brother Tommy is a student at NYU in Manhattan. Supposedly he's in Romania at the University of Bucharest as an exchange student. But I got a postcard in the snail-mail from him. It looked like his handwriting, but it was not from Romania. It was from Asheville, North Carolina. My family lives on the reservation in Cherokee, North Carolina, an hour away from Asheville. I need you three to go down there with me to see what's going on."

Faith smiled and answered, "Of course we'll go with you. But, may I suggest something?" They all silently nodded yes. "First thing tomorrow morning, the four of us should go to the Van Wyck Agency to talk to Ross, Avery and Diana."

"That's a great idea. We can't involve the CIA with personal problems, but we can involve private detectives. If things become dicey and it changes into CIA business, we're with the right people," Hope stated with certainty.

"There is one small detail I failed to tell you. I was late getting here because my brother Joe showed up just as I was leaving. He's already involved. Can I bring him with me to the agency tomorrow?" Grace asked shamefully.

"Hell yeah, bring him. Is he cute?" Faith asked, laughing.

"Yeah, adorable!" Grace answered sarcastically. They all laughed.

Toma Bratu, a large burly man of sixty-five, with thinning gray hair and a thick salt and pepper mustache, sat behind a solid cherrywood desk.

Across from Toma, sitting on a couch, was Costache, a younger man and his wife Stela, Toma Bratu's daughter. Stela looked at her watch, looked at Toma and whined, "It's the middle of the night Papa. When will they be here?"

"Patience, my darling daughter, soon."

Costache kissed his wife's head. "Don't worry, your Papa is right. Those two are in deep, very deep. Their lives and their families are in jeopardy and they know it."

"We have them by their balls. They will do all the dirty work and we will reap the benefits, or we kill them and their families. They know the game. They had their fun, now they pay," Toma explained. There was a knock on the office door. "There, you see, they're here," declared Toma as he pushed his large body out of the chair to answer the door.

Tommy Locklear, Native American, young, tall and lean, and Barnaby Bowen, British, medium height and muscular, were physically escorted into Toma's office by two of Toma's thugs. They were pushed down onto a small couch. The two thugs put the loot collected from the robberies Tommy and Barnaby committed on the floor in front of Toma's desk. Costache stood up and walked over to the bags. He and Toma looked inside each bag, looked at each other and smiled. "We'll see how much this will lower your combined debt of two hundred thousand dollars. In the meantime, I have an important job for the two of you," Toma said as he lit a cigarette, blowing smoke into their faces.

Both Tommy and Barnaby were afraid to speak. They just stared at Toma waiting for instructions. "The job you two will do for me tomorrow is dangerous, but you will manage." Still the boys said nothing. Toma spelled it out for them. "You two will go underground into the tunnels to distribute the merchandise I give you and collect the money. The amount of money you collect for me will be deducted from your debt. The more you sell, the more money you collect to lower your gambling debt. Do you both understand?" Tommy and Barnaby nodded yes.

Toma turned to face Costache. "Costache, go get the merchandise," Toma ordered. Costache obeyed. Tommy and Barnaby were each handed a large envelope containing the merchandise they were to sell. The two boys were going under the streets of Bucharest, where people, drug addicts, lived like feral beasts, armed only with their addiction to drugs. Toma gave Tommy and Barnaby each a revolver without the cartridges, explaining that his two henchmen would take them to the entrance of the tunnel. They would arm the revolvers and wait for them to successfully emerge after selling all the merchandise. Toma's two thugs would retrieve the revolvers and the money. Then, and only then, would Tommy and Barnaby be set free until they were needed again.

Hope, Faith, Grace, Charity and Joe walked into The Van Wyck Detective Agency just as Diana was putting the coffee on. Diana was startled, "What a surprise! I haven't seen you four in a long time. And who is this handsome young man?"

"Diana, this my brother Joe," Grace said, introducing him. Ross and Avery walked in and were surprised to see the five visitors. "Ross, Avery, this my brother Joe and of course you know Hope, Faith, and Charity."

Ross shook Joe's hand. "It's nice to meet you, Joe."

"What brings you guys here?" Avery asked pleasantly, knowing it had to be some sort of situation.

"Please everybody, sit down. The coffee will be ready in a minute and Lester will be here any time now with the donuts," Diana said, gently prodding them to sit. Lester walked in and Grace introduced him to Joe.

Diana looked around, smiled and said, Well, now that we're all settled down with coffee and donuts, please Grace, explain your situation." All eyes focused on Grace as she explained what had transpired the day before.

Joe expressed tremendous concern. "Our brother Tommy is in Bucharest, Romania as an exchange student, yet Grace received this postcard from him." Joe went on to explain, "Our parents are so worried because Tommy has stopped communicating with them. No one in our family has heard from Tommy in over a month. Now, Grace received a postcard, supposedly from Tommy, saying, 'wish you were here,' from Asheville, NC."

Ross asked what he and Avery could do to help. Grace said that she, her three teammates, and Joe wanted to go down to Cherokee to begin searching for Tommy. Grace wanted Diana, Ross and Avery to keep in touch with her team, to be their lifeline.

Diana didn't like it at all. "Lester, we're out of milk. Please go to the store down the block to buy some and take Joe with you." Lester knew exactly what Diana really needed, CIA privacy.

Diana insisted Grace and her team inform Mr. Burke, their boss, and Mr. Sandman, the Hackensack station chief, of the situation unfolding, explaining, "Something is definitely up between your brother Tommy and the Romanian Government and /or Mafia. I would make a bet on it. This could turn into CIA business."

Grace looked pleadingly at Diana. "Will you take us on as private clients, at least for now?"

"Yes, but first you must inform Mr. Sandman and Mr. Burke. Then, and only then can we take you on as private clients". Hope, Faith, Grace, and Charity immediately left the agency to go inform the two men of their plans.

When Lester and Joe came back, Diana told Joe to wait with them at the agency for Grace, explaining that the women had to take care of something at work before they could leave for Cherokee.

Mr. Sandman invited the four young women to sit down, explaining that Mr. Burke would be delayed. "It's good to see the four of you. How are things going?" Mr. Sandman casually asked. He did not expect the answer he got.

Grace leaned forward. "Work-wise, great. Personally, not so good. I have a problem brewing with my brother Tommy that could potentially become work-related, if you know what I mean. It could become a serious situation."

Mr. Sandman looked troubled as Grace explained about Tommy's disappearance and the nature of the postcard she received. Mr. Burke rushed into Mr. Sandman's office apologizing. Grace capsulized the events of the last thirteen hours. Both Mr. Sandman and Mr. Burke gave the team permission to go to Cherokee, NC only if Ross, Avery and Diana were working with them independently through the Agency. Grace and her brother Joe would have to officially hire *The Van Wyck Detective Agency* to search for Tommy. That would mean that Grace and her team were working unattached to the CIA, without pay, until the situation necessitated the CIA to take over.

Early the next morning Hope, Faith, Grace, Charity and Joe left for Cherokee, NC. Their ETA was thirteen hours or so, with stops. Ross and Avery took turns monitoring their trip. They arrived safely. Grace told Ross and Avery that they were exhausted and were planning an early night. First, however, they would stop to see Grace's parents to learn what they knew about Tommy. Grace promised to reach out to Ross and Avery early the next morning.

The Locklear family home was small, as were most homes in Cherokee, North Carolina. Joe opened the door with his key. There was not a sound in the house except for a clock ticking in the living room. "Hello, hey, where is everybody?" Joe yelled, expecting a warm welcome from his parents and ten-year-old sister Susie. There was just an ominous silence. Immediately Grace looked at her teammates, nodded, and they took out their weapons. Grace whispered to Joe, "Stand by the front door. If anything happens, run out and call the police. Don't say a word, just do as I say!" Joe did not question Grace. He obeyed her orders.

Hope, Faith, Grace and Charity knew the drill. Grace carefully walked into her sister Susie's bedroom, stood still and listened. She heard a quiet whimper coming from underneath Susie's bed. Grace got onto her knees and looked under the bed. "Susie, it's me, Grace. Why are you under there?" She gently prodded the frightened child out from underneath the bed. When Susie came face to face with her older sister, she threw her arms around Grace and began to sob. By that time Joe was kneeling on the floor with his two sisters and Hope, Faith and Charity were sitting on the bed.

Susie explained that when she got home from school her parents were not at home. Her mother was always home. Susie waited and waited, but they never came home. The later it got with no sign from her parents the more frightened Susie became. She knew Joe was coming back that night with Grace. She crawled underneath her bed where she felt safe to wait for them. Grace, her team and Joe decided to stay at the house with Susie just in case her parents did come home or tried to communicate with Susie in some way.

Tommy and Barnaby began their journey into the abyss under the streets of Bucharest, each with the merchandise and a loaded revolver. There was no need to seek out customers. The mangy, groping, addicted souls pawed at them from every direction. Tommy was shocked by what he saw. There were children as young as two and three, filthy and living in squalor in this abhorrent underground hell with their drug addicted parents. Tommy wondered what would happen to these babies if their parents died or abandoned them? He decided he would ask Toma the next time they met. Tommy knew the image of those young children would haunt him for the rest of his life.

The hungry, filthy mob was closing in on Tommy and Barnaby. Barnaby took his revolver and shot into the air. The mob backed away. Barnaby held the horde off with his weapon while Tommy made the sales and collected the money, in an orderly fashion. One man refused to pay. Barnaby shot him in the leg. The man payed and so did the others, without hesitation.

With all the merchandise gone, Tommy and Barnaby emerged from the tunnel. They were disarmed and handed the money to Toma's thugs as instructed. They were let go but told to be at Toma's office in three days' time for another assignment. Tommy swore to himself that he would somehow sneak food to the little children he saw in hell. Tommy became obsessed, feeling compelled to help those children.

It was pouring and the rain pounding on the window woke Ross. He looked at the clock, groaned, turned over and began to fall back to sleep, but the sound of his cell phone jarred him awake. He groped for his phone on the nightstand. Avery had awakened. Watching Ross fumbling around for his phone, she leaned over Ross to get it for him. Handing him the phone, Ross and Avery both sat up.

Diana was on the other end telling Ross *not* to go to the detective agency that morning, but to get up immediately and get over to the Hackensack station. A bad situation had developed. Mr. Sandman was calling in the entire group. He wanted them there within the hour.

Ross knocked on Mindo's door to wake him. He was part of Group Eleven and needed to attend the meeting. Mindo called his parents to care for Ralf and Kimmy. They lived close by and were there within twenty minutes.

Ross and Avery showered together as they often did to save time. They threw on sweats and sneakers. By the time Ross, Avery and Mindo were downstairs, Althea and Gabe were pulling into the driveway.

They were to meet in the big conference room next to Mr. Sandman's office. Diana and Lester had gotten there first. They made an urn of coffee and had bought out all the jelly donuts and crullers at their local donut shop.

As Ross, Avery and Mindo approached the conference room Avery said, "They're here." The smell of coffee permeating the air told Avery that Diana and Lester were there, bestowing upon Avery a sense of comfort and security.

The last person to arrive was their boss, Mr. Earl Sandman. Group Eleven in its entirety, was assembled in the large conference room. Mr. Sandman explained, "A team of four female agents from Group Fifteen, named Hope, Faith, Grace and Charity, along with Grace's brother Joe, their younger sister Susie, and their parents Ama and Dustu Locklear have all gone missing from the Indian Reservation in Cherokee, NC. Diana, take over, please."

Diana stood up. "I received, or I should say, our detective agency received a call from Joe. I have it set up that if someone calls the agency and we're not there, the call automatically transfers to my cell phone. That way, we never miss a call or an opportunity. Anyway, Joe was helplessly pleading saying that Tommy and his friend named Barnaby Bowen spent three months straight gambling and borrowing money from a Romanian mafia thug billionaire and casino owner named Toma Bratu. Tommy and Barnaby are in debt two hundred thousand dollars to Toma Bratu. He is a big fish with the Romanian Mafia. Mr. Bratu is threatening to kill Tommy, his parents, Joe, Susie, Grace and her teammates if he is not repaid what he is owed within one month. Great situation isn't it?" Diana asked sarcastically.

"This is totally unacceptable" roared Mr. Burke, the head of Group Fifteen as he came into the room. He was visually upset and explained, "I ordered the rest of Group Fifteen to stand down. They are all too close to the four women to be objective on the job."

"How can we help?" Mr. Sandman asked.

Mr. Burke put his hand on Mr. Sandman's shoulder and said, "Maybe you can lend me a few agents to find my people?" Mr. Sandman stood up, looked at Mr. Burke and shook his head yes.

"I think it's time for the Carter family to take another vacation. This time it will be to North Carolina." Mr. Sandman looked at his people and definitively stated, "Here's who I want on this one. Diana and Lester as the parents Angela and Leon Carter and their three sons and two daughters-in-law. So, Ross and Avery as Rob and Tori Carter. Poppy and Lorelei as Peter and Larissa Carter, and Arlo as Andrew Carter. Mindo, you will work with them also, and make sure they take care of themselves. We will rent a vacation home near the town of Cherokee with all the comforts of home. Any questions?" Sandra raised her hand. "Yes, Sandra?"

"If there are any problems with childcare, Albert and I are willing to help since we're not going on this one," Sandra offered, relieved that she and Albert were off the hook.

"Thank you, Sandra. I truly appreciate that offer and I'm sure your teammates do too," stated Mr. Sandman with a big smile. Ross, Avery, Poppy and Lorelei thanked Sandra, admitting that it was comforting to know that she and Albert were on standby for their kids. Mr. Sandman continued, "Blake and Veronica, I want you two to keep the Hoboken safe house available. Also, work with Caeley and Katrina to monitor our team. When new intel comes in, help them research it."

"Yes, sir. Blake and I will do whatever you need us to do on this one," declared Veronica.

Poppy turned to Caeley and Katrina asking them to check out Tommy's gambling partner, Barnaby Bowen. He then asked Ross to find out all he could on Toma Bratu. "Once we're down there we can decide on how to proceed. My recommendation, however, would be for my parents, Diana and Lester to question all of the neighbors. Ross and Avery, and Lorelei and I will question the people of Cherokee and involve the police only if we need to. Mindo and Arlo, I would suggest you two go into all of the local bars and casinos, questioning everyone," stated Poppy authoritatively. "We need to find out every bit of intel we can on this guy Toma Bratu."

Mr. Sandman stood up to speak to his secretary who opened the door and motioned for him. Irene handed him a printout and left the room, closing the door. "OK, folks, listen up! Carters, your flight leaves from Teterboro tomorrow morning at 09:00. Stop here to see me first at 07:30. I will have the address of your new home and all the intel that Ross, Caeley and Katrina collected. There will be two vehicles waiting for you once you arrive in North Carolina." Mr. Sandman looked at his people, smiled and said, "Thank you all, thank you all so very much." With that said, he walked out of the conference room. They were all suspended on his words of gratitude, not moving for a second or two. Then, one by one, Group Eleven left the room.

At 07:30 the next morning, every member of Group Eleven was seated around the large table in the conference room next to Mr. Sandman's office. He entered the room, looked at Katrina and said, "Katrina, tell them what you discovered."

Katrina stood up and looked directly at Lorelei and then at Arlo and stated, "This may come as a shock to you, unless you already are aware of this. Toma Bratu's daughter Stela is married to a man named Costache Gunther. Your grandfather, Hans Gunther and Costache's grandfather, Horst Gunther, were brothers. Horst Gunther was a captain in the SS during WWII. Toma Bratu's son-in-law Costache is your second cousin once removed or third cousin. I'm not sure how that works. I'm going to look deeper into this. The point is, there is a family connection."

"How does this family connection fit into the scheme of things?" Arlo asked.

"I'm not sure it does. Go to Cherokee, NC and see where it takes all of you," answered Mr. Sandman smiling assuredly at Arlo.

"Yes Sir," Arlo quietly responded.

Avery looked directly at Lorelei and asked, "Did you or did you not know about the German-Romanian connection in your family? You still haven't answered that question!"

Lorelei was fuming mad but worked hard not to show it. "I just knew it would be you asking that question, Avery. Not that it's any of your business, but no, I did not know."

"That's where you're wrong, Lorelei. If that intel or any intel is relevant to the case we're working on, then it is our team's business," snapped Avery.

Poppy put his arm around Lorelei and said, "I'm afraid she's right, sweetheart. But you didn't know."

"Says you!" Avery quickly answered. The verbal exchange was heating up.

Diana instantly turned off the heat. "Put a lid on it, Avery, and that's an order!" Avery obeyed and glared at Diana.

Their flight was short and uneventful, but Diana took the opportunity to speak to Avery about her attitude towards Lorelei. Diana asked Ross to switch seats with her. She sat down next to Avery and whispered, "I'm sorry Avery, I had to turn off the heat, but you know that."

"I'm sorry, too, but you know as well as I do that she can't be trusted."

"She has saved your ass in the past so don't sell her short. Look, Avery, just be open to Lorelei and try to understand where she is coming from. You and Lorelei are two very different people. Try to remember her tumultuous past and have some compassion. You and Lorelei are family, just remember that."

"My level of trust for Lorelei has decreased tremendously since the Moscow incident. I just can't get that out of my mind."

"I understand completely, but just try to remember the times when Lorelei did come through for you and our team."

"OK, I will make a concerted effort to do my darndest to get along with her, for your sake."

Diana gave Avery a quick kiss on the cheek, "Thank you." She went back to Lester and Ross went back to his seat next to Avery, but asked no questions, he didn't have to.

There was an SUV and a sedan waiting for them. Ross drove the SUV with Avery, Mindo and Arlo as passengers. Lester followed in the sedan with Diana, Poppy and Lorelei.

The house was a two-story logged cabin. It was surprisingly bigger on the inside than it appeared from on the outside. The main level was a large open area, consisting of a living room, a very large open kitchen with a dining area, and a bathroom. Upstairs there were four large bedrooms, each with its own bathroom. They were all thrilled with their accommodations but didn't know they wouldn't be there long enough to enjoy it.

As soon as they arrived, they wasted no time. Diana and Lester went to the Locklear home to look for clues and talk to the neighbors. Ross and Avery, and Poppy and Lorelei split up to speak to all business owners in Cherokee and the surrounding area. Mindo and Arlo went to the Cherokee casino to investigate Tommy and whatever they could learn about the family's disappearance, including Grace and her team members.

The door to the Locklear home was not locked, but nevertheless, Lester and Diana knocked. Lester entered first, quietly, with gun drawn and Diana right behind him. They found nothing and no signs of a struggle. Lester and Diana thoroughly searched every room of the Locklear home and found nothing. Diana turned to Lester and whispered, "I have a really bad felling about this, Lester. It's as if they all disappeared into thin air."

Lester agreed adding, "Now we should talk to as many people as we can in the neighborhood. Maybe someone saw or heard something, anything, that we can use as a lead."

Diana made one more sweep of the house before they left. Lester and Diana made it abundantly clear to everyone they spoke to that even the most insignificant piece of information could help their search for the missing Locklears and Grace's friends. One neighbor did remember something. The neighbor next door remembered hearing some sort of muddled noises in the middle of the night. He thought nothing of it, admitting that many people in the neighborhood drink too much. He just assumed it was someone coming home late after a night of too much beer. Lester and Diana agreed that it was not much but it was a place to start.

Ross and Avery and Poppy and Lorelei split the town in half, both couples attempting to check out every business in the small town of Cherokee.

Ross and Avery came across a shop owned by a very friendly older woman by the name of Lily Yazzie. Lily was heavy-set with long graying hair in braids with beads entwined in the braids. She sat on a stool concentrating intently, as her hands quickly did their work.

Avery was enthralled as she watched Lily Yazzie make a beaded necklace by hand. Ross explained the situation to Lily, who was very sympathetic. She knew the Locklear family well and gave Ross and Avery a lot of information regarding Tommy.

Lily told them that Tommy was a habitual gambler. Tommy, she said, was a very smart boy. He went to New York City, graduated college, and was working on a master's degree, the last she heard. Avery bought the necklace Lily had just made to give to Althea as a gift.

Lily then told Ross and Avery that Tommy was at their local casino almost every night when he was around. Avery then bought a bola tie for Gabe. Lily told them that Tommy owed the local casino ten thousand dollars in gambling debts. That was when Tommy left town. Avery bought Althea a bracelet to match the necklace.

Lily then told Ross and Avery that the Locklear family made a deal with the casino owners that they would pay back Tommy's gambling debt in monthly installments. The owners of the casino accepted their offer. Before Ross and Avery left Lily Yazzie's shop, Avery bought herself a bracelet and Ross a bola tie. Just before they left her shop, Lily, with sadness in her voice, told Ross and Avery that all the Locklears, including aunts, uncles and other extended family members were chipping in to pay back, in monthly installments, the ten thousand dollars Tommy owed the local casino. Avery bought a necklace to match her bracelet and received from Lily the names and addresses of every member of the Locklear family.

Poppy and Lorelei spoke to business owners on the other end of town. They found out an important piece of information from the owner of one of the liquor stores. The word was that a Romanian man, who came to Cherokee from Asheville, spoke to the owners of the local casino about Tommy Locklear. The man did not leave his name. The rumor was that Tommy had gotten involved somehow with the Romanian Mafia.

Mindo and Arlo went to the local casino. Everyone there knew Tommy Locklear. It was confirmed. Tommy had a gambling addiction, owing the casino ten thousand dollars. Arlo pushed back, asking the owners of the casino why they allowed Tommy to gamble if they knew there was a problem? The answer was simple. Tommy was an adult. He knew what he was doing. Both Arlo and Mindo agreed that the owners of the casino should have flagged Tommy. They allowed Tommy to put himself into debt, which now fell onto his family. Both Arlo and Mindo were angry, believing that the casino owners had a moral obligation to have flagged Tommy, not allowing him to gamble. They wondered if there was more to this than a simple gambling debt? Was there a connection between the Romanian Mafia and the Cherokee local casino?

That evening, when they were all came together, Mindo and Arlo reported the same information as their teammates, except they asked questions about the possible connection between the Cherokee local casino and the Romanian Mafia. Ross and Avery corroborated that Tommy was deep in debt from gambling to the tune of ten thousand dollars to the local casino. It was also concluded that Tommy did get himself involved with the Romanian Mafia and was probably still in Romania. The question now was, where was Grace, her teammates, Joe, Susie and Dustu and Ama Locklear?

They ascertained that the Romanian man in Asheville must have sent the postcard to Grace to lure her down to Cherokee. "It would have been easy to get her address from Tommy especially if torture was involved," stated Avery.

"You don't know that Tommy is being tortured, Avery," snapped Lorelei.

"And you don't know he isn't," Avery snapped back at Lorelei.

"OK, that's enough! No more talk about torture, and that's an order," Diana insisted, with a hint of disgust in her voice. Both Avery and Lorelei obeyed and backed off. Ross and Poppy just looked at each other and rolled their eyes.

"OK, gang, tomorrow Diana and I will speak to all the Locklear family members helping to pay off Tommy's debt. Then we will head to Asheville to find the Romanian man, if he's there. The rest of you split up and keep questioning the locals. Find out as much as you can about the Locklear family, emphasizing the severity of the situation." said Lester.

"If the Romanian man is not in Asheville, and there's nothing new here, then what?" asked Arlo.

"In that case, I would guess that some or all of us will be going to Romania!" Lester answered, looking straight at Diana, knowing exactly what she was thinking by her smile.

Lester and Diana took the names and addresses Lily gave Ross and Avery of the Locklear family members helping Ama and Dustu Locklear pay back Tommy's ten thousand dollars in gambling debts to the local Cherokee casino. The result was disheartening. Either the Locklear family members denied knowing anything or refused to talk to Lester and Diana completely. Both Lester and Diana agreed on one sure thing, they were all frightened. That was enough to lead them to Asheville to search for the Romanian man.

There were no Locklear family members or Romanian man in Asheville at the locations Poppy and Lorelei had gotten from the post office worker. As both Lester and Diana suspected, it was a dead end. The downside for Lester and Diana was that they had to leave Asheville. The city was alive with history and interesting attractions. It was a place they decided they would return to for a vacation.

The team then got their biggest lead. According to one of the casino workers, to whom Poppy palmed fifty dollars, it became clear that there was a direct connection between a cousin named Integus Locklear, and the Romanians. Poppy reported the intel to Mr. Sandman. He ordered them to stay as long as they needed to explore this new information.

Poppy, Ross and Arlo spent time at the casino talking to the workers and the locals who gamble on a regular basis. Avery and Lorelei were now forced to work alone together, talking again to the local shopkeepers. They asked many people about Integus Locklear. They discovered that Integus Locklear oversaw the private airport in Cherokee. The airport was not for public use, but for mail and other commercial deliveries.

Avery was very anxious to go back to speak with Lily Yazzie. The woman fascinated Avery. Lily had a way about her, something special. Avery knew it and felt it but could not put her finger on it. This feeling kept tugging at Avery from the moment she and Ross first met Lily. She decided to explain her feelings about Lily Yazzie to Lorelei. "Listen Lorelei, I want to take you to meet a very interesting woman Ross and I met. She makes hand-crafted jewelry. There's something special about her, I feel it, I just know it."

Lorelei looked suspiciously at Avery and sarcastically answered, "Of course you do, Avery. You have feelings about everything and everybody, don't you?"

Avery was not surprised by Lorelei's response. "Look, Lorelei, I'm not asking anything from you that's not work related. Please, just trust me on this one and come with me to Lily Yazzie's shop. Put your personal feelings aside. Anyway, I promised Diana I would be more open to you."

"What the hell does that mean, more open to me?" Lorelei snapped.

It took a lot for Avery not to lose her temper, but she took a deep breath and tried to explain what she meant. "I don't blame you for being testy, Lorelei. Basically, what I think Diana was asking of me was to try to get along with you better on a personal basis." Avery smiled, "After all, we are cousins-in-law."

"That's true. I suppose we could try," Lorelei answered, smiling back at Avery, but her smile dissipated. "Look Avery, you know as well as I do that we will never be, how they say, bosom buddies. You don't trust me about certain things and you never will."

Avery was not sure how to answer Lorelei but knew her answer might make a significant difference in their relationship. Avery chose her words carefully. "Believe me Lorelei, I want to trust you one hundred percent, and I do trust you to watch my back when we get ourselves into dangerous situations. But there are things about you that I just don't understand, and right now we don't have the time for that conversation. Maybe when this assignment is closed, we can make the time."

"Maybe, but now, let's go talk to Lily Yazzie," Lorelei replied with a slight smile.

Toma Bratu walked in. He surveyed his guests, opened his arms in a welcoming manor, smiled and said, "It is lovely here, is it not?" Toma Bratu had flown his twelve guests, against their will on private planes, to Romania for Tommy and Barnaby to see, not in person, but on TV monitors. Toma Bratu owned a summer home on Ovidiu Island on Siutghiol Lake, five hundred meters off the coast of Romania. Grace realized that escaping was no option. Toma Bratu made it clear that if even one of his captors escaped, the rest would be executed and disposed of, leaving no trace that they had ever been his guests. Grace's one hope was Group Eleven.

The moment Avery opened the shop door, Lily recognized her. "Somehow I knew you would come back to me," Lily said, smiling warmly at Avery. She then noticed Lorelei and Lily's smile faded. Avery felt a chill up her spine but ignored it. Lily turned back to Avery asking, "And who is this?" Avery saw Lily's eyes piercing through Lorelei and fought off the ominous chill she felt. Lorelei now understood Avery's fascination with Lily, although Lorelei thought it was freaky and a bit unnerving.

Calmly, with a smile Avery answered, "This is my friend and colleague Lorelei." Avery quickly diverted Lily's attention to the problem at hand, believing that Lily knew more about the situation than she let on. Explaining how worried she was about Grace Locklear and the others, Avery divulged that some alarming information, that could be life-threatening, had been uncovered by the other detectives with whom she, Ross and Lorelei were working.

Lily realized she needed to tell Avery what she knew, especially if lives were at stake. Lily said, "I know there possibly was a foreigner in town, some big shot from Europe, possibly Romanian. I know that possibly a private jet may have landed at the local airport. If the Locklears and the others were taken, they would have possibly been taken to that plane and possibly taken out of the country, possibly to Romania." Avery asked Lily Yazzie what people in the community were wealthy enough to keep a private plane at the Cherokee local airport. Her answer did not surprise either Avery or Lorelei. "It is possibly friends of Integus Locklear," Lily answered with a shrewd smile.

Avery found it noteworthy how many times Lily used the word *possibly* and asked, "How close to *sure* does your use of the word *possibly* come, Lily?" Avery picked up a pair of earrings and laid fifteen dollars on the counter.

Lily's eyes stayed focused on Lorelei. She answered, "Very close to *sure*." Without moving, Lily asked Lorelei, "What is your last name?"

Without hesitating Lorelei answered, "Lassiter, my name is Lorelei Lassiter."

Lily shook her head no asking, "No, your maiden name, what is your maiden name?"

Lorelei was becoming unnerved by the way Lily was questioning her, but she answered. "My maiden name is Gunther. Why do you want to know?" Lorelei asked with trepidation.

Once again, Lily's eyes pierced through Lorelei as she answered, "The name Gunther has a black stain on it. I hope you didn't put it there."

Lorelei turned towards Avery, "I've had enough of this woman!" Lorelei quickly walked out of Lily's shop.

Lily put her hand on Avery's arm and warned, "Avery, watch out for that girl. The name Gunther is stained, be careful."

"I will, thank you," Avery quietly answered, shaken at what had just occurred. Lorelei was waiting outside the shop. She and Avery walked away in silence.

That night Veronica and Blake contacted Poppy with a stunning piece of intel. The cousin, Integus Locklear, was paid big bucks to supply Toma Bratu with the intel that lead to the kidnapping of Grace, her team, and her family. They needed to find Integus Locklear, arrest him and bring him back to New Jersey for questioning. Once Integus gave them all he knew, they would send him off to Langley.

Katrina and Caeley dug deeper into Costache Gunther. They found out that Costache's father, Uwe Gunther, was the son of SS Captain Horst Gunther, who married Romanian Irena Radu during WWII. They had a daughter, Ursula and a son Uwe. Horst Gunther was wanted for war crimes he committed in Poland. Horst and Irena hid out in Romania after the war. Horst was never found and put on trial for his crimes but died of cancer in 1955. Irena died in 1970. Their son Uwe Gunther married Maria, Costache's mother, who died in childbirth. Uwe Gunther, Costache's father, died two years ago. In the end, Katrina and Caeley both found the same intel, Costache Gunther was related to Lorelei and Arlo Gunther. Costache's grandfather, SS Captain Horst Gunther and Lorelei and Arlo's grandfather German scientist Hans Gunther, were brothers.

"That's all very interesting, but how is this relevant to the situation we're working on?" Lorelei asked, seeming annoyed.

"There's probably no connection at all. It's just a coincidence that Toma Bratu's daughter is married to a distant relative of yours," answered Poppy reassuringly as he put his arm around his wife.

"That's right." Diana chimed in. "One thing has nothing to do with the other. So, let's just forget about that bit of family history," insisted Diana.

"Diana is right. Let's stay focused and on track," Lester added, putting a period at the end of the Gunther family history lesson.

Diana shared her deep concern with the team, explaining the fear every member of the Locklear family displayed. There was something sinister happening, but Diana feared it was in Romania, not in Cherokee, North Carolina.

Lester and Diana discovered that there was a Romanian man and a Native-American man at the address they were given. Both men had moved out or just left. The landlady wasn't sure. She could not give Lester and Diana a clear description of either man or did not know their names. From there it was a dead end.

Ross, Poppy and Arlo had more luck. By paying a casino worker, Poppy learned more about Integus Locklear. Besides being deeply involved with the Romanians, Integus Locklear ran the small private airport exclusively himself deciding who could land there and who could not.

Avery corroborated the intel Poppy received, explaining what Lily Yazzie told her about Integus Locklear. "Lily Yazzie was very sure that Grace, her team, Joe, Susie and their parents were kidnapped by a Romanian mobster and probably helped by Integus Locklear. Maybe Toma Bratu, himself." Avery, however, did not reveal, to Lorelei's relief, the personal business between Lily, Lorelei and Avery. Lorelei looked over at Avery and smiled. Avery understood and smiled back. Diana noticed and realized that Avery and Lorelei now shared a secret.

Early the next morning Ross, Arlo and Mindo went to Integus Locklear's home to arrest him. They knocked, but Integus didn't answer. Ross gave the signal and tried the front door, but it was locked. Arlo went to the back of the house and Mindo and Ross each took a side. Arlo was able to pick the lock on the back door. He whistled, signaling to Ross and Mindo. Drawing their weapons, they entered the house and separated, searching in different directions. Integus was not in the house. They did not have a search warrant but looked around quickly. Finding nothing, they left the house and headed out to the small Cherokee airport.

As they approached the airport Integus Locklear was just coming out of the hanger, heading for the tower. He saw the car and stopped in his tracks. Ross pulled the car up to him and in a non-threatening way asked, "Are you Integus Locklear?" Ross, Mindo and Arlo all got out of the car.

Integus eyed the three unfamiliar men suspiciously. "Yes, I am. What do you want?" Ross stepped forward while Mindo and Arlo stepped on each side of Integus, almost surrounding him.

Integus began to look nervous and Ross saw that. "We just want to talk to you about your cousin Tommy Locklear. Do you know where he is?" Ross asked benignly. Integus took a step backwards, away from Ross, only to bump into Arlo. Arlo held Integus by his arm.

Integus become defensively agitated, asking, "Who are you? I don't know anything about my cousin Tommy. Leave me alone!" Mindo and Arlo were now each holding Integus each by an arm. Integus began to struggle. Ross handcuffed Integus and showed him his CIA ID.

Ross faced Integus and explained, "We are arresting you for aiding and abetting in the kidnapping of eight people, four of them being CIA agents." Integus stopped struggling and got into the car. Mindo read Integus his rights. They drove to the local police station where Lester and Diana were waiting for them. The police temporarily closed the small airport. Lester and Diana, with Ross, Mindo and Arlo took Integus back to the airport where a private jet was waiting. Mr. Sandman was standing in the doorway waving at them to hurry up and board. The rest of the team was waiting aboard the plane ready to take off. Integus was handcuffed to his seat. He was afraid to speak, but finally asked where he was being taken. Diana smiled and told him not to worry. They were taking him to New Jersey for questioning. That seemed to satisfy Integus. He asked if he could put his seat back to rest. Mindo did that for him. Integus thanked Mindo, closed his eyes and went to sleep.

The flight home was uneventful. Most of them took naps but were awake for their landing. Mindo gently touched Integus to wake him to put the back of his seat upright for the landing. Mindo yelled, "Oh my God, he's dead!" The pilot radioed ahead to have an ambulance waiting to take Integus' body to the morgue for an autopsy. They could not figure out how Integus died. Mr. Sandman called his friend Charley Maher, the medical examiner he trusted and respected the most, to meet him at Teterboro when they landed. Charley agreed to be there.

Tommy and Barnaby sat silently on the couch across from Costache Gunther's glaring stare, waiting for Toma Bratu to arrive. He was a half hour late. Bounding into the room he bellowed, "Hello, boys, glad to see you looking so well. I have another job for you two."

Tommy asserted himself asking, "Mr. Bratu, may I ask you a question?"

"Yes, of course, what is it?" Toma asked, smiling.

"When we were in the tunnels last time, I saw little children, as young as two years old. What happens to them if their parents die or abandon them?

Toma Bratu walked over to Tommy, looked down at him and questioned, "Tommy, Tommy, why are you asking this? I don't know, and I don't care. These people live like rats. I supply them with merchandise, and they pay me. That's all I care about and that's all you should care about." Tommy did not say another word. He knew it was futile.

Toma Bratu then addressed both Tommy and Barnaby. "Look at these two monitors," Toma said pointing to his desk. "Get up, boys. Come see what I have to show you." Both Tommy and Barnaby stood up and walked behind the desk. On one monitor Tommy saw his parents, Susie, Joe, Grace and her team, Hope, Faith and Charity. On the other monitor Barnaby saw his parents and two sisters. All twelve were tied up with tape over their mouths. Toma laughed and said, "The good news is they are all here in Romania as my guests. You two have one more month to finish earning back the rest of the money you owe me. If you fail, all twelve of them will vanish, as if they never existed. What do you say to that?" Barnaby Bowen threw up in Toma Bratu's garbage pail.

Mr. Sandman and Medical Examiner Charley Maher stood in the morgue after Charley completed the autopsy on Integus Locklear. In his gloved hand Charley held a false tooth. He held the tooth up, showing Mr. Sandman and explained, "This is where he hid the small cyanide capsule. He apparently was able to work the tooth off with his tongue. Once the capsule was freed, he chomped on it and it killed him."

"Thanks, Charley, I'll notify the family. Let's have dinner soon to catch up. It's been too long," suggested Mr. Sandman.

"Yeah, I'd like that, Earl. Maybe one day next week? I'll call you." Mr. Sandman smiled and nodded affirmatively as he left the morgue.

They were all at the Hoboken safe house anxiously awaiting Mr. Sandman's arrival. He entered the house, put up his hands to stop them from rushing him and quickly explained, "Integus had a small cyanide capsule hidden in a false tooth in the back of his mouth. Charley ascertained that he must have popped the false tooth off with his tongue and bit down on the capsule."

"Why would he want to kill himself?" Avery asked, puzzled. No one answered the question immediately,

Poppy finally answered. "If there was no way out for Integus, on either side, he probably thought it better he dies by his own hand."

Mindo thought of another reason. "I'm sure Integus must have realized that he brought shame upon his family. He probably couldn't live with that."

"That's true, because his family had no idea how deeply he was involved with the Romanians," posed Lorelei.

"That's right, we were going to arrest him and then ship him off to Langley. Integus had no idea how that would have gone down," added Arlo.

"And on the other side of the coin, if the Romanians got him, Integus knew his death would be painful. The cyanide pill was his only option, so he believed," Lester concluded.

"OK, so who's going to Romania?" Avery questioned Mr. Sandman.

Mr. Sandman walked over to Avery, smiled, and asked, "Avery, who do you think should go to Romania and why?"

At first, Avery was hurt, thinking Mr. Sandman was trying to embarrass her, but when she looked up into Mr. Sandman's eyes, Avery knew he was giving her a compliment, deeming her seasoned and good enough to choose the best people to do the job. He was giving her a chance to show leadership. Avery looked around the room at her team, assessing the situation. "Firstly, I think Lester and Diana should go. We'll be going into a country where we've never been, and they are the most experienced. I'm almost positive we'll have to deal with Toma Bratu, and perhaps his son-in-law Costache Gunther. I don't think Arlo or Lorelei should go because of the family connection." Avery looked at Mr. Sandman, expecting a comment.

He smiled at Avery and said, "Go on Avery, you're doing just fine."

Lester intervened with, "If I'm going, I need you, Arlo, to run the club. We've both been away too long."

Arlo smiled and answered, "Yes, Sir, I was thinking the same thing.

Mindo jumped in with, "I need to get home, Ralf is missing me, but Kimmy couldn't care less when my Mom is around. This way, my Dad can get back to the club with Arlo."

Avery laughed, responding, "Thanks for the help, guys, and I agree with all three of you completely. Of course, Ross and I will go, but we need another couple. How about it, Sandra? You and Albert come with us on this one?"

"I wish we could Avery, but I can't go," Sandra said smiling. Avery cocked her head to the side, silently asking Sandra why she couldn't go. Sandra answered with, "I can't go because I'm pregnant, I'm really pregnant." Avery rushed over to Sandra and hugged her tightly. Avery and Sandra were both crying. Everyone began talking at once, congratulating Albert and Sandra.

Mr. Sandman brought them back on track. "This is wonderful news, but we must get back to the problem at hand. Avery, I turn the floor back to you.

"Blake, Veronica, you need to come with us. We'll bring you up to date on our way to Romania. So, our team will be the six of us. Lester and Diana, Blake and Veronica, and Ross and me. Mr. Sandman, do you approve?"

"Yes, Avery, I approve. Ross, contact Simon and Tessa in London. Tell them we'll have Barnaby and his family flown to Heathrow when the mission has been completed and we've recused all twelve hostages. We'll contact them when we're airborne."

"Yes, Sir," Ross answered as he walked out of the room to make the call.

Mr. Sandman looked around at his people and said, "I want one more person on the team."

"Who?" Avery asked.

"Me", retorted Mr. Sandman, gravely.

The next evening, on a plane headed for Romania, Mr. Sandman explained why he chose to join the team. "I Know Toma Bratu. He's a real bastard. Thirty years ago we had a run-in. He killed my partner and wounded me. I woke up in a Romanian hospital and my partner was dead. Toma Bratu disappeared. I came home and was put on a desk for about five years. I kept him in my sights as best I could over the years." He bent his head down getting lost in his thoughts.

"So, now you want revenge?" asked Blake.

Mr. Sandman slowly raised his head, his eyes blazing, he hissed out the word, "Yes".

"How do you intend to accomplish your goal?" Diana quietly queried.

Mr. Sandman sighed deeply. "I don't know. I'll have to wait to see and assess our situation when get there and how things are played out. I'll know what to do, and then I'll do it."

"Who was your partner that Toma Bratu murdered?" Veronica asked. Placing her hand on Mr. Sandman's arm, she softly whispered, "I hope you don't mind me asking."

"No, I don't mind. Her name was Brenda. She was my wife. We were married a very short time, only two months. I never told Meredith or her mother, my ex-wife, about Brenda." There was an uncomfortable pause. Then, he continued. "I haven't spoken about Brenda in thirty years. Richard Childs was the only one left who knew about her and he's dead. I feel an obligation to tell the six of you now because I may need your help. Toma Bratu is a very dangerous man and I want him dead! I feel I can finally get the closure I've always felt I needed. Granted, it's been a long time, but that kind of pain never leaves. It's always there. That bastard must pay for his actions. We'll rescue our people and I will avenge Brenda's untimely death."

Diana, with a tear running down her cheek, looked at Mr. Sandman with resolve and stated, "Whatever you need, Earl, whatever you need!" They all concurred.

"Are we going to connect with the CIA station in Bucharest?" Veronica asked.

"No, there's no need to involve them," quickly answered Mr. Sandman. After a moment of silence, he added, "Anyway, I don't know them. I can't trust anyone I don't know, and sometimes those I do know turn out to be untrustworthy. No, we'll take care of things ourselves."

"We're always on our own. Why should things be any different this time?" Avery asked. Everyone laughed in agreement.

Mr. Sandman smiled. "Don't worry folks, we won't be entirely on our own."

The Alina Maria Hotel was small, off the beaten track, and very clean. Surprisingly, the manager-owner, Florin Cojoc and his wife Alina knew Mr. Sandman as they both had been his assets for many years. They had met James and Diana years ago once or twice, but they never met Lester. They remembered Brenda and what happened.

That evening dinner was on the house. Over coffee Ross, Avery, Blake and Veronica learned that Florin and Alina were attached to the SRI, Romania's main domestic intelligence service. They often worked in conjunction with the CIA concerning problems in Romania.

Florin explained that they had to be very careful in their dealings with Toma Bratu. Bratu was a very powerful man with many influential and important friends in high places. Florin warned them that If they killed Toma Bratu to save their people, they had better have a plan to get out of Romania as quickly as possible. Mr. Sandman knew that he would kill Toma Bratu but did not reveal that piece of the equation. And, he did have a plan in place to get out of Romania. At this juncture, however, only Mr. Sandman knew the entire plan of events to come. To protect his people and save the people Toma Bratu had kidnapped, he would only tell them what they needed to know when they needed to know it.

That night Mr. Sandman told his team that they flew into Romania under cover not only as the Carter family, but also as guests of billionaire Allister Grimes. The plane was registered in that name and was under constant guard by the Romanian Secret Service, courtesy of Florin and Alina Cojoc.

For their own protection Mr. Sandman informed Florin and Alina that he only wanted information from them, no action. He needed them to stay completely undercover. They all drank a toast to Florin and Alina Cojoc. That night was the last night they smiled.

Two of Toma Bratu's thugs came into the outer office, dragged Tommy and Barnaby inside, and threw them on the floor in front of Toma's desk. Toma Bratu stood up and snarled, "Get up." The two boys pulled themselves up and stood erect. "Unfortunately for you, your situation has taken a turn for the worse. Seven CIA agents arrived in Romania last night. I know one of them. They came to try to save you and the team of four agents that are my guests, one of which is your sister, Tommy. What do you think of that?" Tommy look down, not answering. Barnaby began to shake. "I asked you a question," roared Toma, "Now answer me."

Tommy looked up focusing his eyes slightly over Toma's head. "I don't know what to think. Barnaby and I just want to pay you back the money we owe you and go home safely with our families."

"We will see. You still owe me two hundred thousand American dollars. It's time to go back in the tunnels with merchandise. The more money you collect, the less you owe. Right now, you are paying down the fifty percent interest you both owe." Toma Bruta laughed loudly, as he plopped down into his chair. The boys stared at Toma Bratu in horror. Toma had never mentioned any interest. Tommy and Barnaby realized they were ensnared in a trap with no way out.

Florin suggested the first thing they do was find Tommy and Barnaby. Mr. Sandman disagreed. "No! The first thing we need is a safe house from which to operate. I do not want you and Alina involved. We need a secure place to question and hold people."

Florin thought for a minute, but it was Alina who came up with the solution. "My cousin has an apartment in a building located not too far from here. He and his wife are actually in your country visiting family. I am taking care of the apartment. They won't be back for another month. If you promise not to destroy anything, you can use it."

Mr. Sandman smiled, answering, "I can promise ninety percent that we won't destroy anything."

"That's good enough for me", Alina answered. She wrote down the address on a piece of paper and handed it to Mr. Sandman with the key. They all memorized the address. Mr. Sandman burned the paper. He handed the key to Ross, instructing him and Avery to go there immediately. They were to check and recheck for any hidden cameras and listening devices and set up their own equipment. The rest of them would wait at the hotel for Ross and Avery to return.

Ross and Avery entered the building cautiously. Avery touched Ross' arm and whispered, "I think we're being followed." Without speaking, they took out their weapons and made their way up the two flights of stairs to the apartment. Once in the apartment, they put their weapons away. Avery turned to Ross, shook her head and exclaimed, "I know we were being followed, Ross."

The apartment was clean. There were no listening devices or hidden cameras. Ross set up his computer, his hidden cameras and listening devices. When all was set, they left to go back to the hotel. As they stepped out of the building, two shots rang out, barely missing them. Ross pushed Avery down onto the ground. "Those shots were not meant to hit us, just inform us they know we're here," he whispered in Avery's ear.

Blake and Veronica were next. They went to the safe house to stow away anything breakable or of value into closets and cabinets. Mr. Sandman knew that there was a slight chance things could get rough while interrogating one of Toma Bratu's thugs, whom he fully intended to find. They accomplished their task and left the apartment. Just before arriving back at the hotel, two shots were fired at them, missing each of them by a fraction of an inch. They got the message.

Mr. Sandman set up his own system, using the hotel as his base of operation and the apartment as his black site. Ross had set up cameras in the apartment that, on a computer in the hotel, showed every room and space in the apartment, allowing a continuously secure connection between the two places.

Florin gave Lester and Diana the names of the two casinos that Toma Bratu owned. Their goal was to find Toma Bratu or one of his thugs. They were to inform them that Mr. Earl Sandman wanted a meeting with Toma

Bratu. Diana didn't like it at all stating, "Earl, you can't walk into danger without a plan, and if you have a plan, I would appreciate it if you would inform us of your intent."

He walked over to Diana, picked up her hand and kissed it answering, "I have a plan. We must find out where Toma Bratu is holding our agents and the others. If I let him capture me, he will probably take me to them."

"That could work, but you'll have to hide the wire carefully," Lester conceded.

"No, Lester, I'm not going to wear a wire. I'll have my cell phone. You can track me that way, but no wires."

"Well, if you're sure, OK," agreed Lester.

Diana was appalled. "Are you two crazy? We can find them without you putting yourself in danger. Besides, if these assholes have any brains, they'll destroy your cell phone as soon as they capture you!"

Mr. Sandman smiled at Diana and uttered, "Diana, you've lost your edge!" Lester knew that was the wrong thing for Mr. Sandman to say.

"Please don't patronize me. I have not lost my edge, I've just gotten wiser over the years," Diana snapped back.

Mr. Sandman sat down opposite Diana, so their knees were almost touching. "I'm not patronizing you, Diana. I have too much respect for you to do that. We've known each other a long time. I trust you with my life, you know that too. Now, I'm asking you to trust *me* with my life. I have a plan that I think might work, but I want to keep it to myself right now."

"OK, but at least wear a wire so we can stay with you and jump in if things go sideways," Diana suggested in a controlled manner. She didn't like it but could not order him not to wear a wire. Mr. Sandman was her boss.

"I'll tell you what," Mr. Sandman said after thinking for a moment. "I'll have Ross and Avery follow me wearing wires and disguises. Blake and Veronica will follow them also wearing wires and disguises. You and Lester can always keep in touch with the four of them. How does that sound?" Diana looked at him and thought for a moment.

Diana thought and took a deep breath. "OK, I can go for that. At least we'll know where you are," conceded Diana.

Veronica was the master of disguise and came equipped with an array of disguises. Avery chose a short black wig and Ross a male wig with longish black hair. Veronica became a blonde and Blake wore a cap and a beard. All four changed their looks with makeup. All they needed now was to find the right person to lead Mr. Sandman and them to Toma Bratu and the twelve people he abducted.

Florin Cojoc told Mr. Sandman which of the two casinos he was most likely to encounter Toma Bratu and his thugs. First, Mr. Sandman decided to go to the apartment to become familiar with the lay out. Ross, Avery, Blake and Veronica were following. They did not, however go up to the apartment. Instead the four spread out to survey the area, watch and wait.

Avery noticed him first, a man lurking around the entrance to the building. The man entered the building as Avery said, "He's talking to someone, Let's move in."

"Avery and I will go first. You two follow and cover us," Ross instructed Blake and Veronica.

"OK, and hopefully we all end up in the apartment alive," Veronica joked.

"Let's keep moving, sweetheart," Blake urged as he gently pushed Veronica along. "By the way, darling, are you wearing your ring?" Blake jokingly asked with a slight British accent.

"Yes, Mr. Bond, I am," Veronica answered, also with a slight British accent. They all laughed.

The man was halfway up the second staircase when Ross and Avery quietly hurried up behind him, keeping out of sight. Blake and Veronica stayed just inside the entranceway. When Ross and Avery were rounding the bend, Blake and Veronica took to the stairs following Ross and Avery's lead.

"Keep your mouth shut and do what we tell you or I'll kill you," Avery threatened, as she and Ross opened the door and pushed the man into the apartment. Blake and Veronica followed closely behind.

"Well, well, and who do we have here?" Mr. Sandman asked with a broad smile. Ross and Blake sat the man down onto a kitchen chair and bound his hands and feet to the chair. The smile left Mr. Sandman's face. He walked up to the man and pushed his pointer finger into the man's chest. "Who are you and what do you want?" Mr. Sandman knew the answer to both questions but asked anyway.

The man answered, "I work for Toma Bratu. He knows why you and your people are here, in Romania. Mr. Bratu wants me to tell you to meet him inside the café just across the street in one hour for a coffee. You are to come alone." Mr. Sandman knew this was the beginning. He agreed to meet Toma Bratu.

By this time, Diana and Lester were at the safe house. They stayed with the man while Ross, Avery, Blake and Veronica followed Mr. Sandman clandestinely, spacing their positions so as not to be seen. They looked across the street into the cafe from the entranceway of the building. They watched as Mr. Sandman walked towards the café. "Remember guys, he's not wired," warned Veronica.

"Yeah, but he still has his cell phone," Ross reminded them. "However, if he goes with Toma Bratu, I'm sure, at some point they will take his phone," warned Ross.

"We need to stay on him at all times, and you two need to stay on us," whispered Avery as they watched the two men.

Mr. Sandman walked assertively into the café and headed straight for Toma Bratu. He sat down but said nothing.

"I know what you want, Earl Sandman," stated Toma Bratu with such smugness, that Mr. Sandman had to use all his willpower not to whip out his gun and kill him. He stayed focused on his mission.

"And what is it I want?" he asked coldly, portraying an air of superiority.

"You want the people who are presently my guests," stated Toma Bratu. Mr. Sandman cocked his head to the sided, looked at him, and silently nodded yes. Toma Bratu continued, "Those two boys owe me two hundred thousand dollars. I want my money back. Then, I will let the people go."

Mr. Sandman shrugged his shoulders, smiled and answered, "I think that's only fair, Toma. Those two boys gambled in your casinos, lost and now owe you the money you fronted them to gamble." Toma Bratu was surprised by how understanding Earl Sandman was. Mr. Sandman waited a few beats and continued. "I have a solution. I want my agents back and the other people are innocent. I will pay you the two hundred thousand the boys owe you. What do you say, Toma? We all win. You get your money; the twelve innocent people are set free and the two boys pay back their debt."

"They owe me fifty percent interest, that was the deal," Toma Bratu barked.

Mr. Sandman knew he had full control at that moment. He knew that Toma Bratu was a greedy man. "I'll tell you what, Toma. To sweeten the deal, I am willing to give you a half a million, five hundred thousand American dollars. What do you say to that?"

Toma Bratu leaned forward asking, "What's the catch?"

"No catch, Toma. I just want the twelve innocent people you are holding and the two boys. I will have two private planes waiting at the airport. One for my people and one for the British folks. I will have the money with me. You can inspect it. Then all fourteen people board the planes, I hand you the bag of money, and we both go on our merry way. It's as simple as that. What do you say?"

Toma squinted his eyes and looked at Mr. Sandman suspiciously. Mr. Sandman knew Toma would never turn down half a million American dollars. "OK, it's a deal," Toma answered as he offered Mr. Sandman his hand to shake. As much as he didn't want to, Earl Sandman shook Toma Bratu's hand. "When will this happen?" Toma Bratu asked.

"I need two full days. On the third morning, meet me at the airport's private plane area. It will happen then. And Toma, make sure every one of those fourteen people are unharmed. You bring them in a vehicle with one driver and yourself, that's all. I will let you inspect the money; you release the fourteen people to me, and I release the money to you. Do you understand the plan?" Mr. Sandman asked, as he stood up.

"Yes, I will see you at the airport on Friday morning, 08:00, yes?" Toma asked. Mr. Sandman nodded affirmatively and walked out of the café. He went into the building and told Blake and Veronica to follow Toma Bratu as he handed Blake the keys to their rented car.

At the hotel Mr. Sandman called Poppy who was acting chief at the Hackensack station when Mr. Sandman was not there. He instructed Poppy to take five hundred thousand dollars out of the station safe, put it in a briefcase, and alone, without Lorelei, get on the plane that would be waiting for him at Teterboro Thursday night. Poppy was to deplane at the Bucharest Airport. Mr. Sandman said he would be there to meet him.

As promised, when Poppy deplaned with the briefcase in Bucharest, Mr. Sandman was waiting for him. He took the briefcase from Poppy and told him to get on the other plane. Ross, Avery, Diana, Lester, Blake and Veronica were on board. They explained the situation to Poppy while Mr. Sandman waited for Toma Bratu and his prisoners. A small bus pulled up. Toma Bratu got off the bus and began walking towards Mr. Sandman, who put up his hand to stop him and yelled, "Toma Bratu, tell the fourteen people to get off the bus and line up. I want to see them." There was a pause, a small moment when Mr. Sandman thought things would go sideways. But true to his greed, Toma Bratu was motivated by the five hundred thousand dollars, not his prisoners. He turned around and instructed the driver to open the door and let the passengers out. They all looked haggard and angry until they realized what was happening.

Toma Bratu made Mr. Sandman open the briefcase. Toma examined the money, closed the briefcase when Mr. Sandman grabbed it from him. I want the Americans on this plane and the British folks on that plane. Then you will get this briefcase. Mr. Sandman knew Toma had no choice if he wanted the money.

When all fourteen people were safely aboard the planes, Mr. Sandman handed Toma the briefcase. Toma turned to walk away and Mr. Sandman turned to board the plane. Halfway up the steps, Mr. Sandman turned and called Toma Bratu's name. Toma Bratu and his driver both turned to face Mr. Sandman, who, as fast as lightening, shot them both dead. Mr. Sandman walk down the steps, over to Toma Bratu and quickly collected the briefcase and boarded the plane. In disbelief Avery yelled, "You killed them both. How did you get Toma Bratu to trust you?" Mr. Sandman shrugged his shoulders and buckled his seatbelt as the plane taxied to the runway.

"Toma Bratu deserved to die. It's called pay back. I killed him, and I will never regret it," Mr. Sandman said with conviction.

Diana looked at Avery and said in French, "Ce la vie."

But, Toma Bratu did not die. He picked up his head and watched the plane take off.

CHAPTER 9
REMI

Diana heard her cell phone ringing. She was in a semi state of slumber and thought it was a dream. Lester answered the phone and shook Diana until she was fully awake. She looked at the clock. It was 03:00. A rock hit the pit of Diana's stomach as she grabbed the phone from Lester. "Hello, who is this calling me at 03:00?"

"It's me, Katrina. Mother had a stroke."

Diana sat straight up. "Oh, God, Katrina. I'm so sorry. Where are you?"

"I'm at Hackensack Hospital. The doctors are examining Mother. I urgently need your help."

"How can I help?" Diana quickly answered as she threw her legs over the side of the bed.

"Please take care of Prudence for me. She is very fragile and needs mothering. You are the only one I trust, Diana."

"Of course. Where is Prudence now?" Diana asked as she got out of bed and motioned for Lester to do the same.

She's with me, here in the emergency room. Mother is very frightened. She speaks a little English, but I can't leave her alone." Katrina sounded desperate.

Diana soothed her fears. "Lester and I are on our way. We'll have Prudence move in with us until you get things settled.

"Thank you. I'll explain things to Prudence. You and Lester will be doing a real mitzvah."

"I didn't know you were Jewish, Katrina."

"Neither does anyone else," Katrina whispered.

It was 04:00 and the emergency room was bustling when Lester and Diana arrived at the hospital. Doctors and nurses were running from bay to bay. There had been a bad accident on Route 17 caused by a drunk driver. Diana and Lester couldn't find anyone to direct them to Katrina and Mother. As they began searching, Diana thought she recognized a young woman who was being put into a wheelchair. Before she had a chance to process who the girl was, she heard Katrina calling her name. "Diana, we're over here".

"Katrina, how's Mother and what the heck is going on in here?" Diana asked loudly over the noise as she and Lester greeted Katrina. Prudence looked like a frightened lost soul. Diana realized that caring for Prudence would be a challenge. That realization spurred Diana on.

Katrina explained that ten minutes after she spoke to Diana, she overheard a nurse say there was a bad car accident involving a tractor-trailer truck and five cars. Diana put her arm around Prudence and whispered, "It's probably best if you come with Lester and me." Prudence silently agreed.

Katrina hugged Prudence knowing how frightened she was. She spoke to her softly explaining that Diana and Lester would take good care of her and protect her. "Take Diana and Lester back to our apartment to collect some of your things. You need to stay with them until I get Mother settled in," Katrina soothingly instructed. Prudence hugged Katrina and left walking in between Lester and Diana. No one noticed the young woman peering clandestinely around a bay curtain.

Her suitcase was opened on her bed as Prudence neatly placed in her belongings. She hadn't spoken to either Diana or Lester except to answer questions with a yes or no. Diana was trying to carefully break down the wall of fear and mistrust Prudence had carefully built up over years of being isolated and suddenly finding out her parents, the only two people she fully trusted, were Russian agents and traitors to the USA, the country Prudence grew up in and loved.. Diana knew she had to tread very carefully. "I have a wonderful idea, Prudence. I would like to hire you as my assistant at the *Van Wyck Detective Agency.* I work there every day and could use the extra help. How does that sound?"

Prudence smiled for the first time. "Will Ross and Avery be there?"

"Yes, when they're not out working on a case they will," Diana answered, feeling gratified that she began to break through the wall. The telephone rang. Diana assumed it was Katrina. "Hello! Katrina is that you?" There was a void on the other end, probably a wrong number. But something instinctively told her otherwise. She began to get that old familiar feeling. Diana didn't like it; she didn't like it at all.

At 08:00 the next morning, Andrei Chernov and his wife Caeley were beginning their day. Their three-year old daughter Riley Kristina Chernov was sitting in her highchair gleefully tossing cereal letter shapes into the air wondering where each one would land.

Andrei was reading a letter he had just received from his father Fedor. Fedor and Kristina Chernov lived in Belarus and had never met Caeley or seen their granddaughter Riley. The letter was to inform Andrei and Caeley that a visit was long overdue. They were planning a trip to finally meet Andrei's wife and their granddaughter Riley Kristina. After reading the letter in Russian aloud to Caeley, Andrei stated, "I better call them to find out the details. I cannot understand why they refuse to learn to e-mail or text. I don't want them just showing up unannounced."

"I'm glad they're coming, but we will need time to prepare. We'll move Riley's crib into our room and buy a trundle bed. I'll empty Riley's dresser and put her clothes into a plastic container which I will store under her crib. Your parents can have the room all to themselves."

Andrei listened to Caeley's plan of action smiling all the while she explained in detail how things would be arranged to accommodate his parents. He walked over to Caeley and pulled her up into his arms asking, "How did I get so lucky to have you?"

Diana brought Prudence with her to the agency at 08:30 to show her around. As her assistant, Diana began assigning menial tasks such as sharpening pencils, making coffee, and replenishing the paper towels and toilet paper in the lavatory. She would slowly increase Prudence's responsibilities as she determined how much Prudence was capable of.

Ross and Avery knew nothing of what had happened the night before. They were surprised to see Prudence sharpening pencils when they walked in at 09:00. "Prudence, what a nice surprise." Avery hit Prudence's cold defensive wall as she tried to hug her. Prudence pulled away and turned her back on Avery.

Diana then explained the circumstances regarding Mother's stroke and Katrina's predicament. "I didn't think you two would mind if Prudence helped me out in the office until Katrina got things settled," Diana asserted.

Ross walked over to Prudence and hugged her. "We don't mind at all. It will be nice to have Prudence with us for a while." Prudence nuzzled into Ross. Avery wasn't paying attention, but Diana was. She thought Prudence held on to Ross a little too long but chalked it up to Prudence's immaturity.

As the week progressed Prudence settled in. Every morning she asked Ross and Avery if they wanted coffee and how they liked it. Each time she handed Ross his coffee she placed her hand on his shoulder. Again, Avery didn't notice, but Diana did. Diana said nothing, wanting to see how this would play out. After a few days, Diana was sure Prudence was developing a crush on Ross. Prudence could not take her eyes off him. Diana began to worry, but knew she needed to tread with the utmost of care.

One afternoon after his last class, Andrei stopped by the *Van Wyck Detective Agency* to inform Diana, Ross and Avery that Fedor and

Kristina Chernov would be coming to town. "That's wonderful news, Andrei. We'll have a lasagna dinner in their honor to welcome them," stated Diana affirmatively.

"That would be great, and it certainly would make them feel welcome," Andrei responded thankfully.

"When will they be arriving? Ross and I are looking forward to meeting them," Avery inquired.

"Exactly one week from today. Next Tuesday to be exact." It was then that Andrei realized that Prudence was curled up on the couch in the corner. "Hi, Prudence, I'm sorry, I didn't see you there," Andrei shamefully admitted. "I hope I'm not intruding on something."

Diana quickly answered, "No, of course not. Mother had a minor stroke and Katrina needs to settle her into the hospital and arrange for her rehabilitation. Prudence will be staying with me until Mother is well enough to be moved into a nursing home for rehab."

Andrei looked at Prudence sorrowfully. "I'm sorry Prudence. I know how close you and Mother have become. I hope she has an easy and speedy recovery."

Prudence looked up at Andrei and flatly stated, "Thank you, so do I."

For a moment there was an uncomfortable pause until Diana broke the silence. "Well, that's it, then. A week from Friday we'll have a lasagna dinner at my house to welcome your parents, Andrei."

"Maybe Ross and I should host the dinner at our house. We have more room," Avery suggested. Diana thanked Avery thinking it was a good idea and noticed a slight smile on Prudence's face. Diana was astute and didn't like what she was witnessing.

Ross and Avery left the agency with Andrei, who was beaming at the thought of his parents meeting Caeley and their three-year old daughter Riley, plus all of his friends.

Mother was admitted into the hospital for tests to determine the severity of her stroke. As things were slow at the Hackensack station, Mr. Sandman told Katrina to take the time off to stay at the hospital. Mother spoke little English and was extremely fearful and suspicious of anyone she didn't know.

Katrina began researching rehabilitation facilities where Russian was spoken. There was a large Russian community in northern New Jersey. Katrina found two facilities that catered to Russian and Eastern European immigrants. Convinced both were equally good, Katrina chose the one closest to her home.

The Elmridge Nursing/Rehabilitation Center was a five-year old facility. Katrina was impressed by how clean and welcoming it appeared when she stepped inside. All staff members seemed competent, well equipped and knowledgeable in their own specialties. Many staff members spoke Russian, which for Katrina, was most important. For Mother to succeed in her rehabilitation, she needed to trust and be able to communicate with her caretakers. The Elmridge seemed the perfect fit.

Katrina stopped into the agency for a quick visit. Prudence ran to Katrina and hugged her tightly. Ross and Avery were out working on a case. Prudence served Diana and Katrina coffee. The milk was running low. Prudence asked permission to go to the store to buy a new container. Diana gave her money and told her to go. She wanted to speak to Katrina privately. Katrina turned to Diana and asked, "Prudence seems happy, but I know her extremely well and sense something is not exactly kosher, if you know what I mean."

Diana smiled at her friend of many years. "I'm glad you picked up on that. I was going to tell you that I fear that Prudence is developing somewhat of a crush on Ross," Diana woefully stated. "The last thing I would ever want is for Prudence to get hurt," Diana added.

Katrina sighed and shook her head. "I knew there was something, but I never would have guessed that."

"Prudence is a good-looking young woman. I think she may need a little attention from the opposite sex, but from the right man, and Ross is not it. I'll handle this situation, Katrina. You don't have to worry about Prudence."

Prudence was just coming out of the market with a container of milk, when a stunning woman with dark hair and piercing green eyes came out of nowhere and blocked her way. "Hello Prudence, do you remember me?" Prudence stopped short and dropped the container of milk on the ground. "I'm sorry, I didn't mean to startle you," apologized the woman.

"I need to bring back milk and I have no more money. You made me drop it," Prudence quietly said as she looked at the milk seeping into the ground.

The woman put her arm around prudence. "No worries! Let's go back into the store together and I'll buy you another container of milk," the woman said as she led Prudence back into the store. Prudence chose another container of milk and began to walk towards the register. "Let me buy something just for you to make up for the spilt milk. Pick anything you want, anything, at all," the woman insisted, smiling at Prudence.

Prudence looked suspiciously at the woman. "Why are you being so nice to me?"

"Don't you remember who I am, Prudence?" The woman was perplexed that Prudence didn't seem to remember her.

Prudence turned, looked closely at the woman's face, and stated, "Yes, now I do. You visited us in St. Lucia a while ago." Prudence's face darkened as she flatly stated, "You were a friend of my parents. They were traitors, you know, to our country."

The woman changed the subject. "Pick out whatever you want, and I will buy it for you."

Prudence stared at her for a moment and then picked up a large bag of potato chips and a few candy bars. "Here, you can buy me these," she whispered as she handed them to the woman.

The woman paid for the items and led Prudence out of the market. "Would you like to go for a coffee.?"

"No, I can't. I need to get back to work."

"Where do you work?" the woman inquired.

"I can't tell you. Thanks for the food, goodbye." Prudence turned and began to walk away, but the woman called out to her.

"Prudence, wait." Prudence stopped and turned to face the woman. The woman asked, "Don't you remember my name?"

"Yes, it's Anna," Prudence answered as she turned and walked away. The woman did not pursue her.

As she walked in the opposite direction, the woman spoke into her cell phone. "I made contact. It will take a while, but I am confident my final goal will be attained. He will die, I promise" It was the middle of the night in Romania, but Toma Bratu had waited anxiously for that call. He smiled, ended the call, and sitting paralyzed in his wheelchair, made his way to bed.

Prudence walked into the agency visibly shaken by her unexpected encounter with Sydney Brewer, who she knew only as Anna. Diana noticed at once and asked Prudence what was wrong. Prudence told Diana a distorted truth saying, "On my way out of the market a woman bumped into me. I dropped the milk and the container broke spilling milk all over the ground. The woman was sorry, so she replaced the milk and bought me some snacks and candy to say she was sorry." Diana listened, smiled, but didn't buy the story. She asked what the woman's name was, but Prudence lied stating that she didn't know. Diana decided not to question Prudence any further, but would, however, stay aware of the situation she believed was unfolding.

Mother began to settle in at the Elmridge Rehab Center. Katrina was there with Mother every day for the first week. The staff began to encourage Katrina to leave and get on with her own life. Many of the staff spoke Russian. Mother was feeling more secure and demanded Katrina go home and care for Prudence. Mother knew how fragile and vulnerable Prudence was, enabling her to convince Katrina to move her attention back to Prudence and her job at the G.W. Government Scientific Research Company. Katrina acquiesced seeing how comfortable Mother had become.

That night she called Diana. Prudence loved working at the *Van Wyck Detective Agency* mainly because she was able to see and be close to Ross every day. Ross and Avery were both kind to Prudence, but Ross seemed warmer, as if he genuinely cared for her, Prudence thought.

Diana agreed to have Prudence continue working at the agency to keep an eye on her. She kept thinking about the encounter with the woman at the market. Diana didn't like it; she didn't like it at all.

Katrina brought Prudence back home to live, every morning dropping her off at the agency to work under Diana's watchful eyes. Diana was certain a situation was unfolding but wasn't sure what it was.

Prudence was on her way to the market to replenish some supplies for the agency. She had no idea she was being watched. Sydney Brewer stepped around the corner and walked nonchalantly towards Prudence, pretending not to notice her. Sydney stopped and smiled warmly. "Oh, my goodness, I can't believe we meet again. How are you, Prudence?" Prudence stopped short. She was taken off guard, staring at Sydney as if she had never seen her before. Sydney knew she had to tread very carefully. "I know things were difficult and confusing for you, Prudence. I just want to be your friend. You don't have many friends, do you?" Sydney gently asked.

Prudence stood with her head down looking at the ground. "No, not really."

"Well, neither do I. Please can we meet for a coffee? Maybe later when you get off from work?" Sydney knew that Prudence was extremely vulnerable. "We can sit and chat like two girlfriends. Wouldn't you like that?"

Prudence looked up at Sydney, smiled and said, "Yes, I would like that. I could use a friend."

Sydney knew she got her. "Great! How about tonight? I'll meet you anywhere you say."

Prudence thought for a minute. "OK, meet me at the diner on Stanford street at six o'clock."

"Thank you, Prudence, I'll look forward to it. See you later." Sydney turned and walked away. She wasn't sure Prudence would actually show up, but it was a start.

Because of her age and bad arthritis, Mother was having a difficult time with her physical therapy. After much trepidation in finding the right physical therapist, Remi Levinson seemed the perfect fit. Remi was gentle with Mother. Patiently and soothing, always speaking to her in Russian. Remi never pushed Mother too hard.

Remi and Katrina often met to discuss Mother's progress. She instantly felt a kinship to Katrina. She and Katrina would sit in the cafeteria over coffee talking about everything and anything. Remi began to realize that she could trust Katrina, that she was the right person to confide in. Remi told Katrina that there was something she needed to discuss with her but needed to talk outside of the rehab center. Katrina was curious yet alarmed. She agreed to meet with Remi that evening.

Sydney Brewer arrived early. Choosing a booth, she sat facing the door. Prudence saw her and smiled, feeling happy that she may have genuinely made a friend. But there was nothing genuine about Sydney Brewer. Her motive was clear; to gain Prudence's trust in order to manipulate her into becoming her puppet.

Sydney confided in Prudence that she knew Ross and Avery from being in the army together. She began to speak disparagingly of Avery, putting her down. This made Prudence smile and Sydney more confident. Prudence was shocked to hear that Ross and Sydney had been lovers and that Avery stole Ross from Sydney, even after she and Ross had a son together, whom Avery also stole. Now, Sydney confessed, she no longer wanted Ross but wanted her son back and revenge on Avery. Sydney's lies were enough to get Prudence's juices flowing. They were enough to inflame Prudence's jealous anger towards Avery.

Sydney then asked Prudence what she thought of Ross. How handsome she thought he was. What she thought it would feel like to be held in his arms, and how she would feel when Ross kissed her passionately. Sydney was touching something deep inside Prudence, a primal sexual desire, the sexual connectedness Prudence yearned for. They agreed to meet again at a location of Sydney's choosing.

Katrina suggested to Remi they meet at *The Double O Club* for dinner. Intuitively Katrina knew Remi needed a safe place, telling Remi that the club was owned by her best friend Diana and her husband Lester. Katrina called Diana, explaining the situation. Diana promised that she and Lester would be on site in case they were needed.

Diana greeted Katrina warmly as she and Remi walked into the club. Katrina introduced Remi to Diana in hopes that Remi would agree, at some point, to have Diana to join them. Diana showed them to a table in a back corner. "If you need me, I will be in my office."

Katrina looked at Remi and waited. "I need to feel I can trust someone," Remi flatly stated in a whisper.

"That's why I brought you here to my friend's club. It's a safe place. You can trust me, Remi," Katrina said as she smiled assuringly at her. "You can also trust Diana and her husband Lester," Katrina added.

Remi bit her bottom lip and looked around nervously. "I know you work for the GW Government Scientific Research Company in Hackensack. There are rumors that that place is not exactly what it appears to be," Remi cautiously told Katrina.

Katrina smiled slightly and asked, "What are the rumors?"

Remi shrugged her shoulders and hesitantly whispered, "That it's some sort of secret intelligence place."

Katrina waited a moment and then said, "Come to the point Remi. What's the problem?" It was the way Katrina asked that told Remi the rumors might be valid.

Remi took a deep breath and stated, "I think that the rehab center is in some way being used by spies to pass and receive information."

Katrina sat back in her chair. After a moment she asked, "If that's true, why didn't you go to the police?"

Remi smiled and asked, "Do you really think the police would have believed me?"

Katrina shook her head no and replied, "You need substantial evidence. Can you supply me with that without getting yourself in trouble?" Remi did not reply. Katrina leaned in close to Remi and whispered, "Tell my mother what you just told me. She will believe you. My mother is a very smart woman. You can trust her implicitly, and she will help you, absolutely."

Remi smiled and put her hands over Katrina's hands. "Thank you." She took out a piece of paper and wrote down her cell number, handed it to Katrina and said, "Now give me yours."

Andrei opened the door. Caeley knew they were on their way up. She was standing by the door with Riley in her arms. Fedor and Kristina Chernov were ecstatic to meet Caeley and their new granddaughter Riley. Caeley showed Andrei's parents to their room and told them to take their time settling in.

Fedor and Kristina liked Caeley and immediately fell in love with Riley. They brought Riley a Russian spinning top, a Russian nesting doll and a variety of other toys. They played with Riley until dinner was ready.

Caeley cooked a typical American dinner of roast beef, mashed potatoes, peas and carrots and apple pie for dessert. During dinner Andrei told his parents they were all invited to his best friend's house on Friday night for a welcome lasagna dinner. He explained that all their friends would be there. Fedor asked Andrei the hosts' names. Andrei enthusiastically answered, "Ross and Avery Lisano." Fedor sat back in his chair, crossed his arms across his chest and smiled.

Sydney Brewer did her homework. She instructed Prudence to meet her at the Hackensack public library that evening. Sydney arrived first. She walked through the fiction section and selected books she deemed suitable for Prudence. They were stories of unrequited love, unfulfilled love, stolen loves, losses of love and anything that would fuel Prudence's anger and jealousy towards Avery.

When Prudence arrived, she found Sydney sitting at a table in a secluded back corner scanning through books. Prudence sat down without speaking. Sydney smiled at Prudence and said, "I picked out some good books for you to read. I read them all. If you read one or two then we can talk about them. That's something girlfriends do, you know," Sydney said offhandedly as she carefully watched Prudence's reaction.

"I can take books out. I have a library card. Katrina got me one when I came to live with her," Prudence innocently told Sydney.

"Who's Katrina?" Sydney asked with a smile.

"Oh, I live with her and her mother." Prudence thought Sydney knew nothing about her. But Sydney knew everything about her.

Sydney maneuvered the conversation back to the books. She handed Prudence two books. Sydney began her assault on Avery. She told Prudence that Ross was a pushover for a good-looking woman, and she,

Prudence was much prettier than Avery. If she tried, Sydney told Prudence, she would have no trouble taking Ross away from Avery.

Prudence became confused. "What would *you* get out of me taking Ross away from Avery?"

Sydney smiled answering, "Revenge, my dear, revenge. You can help me. That *is* what girlfriends do, you know. They help each other."

"I wouldn't know where to start," Prudence answered dismayed at what was happening. Yet, Sydney had awakened something inside of Prudence that had been repressed for a very long time.

"You leave it to me. I will take you shopping for the right clothes. Trust me, Prudence, you can have Ross if you really want him," Sydney assured Prudence.

Prudence smiled and stated, OK, I'll put myself in your hands." Sydney now owned Prudence. They planned to shop the following night. That night Prudence read the two books. She could not put them down. As she read the stories, she related to the underdog, the other woman who eventually loses. This again fueled the fires of anger and jealousy towards Avery.

The next day Diana began to notice how withdrawn Prudence had become over the last week. Diana was not one to sit by to watch and wonder. "Prudence are you alright? You seem to have withdrawn into some sort of a shell. How can I help?"

Diana's questions obviously startled Prudence. She clasped her hands and looked down at the floor before answering. She did not look at Diana when she sheepishly whispered, "I'm fine, really." Diana didn't like it; she didn't like it at all.

Ross and Avery walked in before Diana had a chance to address Prudence. As soon as she saw Ross, Prudence seemed to become a different person. It's not what Prudence said that stunned Diana, but what she did. Although Ross and Avery did not see the shy, withdrawn Prudence who Diana witnessed, they were taken aback by the Prudence who was serving them coffee. This Prudence sashayed around awkwardly attempting to act sexy. Ross and Avery were both amused, but not Diana. She was dreadfully alarmed.

Remi walked into the rehab center with a different mindset. Emotionally buffered by Katrina, she was prepared to talk to Mother about the situation. Remi suspected the rehab center was being used as either a person to person exchange or a dead drop zone for Russian spies, but she needed proof. Today her goal was to disclose her suspicions to

Mother. She and Katrina planned to meet later that day at *The Nut Niche* on Washington Street in Hoboken. Katrina promised to give her something helpful.

Mother was aware that Remi was going to need her help. Katrina had called Mother, and once, during their conversation, referred to Mother as "Babushka", which meant there was a situation and Mother was being summoned to help.

Having been born in Belarus, living under the Soviet regime for most of her life, Mother had no choice but to become smart and tough in order to survive. Years ago, when Katrina became a double agent working for the CIA, Mother secretly became Katrina's best asset. Even back then Diana suspected this though she never knew for certain. It was Katrina and Mother's dislike and mistrust of James Kramer, Diana's husband, that kept them from confiding in Diana. Katrina did not disclose any of this to Remi.

Mother was in the dining room just finishing lunch when Remi approached her. "How are you today, Mrs. Duminski?" Remi asked.

In broken English Mother responded, "I fine. Want coffee? Maybe tea?"

Remi laughed and put her arm around Mother's shoulder. "No thank you. I am on my lunch break. Would you like to sit out in the garden for a while?" Remi made direct eye contact with Mother just as Katrina had instructed. Mother smiled, slightly nodding, indicating she understood. Remi wheeled Mother out into the garden. They spoke in Russian. Mother whispered for Remi to check the area as subtlety as possible for listening devices. Although she found none, Remi whispered, telling Mother of her suspicions.

Ross and Avery were in their office just finishing up a case for a client. They were putting together the proof that their client's wife was having an affair. Diana came into the office with a note. "Please do this for me," Diana said with a serious look on her face. Avery read the note and began to speak, but Diana held up her hand and emphatically stated, "Just do it!" Ross read the note and both he and Avery silently agreed.

Remi clocked out of work and drove to Hoboken. The traffic was heavy and parking difficult, but she was lucky, pulling into a spot just as someone was pulling out two blocks from *The Nut Niche*. Katrina was already there buying a bag of almonds. Remi walked in and stood next to Katrina. "Almonds are very good for you," Katrina said.

"Yes, they are. I think I'll buy a bag," responded Remi.

Katrina guided Remi away from the counter after Remi paid for her bag of nuts. "There's an Italian restaurant, *La Casa Mia*, two blocks up. Meet me there in a half hour," Katrina instructed.

"What am I supposed to do for that half hour?" Remi whispered. Katrina sensed that Remi was frightened.

"I'm just being slightly cautious. No cause to worry. Now leave!" Katrina ordered in a whisper. Remi immediately left the shop and walked towards the Italian restaurant, passed it and went into a boutique. Katrina walked into *La Casa Mia*, got a table for two and ordered a glass of wine.

Prudence stood in front of the diner on Stanford Street. Sydney pulled up in her sleek black car. Prudence hesitated and decided not to get into the car. She began to walk away. Sydney rolled down the window and called out to Prudence to stop. Prudence began to run. As Prudence came to the cross-street Sydney turned the corner and blocked her. "Prudence, what's wrong with you? I thought we were friends. I wanted to take you shopping and treat you to a nice dinner in a beautiful mall with exclusive stores."

"I just got scared when I saw this car. I don't like black cars. Avery was my friend. She helped me. I don't want to hurt her."

"OK, let's forget about that for now. Let's just have a fun shopping and having a nice dinner together. Now please Prudence, get in the car." It was the way Sydney smiled that made Prudence hesitate again, but nevertheless, she got into the car.

Remi stepped over the threshold and spotted Katrina. "Boy, I could really use a drink," were Remi's first words. She seated herself across from Katrina, who motioned for the waiter. Remi ordered scotch on the rocks and responded to Katrina's surprised look with, "My father drank scotch. I guess that's where I get it from." Remi laughed at the look on Katrina's face and stated, "I'm a lot tougher than I look, Katrina." She leaned across the table and whispered, "This whole spy thing is new to me, that's all."

"You do realize, Remi, that I'm getting you involved in all of this even though a large part of me is screaming *NO!*"

"If not me, then who? I work there. I am the logical choice. And by the way, I came to you. I inserted myself into the situation."

"Remi, I need to let certain people know what you suspect."

"I understand, but please don't remove me. I know every inch of that place and most of the people who work there. I'm a valuable asset."

"That you are. I just want you to be safe." Katrina smiled at Remi thinking how brave she was to put herself into such a dicey situation. Katrina took a pen out of her purse and handed it to Remi. "Take this. It will help you get what you need."

"A pen? How can a pen help me?"

Katrina leaned forward and whispered, "It's a camera. They've been using these since the 1980's and they still work. As a physical therapist you must fill out charts and reports. In fact, I've seen you many times with pen in hand," Katrina said as she laughed. She then showed Remi how it worked. Remi was amazed how easy and inconspicuous it was. Katrina was sure that Remi was cut from the right stuff.

They drove about forty minutes. The Short Hills Mall was an upscale mall with expensive stores and restaurants. Here, Sydney was sure she and Prudence would not be seen. But they were seen. Ross and Avery obeyed Diana, following Prudence from the time she left the agency. They were stunned to see Sydney Brewer connecting with Prudence. "What the hell could that bitch possibly want with Prudence Krull?" Avery asked herself. Ross and Avery both knew the complexity of the evil webs Sydney was capable of weaving. It gave them pause. Avery called Diana to report that it was Sydney Brewer with whom they were dealing. Diana ordered them to follow it through to the end.

Sydney took Prudence into small boutiques. Sydney knew fashion and was accurate in helping Prudence choose the styles of clothing which made her look her best. Ross and Avery watched from afar while Sydney bought Prudence a variety of stylish, expensive clothing. Avery whispered to Ross, "I wonder who's funding her and why? We need to find that out, Ross, and quickly. I am sure there is so much more to this."

"I agree, but we have to stay on them until this shopping spree ends and Sydney takes Prudence home."

Avery sneered, "That's another thing. Let's hope Sydney does take Prudence home, back to Katrina. That bitch is insane. I fear for Prudence. Diana is right, we need to stay on them to protect her."

On the ride home Sydney asked Prudence where and when she would wear some of her new things. Innocently, without thinking she answered, "Tomorrow night at Ross and Avery's house. We will all be there for a party." Sydney smiled at how well things were progressing.

Sydney deposited Prudence in front of Katrina's apartment building. Ross and Avery watched Prudence get out of the sleek black car with a new haircut and a plethora of packages of expensive clothing, shoes, and high-end costume jewelry. Sydney waited for Prudence to enter the building, then sped away.

Avery called Katrina informing her that Prudence was on her way up. Diana had already spoken to Katrina to alert her as to what was happening. Katrina then told Diana what was suspected of happening at the Elmridge Rehab Center. They wondered if there could possibly be a connection. Diana told Katrina to bring Prudence to work the next day. Diana would keep her busy until Katrina picked Prudence up and kept her busy until they arrived at Ross and Avery's house.

Avery looked up and saw Katrina at the window. She knew Prudence was safe. Ross drove to the club to meet with Lester and Diana in the secure room. Once there, Diana disclosed that she was sure Prudence had a mad girlish crush on Ross. Diana suggested Sydney was using Prudence in some way to hurt Avery. Diana made it clear to Ross that he was to be aware of this at all times, never encouraging Prudence in any way. "I don't like it; I don't like it at all. This is just the beginning of some treachery that we know nothing about. Plus, Katrina was approached by someone at Mother's rehab center who suspects the center is being used as a mailbox for the Soviets. There is no obvious connection to Sydney Brewer, but, as we all know, there never is," Diana explained.

"Well, gang," Lester exclaimed, "It's time to go to the boss. We must tell Mr. Sandman."

"We'll all be together tomorrow night. We could set up a time and place to meet then," suggested Avery. They agreed.

"The next topic is Prudence. We need to grasp her out of the clutches of Sydney Brewer. Katrina and I will talk to her together on Saturday morning. Katrina invited me for breakfast. I think you should be there, Avery. You and Prudence were childhood friends. That should count for something," Diana concluded.

"If it will help Prudence, of course I'll come with you Aunt Diana. We must try to make Prudence understand that Sydney Brewer is not the person she's pretending to be, but is evil, insane and very dangerous. In fact, Dr Payne told me that from the way I described Sydney, she probably has some sort of antisocial personality disorder."

"That sounds grim," murmured Ross.

"It is indeed," concluded Lester.

As they stood up to leave, Diana stated, "There is one more thing." Looking directly at Ross and Avery Diana emphatically stated, "You must keep Ralf and Kimmy hidden and safe until this insane bitch is put away again. Please, put my mind at ease. Tell me you'll do it now!"

Ross put his arm around his aunt and assuredly answered, "We promise. Tomorrow morning Avery and I will escort Ralf into school, speak to his teacher and to the principal. Mindo knows and has already taken the precautions which Avery and I set up."

"Excellent," answered Diana. She then turned to Lester. I want a 24/ 7 watch on all our children immediately. Not just Ralf and Kimmy, but Peter, Albee, and Nika, as well. I will never allow any of our children to ever go through that horror again."

Lester put his arms around Diana and stated, "Consider it done, my darling!"

The next day, Friday, Fedor Chernov asked his son Andrei if he could borrow his car. He wanted to take Kristina, Andrei's mother, to visit an old friend from Belarus who was in a nursing facility nearby. Andrei was happy to oblige.

Fedor and Kristina dropped Andrei at Whyler-Stills University where he taught Russian history and culture, and Russian literature. "Quick, let me out, Papa. There's one of my dearest friends and I would like to introduce you." Andrei jumped out of the car and shouted, "Paul, Professor Paul Richards, please come here and meet my parents." The Professor quickly walked over to Andrei, who introduced him to his parents. They spoke for a few moments. Fedor asked the Professor if he played chess. The two men agreed to get together for a chess game before Fedor and Kristina went back to Belarus. Andrei was exceedingly pleased. Fedor agreed to pick Andrei up after his classes and they headed for the nursing facility.

Katrina dropped Prudence off at the detective agency at exactly 09:00. Diana was waiting at the door with a big smile and a warm welcome. As Prudence stepped out of Katrina's car Diana immediately noticed the transformation. First, Diana saw the high-heeled shoes, then the perfectly fitting short skirt, and the form-fitting shirt. She wore just the right amount of jewelry and makeup to make a statement, but to not be obvious. Her hair had been styled and cut, framing her oval face just right. Katrina looked at Diana and rolled her eyes. "You look very nice today, Prudence," Diana said as she escorted Prudence inside.

"Please, don't patronize me with your false compliments," Prudence sneered, almost to herself, as she pulled away from Diana. Diana stopped moving and watched in amazement as Prudence made her way to the small kitchen to make the coffee. Under normal circumstances Diana would have immediately fired her aide for her rudeness. But, nothing about this was normal. Diana decided not to answer, but to become an observer. In the game Prudence seemed to be playing that was all Diana could do until she understood the game and its rules.

As Prudence went about her morning chores Diana noticed her having trouble maneuvering in her high-heeled shoes but said nothing. When Ross and Avery came in and saw the transformation, they acted happily surprised.

Prudence went about her chores the same as she did every day. What changed was her attitude. She treated Avery with contempt and Ross with kid gloves. Finally, Prudence mustered up the courage to confront Avery. "I know when I reached out to you, Avery, you came through and helped rescue me off of Saint Lucia. But be honest, Avery, you didn't really do it for me. You did it to make yourself look good, like the perfect heroine you think you are." With those words Prudence locked herself in the bathroom. Diana stayed the observer. Avery pulled Ross into their office and shut the door.

"We need to leave, calling it quits for the day. I can't take any more of this craziness. Besides, we need to go home and help Mindo set up for the party."

Ross thought about it. "Do you really think it's wise to leave Aunt Diana alone with Prudence?"

"Absolutely! Aunt Diana can easily handle Prudence, but I can't. Now let's get the hell out of here!" Ross and Avery came out of their office. Prudence was sitting on the couch in the reception area and Diana was behind her desk on the computer. Explaining that they needed to meet with a client, Ross and Avery abruptly left leaving Prudence looking obviously bewildered, but Diana understood completely. Diana didn't like it; she didn't like it at all but continued to remain the observer.

Once they left the agency Avery began texting Diana regarding Prudence's bizarre behavior. Diana told Avery they would deal with Prudence on Saturday morning and not before. Diana told Avery to stop texting her. She was afraid Prudence might get spooked and bolt. Avery agreed.

Fedor and Kristina arrived at the nursing facility. Nadia, Kristina Chernov's childhood friend had moved to the United States many years ago with her husband Dimitri to live with their daughter and her family. Now elderly and ailing, Nadia needed full-time care. Two years ago, Nadia moved into the Elmridge as a permanent patient.

When Kristina and Fedor walked into Nadia's room, the surprise was astounding, and the tears began flowing. It was a momentous, emotional reunion. Dimitri, Nadia's husband, had passed away. The two couples were long-time friends. Seeing Fedor and Kristina brought back memories of the four of them together as young people. Nadia held Kristina tightly sobbing uncontrollably. Nadia began to calm down and the two women talked somberly of the old days and caught up on the years in between.

Fedor excused himself. He walked out into the hall and looked around. A few aids were walking in and out of patients' rooms. An orderly was pushing an old man in a wheelchair. It was late spring, and the days were turning warmer. The doors to the garden were opened and many patients were sitting outdoors. Fedor walked back into Nadia's room. He suggested to Kristina and Nadia they take advantage of the beautiful day and sit out in the garden. Fedor and Kristina sat Nadia in her wheelchair, covered her with a blanket, and wheeled her out into the garden to a bench where Kristina sat next to Nadia's wheelchair. Kristina patted the bench, motioning for Fedor to sit down, but he excused himself to go use the bathroom.

Remi drove in and parked her car. She turned the car off, sat for a moment and took a deep breath. She pulled her purse onto her lap, stuck her hand into her purse and pulled the special pen out just far enough to see it. For a brief moment, a shadow of a doubt passed over her, but Remi knew she was not imagining what she suspected. Unfortunately, Remi knew traitorous occurrences were taking place among her patients whose lives she tried to make better. Because of her findings, Remi believed it was her civil duty to protect those patients she cared for by collecting the proof she needed to substantiate her accusations to Katrina.

Remi clocked in, put her things in her locker, took her special pen out of her purse and put it into her pocket. She looked at her watch. Seeing that she had time for one more cup of coffee, Remi headed to the employees' cafeteria. As she passed the library Remi noticed a strange man looking around the bookshelves as if looking for something specific. This gave her pause. She positioned herself where she could not be seen. Remi instinctively knew to take a photo of the strange man. This was probably nothing, she thought, but if it was something, she had his photo.

The man pulled a book off of the top shelf. He inserted something into the spine of the book and placed it on the very bottom shelf of the same bookcase. He left through a door on the other side of the library. Remi waited in case the man or his contact came back to collect the book.

Remi realized she had a patient in ten minutes. It was now or the opportunity would be missed. Like a flash, she grabbed the book, stuck it under her arm under her jacket and made her way to her locker. No one was around. She opened her locker, put the book inside, closed her locker and went to her first patient. What Remi did not realize was that everything she did was seen on camera.

Later that afternoon when Remi carefully examined the book she found nothing within the book or in the spine of the book. The only thing that was discovered was that Remi Levinson was on to them. Now Remi was in a dangerous situation and could not return to work. Katrina took Remi to the Hoboken safe house and placed her under the protection of Blake and Veronica, where she would stay until the situation at Mother's rehab was resolved.

Diana and Lester were the first to arrive. Avery was unnerved by Prudence's bizarre behavior as was Ross knowing how Prudence felt about him. Because of the amount of people coming, Ross and Avery decided to serve buffet style. They opened the patio doors and set tables and chairs outside as well. Ross and Mindo hung up white lights and Avery lit a candle on each table making the patio's appearance very inviting. People were greeting Fedor and Kristina and each other. Every time Avery was near or passed by Prudence, she smelled her own perfume. Prudence had decided to buy it, thinking Ross had to like it.

It was one of those balmy nights where the first fragrant smell of summer, mixed with a bit of ozone made the air intoxicating and the night alluring. The dinner was in full swing. Albert and Sandra kept the food organized and Ross and Poppy kept the wine flowing.

Everyone was eating, drinking, talking, laughing, joking and having a wonderful time, all except Prudence. Her anger and jealousy were raging, soaring towards Avery. Prudence decided that the next day she would dye her hair blonde. Ross obviously liked blonde hair. She was jealous of Avery's smile and perfect teeth. But, worst of all, she kept seeing Avery in bed with Ross, hearing her moaning as she pulled him in. Prudence was obsessed with that picture. She kept picturing that scene over and over again in her mind. Prudence's mind was working overtime.

The weird stare Avery was getting from Prudence was making Avery very uncomfortable. She knew Prudence was having a very hard time adjusting. Avery decided to sit next to Prudence and speak to her. As she walked close to Prudence Avery asked, "Prudence, are you OK? Can I get you anything?"

Prudence slowly stood up and exploded. "I hate you, Avery, I really, really hate you," she screamed. Everyone stared in disbelief. Prudence turned, ran through the house and out the front door.

Diana put her arm around Avery and explained, "She doesn't hate you, Avery, she wants to be you." As Prudence ran away, two shots rang out. One hit Mr. Sandman and the other hit Avery, missing Diana by a fraction of an inch.

Diana caught Avery's fall as Ross rushed to her side. Fortunately, Avery was only hit in the shoulder. Mr. Sandman was not so lucky. He was hit in the chest. Lester and Poppy worked on him to stop the bleeding while Albert call for an ambulance for both Mr. Sandman and Avery. Avery kept screaming for someone to check on Ralf and Kimmy. A guard had been placed outside their bedrooms. Althea ran up to check and quickly came back to reassure Avery they were fine. She then promised Avery and Ross that she and Gabe would stay with Mindo to watch Ralf and Kimmy.

Sydney waited around the corner. Seeing Prudence run out of the house and down the block, she quickly ordered her driver to speed towards Prudence. Sydney ordered her to get into the car. Prudence was happy and relieved to see Sydney and jumped into the car. They drove back into Manhattan to the hotel where they were based, escaping once again.

Two ambulances had been dispatched. Ross rode with Avery in one and Lester and Diana with Mr. Sandman in the other. He was barely conscious. Diana held his hand, telling him to keep squeezing her hand. Mr. Sandman needed a trauma center. He was being transported to Hackensack Hospital. Ross and Avery demanded they went where their boss went.

Avery was patched up and released. Lester, Diana, Ross and Avery were sitting in a family waiting room when Esther Brouce came bounding in, out of breath and very upset. As soon as she spotted Diana, she ran to her. "He's not going to die, right?" Esther looked at each one of them, not knowing that Avery had been shot also. "Avery, I'm so sorry. I didn't know you were hit also." Esther put her hand on Avery's other shoulder.

"Don't worry, Esther, our man will make it. He wouldn't dare leave us, he wouldn't dare," Avery stated as she stood up and hugged Esther.

Esther looked at Diana and Lester and asked, "Tell me right now, who did this?"

Ross answered, "Sydney Brewer for sure, but we don't know who she's working for ."

"We do know that she has Prudence Krull and it's all my fault. I should have stopped it the minute my gut told me to. I let my guard down and all of this is on me for not doing my job properly," Diana declared somberly.

"No, Diana, don't do this. It's not your fault," Lester answered.

"He's right Diana. You're not to blame, Sydney Brewer is," Esther Brouce responded.

Poppy came into the waiting room alone explaining that Lorelei stayed with Albert and Sandra at the house to take care of things on that end. He also told them that they were tracking Prudence's phone. It led the collection team to a hotel in Manhattan. The team would arrest Sydney Brewer and her people. They would bring Prudence Krull back to Diana and Lester. "Poor Prudence, she really got the brunt of it, didn't she?" Poppy asked.

It was the way Poppy said it that made Diana begin to sob uncontrollably into Lester's chest. The doctor walked into the room. Diana stopped sobbing and they all turned to face the doctor. "It was touch and go. The bullet was very close to the heart. He was lucky. He's strong, in good physical shape and he's healthy. If he makes it through the next couple of hours, then chances are he'll make a full recovery. Take turns going in to see him one at a time. Hold his hand, talk to him, let him know you're here. I'll check in on him in a few hours." They thanked the doctor as he left the waiting room.

"I'm first," stated Esther Brouce as she stood up and walk towards the man she had grown to know and love.

When the collection team stormed the hotel room in Manhattan, all they found was a scared young woman curled on the bed in a fetal position with the gun that shot Mr. Sandman and Avery next to her on the bed. The only fingerprints on the gun belonged to Prudence Krull.

Poppy ordered the team to bring Prudence to the Hoboken safe house where Katrina, Blake and Veronica were waiting to accept her. No charges would ever be pressed against Prudence. They all knew who pulled the trigger.

The moment she stepped into the Hoboken safe house, Katrina asked Veronica where Remi was.

Katrina knocked softly on the attic door. "Remi, it's me, Katrina, please let me in." Remi flung open the door and hugged Katrina as hard as she could.

"Oh, Katrina, I'm so scared," cried Remi.

"Remi, that man, the one whose photo you took, I've seen him before," Katrina whispered. "He was at the party, the welcome dinner I went to. He came with one of the guests, but I don't know who. It all went sideways tonight. I don't know if any of this is connected, but you can never go back to the rehab center or your apartment, for that matter. You have to stay here, hidden until all of these people are arrested. You were right, the center is being used as a mailbox."

Veronica came up and Blake waited downstairs to accept Prudence from the collection team. "We'll get your cat for you and anything else you need from your apartment. Just give me a list," Veronica said smiling assuredly at Remi.

They heard the team arrive with Prudence. Katrina hugged Remi, promising to come back soon for a visit. She and Veronica ran down the stairs. Lester and Diana came in just behind the team and Prudence. Both Blake and Veronica signed off to accept Prudence. Once the papers were signed, the team left.

Prudence had a blank look in her eyes, as if her soul was no longer there. Katrina hugged her warmly and whispered, "None of this is your fault, Prudence, my dear."

Prudence pushed Katrina away exclaiming, "I would have killed Avery if I had that gun, I'm sure I would have. I hate Avery. Why can't I take Ross away from her? What makes her so special? I'm just as pretty, I have nice clothes, I can dye my hair blonde and wear the same perfume...." Prudence kept ranting on, spouting out all of the lines that Sydney Brewer fed her.

Katrina pulled Diana aside while Veronica listened to Prudence. "Diana, we have no choice but to commit her into a mental hospital. She is very damaged. We need to do it tonight for her own good."

"I feel so guilty, Katrina. Maybe if I had stopped it..."

Katrina cut Diana off. "No, it would not have mattered. I began noticing little things. Prudence was beginning to unravel. I never dreamed it would come to this. Think of it this way, Diana, if Prudence had gotten her hands on a gun, she really might have killed Avery. In some weird way, Sydney Brewer may have actually saved Avery's life without realizing it."

Diana stood still, like a statue, staring at Katrina, listening to what she was suggesting. "Yeah!" Diana sighed and hugged Katrina asking, "Has anyone ever told you how very smart you are?"

Katrina laughed, "Yes, a few. You, me and Lester have to take her to Hackensack hospital now, tonight. She needs help. Let's get it for her," Katrina said as she looked to Diana for approval.

"Yes, let's go," Diana said as she and Katrina walked towards Prudence. Lester helped them into the car and that night Prudence Krull began her long road back to sanity.

Veronica stood at the attic window with Remi watching. "There by the grace of God go I," whispered Remi.

Veronica laughed, and said, "It's funny you should say that. My friend Lorelei said the same thing at my funeral!" Startled by those words, Remi turned and looked at Veronica. "It's a long story I don't care to share right now," Veronica responded. Remi smiled, silently acknowledging Veronica's wishes.

There was a knock on the door. Katrina said, "The man in the photo who I saw at the Party was Andrei Chernov's father, Fedor Chernov. Remi, this is very serious. What did you find hidden in that book?"

Remi shook her head as she answered, "That's just it, Katrina, I found nothing. Fedor Chernov is not involved in this. The only thing I did was to let them know I'm now on to them, and believe me Katrina, I'm scared to death."

"Now that we know this is actually happening, the situation will be taken care of and resolved thanks to your bravery, Remi," Katrina assured her.

"What do I do now?" Remi asked, uncertain of where her life was headed.

"Go back to Colorado. Live with your parents for a while. We'll pay for your move and I'll keep in touch with you, I promise," Katrina assured her.

Remi smiled; relieved Katrina was going to help her. "OK, it's a deal," Remi answered, certain that she and Katrina would always remain friends.

CHAPTER 10
JACK PIERCE - PART 1

Amazing as it seemed, it was true. James Kramer, aka, Alexei Stamenov, was dead. A definite kill, but not by Diana, Lester or any other American. James Kramer was suffocated in his hospital bed by Glenda and her Soviet comrade Sergei Alexandrov. Group Eleven was thankful, especially Diana and Lester, for that chapter to have come to a definitive end.

When Lester, Diana, Asa, Barry and JB arrived home from Spain they received the word. Barry and JB had been reassigned. The location of their assignment had not and would never be disclosed. Group Eleven would be getting a new couple. With that announcement, there was much trepidation among the group members. While they were all sad to lose Barry and JB, some suffered higher anxiety levels regarding the change more than others.

At *The Double O Club* secure room, Group Eleven, in its entirety, was waiting for Mr. Sandman to arrive with the new couple. This latest addition, newly trained from the Couple's Program, was hand-picked by Mr. Sandman. They would begin with the understanding that their first assignment was probationary. Lester and Diana would have to approve in order for them to become permanent members of Group Eleven.

Avery and Veronica were sitting at a table in a corner quietly having a lively discussion regarding Barry and JB's reassignment. Both women had worked closely with the two men, especially Veronica. She, Barry and JB had worked as a team together for over a year. The two men had saved Veronica's life more than once.

Avery had worked clandestinely with Barry and JB in regard to Lorelei. Neither man had ever betrayed Avery, which to her was paramount. Trust was a big issue for Avery, and she grew to completely trust Barry and JB. Now they were gone, and Avery deeply felt their loss.

Veronica and Avery both concluded that they had no choice but to give the new couple a chance. Both agreed, however, that the new couple would have to prove themselves to gain their trust, and that would not be an easy task.

Sandra and Lorelei, hearing part of Avery and Veronica's discussion, now joined them at the table. Lorelei immediately voiced her disagreement. "I think you two are starting out in a negatively judgmental way that is not fair to the new couple," Lorelei espoused, looking directly at Avery. Avery felt the angst rising in her chest.

"What right do you have to lecture me and Veronica about trust?" Avery's voice began to fill the air.

Lorelei sensed Avery's angst and responded calmly. She looked at both Avery and Veronica and quietly stated, "I don't believe Mr. Sandman would ever allow anyone to enter our group without completely screening them first."

Avery snidely responded, "Really? He let you in and we don't really know who you are, do we?" Those words heavily hung in the air unanswered.

Ross quickly began to walk over to the table with Albert, Poppy, and Blake, but stopped, changing his mind. "Let's not get involved. Let them work through this themselves."

"Good idea. Let's get a drink instead," Albert sneered amusingly.

"I just don't want them ganging up on Lorelei," Poppy exclaimed.

"Give it a rest. Lorelei still has to prove herself after the Moscow incident," Ross quietly snapped at Poppy.

"Lorelei doesn't have to prove a thing!" Poppy growled, secretly not fully believing his own words. Poppy truly loved his wife Lorelei and would always defend her no matter what his true inner feelings were. That was a dangerous place for him to be; he knew it and so did the rest of the group. Everyone had their eyes wide opened when it came to Lorelei.

Blake had enough of Ross and Poppy's bickering. He told them to shut the hell up and let their wives work out their own issues. He then added, "Believe me, if they don't, Diana will get involved and it won't be pretty. So, let's have that drink and toast Barry and JB, wherever they are."

Lorelei answered Avery's loaded question herself. "This has nothing to do with me or you, Avery, or any of us. We need to accept our new teammates as our equals and start out by giving them the respect they deserve, not negative mistrust. That's all I mean," Lorelei explained.

Sandra had been quiet up to now. She and Avery, over the last few years, had become best friends. She understood Avery and didn't disagree with her assessment of Lorelei. However, in this case Sandra felt she had to accept the new couple without prejudgment. "I know trust is a major issue for both of you. There is no right or wrong. It's a personal choice we all have to make for ourselves. Eventually, this new couple, whoever they are, will have to prove themselves to all of us."

"Ah, finally, words of reason," Diana said smiling as she approached the four women. Diana had overheard most of the conversation. Unless she dealt with this immediately, Diana knew Avery and Veronica could cause potential problems with the new couple unnecessarily within Group

Eleven. She decided to speak to Lester about the situation privately later that night when they were alone. She would meet with Avery and Veronica individually the next day to address each of their personal issues. Both Avery and Veronica knew by the look on Diana's face that she was not happy.

The door to the secure room opened. All talking and activities ceased. The atmosphere in the room changed. Mr. Sandman sensed the change, smiling at his fleeting thought that he walked into a room of mannequins. Behind Mr. Sandman tentatively followed an African American couple in their late twenties. He understood that acceptance was a process, but he needed to integrate Jeff and Chloe Bronson into Group Eleven quickly. Asa Page called in the chips. He needed Mr. Sandman's help to find a missing CIA operative.

Lester and Diana walked through the door of their condo. They stopped short in unison. Lester took out his gun. Someone was in their house and they sensed it the moment they stepped over the threshold. Lester held the gun in his right hand and held Diana back with his left, pushing her back outside because she was not armed. At the same time a light went on in the living room and a familiar voice boomed, "I didn't think you'd mind if I waited in here". It took a moment for them to recognize the voice. Diana pushed her way in front of Lester.

"What the hell are you doing here, Asa? You could have called and told us to expect you, but of course we all know that's not your style." Lester still had the gun pointed at Asa Page.

Asa stood up and walked over to Lester. Turning to Diana he said, "Good to see you again." To Lester he said, "Please put that thing away. Guns make me nervous." Asa extended his hand to Lester. Lester shook Asa's hand and holstered his gun as Mr. Sandman walked into the room.

Upon seeing Mr. Sandman Diana began to laugh. "I'm glad Ross wasn't with us. He can't stand all this clandestine intrigue. He probably would have killed you, Asa." Lester and Mr. Sandman laughed, but Asa did not. Asa Page was serious. He needed their help. "What's this all about"? Diana asked as she gestured for all of them to sit down.

"I need your help in locating a missing CIA operative. His name is Jack Pierce and there are three possibilities. Either he was murdered and buried on the island of Tortola in the Caribbean, which is probable. Or, he's a prisoner in either North Korea or China, or he was a prisoner and is dead, either of which is slim. Whatever the truth, I must know what happened to him."

After a moment of silence Diana asked, "Why is this so important? Who is this guy to you?" Asa looked at Mr. Sandman who gave him the nod to reveal the circumstances.

Asa page took a deep breath. By the look on Asa's face and his long mournful sigh, Diana knew it had to be a grim personal story. "Jack Pierce is my son," Asa flatly stated, casting his eyes downward. Diana thought she saw a tear forming in the corner of his eye. "He was CIA, but the CIA denies any knowledge of Jack. As far as they're concerned, Jack Pierce never existed. So, I want to hire the Van Wyck Detective Agency to help me do the job." Asa glanced at Mr. Sandman silently asking him to continue.

"Look, Asa put his life on the line when we needed his help and now it's our turn to help him," Mr. Sandman quietly stated. Both Lester and Diana silently agreed. "Good, now here's how we're going to play it. Ross and Avery must go, Blake and Veronica must go, Jeff and Chole should go to get their feet wet and you two need to go to supervise."

"Go, go where?" Diana asked with a hint of uncertainty.

"To Tortola." Asa and Diana locked eyes. She knew she owed him more than anyone.

"What if he is in Asia? How will we know that?" Lester inquired.

Mr. Sandman smiled. "Don't worry about that. I've already taken care of that end of things." By his response, Lester and Diana knew not to question him any further.

"It's also about the trust issue that both Avery and Veronica are struggling with, isn't it?" Diana asked.

Mr. Sandman smiled. "Yes and no. I am sending Jeff and Chole with two of our strongest couples. They could learn a lot from them if the opportunity should present itself. And yes Diana, Avery and Veronica are both struggling with trust issues. I know Jeff and Chloe. They can and will win Avery and Veronica's trust in the end. Besides, you and Lester will be there to make sure they do."

Diana stood up and suggested she put up a pot of coffee. "You wouldn't by any chance have any of those great donuts I had the last time I was here?" Asa asked, his face lighting up.

"No, but I can get them in just two minutes," Lester answered as he jumped up and ran out the door.

"Geez, Diana, I didn't mean for Lester to go out to the store to get donuts," Asa answered, stunned by Lester's kind gesture.

Both Diana and Mr. Sandman laughed. "Believe me Asa, unfortunately Lester loves those donuts more than you do," Diana informed him. Diana turned serious. "I'm going to speak to Avery and Veronica individually tomorrow, Earl"

"In all honesty, Diana, I think you should speak to them together. They may find that more helpful," Mr. Sandman advocated.

Diana thought for a moment answering, "Yeah, I see your point. You might be right. OK, I'll speak to them together."

"I'll get the ball rolling right now." Mr. Sandman called Blake and Veronica, ordering them to be at the Van Wyck Detective Agency at 09:00 sharp the next morning. Lester came back with two boxes of donuts and the four of them moved into the kitchen.

The offices of the G.W. Government Scientific Research Company were located in Hackensack, which was the county seat of Bergen County, New Jersey. It was 07:00 and people were just beginning to arrive in the parking garage. Mr. Sandman was thinking about the situation surrounding Asa Page and his son known as Jack Pierce. He called in a favor to a friend and had the Asian piece covered. The Tortola piece would be a bit trickier. Asa would hire Ross, Avery and Diana from the Van Wyck Detective Agency. But how would he justify sending two CIA couples and Lester with them? He knew he would figure it out, he always did.

As Mr. Sandman approached his office, he saw a light emanating from underneath his office door. He stopped and put his hand on his holstered gun. Standing to the side he slowly pushed the door open. "Good morning, Earl," chimed a familiar voice. He stepped into his office.

Esther Brouce, Mr. Sandman's boss, and the head of all stations in the northeast sector, was sitting on his desk with her legs crossed. Without speaking, he went over, took Esther in his arms and kissed her passionately. He then whispered, "I sincerely hope this pleasant surprise means you will be staying with me for a few days?"

"Yes, it does, and I have missed you." Esther kissed him back.

"I've missed you, too." Mr. Sandman answered, smiling. Looking Esther in the eyes he asked, "Besides missing each other, which is reason enough to be here, what's the real situation?"

Esther gently pushed Mr. Sandman away and stood up straight. She stepped back a few steps. "So far, I have turned a blind eye to your... connection, if you know what I mean, to the Van Wyck Detective Agency. But this business Asa Page brought you regarding Jack Pierce...."

Mr. Sandman held up his hand and cut Esther off. "Hold on, let me explain. I owe Asa. He helped me when I needed him, and he came through all the way. I don't know if you know this, but Jack Pierce is Asa's son." Esther smiled and took a step forward.

"Yes, Earl, I do know that." Esther and Mr. Sandman stood still looking at each other. He waited for her to continue. "I feel as if I'm balancing on a tight rope. The CIA has denied any knowledge of Jack Pierce as I am sure you know. It's one thing to use Ross, Avery and Diana as detectives, but to send two CIA couples, one of which is a newbie and Lester...that's not by the book."

"Sometimes you just can't go by the book, Esther. It's his son, for God's sake. From where I'm sitting the CIA owes Asa that much." Mr. Sandman was becoming upset, raising his voice.

"I don't disagree with you, Earl. But we have to look at the wider picture. Who, may I ask is going to pay for this? I know that Diana, Ross and Avery will be covered by their agency, but how can I justify sending Lester, and two CIA couples to the Caribbean?"

Mr. Sandman smiled, avoiding Esther's questions. "There is also a trust issue involved that needs to be dealt with. Plus, one other issue you would be very interested in. It's complicated, but I have it all worked out, my dear."

"What kind of trust issue and between whom? And what other issue?" Esther asked, removing her glasses. Mr. Sandman cocked his head to the side smiling widely. Esther sat down, looked up at Mr. Sandman, sighed deeply and said, "OK, spell it out for me!"

There was a knock on his door. "Oh good, they're here. Now I can spell it out for you, Esther," Mr. Sandman said as he opened the door.

At 09:00 Mr. Sandman and Esther Brouce were having coffee and donuts in the Van Wyck Detective Agency with Lester, Diana, Ross, Avery, Blake, Veronica and Asa Page. Mr. Sandman, in his three-piece suit and tie, took his usual stance; feet apart and hands behind his back. Avery smiled as she remembered him standing that way the first time they met. She remembered wanting to laugh at his name but restrained herself. As he began speaking Avery realized that first memory of Mr. Sandman seemed a lifetime ago.

"This meeting is in regard to the upcoming operation, which is off the books. I purposely did not invite the new couple, Jeff and Chloe, because we need to address the trust issue which both Avery and Veronica seem to be struggling with. All I'll say to you two is that Jeff and Chloe Bronson are now part of our family and you two need to get over it quickly. Jeff and Chloe will earn your trust, but you need to give them the chance to do that without any hindrance." Mr. Sandman paused looking directly at Avery and Veronica. "Do I make myself clear?"

In unison both women answered, "Yes Sir."

"And now I will turn the floor over to Asa. He was there for us when we needed him. He will now explain his dilemma." Mr. Sandman motioned for Asa to take over.

Asa stood up and explained. "A CIA operative using the name Jack Pierce disappeared. Since then the CIA has denied any knowledge of Jack Pierce. I was incensed and took it upon myself to search. I have discovered that he is either a prisoner in Asia, namely China or North Korea, died in Asia or was murdered and buried on the Caribbean island of Tortola. Mr. Sandman has the Asian piece covered. I need to hire the Van Wyck Detective Agency to investigate the Tortola piece." Asa glanced at Mr. Sandman signaling for him to take over.

Avery asked, "Why are you so interested in finding this mysterious Jack Pierce?"

Asa revealed that Jack Pierce was his son and used the name Jack Pierce as an alias, explaining, that's what he was known as so that's who they will search for. Curious, Avery asked, "What's your son's real name?" Avery knew not to ask that question, but nevertheless asked.

"That's irrelevant," curtly answered Asa.

Avery dropped it, to everyone's relief. To herself she whispered, "It may not be."

"What was that?" Asa asked looking directly at Avery.

Avery repeated her words, "It may not be." Asa smiled, not answering Avery but thinking that he liked her tenacity. The atmosphere began to take on a slightly confrontative buzz, but Mr. Sandman neutralized it.

Standing up once again and taking his usual stance, he informed them that this undocumented operation would be mostly a camping trip in the mountains of Tortola for Ross, Avery, Blake, Veronica, Jeff and Chloe. The first two days, however, they would stay at a hotel and spend their time talking to the locals, including the police. Mr. Sandman warned that the locals would be very reticent to speak with them.

Lester and Diana would be based at the hotel where they would monitor the operation. He paused and then explained that for Jeff and Chloe this would be a training exercise enabling them to become familiar with their teammates. Mr. Sandman emphasized that there were two things Jeff and Chloe were not to know. One, that Avery and Veronica have trust

228

issues, and two, that the exercise to find Jack Pierce in Tortola was unofficial and undocumented.

Asa Page stood up and asked, "Where do I fit into this? Will I be staying at the hotel or going with the team up the mountain?"

"I'm sorry Asa, but I can't let you go on this one," Mr. Sandman quietly answered.

"Please! If it's a matter of money, I'll stay at the hotel with Diana and Lester and pay for it myself. I promise not to interfere with the team. I just want to be on Tortola while the search is happening," Asa begged.

Mr. Sandman looked hard at him. "OK, Asa, pay for the hotel yourself and you can come. However, you must remain at the hotel during the entire operation. you are not to participate or interfere in any way. Is that clear?"

Asa noticeably relaxed. "Yes Sir, thank you Sir."

Veronica raised her hand asking, "Jeff and Chloe appeared to be highly intelligent when we met them. They will inevitably ask questions. What then?"

Mr. Sandman clearly spelled it out. "Only tell them what they need to know and do not delve into the past. Treat the search for Jack Pierce as a training exercise because actually, for Jeff and Chloe, it is. OK, that's it, folks. The plane will be waiting at Teterboro at 09:00 tomorrow. Pack accordingly. The mountains in Tortola are very steep and extremely rugged in some places. You definitely will not need formal wear," Mr. Sandman said laughing. "All of your equipment will be on the plane including a tent for each couple. My cousin Tito from St. Lucia will meet you at the plane and be your connection to the Police Chief of Road Town, the main town in Tortola. Blake, will you and Veronica please inform Jeff and Chloe of the situation?"

"Yes Sir. We'll meet with them now," Blake answered as he took his phone out of his pocket. He and Veronica left the agency.

Esther Brouce stood up and wished them all luck. She walked over to Asa Page and gave him a hug. "I sincerely hope they can help you find your son alive and well." Asa hugged Esther back and thanked her. Esther then turned to Mr. Sandman and seductively whispered, "I'll see you later."

Once Esther Brouce left, Avery took the opportunity to ask Mr. Sandman why they had to live in tents instead of at the hotel with Diana and Lester. He looked at Avery and answered, "Because it will be good for you, that's why. You're all becoming too soft. This is a training exercise for Jeff and

Chloe, and you must stay in the mountains to thoroughly search for Jack Pierce. We have intel which you'll receive on the plane. Don't worry, we are not throwing the six of you haphazardly into danger. By the time you arrive in Tortola things will become clear."

Avery explained that it wasn't searching in the mountains that bothered her and Ross but sleeping in a tent that bothered them. Mr. Sandman was astonished asking, "What the hell is wrong with you two ex-military personnel?"

Ross put his hand on Avery's shoulder indicating she should let him answer. "You're right, Sir. I guess we were just surprised. It's been years since we went camping and we're just not used to it anymore."

It was not Avery's nature to remain quiet. "Why aren't you using the money from Eze this time like you've done in the past?" Mr. Sandman was stunned that Avery and Ross knew about the four million dollars Poppy had confiscated from an Iranian agent who failed to complete her mission when she was arrested in Eze, France. Supposedly only three people knew about that money, Poppy, Mr. Sandman and Mr. Childs, who was deceased.

"How the hell do you two know about that?" Mr. Sandman demanded.

"Albert and Sandra told us, but we've kept it to ourselves. Believe me, Sir, it remains a secret," Avery assured him.

"How the hell do they know about it?" he barked.

Diana laughed trying to lessen Mr. Sandman's building anxiety regarding the four million dollars. "There are no secrets among Lester, me and our couples. We keep everything about our family to ourselves. Your secret about the Eze money is safe with us and always has been and always will be."

"It had better be. Esther Brouce knows nothing about that Eze money. If she did, she'd skin me alive. She might even fire me. Richard Childs and I decided to keep that money to use for our agents. A perfect example of that is when I used some of it for Buddy Beisswanger's bone marrow transplant to save the kid's life. Please understand, with Esther in the mix now, I can't put you up in a hotel for more than one or two nights at the most. I had a very hard time convincing her to allow us to move ahead with this undocumented operation," Mr. Sandman expounded.

"Don't worry Earl, your secret is safe with us," Diana reassured him. Lester, Ross and Avery also guaranteed his secret's security. They had never realized that it was Mr. Sandman who saved Victor Beisswanger's son.

Avery walked up to Mr. Sandman, and looking into his eyes affirmed, "So it *was* you who saved Buddy's life. You are quite a remarkable man, Mr. S." Avery gave him a kiss him on the cheek.

Mr. Sandman smiled and answered, "Don't try to butter me up, Avery. You're still sleeping in a tent!" They all burst out laughing.

As Blake and Veronica left the agency, Blake called Albert. Jeff and Chloe were, by trade, bakers. They were excellent and Albert needed good bakers. Jeff and Chloe would work for Albert until they were able to realize their dream of opening up their own bakery.

Blake and Veronica found the new couple in the kitchen up to their elbows in cookie dough. There were a lot of sugar cookies cooling on a large rack. Albert came into the kitchen and immediately insisted that Blake and Veronica taste the cookies. They admitted the cookies were suburb. Blake smiled, swallowed his last bite and said, "We're here on business. I'm afraid Veronica and I must take you away from your baking for a little while." He glanced at Albert asking, "You understand, don't you Albert?"

"Yes, of course," Albert answered. He walked over to the door and called, "Sandra, please come in here." Jeff and Chloe were stunned. They had just arrived and were being beckoned for an assignment. They assumed they would have been given the opportunity to get to know the team before they were sent out into the field.

Jeff looked at Albert, then at Blake and inquired, "Wouldn't it be more prudent for Chloe and me to get to know our team members before we go on an actual assignment?"

"No time like the present," announced an obviously pregnant Sandra, as she walked into the kitchen.

As promised, the plane was waiting at precisely 09:00, as was Mr. Sandman. Albert had called him the day before to explain Jeff and Chloe's sense of apprehension from having just met the team. Mr. Sandman then made the decision to fly to Tortola with them hoping to help Jeff and Chloe acclimate. He also wanted a chance to see his cousin Tito again. He and Tito would stay at the hotel with Lester and Diana. His presence, he thought, might make Jeff and Chloe feel more secure.

Once airborne, Mr. Sandman briefed them on the intel he had accumulated with Tito's help. Around the time Jack Pierce disappeared while vacationing on Tortola, two murders were reported. However, only one of the bodies was found and identified. The other body was never found. The body that was found was that of Sharon Sachs, a woman in her late twenties. She and Jack Pierce were vacationing together. No hint of Jack Pierce was ever discovered; however, some locals spoke of a grave close to the top of Sage Mountain, the tallest in Tortola, rising 1,780 feet above sea level. The alleged grave was supposedly on the eastern side of Sage Mountain. There was no evidence found anywhere that Jack Pierce ever left Tortola.

Mr. Sandman laid out a map of Tortola focusing on the eastern side of Sage Mountain. From what they saw, it appeared the topography was steep and rugged. This appealed to Jeff and Chloe. They loved the outdoors and had gone camping often even before they were recruited into the CIA. To them, this would be an exciting challenge. Ross, Avery, Blake and Veronica were skeptical.

They landed at the Terrance B. Lettsome International Airport, previously known as the Beef Island Airport. As the main airport for the British Virgin Islands, the airport was connected to Tortola by a small bridge.

From the window, as the plane taxied to the gate, Mr. Sandman saw his cousin Tito waiting with his smooth mahogany skin and wide welcoming smile showing off his perfectly white teeth with one gold tooth. He hadn't seen Tito since they rescued Prudence Krull from the clutches of the Soviets on St. Lucia. Seeing Tito, Mr. Sandman knew he made the right decision to join the operation. He smiled remembering the disguise Tito insisted he wear in order to talk to the locals on St. Lucia. Blake, Veronica, Poppy and Lorelei had laughed hysterically and teased him incessantly about the flowered shirt, baggy shorts, worn out sandals and most of all, the wig of long dreadlocks. His memory receded as the plane came to a stop. When the door opened a rush of hot air entered the plane.

Tito was waiting at the bottom of the steps as they deplaned. "Well, well, cousin Earl, you're finally back in the Caribbean," Tito bellowed as he tightly hugged Mr. Sandman.

"Yes, and not a moment too soon," Mr. Sandman replied. He turned towards his team as Blake and Veronica approached. "Tito, you remember Blake and Veronica from our St. Lucia escapade?"

Tito extended his hand to Blake. "Yes, of course. I'm happy to welcome you two again." Blake shook Tito's hand and Veronica gave him a warm hug.

"This is the rest of my team," Mr. Sandman said extending his arm towards the rest of the group. "Lester and Diana, Ross and Avery and Jeff and Chloe." He led Tito towards Asa Page. "This is my good friend Asa. It's because of him we're here." Tito escorted the group to a van and drove them to the hotel.

The Reconnaissance Bay Hotel sat on the side of a mountain overlooking Fort Recovery Bay. Glimmering with different shades of blue, the bay teemed with sailboats of all sizes as well as a few motorboats and yachts.

After checking in they were led into a courtyard where their rooms were located. In the courtyard was a large pool surrounded by a wooden deck. Palm trees and lush foliage supplied ample shade for the lounge chairs surrounding the pool. "Too bad we won't be here long enough to enjoy this," Avery cynically whispered into Ross' ear. Avery was wrong. Mr. Sandman ordered them to get settled in their rooms, put on their swimsuits and enjoy the pool. That order was blissfully obeyed.

After a few hours of swimming, and an authentic Caribbean dinner consisting of jerk chicken, rice, plantains, carrots and green beans with coffee and rum cake for dessert, they began planning their forthcoming operation. They all agreed that Sharon Sachs' murder may hold the key to Jack Pierce's disappearance.

There were many questions to be answered. What, exactly, was Sharon Sachs' relationship to Jack Pierce? Was Sharon Sachs' murder related to Jack Pierce's disappearance? If so, could Jack Pierce, himself have murdered Sharon Sachs? Could she have been a foreign agent? Or, was the murderer a foreign agent who killed both Sharon Sachs and Jack Pierce? Maybe the killer was a local? The consensus was if they could answer those questions, they might be able to fit the pieces together enough to get closer to finding Asa Page's son.

Before the team had arrived in Tortola, Tito, with the help of the local police, discovered where Jack Pierce and Sharon Sachs were staying. Martin and June Konrad, a wealthy couple from New York City, owned a duplex just outside of Road Town. Martin's brother Emil Konrad lived in the first-floor apartment permanently. Martin and June Konrad rented out the top floor apartment to vacationers. Jack Pierce rented the apartment for three weeks. The three weeks were almost up when both Jack and Sharon disappeared.

A local woman and her dog were picking wild mushrooms. The dog unearthed enough dirt to uncover the remains of Sharon Sachs' body buried in a relatively shallow grave. The local woman called the police. Sharon Sachs was identified immediately.

All of Jack's and Sharon's belongings remained untouched in the apartment and there were no fingerprints discovered except those of Jack and Sharon. The coroner determined that Sharon's death was caused by her skull being cracked opened by a hard object. The police cordoned off the apartment until the investigation was completed.

The next morning, Ross and Avery went to question Emil Konrad. Mr. Sandman and Tito went to talk to the locals. Blake and Veronica ventured out to talk to the coroner and the police. Jeff and Chloe stayed at the hotel with Asa Page, surveying their activities on monitors along with Diana and Lester.

The Konrad's house sat perched in a niche on the side of a mountain on the outskirts of Road Town. There was no mistaking it. At the foot of the long, steep driveway there was a bright orange sign painted with the words **KONRAD HOUSE** in bold black letters. Ross pulled the rental car up the steep driveway and around the circular drive, stopping in front of a house covered in weathered shingles and a bright orange front door. "Well, here we go," Avery stated as she opened the car door and stepped out onto the gravel driveway.

There was no doorbell. Instead, a heavy iron door knocker was attached to the bright orange door. Ross grabbed the door knocker and knocked three times. They waited. "What do you think we should do?" Ross tentatively asked Avery as he looked around.

Avery smiled and without hesitation answered, "We should nose around the outside of the house, Ross."

"Yeah, I knew you were going to say that," Ross answered, teasing Avery. As they turned away from the door, a man appeared from around the side of the house. He was wearing denim overalls without a shirt. On his dirty feet were flipflops. There was a straw hat sitting atop a mop of light brown curls. He wasn't tall, standing five feet seven inches, but made up for it by his well-toned muscular body. His green eyes assessed Ross and Avery as he walked towards them. "We're looking for Emil Konrad," Ross announced as the man approached.

"You found him. I'm Emil Konrad. And who, may I ask, are you?" Emil inquired, flashing a wide smile thinking they were potential renters.

Avery stepped in front of Ross, squarely facing Emil Konrad, quickly assessing the man in the overalls and straw hat before answering. "We're detectives investigating the death of Sharon Sachs and the disappearance of Jack Pierce. I understand Mr. Pierce and Ms. Sachs were renting the upper apartment of your house?" That direct question posed with Avery's no-nonsense attitude took Emil Konrad off guard. He stepped back a few steps, his face turning red. Ross marveled at how much Avery sounded like Diana. Diana would ask a question in such a way that the second part of the question, although not verbalized, was understood. The silent part of Avery's question was, "And you killed both Sharon Sachs and Jack Pierce, didn't you Mr. Konrad?"

Emil Konrad hurriedly pulled himself together. "Yes, Mr. Pierce was renting the upper apartment. After about two weeks he just never came back." Ross folded his arm across his chest and leaned against their rental car, indicating to Avery that this was her game now. Avery wanted to rattle Emil Konrad.

"Where is Sharon Sachs, Mr. Konrad?" Avery moved closer to Emil Konrad.

Emil moved back two steps. "If you mean the lady who was staying with Mr. Pierce, then you know she's dead, murdered by a local man. Her body was found in a shallow grave." He took off his straw hat. "It is very sad indeed, Miss… I didn't catch your name." Avery was beginning to dislike Emil Konrad intensely. She knew in her gut this man harbored secrets. That was not all; Avery strongly sensed that he was hiding something about Jack Pierce and Sharon Sachs.

"Who, Mr. Konrad, is this local man you claim killed Sharon Sachs?" Avery asked, smiling faintly. Avery turned and waved at Ross, gesturing for him to come over. With Ross at her side she crisply turned to squarely face Emil. "Answer my question, Mr. Konrad. Who is the local man who you claim killed Sharon Sachs?"

Emil Konrad was sweating profusely. He took a wrinkled handkerchief out of his pocket and wiped his brow as he answered. "His name is Romaine Benta. He owns a local bar in town. Every time I've gone there while they rented the upstairs apartment, Sharon Sachs and Jack Pierce were in there talking to him, being very friendly."

"We need to see the apartment Jack Pierce and Sharon Sachs were renting, NOW!" Avery ordered with military bearing. Emil gaped at Avery, surprised at her forceful presence. Without answering or hesitation Emil Konrad indicated for them to follow him. Ross followed Avery smiling at her finesse.

As they reached the top of the stairs Emil pointed to the yellow tape the police had placed across the door indicating that the apartment was a crime scene. "See, you can't go in there. The police forbid it," Emil stated as he turned on the step to face Ross and Avery.

"That does not include us." Avery sneered as she pushed Emil aside and removed the tape. Ross looked at Emil, pointed to the door and ordered, "Open it, or I'll break it down myself." Emil Konrad was not going to argue. He unlocked the door and the three stepped into the apartment.

Avery immediately firmly stated, "Thank you, Mr. Konrad, you are dismissed!" She gave him the kind of stare-down look Avery was well known for among her peers, especially Lorelei. Emil Konrad backed out of the door and ran down the stairs. This bossy blond bitch frightened him; Emil realized as he slinked into his apartment.

Ross and Avery stood in the middle of the living room like statues only moving their eyes to surveille the area. Then, in their silent language, Ross told Avery to wait outside on the balcony while he checked for hidden cameras or hearing devices. Within ten minutes Ross joined her. He found nothing.

They put on their rubber gloves and searched the apartment thoroughly, including all of Jack and Sharon's personal belongings. Avery found an earring on the floor behind the bed. However, there was no other jewelry among Sharon's belongings. "Ross, look what I found!" Avery held up the earring and dangled in front of Ross.

Ross took the earring from Avery and studied it. "Do you think it's Sharon's?"

"Yes, I do, but where is the rest of her jewelry? This earring is real gold which tells me there must be more where that came from, but where is it?"

Ross looked around answering, "That's a good question?" They searched through Sharon's belongings again but found no jewelry.

"I think we need to speak to Mr. Konrad again, Ross. But don't show him or mention the earring we found." Ross put the gold earring into his pocket, followed Avery out of the apartment and replaced the yellow police tape.

Avery knocked on Emil Konrad's door. He opened the door a crack quietly asking, "What do you want now?"

Ross took the lead this time, realizing that Avery scared the man. "I just want to know a few more things," Ross said smiling, but Emil Konrad recoiled, backing away. In as non-threatening a way as possible Ross asked, "What's frightening you, Mr. Konrad... Emil?" He came out of his apartment and shut the door, which immediately signaled Avery that they needed to search his apartment. He led Ross and Avery out onto the gravel driveway to their car. Ross put his arm around Emil as a caring gesture and said, "Please, what is it you are not telling me?" Emil Konrad's eyes turn onto Avery. Ross knew she scared the hell out of him. Now, Ross needed to play the good cop. He led Emil Konrad out of ear shot of Avery. Avery leaned against the car and smiled knowing it was Ross' game now.

Emil led Ross a little further away from Avery. "I heard them fighting upstairs. Maybe that guy Jack Pierce killed Sharon and ran. Maybe

Romaine Benta helped Jack bury Sharon and then killed Jack and buried his body up on Sage Mountain somewhere."

"Why would Romaine Benta do that?" Ross gently asked.

Emil Konrad avoided eye contact with Ross. "Sharon Sachs was flirtatious with Romaine Benta. He came to the house when he knew Jack was not here and tried to make it with Sharon. Jack came home and caught him. Jack hit Benta, but Benta was able to run away. That's when Jack and Sharon had a huge fight. Shortly after that they both disappeared. I then reported the whole incident to the police. They questioned Romine Benta and arrested him."

Ross got what he wanted. He thanked Emil Konrad and walked towards the car signaling Avery to get in. As they drove away Ross relayed to Avery exactly what Emil Konrad had told him. Both Ross and Avery were skeptical. Avery adamantly stated, "There are three things we must do. First, we must somehow find out about the relationship between Romaine Benta and Emil Konrad because Emil is obviously pointing a finger at him. Secondly, we need to question Romaine Benta who is now sitting in jail. And lastly, we must search both Emil Konrad's apartment and Romaine Benta's home. One of them has Sharon Sach's jewelry, I just know it, Ross."

"I agree, Angel. We'll report back to Lester and Diana and with their approval, move ahead with our plan."

"We need to do this quickly. Tomorrow we go camping to search for Jack's grave."

"I have been thinking about that. You know Avery, sleeping in a tent together might be fun. We could share a sleeping bag. You know what I mean?" Ross asked raising his eyebrows.

Avery smiled answering, "Yes Ross, I know what you mean, and I'm in!" They drove back to the hotel both silently thinking about sleeping in a tent sharing a sleeping bag.

It was one in the afternoon by the time Ross and Avery arrived back at the hotel. They were an hour late. "I take it you two had a successful morning?" Diana asked, rising out of her chair.

"If you were on us then you already know we had a very interesting morning interviewing Emil Konrad," Avery answered smiling at her surrogate mother sweetly.

Mr. Sandman picked it up. "We knew you two were doing well and we had other fish to fry, so no, we were not on you. I heard from my Asian connection. They have a lead on Jack, it's thin, but it is a lead.

Disappointedly Ross asked, "Does that mean we won't be camping?" Avery gave Ross one of her looks, knowing exactly what he was thinking; no sharing a sleeping bag.

Mr. Sandman continued, "However, there is no evidence anywhere to be found that Jack ever left this island. So, to answer your question Ross, yes you will be going camping tomorrow"

Avery took over, explaining her thoughts and impressions regarding their encounter with Emil Konrad. "My instincts are screaming not to trust Emil Konrad. He fingered Romaine Benta for Sharon Sach's death and possibly Jack's death as well." Ross took the gold earring out of his pocket and held it up.

"We found this solid gold earring in the apartment. Avery and I both agree that either Emil Konrad or Romaine Benta stole Sharon's jewelry," Ross added.

Avery rapidly fired, addressing Mr. Sandman, "Sir, Ross and I would like your permission to speak to Romaine Benta. We also want to search both of their homes. One of them has the jewelry. If they already hocked it, we have this earring to show to any pawn broker who might have the match. Then we may find out or at least get a good lead as to who stole the jewelry."

Tito stood up. "I'll get search warrants immediately for permission to search both premises."

"Thank you, Tito. We may need search warrants. So, yes get them. However, Ross and Avery have their own method so as not to arouse suspicion. Why don't you two explain," Mr. Sandman suggested, looking at Ross and Avery.

Avery stepped up. "It's really very simple. We never mentioned the earring we found to Emil Konrad. He has no idea we know anything about the missing jewelry. We clandestinely search his home when he isn't there. If we find the jewelry, we go back with the search warrant. If we don't find the jewelry, it's like they say, nothing ventured, nothing gained. The same applies for Romaine Benta. If we find no jewelry in either place, we start hitting every pawn shop on this island"

Ross took the lead. "We need to speak with Romaine Benta to find out about his part in all of this and the nature of his relationships with Emil Konrad, Sharon Sachs, and Jack Pierce."

Mr. Sandman looked at Tito and then at Ross and Avery. "Here's how we're going to play this. You have my permission to search the two homes but stay away from Romaine Benta. Tito and I will speak with him.

We will pick Emil Konrad up for questioning right after we eat lunch. That's when you two search his apartment. Tonight, Tito will go with you and stand guard while you search Romaine Benta's home. The search warrants will be in our hands by tomorrow morning. Any questions?" There were none.

Veronica then said, "Blake and I spoke with the coroner. Sharon was definitely killed by having her brain smashed in by a very hard heavy object. There were no other injuries, either externally or internally."

"What would you like us to do now, Sir?" Blake asked.

Mr. Sandman smiled. "Nothing. You and Veronica stay here at the hotel." He then turned his attention to Jeff and Chloe. "You two go with Ross and Avery this afternoon and tonight. Just do everything they tell you."

The new couple was happy they were finally being included in some way. "Yes, Sir, thank you," Jeff answered as both he and Chloe stood up.

Tito walked over to Ross. "Give me the earring if you don't find the missing jewelry. I am the best one to hit the pawn shops, if it comes to that. If you do find the jewelry today, Earl and I will make the arrests along with the local police."

"That's it then. Tomorrow the six of you begin your camping trip," declared Lester.

Mr. Sandman and his cousin Tito collected Emil Konrad for questioning. Ross and Avery left their car parked on the road and walked up the steep driveway with Jeff and Chloe following, staying close to the foliage to avoid being spotted. Reaching the house, they searched for an easy means of entry. Ross was able to pry a window open. They immediately put on their gloves for the search. Avery turned to the new couple and authoritatively ordered, "You two stay out here. Keep watch in case anyone approaches, in which case, call us immediately."

"Can't I go in with you? Jeff can keep watch," Chloe questioned.

"No! I just gave you an order." Avery was annoyed and Chloe knew it.

"I'm sorry, I just thought…"

"Don't apologize. Just do as you are told!" Avery gave Chloe one of her looks that sent chills down Chloe's spine.

Jeff put his arm around his wife who he knew felt demoralized by Avery's tyrannical behavior. He knew crossing Avery now would be a big mistake. Chloe, by nature, was pugnacious and could never let an opportunity pass without grabbing it. Jeff knew he had to stop her before the situation escalated. "Avery is right, Chloe. It's safer if we stand guard together."

Chloe leaned into Jeff and nodded. As they walked towards the front of the house she whispered, "Thank God you keep me grounded."

Ross and Avery quietly climbed through the window. Ross was annoyed, but not surprised, by the way Avery spoke to Chloe. "Why did you treat Chloe as if she were an underling and not a member of the team?"

Avery turned to Ross answering, "Because she is. They're newbies and need to learn to follow orders without questioning every little thing."

Ross grabbed Avery by the shoulders and turned her towards him. No one treated us that way. What's wrong with you, Avery? I know there's something wrong."

"Everything is wrong. I just feel it, Ross. I don't think Jack Pierce is even on this island."

Ross took Avery into his arms and held her tight. "I love you Avery and I'm with you all the way. But please, try to be more tolerant and kinder towards Jeff and Chloe. I understand why you have all this angst. We have enough to think about right now."

Avery took a deep breath and smiled. "I always have angst, you know that. I'll try to be kinder to the newbies. Now let's search for the jewelry and get the hell out of here!"

Ross kissed Avery on the forehead. "Okay, boss." They stood still, looking around to assess their surroundings.

"This place is a pig sty," Avery whispered, astonished at the mess. There were old newspapers strewn on the couch and coffee table. A small table and chairs sat next to the kitchen. The table had piles of books upon it and clothes draped over the chairs. The kitchen, however, was spotlessly clean.

"Would you look at this," Ross stated in amazement. "Why is the kitchen so clean and the rest of the apartment a mess?" Ross asked as he walked towards the bathroom to check that out. "The bathroom is spotless, too, Avery, but the bedroom is messy. Now why would a guy keep his kitchen and bathroom immaculate, but not care about the rest of the house?"

"It's simple Ross, bugs and critters," Avery declared.

"What the hell does that mean"?

Avery laughed and answered, "You amaze me Ross. For such a smart guy, sometimes you don't get the simplest things. We're on a tropical island where it's hot all the time there are all kinds of weird bugs and critters. Leaving food around would attract them. As we search for the jewelry, I assure you we will not find one single crumb of food." They began their search in earnest.

Mr. Sandman and his cousin Tito took Emil Konrad to the police station for questioning. The police sequestered him in a room. In a friendly manner, Mr. Sandman offered Emil coffee and cake while they spoke about Sharon Sachs and Jack Pierce. Emil Konrad gave Mr. Sandman the identical story he had given to Ross and Avery.

At the same time Tito went to see Romaine Benta. Tito offered Benta coffee, but he refused. Romaine Benta paced back and forth pleading with Tito and the police officer who was also present, to believe that he was being set up. He swore that although he knew Sharon Sachs and Jack Pierce because they came into his bar every night for almost two weeks, he had nothing to do with them socially. Romaine Benta cried explaining that he never stepped foot on the Konrad's property. He stated over and over again that he didn't understand why Emil Konrad would accuse him of such an atrocity. Romaine Benta was so distraught and confused, explaining that Emil Konrad would come into his bar to have a few drinks and was always friendly. Nothing about this made sense to Romaine Benta. Listening and assessing Benta's story, Tito tended to agree; Romaine Benta was being set up, but why?

Ross and Avery discovered a large pouch of gold and sterling silver jewelry under a floorboard in Emil Konrad's bedroom closet. The match to the earring Avery found was in the pouch. Ross immediately contacted Mr. Sandman. Ross put the jewelry back exactly as he found it. Emil Konrad was released and driven home. An hour later Ross and Avery arrived with a search warrant and the police. Emil Konrad was arrested for theft. Once the DNA on the jewelry found in Emil's apartment was matched to Sharon Sach's DNA, Emil Konrad was officially charged with theft. His bail was set, and he was locked in the jail cell next to Romaine Benta.

While each man was escorted out of his cell and taken for a shower and to change into bright orange prison garb, listening devices were installed in both cells. Mr. Sandman would listen while Tito went with Ross and Avery to search Benta's home. Before Mr. Sandman had a chance to hear anything, Emil Konrad was being released on bail. Martin Konrad, Emil's brother, had wired the bail money to the police from New York. Emil was escorted home and instructed not to leave Tortola.

Romaine Benta lived in a small apartment attached to the back of his business, a very popular hangout called *Benta's Bar.* Tito stood watch while Ross and Avery carefully and methodically searched the small apartment. To their amazement they found another pouch of jewelry consisting of some sterling silver, but mostly good costume jewelry. Ross contacted Mr. Sandman.

The DNA matched that of Sharon Sachs. Mr. Sandman then presented Romaine Benta with a search warrant informing him that his home and bar would be searched.

An hour later Romaine Benta was charged with theft. Sitting in his cell with his face in his hands, Romaine Benta sobbed like a little boy exclaiming, "Why is the Lord punishing me? What have I done to deserve this?" It was at that moment that Mr. Sandman was sure that Romaine Benta was innocent. Someone wanted to destroy him. Mr. Sandman began to wonder if Emil Konrad was being set up as well. The one thing he guaranteed was that this was all connected to Jack Pierce.

Mr. Sandman was a good judge of character. He had conversed with Romaine Benta for a long time. He spoke to locals who knew Romaine well. Everyone agreed that Romaine Benta was a kind, honest man just trying to run a good business. He had never been in trouble or hurt anyone. Mr. Sandman made the decision; he anonymously bailed Romaine Benta out of jail.

It was 11PM, nevertheless, Ross and Avery were determined to break Emil Konrad. They persuaded Mr. Sandman, Lester and Diana to allow them to interrogate Emil that night, arguing it was late and Emil would be exhausted. It would be easier to break him, especially if they played good cop, bad cop. Ross and Avery won. Mr. Sandman let them loose.

So as not to signal Emil they were coming, Ross parked on the road and they stealthily made their way up the steep gravel driveway. There was a light in a window. They saw a shadowy figure move behind the wispy curtain. Ross and Avery quietly approached the door. Ross knocked and as Avery glanced towards the shadowy figure in the window, she thought she saw two shadows, but when she looked back, she only saw one. The shadow then disappeared.

Emil Konrad opened the door a crack. "Why can't you leave me alone? I've answered all of your questions. Please, just leave me alone." Avery now knew how vulnerable Emil was and planned to take full advantage of it.

"Not quite, Mr. Konrad," Avery answered as she put her foot in the doorway. Ross pulled the door open. "May we come in!" Avery said as a statement, not a question. Again, Ross noted how much like Diana Avery had become. Ross allowed Avery to play the bad cop. With precise timing Ross, as the good cop, would know when to take over with Emil. This is what they did best.

Avery began. "You have already been charged with theft, Mr. Konrad. Why did you plant the rest of Sharon Sach's jewelry in Romaine Benta's home?" Emil Konrad was speechless. He began slowly backing away from Avery as if in fear of his life. "We know what you did, and you will go to prison, Mr. Konrad. Do you know what it's like in prison, Mr. Konrad?" Emil kept backing away. He shook his head no, afraid to speak. Avery walked towards him, her voice becoming louder and very militaristic. She spoke as if she were barking orders. "I'll tell you what it's like in prison, Mr. Konrad." She continued in a fevered pitch, barking, "You will be thrown into a cell with very bad men. They will beat you and steal from you and…" Avery, for a moment. switched to German. The loud guttural sound of German barking at the frightened man brought forth a certain connotation which paralyzed Emil Konrad, pinning him against the wall. He began to cry and dropped to the floor begging Avery to stop, promising to tell her everything. This was the right moment. Ross intervened.

Emil was sitting on the floor crying. Avery had verbally beaten him into a helpless funk. Ross knelt down to help Emil stand up. He looked up at Avery and handed her the car keys. In their silent language Ross indicated she should get the car and bring it up to the house, then wait outside until he was finished. Avery tacitly agreed and silently left.

Ross turned his full attention to Emil. In a subdued kindly manner Ross put his arm around Emil Konrad as if he were his best friend. Ross noticed a bottle of whiskey on the kitchen counter. "How about a drink? I know I could use one," he asked Emil as he help him up and guided him towards the couch.

Emil Konrad was extremely shaken by what Avery had done to him. He managed to whisper, "Please, I need a drink badly." Ross saw a stack of plastic cups next to the bottle of whiskey. He brought the bottle and cups over to the couch. He poured them both a drink and sat down next to Emil.

"Cheers," Ross said as he held up his cup. Emil held up his cup and downed the whiskey in one large gulp. Ross poured them each another. Emil downed it again in one huge gulp. Ross poured Emil a third.

Ross began. In low even voice he said, "Listen Emil, so you took the jewelry. The woman was dead, so she had no use for it. I can understand why you did it. It was a tempting situation. Anyone might have done that." Ross was watching Emil very carefully and saw he was beginning to relax. Ross smiled, indicating that he understood. Ross then said, "But what I don't understand is why you planted the rest of the jewelry in

Romaine Benta's house. Why did you do that? What's your beef with Benta?"

Emil looked up and then down at the floor. He was stalling. Ross wasn't sure he would get the truth out of him. Or, Emil would only tell him part of the truth. Emil Konrad spoke, but never looked directly at Ross. "OK, I did put the rest of the jewelry in Benta's house. I had a crush on Sharon. I was jealous of the attention she paid to Benta every time we saw him."

"How often was that?" Ross asked.

"Every night when the three of us went to Benta's Bar. Sharon was very flirtatious towards Romaine Benta and totally ignored me."

Ross wasn't buying it completely. He acted perplexed to keep up the ruse. "I'm confused. Where was Jack Pierce when all of this was happening?"

"Oh, he was there, but circulating around, talking to everyone who was in the bar. He was a very friendly sort of fellow. He was always talking to people. Sharon complained to me. She told me Jack ignored her. I was very attracted to Sharon. It made me angry that Jack treated her so badly. I would have done anything for Sharon, but she didn't like me that way. She said she liked me just as a friend."

Ross looked straight at Emil Konrad and asked in a controlled even voice, "Were you also jealous of Jack Pierce?"

"Nah, I was angry at Jack more than jealous," Emil answered looking down at the floor. Ross poured Emil another drink and waited until he downed it.

"Is that why you killed Jack Pierce?" Emil did not expect that question. He was stunned.

"No, I did not kill Jack Pierce. I don't even believe that Jack is actually dead," revealed Emil.

Ross looked at Emil Konrad, smiled and asked, "Well, where the hell is he then?" Ross forced Emil to make direct eye contact with him.

Emil yawned, stretched his legs out and stretched his arms over his head. He was beginning to slur his words. "I don't have a clue where Jack is, nor do I care. He and Sharon had a big fight about something. I was outside in my garden so I couldn't really hear what they were fighting about, but I did hear Sharon say that she saw him on the beach with another woman. Shortly after that, they both disappeared. I reported the whole thing to the police." Emil began to cry. "When they found Sharon's body I was devastated. I thought it was either Jack or Benta who killed her. That's the real reason I planted the jewelry in Benta's home. I loved
244

Sharon, and that's the truth." Emil was having trouble keeping his eyes open. Ross believed he was telling the truth.

Ross put his hand on Emil's shoulder. He quietly asked, "Do you have any idea who the woman Sharon saw Jack with on the beach was?"

"No. She was probably just some woman who happened to be there the same time as Jack. Sharon didn't trust Jack. That much I do know."

"Why didn't she trust Jack?" Ross inquired.

"I'm not sure except she did once say that Jack was very closed off, very secretive. Sharon thought he was hiding something." Emil was struggling to stay awake. Ross needed to ask one more question.

"Emil, think hard. What do you think Jack was hiding?"

"I'm sorry, Ross. I have no idea. It's all so confusing to me. I don't understand why someone would want to kill Sharon."

"We'll do our best to find out. And Emil, I'm sorry my wife Avery was so hard on you." Ross stood up and extended his hand. Emil Konrad struggled to stand up. Ross helped him and the two shook hands. Ross smiled, but before walking out the door he said, "Stay put, my friend and I'll be in touch." Emil Konrad smiled but said nothing.

On the way back to the hotel, Ross told Avery what had happened between him and Emil Konrad. "The bottom line is that Emil Konrad is a loser who is afraid of his own shadow. He was in love with Sharon Sachs. I honestly believe that he had nothing to do with Sharon's death or Jack's disappearance. Emil Konrad is guilty of two things; theft and planting the other half of the jewelry in Romaine Benta's home to punish him for having Sharon's attention every night, nothing more."

"Are you sure, Ross?" Avery asked, surprised at Ross' conclusion.

"Yes, I'm positive," Ross asserted. They road in silence for a while. Ross turned to Avery asked, "Why the hell did you start screaming at Emil Konrad in German? Was that really necessary?"

Avery was annoyed. "It worked, didn't it?"

"Yes, it worked, but I think it was a cruel thing to do."

"By screaming at him in German it got you what you needed, did it not?"

"Yes, it certainly did," Ross quietly answered.

"So, to answer your question, yes, it was necessary."

"When you were screaming in German, Avery, for the moment, it scared the hell out of me. I didn't recognize you. I didn't know who you were," Ross confessed.

Quietly Avery conceded, "Neither did I, Ross."

It was a beautiful night. Fire torches surrounded the pool, their light reflecting off the water. Ross and Avery walked over to where their group was sitting. "What's everybody drinking?" Ross asked as he looked around.

"Dirty martinis, do you want one?" Blake asked as he held up his glass.

"Sure, I'd love one," Avery answered. Ross declined. Blake ordered a martini for Avery and Ross pulled over two chairs. Where are Mr. Sandman and his cousin Tito?" Avery asked, as Blake handed her a Martini.

"They're at Benta's Bar talking to the locals. They should be back any time now," answered Diana as she and Lester came outside.

Lester pulled over two chairs for himself and Diana. "You two did a great job tonight with Emil," he said smiling at Ross and Avery.

Diana smiled adding, "You sure did. I'm proud of both of you. Avery I was impressed the way you so naturally switched to German at the exact right moment. You brought him down to a place where it made it easy and more natural for Ross to take over. Good job, both of you."

"Thank you. Who do you think that woman was who Sharon saw Jack with on the beach?" Avery mused, almost to herself.

"Who knows, but we better find out. Maybe Earl and Tito will come back with some answers," Lester suggested.

"We can't just dismiss that, Lester. She may be more than just some random woman he met on the beach. I have a funny feeling about all of this. We have a lot of little pieces which need to be put together correctly in order to understand what actually occurred.," Avery espoused.

Mr. Sandman and Tito joined them without any new information regarding Jack Pierce or Sharon Sachs. "A local fisherman told us he saw Jack Pierce talking to a dark-haired woman on the beach. The fisherman thought the woman maybe could have been Asian," Mr. Sandman informed them.

Asa Page had been surprisingly quiet up to now, as if he was thinking about something else. "I've been thinking about a conversation I had with Jack the last time I saw him. We were in a bar having a couple of beers talking casually. I asked him what he was up to. He said he was working for a good friend of his. I asked him his friend's name and he said it was Martin. Jack was drinking a little too much, but he knew he could when he was with me. He confided that this Martin had business dealings with the Chinese Government. I wonder if it was Martin Konrad who rented Jack the house here in Tortola?"

"I'm sure it was," retorted Avery.

"I checked Martin Konrad out and contacted Poppy to check him out. Poppy is exceptional at that. Martin Konrad is not on the CIA's nor the FBI's radar. Now that you tell me he is doing business with the Chinese, we will put him there," Mr. Sandman stated.

"Wait Earl, that's not all. If I remember correctly, Jack told me he thought Martin Konrad was somehow colluding with the Chinese, being paid big bucks. I told Jack to cut himself loose from that guy. I explained that he might be getting himself into dangerous waters. It was a casual conversation and at the time Jack agreed with me, saying it was not worth getting involved. Now I realize he was probably involved up to his eyeballs and agreed with me just to shut me up," Asa divulged. Asa was now clearly upset.

Diana stood up, walked over behind Asa and placed her hands on his shoulders. Don't worry, we'll get to the bottom of this and we'll find Jack."

"I have a very strong feeling he is alive. Emil Konrad thinks so also, right Ross?" Avery was looking for affirmation from Ross to help reassure Asa.

Ross gave Avery what she wanted. "Yes, that's right. We start our search tomorrow and I bet we won't find anything."

Asa smiled, answering, "Jack is a good boy. He's CIA and very patriotic. He would never commit treason against our country, I swear it because I know my son. He would never do anything to hurt the United States. If he is doing something covert to uncover something about Martin Konrad's dealings with the Chinese, I just pray he is not found out."

Mr. Sandman stood up and stretched. "Tomorrow you three couples will begin your camping trip and I will contact Poppy again and have him investigate Martin Konrad's company and business dealings. Diana is right. We will get to the bottom of this. I think we should all go to bed now." Everyone began to stand up to head to their rooms.

"Just one more thing," Avery said. They all stopped in their tracks. "Who killed Sharon Sachs? We should really check it out." They all agreed. As everyone walked off to their rooms Avery quietly declared, "Who was the woman on the beach? She very well may have killed Sharon Sachs."

CHAPTER 11
JACK PIERCE - PART 2

By 08:00 the next morning Ross and Avery, Blake and Veronica and the newbies, Jeff and Chloe were ready to begin their hike up the eastern side of Sage Mountain to search for an alleged grave at the top of the mountain that might belong to Asa Page's son Jack Pierce. Using a map with a route mapped out by the local police, they slowly began to climb the steep and rugged terrain covered in foliage. Their goal was a shallow cave the police pointed out on the map halfway up the mountain. It appeared that the cave might make a good place to set up camp.

They hiked until dusk when they found the cave. Although it was shallow, there was enough room for their three tents. Jeff and Chloe volunteered to gather wood to make a fire just outside the opening to the cave.

Once they were all settled, and as they ate their prepackaged dinner, Ross and Avery, and Blake and Veronica took the time to talk to Jeff and Chloe, trying to get to know them and to understand what made them tick. The couple was very open and happy that they were finally able to share who they were with them. Albert and Sandra already knew their story as they were now working for them at their catering facility as bakers. "Chloe and I met in college on the very first day of classes and for me it was love at first sight," Jeff said as he pulled Chloe close to him.

Chloe snuggled into Jeff. "It was for me too. We had so much in common, including where we both grew up."

"Where was that and where did you both go to college?" Avery asked trying to sound friendly and nonchalant.

Chloe answered, "We both grew up in Columbus, Ohio and never knew each other until we met at Ohio State. That's where we went to school."

"What kind of degrees did you both graduate with?" Veronica inquired.

Jeff answered, "We both majored in criminology and minored in psychology."

"What in hell could ever have made you join the CIA?" Veronica asked sarcastically, laughing.

Chloe answered, "Yeah, but we didn't join we were recruited by a good friend of my father. You see, my dad is an attorney and knows a lot of people in law enforcement."

Avery smiled and asked, "Your father's friend wouldn't happen to be our Mr. Sandman, by any chance, would it?"

In amazement Chloe responded, "How did you know?"

"I thought it might be the case just by remembering what he told us. He said he knew you well and we could trust you and Jeff completely," Avery answered. By this time, they were all very relaxed.

"As a matter of fact, his daughter Meredith and I are friends," revealed Chloe. "Do you know Meredith?"

"Yes, we do," answered Avery, not wanting to say anymore. Chloe got the hint.

"What about you, Jeff? What's your background?" Blake gently probed.

Happy to answer, Jeff explained, "My parents own a string of bakeries throughout Columbus. I began learning to bake when I was very young. My parents were very strict with me as I was growing up. I had to work in the bakeries after school every day and on Saturday mornings. Saturday night I could spend with my friends, but only if Dad approved of who they were. Sunday was always the same, church in the morning and family dinners in the afternoon. Dad kept a short rein on me. I resented it then, but now I'm grateful. I stayed out of trouble and became the man I am today. Yes, I'm very grateful to Dad, and I have told him so." There was a lull in the conversation.

Veronica noticed Avery listening intently, looking around with her eyes without moving her head. She was just about to question Avery when Ross asked Chloe, "What was it like for you growing up, Chloe?"

Chloe also noticed Avery was distracted by something. She quickly turned her full attention to Ross. "When I was young, I went to camp every summer. Believe it or not, I still have two close friends from my childhood days camping. As a teenager I worked in my father's law office. He wanted me and Jeff to go to law school after graduation and work for him, but Jeff and I had other plans." Chloe paused, laughed and continued, "We went to chef's college to become bakers, figuring it might come in handy someday. Jeff and I graduated, got married and took over one of Jeff's father's bakeries in Columbus. We never imagined it would become our cover as agents."

"What did you tell your parents after Mr. Sandman recruited you?" asked a curious Blake.

"Simply that we needed space, to go off on our own. We wanted to open a bakery in New York. They weren't very happy, but we told both sets of parents it was non-negotiable. We, of course, went to Montana for training and you all know the rest," Jeff explained.

"Avery, what are you looking for and listening to?" Veronica whispered.

"I'm sure I saw a glint, a reflection. I also thought I heard twigs breaking like someone was walking on them," Avery whispered.

"What you probably saw was an animal's eyes and heard the animal walking and rustling the bushes. It's nothing to be worried about," Ross assured Avery as he put his arm around her.

"Yeah, you're probably right," Avery said as she yawned and settled in closer to Ross.

"Why don't you guys go to bed and Jeff and I will keep watch for a while?" suggested Chloe. They thanked Jeff and Chloe and the two older couples went into their tents.

Ross and Avery quickly stripped naked and got into one sleeping bag. That made them vulnerable, but they took a chance. Ross maneuvered his way on top of Avery. As he kissed her deeply, his hands moving down both sides of her body and back up to her breasts. He slid down slightly and gently began kissing and sucking each breast. Avery felt Ross' erection pushing against her leg. She wrapped her hand around his hardness and began to softly moan. Ross slid his right hand down between Avery's legs and entered her with two fingers. She leaned hard into his hand. Ross knew she was more than ready. He replaced his fingers with his very hard erection as Avery slowly guided him into her. It didn't take long. Avery buried her face into Ross' chest, digging her fingers into his back. Ross pushed deeper and moved faster until they released at the same time. They switched positions with Avery now on top of Ross. They made love all night switching positions.

The next morning, the team decided they would use the cave as their base of operations. It was half-way up Sage mountain and central to where they needed to search. Leaving their tents in the cave, they got rid of any traces of their fire and covered the cave opening with piles of rocks and an abundance of foliage.

Just as they were marking their coordinances as to the location of the cave, Mr. Sandman contacted them. "I Have a very interesting piece of intel for you. Sharon Sachs was FBI. She was trying to find out what Jack was up to."

"Well, I'll be damned! What *was* Jack Pierce up to?" Ross exclaimed.

"Jack Pierce was definitely CIA, either working for us as a double agent or gone bad, going over to the Chinese or even possibly the Russians. Keep searching for that grave. It's important you find it or confirm that it doesn't exist."

Avery quickly asked, "Who was that women on the beach? She may have killed Sharon Sachs."

"You're right, Avery, and we're working on it. Just search for that grave and keep me informed." answered Mr. Sandman.

As they climbed higher and higher up Sage Mountain, they spread out to search the area thoroughly. Avery began to sense that she and Ross were being followed. Avery trusted her instincts as they always proved to be right. "Ross, I strongly sense we are being followed," she whispered. Ross knew to trust Avery's instincts.

"I believe you, Angel. We better quickly gather the others and inform them," Ross concluded. Within five minutes the three couples were sitting hidden in a copse of bushes and thickets. They sat close together speaking in whispers.

"I sense very strongly that we are being followed. The glint I saw last night was not an animal, I'm sure of it," Avery disclosed. They all believed her.

"This changes things, a bit, doesn't it?" questioned Veronica.

"It does, indeed. Blake answered

"However, we are committed to complete our assignment." Asserted Ross. Jeff and Chloe took a back seat, allowing the two experienced couples to make all the decisions.

"One thing is obvious, whoever is following us knows about the cave. We can never go back there," solemnly stated Blake.

"That's no big deal. The only things we left there are the tents, but unfortunately our flares are in the tents. We have all our other equipment including out sleeping bags," Veronica said playfully, smiling at Avery, who gave Veronica a sideways smile, shrugging one shoulder.

"Not all the flares. Chloe and I took ours," proudly stated Jeff.

"Good thinking," said Ross. They all agreed. Avery and Veronica looked at each other smiling slightly, acknowledging that Jeff and Chloe were beginning to win them over.

They were being monitored, but neither Diana, Lester, nor Mr. Sandman spotted anything suspicious. "Just stay with it, and keep on your toes," Mr. Sandman ordered. He and his cousin Tito were going into town. Lester and Diana took a short break, leaving Asa on the monitors. Asa's eyes kept closing. He was trying very hard no to drift off to sleep.

The team moved closer together as Ross took out the map. "OK, look, let's move for about another hour in this direction. Keep your weapons drawn and eyes and ears open. We'll spread out as we did before but be ready for anything. We don't know who, what, or how many we're dealing with. OK, no talking from this point on. Let's move, ordered Ross.

As each couple began to stealthily move away from each other, Chloe whispered, "I'm scared, Jeff. I didn't expect this." They were the most vulnerable. They got it first.

It was just before dusk. Diana and Lester had taken turns monitoring the three couples all day. They saw what had occurred, but so far there was nothing to be concerned about. Diana had been wanting to take a swim in the pool. Lester and Asa took over the watch, telling Diana to take her swim.

Diana was reclining on a lounge chair with her eyes closed. She felt a presence, opened one eye and saw Mr. Sandman walking briskly towards her. "Don't get too comfortable, Diana. As soon as the team gets back from Sage Mountain, we're leaving. We need to get back to the Hoboken safe house."

"Why, what's happened?" Diana asked as she sat straight up.

"I didn't see Esther before I left to come down here with you. I didn't have time. I texted her and apologized, but I think she's madder than a wet hen, as they say."

Diana stood up and wrapped a towel around herself. "Don't worry, Earl. Esther is a reasonable person and she'll get over it. I think your presence is really helping Jeff and Chloe. Esther will understand that." Diana knew there had to be more regarding Mr. Sandman's angst, but didn't have a chance to ask.

Lester came running out shouting for Diana and Mr. Sandman to come in quickly. Once they were inside Lester stated, "They're off the monitor. I can't connect with any of them."

The five assailants dressed in black with black masks quietly got as close to each couple as possible for the spray to knock them out. The five assailants carried the three women and Ross back to the cave. Inside the cave they tied Avery, Veronica and Chloe up, binding their hands and feet and taping their mouths. They bound Ross up the same way outside of the cave. The five assailants then blocked the cave with large rocks and a lot of foliage. Four of the five assailants went to collect Blake and Jeff. Both men were still knocked out. They were brought back to the cave, put inside and bound up and gagged the same as the women. They then blocked the cave with more rocks and foliage. One assailant with a gas cannister stood next to Ross. Once the cave was blocked, the assailant told the other four to leave. The assailant then took the cannister with the gas and positioned the hose into the cave just enough so that it would kill the five agents if left on. Ross began to stir, as did the others inside the dark cave.

There was now an all-out search taking place for the six agents. Asa and Diana were on the monitors just in case. Mr. Sandman, Lester, Tito, and a plethora of police were searching furiously with flashlights. As they headed towards the cave that had been the agents' base camp, they realized it was a futile effort in the dark. They went back and boarded a helicopter with night vision and a large search light, deciding if they were not successful that night, they would go on foot with dogs and use the helicopter at first light.

The man with Ross knew he had to act fast. The helicopter searching the mountain could be heard in the distance. "OK Ross here is what you need to do to save the lives of your comrades inside the cave. If I turn this gas on full force, they will all be dead within an hour. "I want you to come with me without a struggle." Ross was furious and did not answer. I will leave your comrades alive in the cave or I will turn on the gas, it's your choice. Ross nodded, agreeing to go with the man.

Avery was struggling fervently to get loose from her bondage, as were the other four. The two couples managed to sit back to back trying to untie each other's hands while Avery struggled on her own. Blake and Veronica managed to free their hands. They unbound their feet and quickly freed their comrades. The problem was moving the large rocks in front of the cave. Through a small crack in the pile of rocks and through the foliage Avery saw the man leading Ross away. "They're taking Ross away. Where the hell are they taking him and why? We have to get out of here," frantically Avery screamed as she clawed at the heavy rocks trying to move them.

The cannister of gas was wedged between two rocks with the nozzle of the hose wedged into a small opening in between the rocks. Avery managed to move the large rock just enough that the cannister of gas moved in such a way that the switch turned itself on. Gas began to lightly spray into the cave.

Ross was blindfolded as the man led him through the rugged mountain terrain. Ross kept tripping and sprained his ankle. The man became angry but knew that he had to get Ross to their destination as fast as possible. The man put his arm around him, helping Ross move faster with his sprained ankle. Ross was in pain and could feel his ankle swelling. He asked the man if they could stop so he could bind his ankle. The man refused and kept pushing Ross forward. The man and Ross both heard the police helicopter high above. A light shown in the distance. The noise from the helicopter grew louder as the light approached them. The man pushed Ross down under some thicket, ordering him not to move. The light was now all around them. The light faded. The helicopter moved away in a different direction. Ross begged the man to allow him to bind his ankle. Again, he refused, roughly pulling Ross up and pushing him forward.

They realized they had to do something to stop the gas from spraying into the cave, but the rocks were wedged in such a way that made them almost impossible to budge. Blake suggested they lift Chloe, who was the smallest, up to where the nozzle spraying the gas was located. With her nose and mouth wrapped in a towel, she would try to push the nozzle out. The plan worked; however, they were all very groggy from the gas spray. They moved to the back of the cave where the gas was sparse.

Once all of the gas dissipated, the five of them together were able to move the rocks to create a small opening. Chloe, assessing the size of the opening, suggested she try to squeeze through to set up the emergency flares they had in their tents. After a brief discussion, they all agreed, Chloe might be able to make it. There was one concern; that the assailants were watching the cave. It was a tremendous risk. "Chloe, you could be killed the moment you emerged from the cave if they're watching" Jeff said with trepidation as he held her by the shoulders.

Chloe stroked Jeff's face lovingly. Looking into his worried eyes she whispered, "It's a risk I'm willing to take plus I'll be armed. We signed on for this. You have to let me go." Jeff hugged Chloe tightly, indicating his acceptance of her decision. Avery and Veronica smiled at each other. This was the moment Mr. Sandman alluded to when he told them that Jeff and Chloe would prove themselves trustworthy and a valuable part of their team.

Chloe was able to squeeze through the opening easily. In her favor, the assailants had placed an abundance of foliage in front of the rocks. She hid crouched down in the thicket, turned off the gas cannister and retrieved her weapon. Without moving, Chloe scanned the area with her eyes. Searching the ground around her, she picked up a large pebble and tossed it out as far as possible. Avery stood with her weapon pointing out of the opening to cover Chloe. The pebble landed in a bush. Some small birds flew away. After Chloe threw two more large pebbles in different directions, Avery loudly whispered to her, "OK, Chloe, start clearing the foliage. Keep out your weapon and I've got you covered from here."

Chloe turned slightly, answering, "Thank you, Avery."

"Thank you, Chloe," Avery answered back as the tears rolled down her face thinking about Ross and what he must be going through.

Ross and the masked man arrived at a cabin about two miles west of the cave. Ross was pushed into the cabin and placed in a chair. "He sprained his right ankle," the man said to another person. Ross listened carefully. He was sure the man left. He was left alone with an unknown person.

His ankle was throbbing. Someone took off his boot and gently took off his sock. He was left alone until the person came back and began binding his ankle. He could tell by the touch it was a woman. The hands touching him were smaller and more delicate. He moaned, indicating he wanted to know who she was. The person removed the tape from his mouth. "Thank you for binding my ankle and doing it so gently and carefully," Ross quietly managed to say. Ross was sure it was a women because she knelt down, placing her hands on his thighs. She laid her head on his lap, pushing into him. Ross began to feel aroused and moaned as he felt her open his pants.

They passed the flares through to Chloe as soon as she cleared the foliage away. The flares lit up the area brightly. They heard the helicopter and saw the light approach. Chloe stood in the middle of the light waving her hands. They were found. Within a short time, Mr. Sandman and Lester were lowered to the ground with four policemen. The helicopter hovered above lighting up the area. The heavy rocks were removed from the mouth of the cave.

Avery immediately ran to Mr. Sandman and Lester screaming, "They took Ross, they took Ross and I don't know why." Avery was sobbing as Lester held her in his arms.

"We'll find him Avery, don't worry," assured Mr. Sandman, but he told Lester he was worried, very worried because he already knew who had Ross.

Lester held Avery and said, "Let the police take you back to the hotel. You stay with Diana while we search for Ross."

Avery pushed Lester away and adamantly stated, "No, I will not go back. Ross is my husband and the father of my children. I am going with you. For his sake, I must be there when we find him." Lester knew there was no argument. They agreed to let Avery remain with them. The police left in the helicopter but promised to return with dogs at first light when they could begin searching for Ross.

Avery laid in her tent quietly crying clutching a shirt Ross had left behind. She thought about the night before. They had crawled into one sleeping bag and made love silently so as not to disturb the other couples. Through her tears Avery smiled recalling how she and Ross quietly talked about how they missed their son, Ralf and daughter, Kimmy. Now Avery's most dreaded fear had come to fruition. She knew in the deepest part of her heart and mind who had Ross; the dark-haired woman seen on the beach. She knew she had to trust Ross to do the right thing.

The woman unbuttoned Ross' shirt and slid her hands up and down his chest. He relaxed and went with it. She took Ross' hardness in her mouth. She stood up and straddled Ross plunging him deep inside her. At first she moved slow to get Ross going. She kissed his neck and around his ears. Then his lips, gently then passionately, using her tongue. As he responded, he realized it felt familiar and very good. They moved together like two sexual athletes running as a team, faster and faster until together they achieved final victory. "Sydney," Ross sighed as he collapsed into a state of momentary bliss. "God you're good!" That was an honest statement, but then Ross was pulled back into reality. He made an instant decision to keep it sexual with Sydney. If he could get her into a vulnerable position, he could kill her.

As Sydney moved to get off Ross, he stopped her. "No Syd, stay. Let's do it again. But please, Syd, take off my blindfold so I can see your gorgeous face and your magnificent green eyes." Sydney's heart raced and she smiled, not quite believing what she was hearing.

"OK, my darling Ross, whatever you say." She slowly removed the blindfold from Ross' eyes. Ross looked into her beautiful green eyes.

"You are so gorgeous. Thank you, Syd for our beautiful son."

They looked at each other for a long moment. Ross saw her eyes darken at the mention of their son. Ross seductively whispered, "Kiss me Syd, I want you so bad." Sydney kissed Ross the way she knew he liked it. As she increased the pressure on his lips, she and Ross attained their rhythm. As they moved together Ross cried, "Oh God, Syd, I wish I could touch you. I want to touch and feel all of your perfect body." Sydney reached around and untied Ross' hands. He wrapped his arms around her pushing deeper and faster into her. He ripped her top off and held her breasts, one in each hand kissing and fondling them as they moved together. Ross took her face and pulled her lips to his kissing her. Sydney responded and they exploded together into blissful victory once again. Without speaking, Sydney untied Ross' feet and gently helped him up, leading him into the bedroom. They silently stripped off their clothes and got into bed. Sydney lay in ecstasy as Ross kissed and caressed her entire body, putting his tongue inside her teasing her most sensitive parts.

Sydney was sprawled out naked and completely vulnerable. Ross knew if he was going to kill her, this would be the time. He laid on top of her between her legs which were wrapped around him. She whispered, "Please Ross, my darling, all I want is to feel you inside me forever. They found their rhythm again. He realized he couldn't kill her, the woman who gave him his beautiful son. A part of him loved her, though he was not in love with Sydney. He was deeply in love with Avery. No, Ross thought, he could never kill Sydney Brewer, the mother of his son. "Ross, does Avery know or even realize what an amazing lover you are?" Sydney asked as she fondled him.

"Ross looked at her smiled slightly and answered, "Yes, I think so." Ross began to become aroused again.

"I'm better than Avery aren't I Ross?"

Ross knew what she wanted to hear.. "Yes, Syd, you are." He gently pushed her hand away. "Just lay here with me and relax for a while," Ross suggested. Sydney was exhausted and obeyed Ross.

Ross and Sydney were both spent. She laid with her head on his chest. "Syd, I'd like to make a deal with you," Ross quietly said.

"What kind of a deal?" Sydney climbed on top of Ross. She began kissing his neck, but he gently pushed her off and turned on his side.

Looking into her eyes Ross said, "Let's be lovers, let's have an affair. I don't want to live the rest of my life without you, without this. However, you have to promise me you'll leave Avery, Ralf, Kimmy and the rest of my family alone and never bother them again. What do you say?"

"I'll agree to that if you make me a promise. I desperately want to see our son. I want the three of us to be a family, even if it's just for a few days. We can go somewhere where nobody can find us." Sydney watched Ross thinking.

"OK, I agree to that, but we have to leave now, before they start searching for me again." She threw her arms around Ross and began to cry. Ross knew he needed to tread carefully. He was dealing with a very damaged woman.

"Ross my darling you've made me so happy. Yes, let's leave now, right now." Ross and Sydney got up and put on their clothes. Sydney packed her things and said, "You wait here, my darling while I get the car." She pulled up in a non-descript small compact car. Sydney helped Ross down the porch steps and into the car. Then, they were gone.

At dawn's first light a helicopter landed in a clearing near the cave. The five agents came out of the cave as soon as they heard Mr. Sandman calling their names. He was accompanied by Lester and two FBI agents with dogs. "Finding Ross will be a joint mission. Sharon Sachs was an FBI agent. We all agree that whoever instrumented Ross' kidnapping also killed Sharon Sachs," Mr. Sandman announced.

"It was the dark-haired woman on the beach, name: Sydney Brewer. I'd bet my life on it," proclaimed Avery.

"We think so," definitively stated one of the FBI agents. Avery handed him Ross' shirt for the dogs to pick up Ross' scent. The dogs picked up the scent easily and began going in a definite direction. The two FBI agents were in the lead with the dogs, followed by Mr. Sandman and Lester, followed by the five CIA team members.

It was about a two-mile hike before the dogs lead them to the cabin Ross and Sydney had fled from hours earlier. Once it had been determined that the cabin was deserted, Avery ran in, stopping short when she saw the ropes Ross had been tied up with on the floor next to a chair. She looked around and noticed the bedroom door was partly opened. Avery was beginning to feel the angst rise within her as she slowly walked over to the bedroom door and pushed it opened with her foot. She stood staring at the bed with its wrinkled sheets and misplaced pillows. As Avery approached the bed she leaned forward as if examining evidence. A wailing scream came from deep within her, "He slept with her and left with her willingly, I just know it." Mr. Sandman, Lester, Blake, and Veronica ran to Avery. Jeff and Chloe hung back out of respect. Lester took Avery into his arms pleading with her not to jump to any conclusions. Avery was suffering from both heartbreak and extreme anger. She pushed Lester away, threw herself on the bed and screamed, "They had sex right here in this bed. Ross is my husband and I know he had sex with that fucking psychopath in this bed." Avery was sobbing uncontrollably. Chloe was crying silently into Jeff's shoulder.

Veronica tried to comfort Avery. "Avery, you don't know what really happened. They may have taken Ross away and it was totally someone else who was in this bed."

Avery looked forlornly at Veronica. "Don't you understand? I smell him, his scent is all over this bed. Ross is my husband. Believe me, I know it was him and I know what he did with her." Veronica did understand. She sat on the bed and put her arms around Avery. Veronica rocked Avery back and forth in her arms until Avery was all cried out.

The FBI collected what they needed. Lester put his arm around Avery and lead her out of the cabin, with Jeff and Chloe following. Chloe was hurting for Avery. She wanted to talk to Avery, to comfort her, but knew she couldn't, at least not now.

Mr. Sandman walked out last with Blake and Veronica. As they walked, he said, "Listen, do me a big favor, Keep an eye on Avery. This is very worrisome. It might be the beginning of something really bad."

Veronica put her arm through Mr. Sandman's arm as they walked and said, "Don't worry, we'll keep a close watch, we all will. We're a family and Avery will be surrounded and kept safe by our love and strength."

Lester contacted Diana to tell her about Ross. Diana was devastated and knew she would have her hands full with Avery. Diana knew how high-strung Avery was, how angry she could get and how mistrusting she was of people. But Ross, her own husband, that was crossing a sacred line. Diana was not sure Avery would ever be able to recover from this. She was not sure Avery would ever forgive Ross. Diana was not sure she would ever forgive Ross.

By the time they arrived back at the hotel, there was news. The police did find a grave on the top of the eastern side of Sage Mountain. It was not Jack Pierce. But there was more relevant news. Mindo had contacted Diana. Ross had come home and had taken Ralf away. Ross gave no explanation except a message for Avery. Ross instructed Mindo to tell Avery that he loved her and Kimmy and would be back with Ralf as soon as he could. He would explain then and she should trust him. Diana knew Avery would not believe or trust anything Ross said. Lester and Diana decided not to tell Avery about Ralf until they returned to Hoboken to debrief.

When the team returned to the hotel Avery was in total meltdown. Diana insisted Avery take an anxiety pill. She had packed all of Ross and Avery's things. Blake and Veronica and Jeff and Chloe quickly packed. Mr. Sandman made it clear that they needed to get back to the Hoboken safe house as soon as possible but was secretive about why. None of them cared. It was Ross and Avery they cared about. Not one of them believed that Ross would go willingly with Sydney Brewer.

Avery slept with her head on Diana's lap for most of the flight. She woke up once, looked at Diana and asked, "Please tell me I had a terrible nightmare and that my Ross is with the rest of the team. Please Aunt Diana, tell me that." Diana's heart was breaking for Avery who she loved as if she were her own daughter.

Diana stroked Avery's hair answering, "Go back to sleep, sweetheart. We'll be home soon, and all of this will get straightened out. You'll see, it'll be fine." Diana didn't believe one word she said. Both she and Lester agreed with Mr. Sandman, that this might be the beginning of something very bad. The anxiety pill Diana had given Avery was working full throttle. Avery obeyed Diana and went back to sleep.

Avery was eerily calm and looked numb when they arrived at the Hoboken house. Albert and Sandra and Poppy and Lorelei had been told what had occurred. Avery and Sandra had become best friends, like sisters who told each other everything and shared personal secrets. Sandra ran to Avery and hugged her. She took Avery by the hand and guided her to the couch. Sandra sat on one side of Avery and Albert on the other. Albert put his arm around Avery and whispered in her ear, "Don't you worry, I will find him and bring him back to you if it's the last thing I ever do."

Avery looked at Albert and whispered, "He went with her willingly. He made love to her willingly. I saw the bed. I smelled his scent in the bed." Avery paused and turned to Sandra. "I don't know how I'll ever get passed this?"

Sandra looked at Albert sideways and stated, "You'll get through it, Avery. I understand completely how you feel. Besides, you don't know what really happened, why Ross did what he did. He had to have had a good reason," Sandra answered trying to be the voice of reason.

Diana walked over to Avery. "There's something else you need to know Avery. Mindo contacted us. Ross showed up at your house and took Ralf. He told Mindo to tell you that he loves you and Kimmy. He and Ralf will be back as soon as possible, and you are to trust him. Those were his exact words."

Avery did not respond for a few moments. She stood up stating, "I need to go home right now. I want to get my daughter. I feel Kimmy is not safe there."

Mr. Sandman heard Avery. He took her by the shoulders and said, "I can't let you leave, but I understand how you feel. I will send two agents there to protect your family. Mindo, Kimmy, George and your dog Dixie will be safe, I promise. Now I suggest you go upstairs and lay down. Diana, go with Avery to settle her in."

Avery looked soulfully at Mr. Sandman. "He took my little man away."

"You need to sleep and let the team take care of this situation. It's out of your control now," Diana said as she put her arm around Avery and led her up the stairs.

Ross and Sydney walked along the beach holding hands. Ralf ran ahead picking up seashells as he scampered in front of them. "I heard him last night, crying for Avery."

"I'm sorry, Syd. Avery loves Ralf and has been a good mother to him. He's become very attached to her.

"In the long run, I guess that's best, as long as I can see him once in a while." Sydney ran ahead to Ralf and looked at all the shells he had collected. Ross stood watching, thinking of the night Ralf was crying asking Avery when Sydney would be coming back for him. He remembered how Avery held Ralf and comforted him. He remembered how Ralf asked Avery if now she would be his mommy. He remembered Avery's tears of joy as she accepted Ralf's offer. He remembered how Avery comforted Ralf as he fell asleep.

Ross was jarred out of his memory bank when Ralf came running up to him yelling, "Daddy, Daddy, look at all the great shells I collected. I want to bring them home to Mommy because she loves seashells. Auntie Syd said I should do that. Can we do it soon, Daddy?" Ralf looked up pleadingly at Ross with his big brown eyes. "I want to go home. I really miss Mommy, Kimmy, Mindo and Grandpa and Dixie."

Ross knelt down and smiled at his son. "I know you miss Mommy and everyone. I'll take you home today." He stood and walked over to Sydney. "I'd better take him home. Anyway, I want to be alone with you. I'm craving you, Syd."

"Likewise!" Sydney took a deep breath. "How do you suggest we do this, my darling?"

"A friend of mine owns a brownstone in Hoboken. He's away and I have the key. We could go there. No one would know," Ross whispered, smiling seductively at Sydney.

"But Ross, I can't possibly go with you to take Ralf home. Where will I meet you?"

"Before I take him home, I'll drop you on Washington street in Hoboken. It will take me at least an hour and a half to get back. After an hour or so, stay near eleventh street. There's a coffee shop on that corner. I'll pick you up there. Then we'll be alone. God, Syd, I can't wait."

"Neither can I. Let's go back to the beach house, pack and leave now," Sydney suggested.

Ross grabbed Ralf from behind and swung him around. "Guess what Buddy? Being you miss Mommy and everybody so much, I'm taking you home today."

"Look at the pretty shell I found for Kimmy, Daddy. Can I give it to her today?" joyfully squealed Ralf.

"Yes, you can, my little man," Ross said as he picked Ralf up piggy-back style.

"Hey, that's what Mommy calls me." Ralf yawned and laid his head on Ross' shoulder.

Sydney's plan of getting Ross back by using Ralf as bait, thinking Avery would reject Ralf and leave Ross failed. A part of Sydney was grateful to Avery for accepting Ralf and being a good mother to her son, but another part was jealous that Avery had Ross and Ralf. Now, however, she would have both Ross and would be able to see her son. It was a good deal.

Diana sat with the distraught Avery until she fell into a deep sleep. As she quietly closed the bedroom door, Diana heard a commotion occurring downstairs. She ran down the stairs and saw Asa hugging a young man who she assumed was his son Jack Pierce. When she got to the bottom of the stairs, she spotted Barry and JB. Diana smiled, surprised to see them. As she hugged them both she asked, "I thought you two were reassigned?"

Barry answered, "We are reassigned, but we took a little side-trip for Mr. Sandman before we started our new assignment."

Mr. Sandman asked everyone to sit down and be quiet. "Before we went to Tortola, an interesting piece of intel crossed my path which indicated very strongly that Jack was alive and imprisoned in a Chinese work camp. Barry and JB went to China and connected with two of our agents. The four of them began a mission to rescue Jack."

"Why the hell did we have to go to Tortola"? Blake asked.

"Yeah, well, until they actually found Jack in China and alive, we still weren't sure. Plus, there was no evidence that Jack ever left Tortola," Mr. Sandman answered somewhat hesitantly. "I better let Jack explain."

Jack Pierce stood up next to Asa who was beaming. "First of all, I want to thank all of you for your time and effort to find and rescue me."

"You have your father to thank for that. That man is relentless," Lester commented, laughing. Agreeing, they all began talking at once.

"Let me continue, please," asked Jack as he held up his hands. Once they all settled down, Jack continued. "I also must thank Barry and JB for going above and beyond the call of duty."

"We were happy to help," answered JB.

Jack continued. "I didn't realize that Sharon Sachs was FBI. You see, I met this woman on the beach. She was very friendly, and we struck up a casual conversation. I was in vacation mode and told her where Sharon and I were staying. I stupidly let my guard down."

Diana sensed Jack's guilt and answered, "It's happened to all of us at one time or another. After all, we are only human."

"Thanks. Later that night the woman I met on the beach killed Sharon and I was knocked unconscious. When I came to, I was in a dinghy headed for a boat that was waiting offshore. As soon as they got me onto the boat, they shot me up with something. When I awoke, I was on a plane headed for China. You know the rest.

Mr. Sandman walked over to jack with a photo. "Jack, was this the woman who killed Agent Sachs?" Jack looked at the picture and immediately confirmed it was the same women. "Her name is Sydney Brewer," said Mr. Sandman.

Jack looked perplexed. "She told me her name was Beatrice Downing."

"That's just one of her many aliases. We know of three. In the United States she calls herself Sydney Brewer, in Europe it's Beatrice Downing, and in Eastern Europe and Russia it's Anna Vavara," Veronica explained.

Avery appeared in the doorway and yelled, "And that fucking woman stole my husband."

Sandra began to get upset. "I just don't understand how Ross could go off with that psychopath and hurt Avery." Sandra exclaimed. Albert got up and ran to Avery, escorting her to the couch to sit between him and Sandra.

"That's the next situation we are going to deal with," announced Mr. Sandman. "I suggest we all disperse for now and meet back here tonight as my guests for pizza at 19:00. Diana, will you and Lester please take Avery home." They all left. The Hoboken house was empty.

As planned, Ross dropped Sydney on Washington Street in Hoboken. He then drove Ralf home to Tenafly. Ross opened the door with his key. Avery had just come down the stairs with Kimmy in her arms. She turned when the door opened. They made eye contact for a brief moment until Ralf bombarded Avery with the seashells he brought home for her. Kimmy beamed stretching her arms out for Ross to take her. Ross took Kimmy and held her close to him. At almost three, she hadn't quite lost that baby smell Ross loved.

Avery went into the kitchen with Ralf to spread the shells out on the table to examine them. Mindo was at the sink and looked at Ross without speaking. Ross put Kimmy in her highchair. Kimmy began to cry, but Ross just turned to Avery and said, "Mr. Sandman wants to see me. I'll be back in about two and a half hours." Avery looked at Ross but did not answer him. Ross turned and left to return to Sydney in Hoboken.

"I love these beautiful shells you brought me," Avery said to Ralf as she hugged him tightly.

"I found a special one for Kimmy." He showed Avery the shell.

"Oh, it's beautiful. Thank you, my little man, for thinking of your sister. Give the shell to Mindo so he can clean it properly. Kimmy might put it in her mouth." Ralf handed Mindo the shell. He then went to sit on Avery's lap.

"I love you Mommy," Ralf said as he threw his arms around Avery.

"I love you too, my little man, so much," Avery answered as she held Ralf tight and kissed him on the head.

In a timid voice Ralf asked, "Are you mad at Daddy?"

Avery hesitated for a moment. "No, you have nothing to worry about." Avery hugged and kissed Ralf again.

Avery took Kimmy out of the highchair and said, "You, my little girl, need a new diaper." Avery walked out of the kitchen with Kimmy. Mindo watched the entire scene with trepidation, without saying one word.

Ross picked Sydney up on the corner of Washington and Eleventh just as he instructed. When she got into the car, Sydney threw her arms around Ross' neck and kissed him passionately. She touched him and felt Ross getting hard. "You came back. I wasn't sure if you really would." She was rubbing her hand up and down on him.

"Of course, I came back." Ross was extremely aroused and breathing heavily. "Now let's go to the brownstone so we can be alone, please!" Sydney laughed as Ross headed towards Park Avenue. It was difficult to find a parking space. As they rode around looking, Sydney opened Ross' pants. As she stretched the waistband of Ross' briefs, his erection sprung up and out. Sydney took him greedily deep into her mouth. Slowly pulling up, she teased the tip of him with her tongue, biting him gently. "Oh, God Syd, can't you wait until we get inside the house. What if someone sees us? Oh God, don't stop. I have to pull over" Ross pulled the car over until he was satisfied. Just as Ross pulled himself together, a spot opened up and Ross grabbed it. "That was wild, but dangerous."

"I love danger," Sydney whispered, as she got out of the car. They walked hand in hand to the brownstone. Ross took out the key and opened the door. Sydney looked around as she stood inside the door. This is nice. What now, my darling?"

"Let's go upstairs and find a bedroom," Ross said as he grabbed Sydney's hand an led her up the stairs.

Avery walked back into the kitchen holding Kimmy, put her back in the highchair and gave her the crackers she loved. "Mindo, Mr. Sandman just called me. He wants to meet with me. I'm not sure when I'll be back."
264

Mindo looked so sad that Avery walked over to him, hugged him said, "We're so lucky to have you in our lives. You're the brother I never had."

"You, Ross, Ralf, Kimmy and George are my family. I would do anything for you and Ross. If I can help in any way just let me know." Mindo and Avery made eye contact and held it for a few seconds.

Avery smiled answering, "Thank you, I appreciate that." She turned and walked out of the house, got into the car and headed to Hoboken.

Ross led Sydney into a bedroom. He turned her to him and took her face in his hands and began kissing her lips gently. Sydney and Ross began undressing each other frantically as their kisses became deeper and more passionate. Ross picked Sydney up and carried her to the bed. He laid her down and got on top of her. She wrapped her legs tightly around him as he plunged into her. Ross moved faster and faster until they caught their rhythm.

Avery drove around looking for a parking spot. It took her a while, but she finally parked four blocks away. She checked her watch. As she walked, her entire life with Ross flashed in front of her face. Avery picked up her pace walking faster and faster.

Ross turned Sydney over, so she was on top. Sydney sat low on Ross, rotating her hips so he rose deeper and deeper inside her. Ross began moaning in ecstasy and Sydney leaned forward as Ross held and caressed her breasts while she kissed Ross fervently.

Again, Avery checked her watch. Her heart was racing. She didn't want to be late. She felt a bit light-headed and slowed down her pace.

They were spent. Ross stroked Sydney's hair as Sydney caressed Ross' body. As her hand lightly ran across Ross, he began to get hard again. "Go down on me Syd, Please. It felt so good in the car today," begged Ross.

"Anything for you, my darling. Sydney moved her head onto Ross' stomach. She played with him gently until he was very hard. Then she tickled and teased him with her tongue.

Avery took the key out of her purse and opened the door. She looked around, but there was no one there. She listened and thought she heard someone upstairs. Slowly and quietly Avery began to climb up the staircase.

Sydney continued to tease Ross with her tongue until he pleaded with her to take him completely into her mouth. Sydney sucked hard, biting him gently and pumping him in and out of her mouth. Ross moaned and moaned, louder and louder, until he screamed out as Avery opened the bedroom door.

Avery stood in the door frame smiling for a few moments before they noticed her. Ross sat straight up and breathlessly asked, "Avery, what are you doing here. How did you know where I was?"

"I followed you, Ross." Sydney was curled up in a ball hiding behind Ross fearing that Avery was armed. Avery walked over to the bed. "Show yourself Sydney, don't be afraid. Look, I'm not armed, I promise."

Sydney sat cowering behind Ross covered with the sheet. Looking at Sydney Avery said, "Sydney, I've come to a decision." Sydney pulled the sheet up almost to her face. Avery knew Sydney was nervous. "Listen, I love Ross and you love Ross. We've been battling over him foolishly for a long time. So…I think we should share Ross. And also, I think you should see Ralf sometimes, too. Well, what do you think?"

Sydney sat straight up. "I think it sounds too good to be true."

"It's true. I fear for our children. We each have a child and Ross is their father. Your son and my daughter are brother and sister. That, in itself, makes us family. We can share Ross."

Sydney was dumbfounded. "Yes, I will agree to that for the kid's sake. We will share Ross."

Ross looked astonished. "Don't I have a say in this?"

Avery quickly answered, "No, Ross, you don't. As of now you have me as your wife, Sydney as your mistress and a beautiful child from each of us. What more could any man ask for?"

Avery, biting her bottom lip, looked seductively at Sydney. She slowly began taking off her clothes and said, "You Sydney, are the most beautiful woman I have ever seen. I have been with a woman before, Ross knows that. I know it would be a big turn on for him. In fact, Ross admitted that to me, remember babe?"

Ross remembered and smiled. "Oh, yeah, I remember that. Syd, I would love to see the two of you together." Avery was stripped down to her bra and panties.

Sydney looked at Ross and said, "If that's what you want, my darling, that's what you'll have. What do you want me to do?"

Ross looked over at Avery and then at Sydney. "Syd, I want you to take Avery's bra and panties off and I want to see you nibble her all over before she gets into bed with us."

Sydney stood and inch or two taller than Avery. She ran her hands over Avery's long, blonde hair and kissed her gently while unhooking and removing her bra. Sydney kissed and fondled Avery's breasts as she worked her way down to her panties. While kissing Avery's stomach, Sydney began slowly removing Avery's black lace panties. Sydney moved Avery backwards, gently pushing her down onto the bed. She began exploring Avery with her fingers and then entered her with her tongue. Avery moaned and spread her legs wider. "Oh my God, are you good!" Avery moaned and began to move her hips to the motion of Sydney's tongue, until exploding in a huge crescendo.

Sydney took Ross into her mouth again to relieve him. Ross kissed Avery. He knew her body very well, gently touching and working her most sensitive parts the way he knew it would satisfy her the most.

Ross laid Sydney on her back, spread her legs and entered her with his tongue while Avery straddled her torso, kissing and caressing Sydney's breasts. Sydney began moaning, slightly rotating her hips to the movements of Ross' tongue. As he brought her to orgasm. Ross reached up and held Sydney's arms down to give Avery the freedom to do the deed. Avery placed her hands upon Sydney's shoulders, kissing her as she inched her hands towards Sydney's neck to strangle her. Avery hesitated, kicked Ross gently in the head and motioned for him to stop, but that was not in the plan. Ross was confused. He was now in unknown waters. The three of them were sweaty and satisfied. Avery rolled off of Sydney and Ross and Sydney sat up. Ross excused himself to go to the bathroom. Sydney and Avery talked until Ross returned.

Ross saw Avery and Sydney sitting quietly looking at one another as if they had been best friends forever. Avery spoke first. "The truth is Syd, that Ross and I were supposed to kill you. Ross was going to kill you in the cabin on Tortola, but you are the mother of his son. He just couldn't do it. I was supposed to kill you two minutes ago, but after the most unbelievably orgasmic sex I've ever had, I couldn't kill you either. Besides you are Ralf's biological mother and I love Ralf too much to kill his birth mother. As I said before, we're family."

Stunned at Avery's honesty Sydney asked, "So what do you propose we do?"

Avery answered, "Work with us undercover, Sydney. The three of us together, with our combined skills and training could save the world, making it a better place for our kids."

"I need to have input here, ladies," Ross asserted.

Avery came back at him quickly. "No Ross. When you went to the bathroom Sydney capsulized the story of how you and she first met in. You and I had just started dating, yet you lied to Sydney and told her you were engaged to be married. Were you engaged to someone when I met you? Was that really true?"

"For Christ sakes Avery, you know damn well I wasn't engaged to anyone when we met?"

"Yeah, well, I'm not sure of anything anymore. You see, Syd, I knew nothing about you. When Ross and I were very close to getting engaged and I began to trust him completely, he abandoned me. Ross walked out on me when he walked into my apartment and witnessed his brother Marco beating me up and raping me. Marco told him I was a slut and slept around. He believed Marco and broke it off with me. I, too, became pregnant but with Marco's child. I immediately had an abortion. So, you see, Syd, you're not the only one Ross abandoned. And you Ross, as much as we both love you and your sexual prowess, must face the consequences for your past behaviors.

"What consequences?" Ross asked tentatively. A part of him was beginning to fear Avery. He had noticed subtle changes in her but wasn't sure what they meant. Avery had taken full control of this new situation and it bewildered and slightly unnerved Ross, while at the same time turned him on.

Avery answered without hesitation. "With me as your wife and Sydney as your mistress, we will have full control over you. You will do what we tell you when we tell you, within reason, of course."

"That's right Ross," Sydney agreed, smiling at Avery. Sydney liked where this was going.

"OK, I'll agree to that," Ross answered, relieved for the moment that nothing weird was in the mix.

"I'm sorry, Avery, I didn't know about your past with Marco. I know him. We were actually hooked up for a while. Now, I believe he's hooked up with a Polish woman in Warsaw named Adriana Drago. Your brother, Ross, is a traitor. He's working for the Russians to undermine the United States anyway he can."

"I knew he was doing something sinister, but that I didn't know," Ross admitted.

Avery changed the subject. "Let's talk about the three of us. What do you think of my plan for our future, Syd?"

"Yeah, I can see it working. We can have the best of all worlds. Amazing sex and we can be a family. I can get to see Ralf and get to know Kimmy, Ralf's sister. I'm sorry about the kidnapping. I would never have hurt Kimmy. I hope you know that."

"We can't change the past, but we can drastically improve the future. But thank you for that, Syd," Avery declared.

"Never look back. Only look ahead," Whispered Ross as he fingered both of his women gently and slowly at the same time. Both Sydney and Avery spread their legs while Ross sat in between them, entering Avery with his right hand and Sydney with his left, working their most sensitives areas. Avery and Sydney held hands until they screamed, achieving victory at the exact same time. "Well, that was a first," Ross proudly stated.

"Yes, that was a first, but I promise you it will never be the last," Avery answered, as she and Sydney laughed, both hugging Ross.

Avery laid down the rules. "OK, here's how it will work. Sydney, you get us the intel on all these bad-ass people who don't deserve to live in our world. Ross will be in charge of reconnaissance, luring them out into the open, and I will do the killing," Avery proudly stated. Both Ross and Sydney concurred.

Sydney smiled, pleased with the setup. "Great, let's start with this. I know that Toma Bratu, who has it in for your Mr. Sandman, will be in Manhattan early next week to attend his niece's wedding. I know he is paralyzed and in a wheelchair. That might make him an easier target. You Ross will plan the setup and Avery will execute Toma Bratu's execution. You can't get rid of a much worse bad-ass than that asshole," Sydney ascertained.

"Yes, that is the perfect way to begin our new endeavor to save the world. We will have to figure out a lot of things but killing Toma Bratu is the perfect way to begin!" Avery stated with conviction.

It was time to leave the Hoboken house. Ross and Avery carried Sydney out, wrapped in sheets, as if she were dead and put her into the trunk of their car. There was a hatch from the trunk to the back of the car. It was a tight squeeze, but Sydney managed to get out of the trunk and into the back of the car. In the dark of night, Ross and Avery carried a large empty toolbox wrapped in the sheets up to the cave with the hole spewing a putrid mist and threw what looked like a body down into the hole, ridding the world of Sydney Brewer forever. Sydney slinked out of the back of the car and disappeared into the night.

"I'm sorry I couldn't kill her in Tortola as we originally planned and I'm sorry I put you through all of that," Ross said when they got back to the car.

"It had to look real. For this plan to succeed, everyone had to believe it was real except Mr. Sandman, Esther Brouce and us. So, we implemented plan B. Ross, I understand why you couldn't kill her. It was just like Diana; she couldn't kill James. I think our new plan is better, but Ross, no one must ever know. Promise me you will honor that," Avery solicited.

Ross faced Avery, holding her by the shoulders and proclaimed, "I'm so in love with you, Angel, more than you'll ever know." Ross pulled Avery into his arms and devotedly and adoringly kissed her.

At 19:30 Ross and Avery went back to the Hoboken house. When they walked in everyone from Group Eleven was there, applauding and shouting, "Good job," and "Bravo, you killed the psychopath Sydney Brewer, you did it!" Mr. Sandman had revealed and explained the entire operation to the group. They were shocked that the five assailants were actually CIA operatives Mr. Sandman used to lure Sydney in, telling her that the Chinese hired them to help her kill the CIA team and present her with Ross Lisano as part of her reward for killing Sharon Sachs. Everyone was astonished with the incredible acting job both Avery and Ross performed. Diana was especially amazed and very proud.

Ross and Avery thanked everyone and asked if they could be excused from dinner. Ross explained that all they wanted to do was to go home to their family and sleep in their own bed together. Everyone understood. On their way out the door they heard Mr. Sandman say, "God, I wish I could give you two a medal and an Oscar!" Ross and Avery stopped, turned around, smiled, and left. They called Sydney's cell phone as soon as they rounded the corner on their way to the car. That was the night Felicia Hagar was born.

CHAPTER 12
SHENANIGANS

There was a momentary lull, it seemed, in their world that summer. Things were quiet and life was good, moving slowly along. Sandra was eight months pregnant and working only part-time at the catering hall. Arlo and Ramona were planning their wedding for the middle of October. Almund and Inger Good, Albert and Ramona's parents, applied for citizenship to be able to stay with their family permanently. Albert's aunt and uncle offered to buy their bakery in Berlin. Everyone was focused on Albert and Sandra's upcoming baby and Arlo and Ramona's wedding, not on each other. And for Ross and Avery, that was the way they liked it.

The covert partnership Ross and Avery ventured into with Sydney Brewer was working out better than expected. Over the summer they were successful in eliminating six very bad people. Their manage a trois was exciting, quite satisfying and addictive.

Mr. Sandman was unnerved because Toma Bratu, who he thought he killed, was alive, showing up in Manhattan for his niece's wedding. But his angst turned to jubilance. While sitting in front of the church in his wheelchair, Toma Bratu was assassinated by a sniper's bullet. The assassin was never found. In the end, no one cared. Toma Bratu was an evil man. Most who knew him despised him.

The summer was coming to a close, and the week after Labor Day Ross and Avery took Ralf and Kimmy for a quiet week to Long Beach Island, off the coast of New Jersey. They rented a beach house on the north end of the island near the lighthouse. Being the most seclusive place that time of year, they felt safe with Sydney joining them.

Previously, during the summer, Ross had thoroughly researched the possibility of anyone working in the Hackensack station or in any station in the northeast district, owning or renting a house on Long Beach Island. The results were negative. Ross, Avery, and Sydney felt secure that they would not be seen or recognized.

It was a glorious week for all five of them. During the day they focused on Ralf and Kimmy. At night, once the kids were asleep, they focused on each other. The three had grown to know each other's bodies intimately, trying every position possible. By week's end they were not only a well-orchestrated killing machine, but also a well-tuned sexual team.

Kimmy was three and her outgoing personality was becoming more evident and endearing to everyone. Sydney grew to love her own son Ralf and Kimmy, Ross and Avery's daughter. To make Ralf's life easier, Avery asked Sydney if they could change the spelling of Ralf's name to the usual spelling of the name, Ralph. Sydney agreed.

Avery and Sydney spent time together. They had more in common than they thought possible. They compared notes on what it was like for each of them growing up. Despite the fact that their backgrounds were vastly different, they shared similar fears and emotional deficiencies. Avery and Sydney began to develop empathy for one another. They became friends.

The house was directly on the beach. Ross or Avery went for supplies when needed. Sydney never left the house or their beach area. For the first time in a very long time, Sydney Brewer, aka, Felicia Hagar felt safe and happy.

It was difficult to leave the beach house at the end of the week, but necessary to protect the game they were playing. Sydney promised to get in touch with Ross and Avery for their once a week connection. If there was a potential target, they would meet and plan in a secure location.

Mindo was five minutes early for his appointment with Mr. Sandman. Mindo was sure that what he was doing was the right thing. In the end, Mr. Sandman thanked him, agreed with him, and asked Mindo if he would do things for him in the future if he needed him. Mindo was happy to oblige.

Diana planned a Lasagna dinner for the team as soon as Ross and Avery arrived home from their vacation. Poppy and Lorelei offered to host the dinner in their home. There was the usual joking around and storytelling. Poppy began questioning Ross and Avery about how they got rid of Sydney Brewer's body after they killed her. Avery answered with, "We're eating and it's much too gruesome to discuss during dinner. Anyway, Ross and I decided that since the Sydney Brewer issue was just about us, and we dealt with it alone, we would keep the details to ourselves." Everyone agreed that was fair. However, Diana said nothing. She just smiled.

Ross felt he had to say something so he added, "Let's just say that Sydney Brewer will never bother us again." With that said, the Sydney Brewer saga was closed. Ross and Avery looked at each other in a knowing way and Diana noticed. She was about to say something when the doorbell rang.

"That would be Earl, I'll get it," Lester said as he went to answer the door.

Diana got up to greet Mr. Sandman, stopped by Avery and whispered in her ear, "Saved by the bell." Avery looked up at Diana, who gave Avery a sideways glace with a subtle smile. Avery was perplexed by that look and Diana's words. What did she mean by that? Avery wondered if she knew they hadn't killed Sydney. She desperately wanted to talk to Ross alone but knew it would be a dangerous move. It would seem odd, especially to Diana.

Lester and Mr. Sandman came into the room. "Are you hungry, Earl? Do you want some Lasagna? Diana asked, glancing at Avery every so often with that knowing, subtle smile that Avery knew so well. Avery was becoming unhinged but was able to control her anxiety.

"No thanks, Diana, but some coffee would be great," Mr. Sandman responded. "Listen up, people. We have a situation brewing in Poland which needs attending to immediately. Four of our best agents have disappeared without a trace. Their bodies have never been found. As you know, that means they could be held captive somewhere by who knows who." Avery's anxiety began dissipating, being replaced with a sense of excitement. She wanted to go to Poland with Ross and Sydney. Sydney, as Felicia Hagar, could covertly help them find their missing agents and the bastards who abducted them, if they were still alive. Avery focused on Mr. Sandman as soon as she heard him say, "The way I see it, sending couples in may be the only way to go. I'm thinking two couples, maybe three."

"Ross and I will go, Sir," volunteered Avery.

Albert and Sandra seemed upset. "Avery, you and Ross are going to be our baby's Godparents. We thought for sure you two would be here when the baby was born," stated a disappointed Sandra.

Mr. Sandman intervened. "Sandra, you know that assignments come first. I promise, after the baby is born we will have a big party to celebrate. But right now, we must find our four agents in Poland. Thank you, Avery." Mr. Sandman stood up and announced, "I'll make my final decision before the night is over, but you will not know who is going until tomorrow."

Chloe stood up and asked Mr. Sandman if he would consider sending and Jeff and herself to Poland. Before Mr. Sandman could answer, Avery answered Chloe. "Absolutely not. It's much too complicated and dangerous an assignment for newbies."

Chloe came back with, "We did well in Tortola. How are we ever supposed to gain experience if we can't go on assignments?"

Mr. Sandman answered. "Avery is right, Chloe, you and Jeff can't go on this one, I'm sorry."

For the rest of the evening Avery was relatively quiet, spooked by Diana's sideway glances and subtle smiles. Under normal conditions Avery would have confronted Diana. But the conditions now were not normal. Avery was terrified that somehow Diana found out about the game she and Ross were playing with Sydney Brewer. For Avery, the shocking part was that she actually liked Sydney and felt a comradery towards her. But down deep inside Avery realized that this game of theirs could not end well for any of them.

As soon as they opened the door, Mindo came at them with a message from Lester to get over to his house immediately. Ross and Avery rushed to Englewood as fast as possible thinking something happened to Diana. On the way Avery told Ross about the strange looks Diana was giving her during dinner and afterwards. Ross told Avery she was being paranoid.

Lester was waiting for them at the door, pulling them in and slamming the door shut. Mr. Sandman was sitting on the couch with Diana. Avery knew she got it right, Diana found out. "Paranoid, really?" Avery whispered to Ross.

But it was not Diana who found out, it was Mr. Sandman and purely by chance. Mr. Sandman stood up, smiled and said, "My dear old Granny was a very wise woman. She used to always tell me that "man plans, and God laughs." He held up his cell phone with a picture of all five of them on the beach. "Now, I want to know what the hell you were doing on Long Beach Island with Sydney Brewer?" He sat back down, took a deep breath and asked as calmly as he possibly could, "Why didn't you kill her at the Hoboken house?" Ross' mind went blank, but Avery's was working on full power trying to come up with a viable explanation without exposing the sexual aspect of their relationship.

"How did you find us, Sir?" Avery whispered.

"Irrelevant! Now answer my question. I repeat, why didn't you two kill Sydney Brewer at the Hoboken house as planned?" Ross was feeling guilty for letting Avery take the brunt of this.

Ross answered, "It's very complicated, Sir. If you want to blame someone, blame me. It was all my fault for not killing her in the cabin on Tortola the way we planned in the first place. This is not Avery's fault."

"Bottom line, Sir, I think if Ross and I should go to Poland with Sydney. She could and would help us find the missing agents," Avery advocated.

Mr. Sandman laughed, asking, "And what makes you think I would trust Sydney Brewer on any level, Avery? That crazy psychopath almost killed me not that long ago!"

Avery looked over at Ross and decided to go full throttle. "Sir, do you remember finding out that Toma Bratu was assassinated in Manhattan?" The question hung in the air like a lead balloon ready to drop.

Diana stood up looking worried. "Are you suggesting that Toma Bratu was killed by you, Ross and Sydney Brewer?"

Avery stood up, faced Diana and squared her shoulders. "Sydney got us the intel, Ross did the reconnaissance work and I was the assassin." Diana stared at Avery with her mouth open and sat back down trying to process what she just heard.

"You're telling us that you took it upon yourselves, without any orders from anyone to kill Toma Bratu?" Lester asked.

Avery jumped on it. "Yes! The intel Sydney obtained strongly indicated that he was going after Mr. Sandman. We couldn't let that happen. We had to get him first." Avery turned to Mr. Sandman and said, "That intel Sydney obtained saved your life, Sir." Mr. Sandman was too astonished to speak.

Diana was dumbfounded asking, "Have you three killed anyone else?"

Ross began to speak, but Avery stopped him. "Yes, I do the killing, so I'll answer. We've eliminated some other very, very bad people to make the world a better place for all of our children. You see, Sydney knows where to find these scumbags, Ross lures them out, and I, operating as a sniper, kill them."

Diana was beginning to feel both anxious and nauseas. "How many people have you've killed besides Toma Bratu?" Diana breathlessly asked.

"Six, including Toma Bratu," Avery admitted.

"The names, Avery, write them down on a piece of paper and give them to me. Do it now," Mr. Sandman ordered as he paced back and forth madder than Avery and Ross had ever seen him. The room was silent. Everyone was trying to process what they had just learned. Diana took an anxiety pill. Avery wrote down the five other names and handed the paper to Mr. Sandman. He looked at the names, looked at Avery and, with clenched teeth said, "Yes these were bad people, but this kind of killing must stop. We are not vigilantes. That is not what we do. Is that clear?"

"Yes Sir," Avery softly answered.

Diana stood up and pointing her finger at Ross and Avery screamed, "You are not permitted to leave this family we've created. It is not allowed. You cannot go rogue or outside the boundaries of our family!"

Avery could see Diana's anger and feel her pain thinking that she and Ross betrayed her, Lester and Mr. Sandman. Calmly Avery explained, "Ross and I have not nor would we ever leave the family. We just...uh, brought in a guest."

"We don't allow guests. You have to eliminate Sydney Brewer and if you can't do it then Ross will!" Diana asserted.

Ross looked at his aunt and answered, I couldn't do it in Tortola, at the Hoboken house, or anytime, not ever. Sydney is Ralph's biological mother. I could no more kill Sydney Brewer then you could have killed James Kramer in Spain," Ross explained as he put his arm around Avery. Diana stared blankly at Ross and Avery.

"OK, you got me there. I get it. So, who will do the deed? She must be eliminated," Diana insisted.

"No!" Avery said forcefully. "Why does she have to die? Let her work for me and Ross as an asset. She could be very valuable to us."

"I bet." Diana stated sarcastically. A light bulb went on in Diana's head. She now figured out the missing piece to this whole thing. She leaned forward towards Ross and Avery and bluntly stated, "You three are involved in a manage a trois." Neither Ross nor Avery answered, but stared at Diana in shock amazed that she figured that out. "Well? I'm right, Aren't I?"

Mr. Sandman stood up and began pacing back and forth. "Damn it, this is getting worse and worse." He turned to Ross and Avery and said, "You'd better give me the bottom line. I can't take much more."

Avery explained. "The bottom line, Sir is that under that psychopathic, evil woman is a beaten down, sad from being alone, untrusting from being lied to and used human being. Ross used her and lied to her. Ross had a two-week affair with Sydney in where he told her he loved her. After the two weeks were up, he told her he was going home, back to his fiancée. Sydney begged him to take her with him as he promised he would, but then he told her he lied; that he didn't love her. Ross left Sydney there brokenhearted, alone, and pregnant with his son." Ross tried to intervene, but Avery stopped him. "Shut up Ross. I'm not finished. Ross told Sydney he was going home to his fiancée, but actually we had been together for about one month when this all took place." Avery looked directly at Diana. "Aunt Diana, please tell me the truth. Was Ross engaged to someone else when he met me?"

Diana gave Ross a disgusted look and asked, "Ross?" assuming Ross had told Avery about this years ago. She then answered

Avery. "Yes, he was but it wasn't what you think." Avery began to speak, but Diana stopped her. "Avery, I just assumed Ross told you about this. It was sort of an arranged marriage. It was with my sister Adreena's best friend's daughter. They didn't love each other. Today that girl is married with about four kids. It was a nothing thing."

"OK, so it was a nothing thing, but what's important is that Ross never told me about it," Avery said.

Ross turned Avery towards him. "Please forgive me, Avery. When I first met you, I fell so head over heels in love with you that I couldn't see straight. You're the love of my life. I have never loved anyone as truly and as deeply and completely as I love you..." Avery cut him off.

"Give it up Ross, you're making me sick!"

Ross would not give it up. "You are the only woman I ever wanted to marry and spend the rest of my life with. That is the honest truth. Aunt Diana remembers, she can confirm that for me."

Avery looked at Diana. "I have to be honest, Ross is telling you the truth, you are the only one Ross ever truly loved and wanted to marry, as far as I know," Diana confirmed.

"Aunt Diana!" Ross choked out.

"OK, Ross, you're forgiven." Avery then turned to Lester and Mr. Sandman who were standing together. Avery stood up to speak. "Mr. Sandman, Sir, Uncle Lester, please, I beg you, let me and Ross go to Poland with Sydney as our asset. We can at least find our agents. You can send Poppy and Lorelei with us. I think Lorelei speaks a little Polish. Please, seriously think about it."

Avery sat back down next to Ross and they nestled together waiting for Mr. Sandman's answer. He took Lester and Diana into another room to discuss it. They came back into the room. Lester and Diana sat down. Mr. Sandman stood in front of Ross and Avery, looming over them, in his usual stance, feet slightly apart and hands behind his back. Avery could smell his intoxicating cologne. He stood looking down at them as if he forgot what he wanted to say. Then, he spoke. "First of all, let me just say that I could wring your necks. You two caused me one big headache, your aunt panic attacks, and your uncle bad indigestion. I should

278

throw you two out of the CIA for going rogue with Sydney Brewer and rolling around in the sac with her instead of killing her. But I can't. I need you two." Mr. Sandman began pacing. "Let me make myself crystal clear. What happened here tonight never happened. Sydney Brewer is dead, as well as her aliases." Mr. Sandman began to pace back and forth. He stopped and stated, "She needs a new identity in order to go to Poland. You two take care of it.

"We already did. She has a new name and a new look. All she needs now is a passport, Sir," Avery advised him.

"Good!" Mr. Sandman continued, "She is not permitted near any of our team or agents in the field. I will send Poppy and Lorelei with you two. They will have a separate contact who goes by the name of Carmen Sabian. Poppy and Lorelei must never know anything about your misguided shenanigans. Is that clear?" Both Ross and Avery nodded indicating they understood. "Don't think you two are off the hook. Sydney Brewer must be eliminated before you leave Poland. I want the Sydney Brewer saga dead and buried. That is a direct order from me to you!"

Ross and Avery stood up. Ross thanked Mr. Sandman, then went over to Diana and hugged her, and then to Lester and hugged him. Avery stood facing Mr. Sandman. "Thank you, Sir. I am confident we will find our missing agents, or at least what happened to them."

Mr. Sandman smiled and said, "Oh, and one more thing. No more hunting and killing unless it's ordered by me. Tell your friend the two of you are out of that business. Is that clear?"

"Yes Sir," Ross and Avery stated together.

"We better meet tomorrow at 09:00 at the Hoboken house instead of my office at the station. I'll call Poppy when I leave. Lester, I want you and Diana there also. I'm considering sending you along with them."

"Is that necessary?" Ross asked sheepishly.

"I'll make that decision, Ross. Why is it always so damn complicated with you two? What you and Avery do with your sex life is your business. If it begins to interfere with our assignment in any way, then it becomes my business. Do we understand each other, Ross?"

"Yes Sir," Ross uttered, ashamed that he had even asked that question.

The jig was up, but in the end Avery got her way. She and Ross were going to Poland with Sydney Brewer, aka, Felicia Hagar. There was one problem. Mr. Sandman gave them a direct order to kill Sydney. Both Ross and Avery knew neither of them could ever obey that order. They would have to figure out a way to make Sydney disappear as if she were actually dead. That was a common story in the world of espionage. It was too easy. They had to think of something drastic, something different, complex and never done before, and Sydney had to agree to whatever scheme they hatched. They also realized they were, once again, on their own. There was no one to turn to for help. Avery opened up the back of her cell phone, took out the tracking device and did the same for Ross while he drove to Hackensack. Avery called Sydney to tell her to expect them shortly.

Ross parked the car underneath a flickering streetlight just like the one outside the seedy apartment building where Blake Ramos used to live. Sydney lived in a basement apartment under the name of Felicia Hagar. As soon as they came back from Long Beach Island, Sydney had cut her hair short and died it red, which looked wonderful with her piercing green eyes. She was still stunning.

Ross knocked softly on the door. Sydney opened the door and pulled them both in, throwing her arms around both Ross and Avery. Ross closed the door behind him with his foot. "I've missed you two so much, I'm craving us. Ross, before we get down to business, please do me and Avery together again like you did that time. OK, Avery?" Avery was more than happy to oblige.

Both Avery and Sydney reclined on the bed together, holding hands. Ross was between them. Ross was very good at this, moving his fingers in and out and around, while each time going a little deeper and a little harder and faster until both Avery and Sydney, knowing not to scream, squeezed each other's hands until they were spent. Ross rolled onto Avery and pushed into her as Avery wrapped her legs around him. Ross put his fingers inside Sydney, who moaned and rotated her hips on Ross' hand as he pumped hard into Avery. Once victory was triumphed, they got down to business.

Avery began to explain. "There's a serious situation in Poland. Four CIA agents have disappeared without a trace. Other Agents have gone missing in other Eastern European countries, but most have turned up either dead or alive. In this case, none of them have turned up at all. We're convinced they're being held by someone, but we don't have a clue as to who might have them. Our analysts have come up with nothing as of yet."

"Avery convinced Mr. Sandman to send us and one other couple to Poland to find the missing agents. He knows about us, Syd. Somehow he saw you me and Avery on the beach with our kids," Ross revealed.

"We got off really easy and honestly, I'm surprised. They know we killed Toma Bratu plus the five others. Mr. Sandman was furious, ordering us to stop the killings. That part of our plan is over," Avery stated.

"How can I help?" Sydney asked.

"We want you to go to Poland with us to help us find our agents. You know a lot of people over there. We'll take your picture now and tomorrow we'll come back with your passport. It will be under the name of Felicia Hagar. We'll have to travel separately. The other couple we're working with cannot see us together. We will give you the name of the hotel we we'll be staying in," Ross explained.

"You can stay in the room with us. Please Syd, we really need your help. You'll be our contact. You will only be known from now on as Felicia Hagar." Avery stated.

"Does Mr. Sandman know about our sexual arrangement?" Sydney asked hesitantly.

Ross answered, "Yes he does, but he doesn't care as long as it doesn't interfere with our mission."

"Well, in that case, of course I'll help you in any way I can," Sydney agreed.

There was a momentary lull. Avery spoke. "There is one more serious issue we need to deal with, which is one of the reasons we must insist you come to Poland with us." Avery's face darkened. "Ross, you explain," insisted Avery.

"I'll just come right out with it. Mr. Sandman ordered us to kill you once the Poland assignment was fulfilled. Avery and I can't obey that order. We both care about you and want to protect you," Ross declared. Sydney sat motionless, staring at Ross and Avery.

Avery put her arm around Sydney. "We need to come up with a plan to make you disappear. We'll come up with some kind of a story where your body was destroyed somehow." Avery began to choke up. "You do realize that you'll have to stay in Europe. You can never come back to the United Sates." Avery had to pause.

Sydney cried, "I can't bear the thought of the three of us not being together." Sydney and Avery held on to each other. Sydney began kissing Avery and Avery began to respond. Ross stopped them.

"Please, will the two of you stop. We need to keep grounded and figure out what to do," Ross forcefully ordered. Avery and Sydney apologized to Ross. Ross was upset and snapped, "You two better pay attention. Your life depends on what we do and how well we execute our plan, Syd."

"Ross is right. Tomorrow morning we're meeting with Mr. Sandman and the other couple. When we come back with your passport we'll have a more concrete understanding of how this op is going to play out. Tomorrow we'll formulate our plan of action to protect you. It's late, Syd. We all need to get some sleep. Just hang loose until tomorrow." Avery looked at Ross and said, "We'd better go." The three of them hugged and Ross and Avery disappeared.

Sydney watched as Ross and Avery walked out under the blinking streetlight, got into their car and drove off into the darkness. Sydney took off the sheet that was wrapped around her, got into bed and began to cry, "Why did this have to happen? Now I'm passionately in love with both of them!"

Once in the car, Avery turned to Ross and said, "I think I've figured out the perfect plan to keep Syd safe and here with us. Don't go home, Ross. Go to the Hackensack station. We are going to do what Caeley did for her and Andrei, remember that crazy scheme? It was nuts and illegal, but it worked. We will fake Syd's death in Poland, but she will come back with us as a completely new and different person with all the correct documentation to begin a new life. I believe if you really want to hide someone or something, do it right out in the open. People never notice the obvious."

Ross laughed. "You, Angel are brilliant, the perfect spy." He pointed the car towards the Hackensack station. "Tomorrow when we go back to Syd with your plan and all of the documentation with her new identity, she'll be thrilled."

At 08:55 Ross and Avery walked into the Hoboken house. The smell of freshly brewed coffee permeated the air. "They're here, Ross," Avery bluntly stated.

"We certainly are," Diana said as she walked out of the dining room greeting them with hugs and a smile.

Ross and Avery were the first to arrive. Diana quickly stated, "When this Poland operation is completed, we have to sit down together and you must tell me how this odd relationship developed between you two and your arch enemy, Sydney Brewer, OK?" Diana was on the verge of tears. Ross and Avery could see how much Diana agonized over this unexpected circumstance. Before Ross and Avery had a chance to answer, Poppy, Lorelei and Mr. Sandman walked in. Behind them came Lester carrying a large box of donuts. Without speaking Mr. Sandman walked over to Ross and handed him an envelope. Ross knew it was a passport. Ross looked up and thanked him with a smile and a nod.

Mr. Sandman stood at the head of the table and began to speak just as Caeley and Katrina, the Group's two top-notch analysts walked in. "Oh, good, you two are here. Have you found anything at all?"

As Caeley and Katrina sat down, Katrina said, "Not really, however we are almost certain that those agents never left Warsaw. There's no evidence of it."

"That's right, we're almost certain they are still in or somewhere near Warsaw," Caeley said, confirming Katrina's findings. Then Caeley asked, "What if Katrina and I connected with your contacts in Poland? That might lead us somewhere."

Mr. Sandman answered, "Unfortunately, that's not possible. These people are very skittish. They are not likely to connect with anyone accept Poppy, Lorelei, Ross and Avery."

"Ok, then all I can suggest is to go on the assumption that the four agents are still somewhere in or on the outskirts of Warsaw, but we'll stay closely on top of it," Katrina submitted.

Mr. Sandman gave Poppy and Lorelei their contact information and plane tickets for the next day. They thanked him, kissed Diana and Lester goodbye and left, sensing there was something going on that was none of their business. They were very perceptive. Poppy told Lorelei that if whatever it was that was not their business began to become their business, they would learn what it was. Poppy trusted Mr. Sandman.

Ross and Avery stayed behind after Poppy, Lorelei, Caeley and Katrina left. Mr. Sandman handed Ross two more envelopes and said, "One envelope contains your plane tickets on the same flight as Poppy and Lorelei. The other envelope contains a plane ticket, on a different flight, for Felicia Hagar and the name of the hotel where you two will be staying. I put Poppy and Lorelei in a different hotel."

Avery looked up at Mr. Sandman and confessed, "I don't feel good at all about this one, Sir."

He uncharacteristically barked, "You shouldn't Avery, because it sucks!" Mr. Sandman turned and walked out the door. Avery felt bad because she knew he felt frustrated. He was angry with her and Ross and probably felt betrayed. But nevertheless, they had to keep moving forward even though feelings of guilt were eating away at her.

In the car, on the way to see Sydney, Avery said, "I don't think I can do this anymore, Ross."

"Do what? What are you talking about?"

"You know, the three of us together sexually. It's becoming too much for me. I honestly don't think I can handle the stress that comes along with it anymore."

"Don't worry about it, Angel. Let's deal with one thing at a time. We'll protect Syd by finding her a safe place when we come back. Then we'll slow it down. Things will go back to normal," Ross asserted.

Avery asked, "What the hell is normal for us, Ross?"

Ross thought for a moment, looked at Avery and said, "That's an excellent question. I don't know the answer."

They arrived at Sydney's apartment. Ross knocked on the door, but there was no answer. Ross knocked harder, but no sign of Sydney. "Ross, break in, something is very wrong," Avery nervously whispered. Ross kicked the door in.

They found Sydney sprawled out on the bed naked with an empty bottle of pills next to her. "She's still alive. Make her throw up, Ross, hurry make her throw up," Avery screamed in a panic. They quickly laid her on her stomach with her head hanging off the bed. Ross stuck his fingers down Sydney's throat. Avery had gotten a bucket. Sydney began heaving and finally threw her guts up. Most of the coated pills had not dissolved and could be seen in her vomit. Avery ran a shower, stripped and got in the shower with Sydney just to wash her off. Ross took care of cleaning up the vomit.

Avery made Sydney a hot cup of tea and made her drink it. "Why the hell did you do that? We have your new passport, a plane ticket and the name of the hotel we will be staying at. You'll arrive the day after us. Come straight to the hotel. Ross and I will be waiting for you in the lobby to take you up to our room. You'll stay in our room with us. We'll be together for as long as the mission takes, I promise, Syd. Please promise us you'll never do that again."

Sydney gathered her thoughts. "Thank you for saving my life, but I'll never be able to come back here. I can't bear the thought of never seeing you two again.

Ross put his arm around Sydney and pulled her towards him. "Listen Syd, Avery came up with a brilliant plan to keep you here. You will fly to Poland as Felicia Hagar, die there as Sydney Brewer, and fly back with us as Sloane Mitchell. We will keep in constant contact with you. When we come home from Europe, the three of us will be together, I promise, Syd," Ross said as he kissed Sydney's head. Avery showed Sydney all of her new documents, all under the name Sloane Mitchell. Sydney was thrilled with the plan as Ross and Avery explained it in detail. For security reasons, Ross and Avery kept the Sloane Mitchell documents with them. They would give them to Sydney right before leaving Poland.

Sydney looked at Avery and asked, "What time is your flight?"

"19:00 tonight. We arrive in Warsaw tomorrow morning. Your flight is tomorrow night and we know exactly when you'll be landing. Ross and I will be sitting in the lobby waiting for you. And damn it, Syd, you better show up. Then we can go up to our room and be together, really together," Avery said seductively.

Sydney stroked Avery's cheek. "Wild horses couldn't keep me away. I'm so in love with both of you, so much."

"I think you should eat something. Ross can get you some chicken noodle soup," Avery suggested. Ross ran across the street to the small market and brought back a few cans of chicken noodle soup. Avery heated it up and made Sydney eat it. Sydney admitted it made her feel better.

"Can you two stay with me for a while? I don't want to be alone," Sydney asked pleadingly.

"What do you say, Avery? Can we stay for a bit"? Ross asked, knowing Avery would agree.

Sydney looked at them, smiled and asked, "Can we be together, I mean really connected together?"

Avery was surprised. "Are you up to it Syd?" Sydney smiled and put one hand on Avery's breast and the other between Avery's legs. Ross was getting hard watching them.

"Let's go," Sydney said as she tried to pull Ross and Avery into the bedroom. Ross began to go, but Avery was resistant. "Avery, what's wrong?" Sydney was confused, thinking Avery was rejecting their closeness.

"Ross and I have a long trip ahead of us tonight and we will probably not get much sleep. I just think we better wait until we're together in Poland," Avery said, sounding very sensible. Ross knew if Avery said no, it was no, and he was disappointed, but agreed with Avery. Sydney had no choice but to go along with their plan.

Ross gave Sydney her passport and plane ticket under the name of Felicia Hagar to use for the trip to Poland. Avery made Sydney promise not to do anything stupid. The three hugged and said goodbye.

Ross and Avery sat across from Poppy and Lorelei on the plane. Ross and Poppy were in the aisle seats. Avery and Lorelei were asleep. Poppy leaned towards Ross and quietly called out, "Ross, what's going on with you and Avery?"

"Nothing, why?" Ross answered with a disgusted look on his face.

"Hey, cousin, I wasn't born yesterday. Now what's going on?"

"None of your business. It's personal, but it's not about me and Avery. It's about a friend who's in trouble. It has nothing to do with our trip."

"OK, Ross, why are we staying in two separate hotels?"

Ross leaned towards Poppy. "Because the people we are supposed to meet claim they can't see each other. That's what Mr. Sandman told me when I asked him."

Poppy looked hard at Ross and stated, "If your problem starts becoming my problem, then you damn well better tell me what the hell is going on. Do you understand me Ross?"

Ross sat back in his seat and answered with, "My problem will never, and I mean never, become your problem. Do you understand that, cousin? Ross said through clenched teeth.

"Yes, and it had better stay that way!" Poppy spit back at Ross, but Ross pretended he was asleep and didn't hear him.

Ross was looking at Avery, watching her sleep. He became aroused and began to get hard. He loved Avery so much more since the whole Sydney thing started. Even when he and Avery were home alone in their own bed, he needed her every night. He thought about how he would lay between Avery's legs. Ross had to put a pillow over his lap when he started thinking about it. Ross was so turned on he began squirming in his seat. He realized it was his own fault. He had to stop thinking about sex in order to calm himself down. His movements woke Avery up. She saw he was in distress and asked, "What's wrong, babe?" Ross pointed to the pillow on his lap. Avery gently put her hand under the pillow and felt his throbbing hardness. They were both traveling in sweats. It was the middle of the night. Most of the people around them were asleep, including Poppy and Lorelei. Avery put the arm rest up and laid her head in Ross' lap, covering her head with a blanket. She pulled Ross' sweatpants down just enough to bring him out. She held him moving her hand up and down, while taking just the tip of him into her mouth, using her tongue as a stimulant. Just before he exploded she released him from her mouth. Avery pulled Ross' pants back up and sat up. Ross thanked her, taking her in his arms and kissing her.

Avery put the blanket over them and nuzzled into Ross. He put his left arm around Avery, pulled her to him and kissed her passionately again. "I love you so much, Avery," Ross whispered as he put his right arm under the blanket and began inching his hand down into her sweatpants until he reached her panties. Ross began kissing her again, holding her tight with his left arm. Ross rubbed her up and down on top of her panties. Avery wanted more but pulled Ross' hand out of her pants. This was the first time they ever done this or anything like it without complete privacy.

Avery looked at Ross and asked, "What's wrong with us, Ross? We are out of control. We were never like this before, even that first time when we were on the run in Germany"

"I know, I agree. Every time I look at you when you don't know I'm looking at you, I get a hard-on. I can't stop thinking about sex, the things we do to each other and how we make each other feel. The funny part is that Sydney is never in the mix when I think about you and me."

Avery smiled and stroked Ross' cheek. "Yeah, for me too. She's never there with us when I think about us together." Avery turned to face Ross and said, "Maybe we should reconsider this whole thing with Sydney. We're getting ourselves deeper and deeper into trouble."

"Yes, we are. When we get to Poland we'll reassess things," Ross said as he pulled Avery to him and kissed her again.

Avery held Ross tight and said, "I was going to wait, but I think I better tell you now. As our son, my little man would put it, Mommy and Daddy made another baby. I just found out that I'm about ten weeks pregnant."

Ross was taken by surprise but quickly pulled himself together. "Does Diana or anyone else know?" Ross asked Avery as he touched her belly. Avery kissed Ross gently assuring him that only he knew.

"This changes things with our arrangement with Syd." Ross put his hand back onto Avery's belly. "I have to protect you and our baby. We complete the assignment as ordered and we go home. No more shenanigans, Avery," Ross said as he lovingly rubbed Avery's belly. Avery tacitly agreed, with Ross' left arm around her and his right hand on her belly. Ross was elated stating, "Maybe this new baby will bring us back to sanity."

Avery looked up at Ross and said, "We're meeting Syd tomorrow morning in the lobby of our hotel. We should get her a room for herself. We need our privacy, Ross, especially now." Avery's demeanor quickly changed, "Oh my God, what if Syd's pregnant, too?"

Ross was horrified. "Shit, I never thought of that. Forget about Sloane Mitchell. We have to follow orders and eliminate Sydney in Poland," Ross stated without hesitation.

"What, no, why?" Avery protested, but Ross, explaining how complicated it would be, finally convinced Avery it was the only way out. The problem was that neither of them had the heart to do it.

From the airport Ross and Avery took a taxi to their hotel. When they checked in they got a second room for Sydney, aka Felicia Hagar. They planned to explain to Sydney that Avery was pregnant and the nature of their relationship had to be altered.

By the time Ross and Avery got to their hotel room, they were both exhausted. They took a shower together and climbed into bed. Ross kissed Avery's belly. "It's a boy, Avery, I just know it." Avery was half asleep. Ross laid between her legs, his head resting on her thigh. "Have you thought of a name for our son yet?" Ross asked putting his hand on Avery's belly.

"No, I haven't. do you have any suggestions?" Ross smiled.

"I want to name him Dillon Ross. Do you like that Angel?"

Avery laughed answering, "Yes, I love it." Ross kissed Avery's belly. He laid his head back on her thigh.

Avery stretched and put her legs on top of Ross. Avery moaned, "Ross, please, come up here. I want to feel all of you on top of me as if we were one."

Ross went on top of Avery, kissing her as he entered her gently, thinking of their baby. "We are one Angel, and always will be." Ross whispered as they made love.

They slept in each other's arms for hours. It was midafternoon when they awoke. Ross had made arrangements to meet Poppy and Lorelei for a late dinner that evening at their hotel. Ross ordered room service for lunch and Avery decided they would not leave their room until they had to walk the two blocks to the other hotel.

While eating lunch Avery looked hard at Ross and said, "Tonight we must tell Poppy and Lorelei what's been going on, the whole story, because we need them to eliminate Sydney."

Ross stared at her in horror. "Are you crazy. We were ordered not to tell them. And besides, they'll probably tell us no and to do the deed ourselves."

"We'll tell them about the baby, that I'm pregnant and can't take the risk." Avery paused, changing gears. "You know Ross, this is not our first baby. I'll never forget when my little man came into our bedroom after I lost our first one, asking us if we could make another baby. And, we made Kimmy." Ross began to beam at the mention of his daughter's name.

"We sure did. I love that kid. She's really something because she has your personality and temperament," Ross stated.

"Yeah, and she has my blonde hair, but curly like yours and your brown eyes, and she looks just like you. She's so cute. But you and I, we grew apart for some reason after Kimmy was born." Avery started to cry. Ross ran to her and put his arms around her. "Why are you crying, Angel?" Ross whispered. Avery began to lose control of her emotions. Ross held her tighter. "Talk to me Avery, please."

Avery began to verbally explode. "I love you and need you more than you'll ever know, Ross. I love our life together. I love our family. I love our kids, including our new baby. I want to be a good mother to them, a real mother. But we're sitting here in fucking

290

Poland planning to betray and kill a woman we care about and go running around in circles searching for people we don't even know. I want to go home, Ross. I want to go back to our children, our home and our family. I want a normal life. I want us to be a normal family, please Ross, please," Avery sobbed. All Ross could do was to hold Avery in his arms and comfort her.

Ross lead Avery over to the bed. He laid down with her, wrapping her in his arms. As they laid wrapped up in each other Ross talked softly to Avery. "A very large part of me feels exactly the same way you feel. But you know as well as I do that we have to see this through. It's true, the baby changes things, but those things needed to be changed." Ross sat up and pulled Avery up. "Two wonderful things came out of this fiasco. First our new baby, and second, you and I fell in love all over again, but so much deeper this time." Ross kissed Avery fervently and she responded.

Wiping her tears away with the bed sheet Avery answered, "You're so logical, Ross. You're right about everything. You keep me grounded."

Ross smiled lovingly. "Yes, I do, I know." Avery laid back down happy, feeling that a great weight was lifted off of her.

"I know exactly when our baby was conceived. It was just before we started with Sydney. It was the night in Tortola in the cave in our tent when we stripped down naked and got into one sleeping bag, remember? We made love long and hard all night, knowing what was coming the next day. Do you remember that?" Avery knew he remembered by how aroused Ross had become.

"I sure do. I'll never forget it," Ross replied.

Avery pulled Ross on top of her. When her hand touched Ross it made him harder. As Avery guided him into her she said, "This baby represents a new beginning for us. I love you, Ross Apollo Lisano." They made love long and hard.

Poppy and Lorelei were waiting for Ross and Avery at the bar in the hotel restaurant. They moved to a table and Poppy announced the first round of drinks was on him. Avery ordered a seltzer with lemon. Immediately both Poppy and Lorelei noticed. "Not drinking?" Poppy asked.

Avery thought that was the perfect vehicle for informing them that she was pregnant. "If you want to know why I'm not dinking it's because Ross and I are having another baby. I'm pregnant. Poppy and Lorelei congratulated them. Avery looked at Ross and said, "We're going to tell them everything, Ross. We have to, we need their help."

Poppy looked at Lorelei, smiled and stated, "I told you something was off, or on." Poppy turned to Ross and Avery. "OK, Ross, start talking." Ross began to explain from the beginning, how Mr. Sandman, Esther Brouce, he and Avery concocted an elaborate plan to lure in and kill Sydney Brewer. They used their mission of looking for Jack Pierce in Tortola as a lure. They had received intel that a large Chinese conglomerate hired Sydney to go to Tortola for a hit and/or a kidnapping job. It was purely by coincidence that Asa Page asked Mr. Sandman to see if his son was or had been on the island of Tortola. Mr. Sandman had arranged for six CIA agents to approach Sydney telling her that as a bonus, the Chinese were giving her Ross Lisano. The CIA rented the cabin where Sydney waited. The six CIA agents, dressed in black and wearing masks ambushed the three couples, knocking them out with a harmless sleeping mist and barricaded them into the cave, except for Ross. Five of the CIA agents left and one delivered Ross to Sydney Brewer, as planned.

Ross divulged how Sydney immediately hardened him up with a blow job, sat down on him and fucked him. He played the game. Sydney untied him and took him to bed. That's when he was supposed kill her but couldn't because she's the mother of his son Ralph. They then had to go to "Plan B", which was for Avery to walk in on Ross and Sydney at the Hoboken house, join them in bed and kill Sydney, but Avery couldn't kill Ralph's mother either. Ross asked Avery to explain the rest.

Avery explained how they made a deal to work as a team to kill bad guys, killing six, including Toma Bratu. Ross and Avery allowed Sydney to see Ralph. They faked Sydney's death and entered into a manage a trois. At first it was great sex and very arousing. By chance Mr. Sandman, or someone he knew saw the three of them with Ralph and Kimmy on the beach on Long Beach Island. Avery confessed that Diana and Lester also knew everything.

292

Avery shared how she and Sydney talked, getting to know one another. Avery said she was surprised how alike they were in so many ways, developing a strong bond and a sense of comradery for one another. Sydney cried to Avery explaining how devastating it was for her to have to give Ralph to them because her mother passed away and she had no one else to care for him. Sydney thanked Avery for loving Ralph and taking such good care of him. Avery choked up, asking Ross to finish explaining.

Ross described how Avery convinced Mr. Sandman to allow Sydney to come to Poland with them as an asset to help find the missing agents. However, he ordered them to eliminate her when the assignment was fulfilled. That was what they needed help with; killing Sydney Brewer. Poppy and Lorelei sat staring at Ross and Avery with their mouths opened, shocked at what they were hearing.

Avery took Lorelei's hands in hers and said, "I want to apologize to you for everything. I realize you and I are two very different people, but I gained an understanding of how a person can love someone but be in love with someone else at the same time. I understand that you love Sergei, but I know in my heart that you are totally in love with Poppy. I'm so sorry for being such a bitch, saying all those awful things to you. I trust you and will never doubt your loyalty again. Can you find it in your heart to forgive me?"

Lorelei smiled answering, "Yes Avery, I do forgive you. Let's you and I start over from this moment on."

"Thank you Lorelei. I know Diana will be relieved and happy because we're family." Their table was ready in the dining room. When they stood up Avery hugged Lorelei, thanking her again for her forgiveness. After they were seated, Avery looked at Poppy and Lorelei and said, "Ross and I would be honored if you two would be our baby's Godparents?" Stunned, but happily surprised, Poppy and Lorelei readily agreed.

"How do you want us to do it?" Poppy asked, looking at Ross.

Avery answered. "Ross and I thought it would be best if you did it between her arrival in Poland and her arrival at our hotel. But before we decide, I must ask you, how reliable is your contact, Carmen Sabian?"

"As far as I know, she's very reliable, but afraid of being discovered as a traitor," Poppy answered.

Ross added, "Sydney is travelling under the name Felicia Hagar. She knows a lot of people and might be very helpful in finding those four agents. We might want to rethink our plan. Poppy, what time are you and Lorelei meeting Carmen?"

"09:00 tomorrow. Isn't that just about the same time your friend will be arriving?" Poppy inquired. Ross and Avery realized their plan wouldn't work.

"Yes, it has to be done at a different time." Ross thought for a moment, then asked, "Would it be possible to bring Carmen over to our hotel? We have to wait in the lobby for Felicia Hager to arrive. Together, Carmen and Felicia may make it easier for us to find the missing agents." Both Avery and Lorelei agreed.

"Once we find the agents or what happened to them, we'll do the deed. Don't worry, it will be done. Am I right in assuming that your Felicia Hagar suspects nothing?"

"I'm quite sure she suspects nothing. She expects to stay in our room with us tomorrow tonight, however, we got her a room of her own. Ross and I decided to back out of that sexual relationship we had with her," Avery whispered secretly.

Ross raised his glass and said, "To our baby, my son, Dillon Ross Lisano, or, my second little girl." They all raised their glasses and toasted the new baby.

The next morning Poppy came running into the hotel. Ross and Avery stood up and hurried to meet him. "Lorelei and Carmen are in the SUV. Carmen got a very hot lead on the location of the four agents, but we have to go now," Poppy demanded.

"I must leave Felicia a note at the desk" As Avery hurried to the desk she looked over her shoulder saying, "She expects us to be waiting for her. I'll be there in one second." Avery left a note explaining that they had to follow up a hot lead. She should go to her room and wait. She and Ross would meet her there and explain later.

Ross and Avery jumped into the SUV with Poppy. Lorelei introduced them to Carmen Sabian. Ross thought she looked vaguely familiar but couldn't place her. Carmen was able to obtain ambiguous directions to a place abandoned many years ago. The rumor, Carmen explained, was that the facility was haunted by angry spirits because terrible things had happened there.

They drove to the outskirts of Warsaw to the edge of a forest lane. Poppy stopped and asked Carmen which way to go. Looking at the map she told Poppy to turn right onto the lane and follow it for two or three kilometers. The dirt lane was littered with potholes. Ross began to get agitated. "Slow down, please. Remember, Avery is pregnant." Ross regretted allowing Avery to go with them.

On the right side of the lane they came to the beginnings of a broken-down brick wall. Along the top was barbed wire, broken in many places. The old dilapidated brick wall stretched for about one kilometer. At the end of the lane they cautiously approached a large, rusting heavy iron gate hanging loosely by its hinges. "What the hell is or was this place, Carmen?" Poppy questioned.

As they all looked in dismay at the scene in front of them, Carmen answered, "I think I know but I'm afraid to say it."

"Well, we better find out. Come on Ross, lets open the gates so we can drive through," Poppy suggested. Ross followed Poppy and slowly, pushing hard they were able to budge the gates open far enough for their SUV to fit through.

As they drove through the large rusted gates Carmen said, "My grandmother told me that long, long ago this was a psychiatric hospital for the insane. During the war when the Germans occupied Poland, they murdered all the patients and burned their bodies in a large ditch. Once the facility was emptied the Germans used as a holding facility for Jews, Polish resistance fighters, and others who opposed them until they could be evacuated to extermination camps around Poland. Many people were tortured and died in this place, so the story goes." They passed many dilapidated buildings that looked like army barracks. Carmen said, "My grandmother and my parents had forbidden me to ever come here, but you know how kids are. If they're told not to do something, they'll do it." Looming straight ahead was an expansive three-story red brick building.

"So, Carmen, you've been here before?" Poppy asked.

"Yes, but not lately. I think, over the years, people have probably intentionally forgotten about this place," Carmen speculated.

Avery pushed into Ross and whispered, "This place gives me the creeps."

"I will not allow you to go in there, Avery," Ross adamantly stated. "Lorelei, will you please say in the SUV with Avery?" Ross asked. Lorelei looked at Poppy for an answer.

"Of course, Lorelei you should stay here with Avery," Poppy agreed. "Ross and Carmen will go in with me," Poppy uttered as he looked precariously at the large brick building which was in total disrepair."

Avery called Ross over as she got out of the SUV. Ross took Avery into his arms knowing exactly what she was feeling. "Don't worry Angel, I will be careful."

"Ross, just remember you have almost three children, Dixie, and me." Avery took Ross' hand and placed it on her belly. Ross felt something stir inside of him he had never felt before. Avery's words and the look on her face touched the inner depths of his soul.

He held Avery tight, kissed her passionately and declared, "I am so in love with you."

"And I am so very much in love with you," Avery whispered. Their eyes connected for a moment before Ross turned and joined Poppy and Carmen as the three of them entered the historically nightmarish red brick structure.

The old dark green double doors, with most of their paint chipped away, were locked. "Someone doesn't want us or anyone to enter," Ross sneered sarcastically. He looked at Poppy and stated, "This is bullshit. Let's get in there!" When Ross examined the nature of the lock, he discovered the door were chained on the inside. "Maybe we should just shoot our way in," Ross suggested.

Poppy disagreed and began running around the side of the building. "No, come on, let's look for another entrance or maybe a window. No guns and make as little noise as possible. I'm getting a weird feeling about this place that I don't like. Carmen, are you armed?"

"Yes, I'm carrying two weapons; a gun and a knife. Why did you ask me that?"

Poppy answered, "Carmen, listen to me, go back to Avery and Lorelei in the SUV. I feel they need protection. Please go, and Carmen, stay alert." Carmen nodded and quickly ran back to the SUV.

When she got there, she overheard Avery telling Lorelei about some false documents under the name of Sloane Mitchell she and Ross created for a woman named Felicia Hagar. Avery told Lorelei that they were going to give them to the woman named Felicia but changed their minds. Avery made Lorelei promise never to tell anyone about the Sloane Mitchell documents. Lorelei hugged Avery promising to keep it to herself. Carmen ran, hid and made a phone call.

When Carmen went back to the SUV Avery and Lorelei were gone. She immediately ran back to Ross and Poppy, who were trying to open windows.

As soon as she spotted them Carmen whistled. When they looked her way, she motioned for them to come quickly. "Avery and Lorelei are not in the SUV, they're gone." Ross and Poppy both took off like two racehorses out of the gate. Carmen ran behind them.

As they reached the SUV Ross became out of control screaming, "We have to find them. Avery is pregnant."

Poppy grabbed Ross by the shoulders, looked at him and said, "So is Lorelei. We were going to tell you tonight." Ross and Poppy hugged, keenly feeling their family connection as cousins for the first time.

Carmen checked out the other side of the building, discovering an open window. She ran back to Ross and Poppy and told them to hurry. Showing them the open window, she said, "They may be in here, let's go." The three climbed through the window, landing three feet down into what seemed like a basement. It was damp and musty with a slight smell of urine in the foul air.

As they cautiously moved forward, they began to hear a faint moan, and then another, which was different from the first. "Listen, follow that sound," Ross said. Moving towards the moans they discovered Avery and Lorelei tied up with tape over their mouths. Poppy and

Ross quickly untied them. Both men hugged their wives. Avery had to assure Ross that their baby was safe. Ross held Avery by the shoulders and asked, "Who did this to you and Lorelei?"

"It was two men or maybe a man and a woman, I'm not sure. Both had their faces covered. They took us by surprise, tied us up and just left. They used me and Lorelei to lure you, Poppy and Carmen in. You were looking for an entrance, well they showed you one. They wanted us all in here, but why?"

"This is all fucked up," Poppy uttered.

"No, it's fucking bullshit, that's what it is," Ross yelled, his anger seething.

Avery turned to say something to Ross, hesitated, then said, "There's one more thing I have to tell you. It's crazy…it's nuts, but I think one of them, the one who took me, was your psycho brother Marco." Ross was stunned but believed Avery. Ross began cursing, calling Marco a fucking little piece of shit. Poppy let Ross vent. He understood where all Ross' anger towards Marco was coming from. Ross almost killed Marco when he found out that Marco had raped Avery when she and Ross had just gotten engaged.

Poppy was curious and asked Avery how she could be so sure it was Marco. Avery answered with bitterness and disgust, "I smelled his scent."

"Jesus Christ." Avery's words set Ross off again. Both Poppy and Avery had to calm him down. Ross held Avery tightly in his arms until he calmed down. "Avery, I'm not letting you out of my sight, not for one second," Ross stated. He turned to Poppy. "We should all stay together while we're searching. There's safety in numbers and our wives are not armed."

"Are you serious, Ross?" Avery asked as she pulled a gun with a silencer out of her shoulder bag. Lorelei partially pulled out the wire she always kept for strangulation purposes in her bra and a gun from her shoulder bag.

Carmen laughed. Looking at Ross and Poppy she said, "I feel much more secure with your wives with us." Avery and Lorelei both laughed and told her she should.

They checked the first and second floors and found nothing. As they headed up to the third floor, they began to smell a very unpleasant odor. Ross, Avery, Poppy and Lorelei knew exactly what it was. At the top of the stairs they turned left and began slowly walking down the long hall with their weapons drawn. As they walked, the bad smell diminished. "We have to turn around and walk the other way," Poppy ordered. Once they passed the staircase, the bad smell grew stronger. Poppy stopped, turning to Avery, Lorelei and Carmen. "You three stay here and keep your weapons out."

Ross and Poppy slowly walked down the hall, Ross on the right and Poppy on the left examining each room. More than halfway down the hallway, Ross stopped and yelled, "Poppy in here." Avery, Lorelei, and Carmen began to walk towards Ross and Poppy. "No, go back, do not come any closer, and that's an order," Ross yelled. They obeyed, going back to the staircase. Poppy immediately called it in. Ross came out of the room, leaned against the wall, slid down to a squatting position with his hands covering his face. Avery knew the scene had to be horrific because Ross was crying, and Ross never cried. Poppy helped Ross up and they walked back to the staircase. "Let's get out of here. Poppy called it in, but we have to wait for the collection team to come. Let's wait outside," Ross suggested.

Avery put her arm through Ross' as they walked down the stairs. "Ross, what was in that room?"

"The four Agents. They were murdered, probably tortured and dismembered. Whoever did this used the victim's blood to paint Jewish stars and swastikas all over the walls."

"Three out of four of those agents were Jewish. Antisemitism is running rampant in Europe again," Poppy alleged. When they left the building, Poppy said, "I'm calling Mr. Sandman while we wait for the collection team to find out what's next. He may want us to stay to find out who killed those four agents."

"Why can't the agents posted at the Warsaw station do that job?" Avery asked.

Ross walked over to Poppy and whispered, "You have a job to do for me. Please don't forget. It was an order directly from Mr. Sandman."

"Don't worry, I keep my promises," Poppy assured Ross. The collection team arrived. Poppy told them where to find the bodies. "Everybody into the SUV," ordered Poppy. Once they were all in, he informed them that Mr. Sandman wanted them to go back to the hotel and wait for his orders.

Avery whispered in Ross' ear, "I want to go home!" Ross put his arm around Avery and leaned his head on hers but did not respond. He was just grateful that Avery did not see the horrific sight he witnessed in that room.

When they arrived back at the hotel they were saying goodbye to Carmen who asked Avery and Lorelei if they could speak to her in private. They walked off to the side and Carmen whispered, ""How could I become a CIA agent?" Avery and Lorelei laughed, each putting an arm around her.

"Go to the Warsaw CIA station and they will tell you exactly what to do," Avery instructed.

"Avery's right. We think you have what it takes, Carmen," Lorelei said, encouraging Carmen to do it. They all wished her luck and walked into the hotel. Ross and Avery went up to the desk to find out if Sydney checked in under the name Felicia Hagar. The desk clerk gave them her room number.

"Do you want us to go with you to her room?" Poppy asked.

"Yes, we might need you. Thank you," answered Ross."

"We can do it now if you want. We'll get her to sit in a chair and I will walk behind her. As soon as I begin to strangle her and Poppy lunges to hold her down, you two leave, ok?" Lorelei proposed. Neither Ross nor Avery was happy about it but knew there was no choice. It was their only way out of the trap they were caught in and a direct order from Mr. Sandman.

Ross knocked on the door saying, "Open up Felicia, it's me and Avery." They waited, but nothing.

"We have to get in there. She tried to kill herself once, but Ross and I showed up in time to save her life," Avery explained. Lorelei immediately took her kit out of her shoulder bag and began to slide certain instruments into the card key slot. The door opened. They stood transfixed, unable to move or speak until Avery began screaming. A hook had been implanted in the ceiling with a strong rope attached to it. Sydney Brewer, aka, Felicia Hagar was dangling at the end of the rope strangled to death. Avery ran over wrapping her arms around Sydney's legs, spoke to the dead woman. "Why, Syd, why? Her words were staccato in between sobs "You promised me you would never try to kill yourself again." Ross ran over and pulled Avery away from Sydney, prying her arms off of her legs.

Poppy looked at her body and with certainty stated, "Sydney did not commit suicide, she was murdered. Look, someone put a bullet through her head." They all stared in horror at the bullet wound in Sydney's skull while Poppy called Mr. Sandman. He told them to check out immediately, get into the SUV and drive to Berlin. Col. Ramsey would be waiting to fly them home from Ramstein AFB. He instructed them to make an anonymous call to the police directing them to Sydney's body once they were safely on the road to Berlin.

Ross and Avery went back to their room to quickly pack and retrieve the Sloane Mitchell documents out of the safe. They were going to burn them. But that was not to be. The safe had been broken into and the Slone Mitchell Documents were gone. Ross was seething mad. Avery calmed him down and they agreed that whoever stole the Slone Mitchell documents most likely murdered Sydney. They illegally created the Sloane Mitchell documents. That meant they could not involve the CIA in any way. After much discussion they concluded that the only two people they could completely trust were each other.

Mr. Sandman stood on the tarmac watching the small jet taxi towards him. Only one person was on the small jet, the one person Mr. Sandman trusted the most. He walked down the steps of the plane directly to his boss. "It's done, Sir, finally and forever!"

"Thank you Mindo, I am so glad you came to me with those photos. I know how much you care about Ross and Avery. By helping me you saved them," Mr. Sandman said as he shook Mindo's hand.

"I would do anything to protect Ross, Avery, the kids and George." Mindo smiled. Anytime you need me, just call."

"Don't worry Mindo, I trust you more than anyone. They'll be back soon. I better get you home." They got into the car and drove off.

The two couples followed Mr. Sandman's instructions to the letter. Using their UN documents at the border, they left Poland with ease, driving directly to Berlin. Col. Ramsey got them on a transport plane and flew them directly to JB MDL. They were all exhausted, especially Avery and Lorelei who were both pregnant, due to have their babies around the same time. Flying home the four decided to immediately inform Mr. Sandman, Diana and Lester at their debriefing that Avery and Lorelei were pregnant.

Lester and Diana were waiting for them when they landed. Immediately Diana informed them that during the night, while they were airborne, Sandra gave birth to a healthy baby girl. They named her Sarah Jillian Goode.

Mr. Sandman was not pleased with the outcome. There was the unanswered question of who killed the four agents whose bodies were torn apart and mutilated? Ross and Avery looked at each other, silently communicating that since Mr. Sandman assumed they killed Sydney, they would only concentrate on the missing Sloane Michell documents.

The debriefing was winding down. Mr. Sandman asked his usual, "Are there any other issues to be addressed?" Avery and Lorelei were sitting together, which Diana was keenly aware of during the entire debriefing. They both raised their hands. "Who wants to go first?" Mr. Sandman asked. Lorelei whispered something in Avery's ear. Avery smiled and nodded.

Avery stood up and began. "First of all, it is important that you know that I have apologized to Lorelei for all the grief I have bestowed upon her over the last few years. I have asked for her forgiveness and Lorelei graciously accepted my apology and forgave me. Lorelei and I understand each other better now and we have decided to start over. I will never question her loyalty again," Avery said, smiling at Lorelei. Diana was speechless but elated. Avery continued. "And now for the best part. We are both pregnant and due at the same time." Ross thought how beautiful Avery looked.

She was absolutely glowing. Looking at Avery, he thought about his son growing inside of her. He was so proud he thought his chest would burst open. The congratulations lasted for a while longer before they all dispersed and went home.

Ross pulled the car into the driveway and shut the lights off. It was dark. There was no moon. "Well Angel, the last four months have been one hell of a ride, wasn't it?" Ross unhooked his seatbelt and Avery followed. "Come over here and let me hold you in my arms for a while before we go in," Ross said as he pulled Avery into his arms. He put his hand on Avery's belly. "I just want to feel my son," he whispered in Avery's ear.

"How can you be so sure it's a boy? At my next doctor's visit, you should come with me. We may be able to find out what we're having, but we won't tell anyone. I just want you to be prepared in case it's our second little girl." Ross took Avery in his arms and kissed her with one of those tongue twisting kisses that last and last.

As they slowly came apart, Ross took Avery's face in his hands. "As long as our baby is healthy, I don't care what we have, Angel."

Avery laughed and teasingly said, "Liar, you want this to be a boy, so just admit it." Ross knew she was on to him.

"OK, so I want us to have a son together. We have a beautiful daughter. Now I want us to have a beautiful son."

"We have a beautiful son. His name is Ralph." Avery sighed and said, "Ross, now with Sydney gone, I want to adopt Ralph legally as my son so no matter what happens he's mine."

"OK, I'll call our lawyer tomorrow. It's just that I want you and I to make our son together."

Avery stroked Ross' cheek lovingly. "It doesn't matter who Ralph came out of because I love him as if he did come out if me and you. He is our son just as much as Kimmy is our daughter and this baby is our child." Ross took Avery in his arms again and kissed her. Avery pushed her hand onto Ross' pants and felt him getting hard.

"Oh, God Avery, Lets go take a hot shower together and climb into our bed so I can kiss you all over," Ross said as he hit the button to open the garage door. As the garage door opened an automatic light went on displaying the strangled body of George Lisano hanging from the rafters." Avery screamed and after the initial shock Ross called Mr. Sandman, Lester and Diana. Mindo ran out of the house half asleep. He stood staring in horror as George Lisano's limp body moved ever so slightly back and forth. Mindo was the first to notice; there was a bullet hole in George's head.

It was confirmed by all the professionals, including Medical Examiner Charley Maher, Mr. Sandman's friend, that George Lisano was murdered!